GOERING'S GOLD

STAN MORSE

Published by Stan Morse

Copyright © 2014 Stan Morse

ISBN: 0989851338
ISBN: 978-0-9898513-3-6

Thanks to: Doug Shea, H.T. Miller IV, and Michelle Minor who read early drafts of this novel and offered their comments; and special thanks to Gaylen Willett who so very kindly lent editorial help.

Thanks to graphic artist Tim Oldfield for the excellent book cover.

OTHER BOOKS BY STAN MORSE
Circling the Earth in a Wheelchair
Brothers of Summer

Author's Note

I learned in 1976 that a local hydro powerhouse, constructed prior to WWII, had pipes with swastikas cast in the metal. The cover of this book was derived from a photo I took of one of those pipes.

How the swastikas came to be there remains a mystery. But the possibility that the pipes were manufactured by Nazis in pre-war Germany got me to asking the question novelists are compelled to ask:

What if?

CHAPTER 1

Central Washington State – 2002

To the dead assassin it seemed the perfect hiding place.

The olive colored dome tent appeared in early May, embedded within a tangle of cottonwoods in the wild gorge of north central Washington's Little Cascade River. By June, the tent was practically invisible under a leafy canopy; further protected from unwanted visitors by thick fields of sagebrush spreading into the nearby foothills.

The tent's owner, a man now using the last name of *Wells*, awoke soaked in sweat shortly after dawn, his sleep plagued by a vortex of jungle and death, sighting through a high power scope with one finger burning against the smooth curve of a trigger, a sea of dead faces swirling in the crosshairs.

The intensity and frequency of the dark vision had been easing. Up until now. Something had changed during the night.

What?

The man, whose real name was Jerry Allen Dearborn, pulled the tent's zipper and eased back the flap, squinted at the sun cresting the horizon, crawled out into the morning light. He stood and stretched and ran one hand through his thick sandy hair and took a deep breath of clean steppe desert air, scanned the fields of wild grasses and sage, up and down the riverbank and into the rolling brown hills, and was satisfied he was alone.

Wearing only faded jeans and his dog tags, Jerry rummaged in the khaki duffle bag that lay beside the tent, pulled out a worn blue towel and a bar of soap, and side stepped down the rocky bank to the riverbed. At the bottom he paused and turned in a slow circle and when he saw no one he picked his way across the rounded stones to a place where the river had carved a deep pocket into the bedrock.

He stood on the worn granite and stripped off his jeans. Naked except for his dog tags, he plunged feet first into the deep well and remained submerged for several seconds before breaking the surface with a little shout, pawing at the brisk water. He grabbed the ledge and levered with tanned arms and sat on the smooth rock. Holding the bar of Ivory and facing the pool, with his feet dangling in the water, Jerry scrubbed the flaky soap into his scalp until there was a thick lather. He cupped gobs of suds and spread them over the rest of his body. Now covered in white from head to knees he stood and plunged back into the pool. He surfaced and flailed the soap from his body, and for just a moment he acted more like a teenager than a man of fifty.

Climbing back onto the smooth granite, Jerry toweled off, pulled on his jeans, and took a few steps to a slab of bedrock where he begin a ritual dating back to the early killing years; finding a focus and breathing evenly; stretching and relaxing muscles and joints that had withstood three decades of soldiering; pushing dark thoughts aside and replacing them with the gentle rushing sound of the river and the sharp angle of morning sunlight warming his body.

His last flight from danger began in Texas. When the silvery bus pulled into Langston he saw the promise of solitude and safety in the wilderness surrounding the rural town. He was nearing Seattle and wanted to stay away from the large city where federal agents would be all too common. There was nothing for him there or beyond; no decent chance of crossing undetected into Canada; no possibility of boarding a jet or a cruise liner. Jerry climbed off the bus and shouldered his backpack.

After walking the streets and finding the community populated by mind-your-own-business working class folk, he picked the west side of the river that flowed from the lake and ran for two miles through a gorge until it reached the Columbia River. To a casual observer he might have looked like a backpacker returning from a trek in the nearby Cascade Mountains and now searching for a place to set up camp.

He followed the paved road through a neighborhood of modest homes. Near the edge of town a man wearing a Seahawks cap and slouched behind the steering wheel of a blue Chevy pickup sporting a faded *Reagan/Bush* bumper sticker slowed to ask if he was lost. When he told the man he was "just doing some exploring" it seemed to satisfy the fellow, who drove off with a short rev from his engine.

When Jerry reached the concrete dam, both the paved road and the houses ended. Beyond the dam he followed a dirt road that meandered through an increasingly wild and narrow canyon for a quarter of a mile until it became choked with brush. Afterwards there were just two ancient tracks of compressed earth with a hedge of native plants down the middle. The primitive track quickly faded until he was often pushing through brush that had taken over.

He kept walking.

A bit further on he found a field cleared for a large campsite in the distant past but now fallen back to grass and bush. It was here he discovered the promise of privacy amongst the cottonwoods.

For the past six weeks Jerry had only once encountered invaders: two teenage boys, each carrying a six-pack of beer. The moment they saw him they gave the solidly built stranger a wide berth, hurrying around his campsite and disappearing into the thick brush downstream.

λ

After his meditation beside the river, Jerry climbed back to his camp, took an apple from the small white Styrofoam chest, bit into the juicy fruit, and reflected upon how this place had changed him for the better. For recreation, the nearby Columbia held fish free to anyone with a pole and patience. He trekked into town once a week to buy rice and vegetables and the treat of a chocolate bar. A diet of unprocessed foods and the rigors of outdoor life shaved off twenty pounds. His body tightened. Muscles again defined his midsection.

Jerry ate the apple down to the seeds and tossed the core back into the cottonwoods. He grabbed up his fishing pole and lures. It was still early enough to expect trout to be rising in the race below the powerhouse. He'd caught pan-sized rainbows in a deep hole that lay just before the stream passed beneath a railroad trestle and emptied into the Columbia. And if he landed no trout, then small mouth bass were plentiful beyond the trestle in the deeper water.

He skirted the cottonwood grove and came to where the barely defined rut of the old road followed on. It must have once carried some measure of traffic, but now there remained little evidence of humanity: a shard of blue glass; an edge of rusted sheet metal angling from parched ground; a few bits of charred wood from an ancient campfire.

The sun felt warm against his face and Jerry was in no particular hurry. Soon enough he would reach the graveled access road a quarter mile below his campsite. Until then he was in familiar and safe territory—his backyard so to speak. He could relax in the solitude, let his mind wander; enjoy the fading yellow blossoms of balsam root; the musky sage; a redwing blackbird; a soaring eagle; the western range of foothills rising toward a jagged line of snow-capped peaks.

He had nearly reached the beginning of the access road, musing about how pleasant the day was, when he saw something he might have tripped on if he'd been looking at a slightly different angle. It protruded from beneath a thick grouping of sage. He froze, mid-step, as he realized it was a human foot.

CHAPTER 2

North Atlantic – March 1934

A great wave slammed into the small Danish freighter, rocking it sharply to one side. Cargo in the main hold shifted, and two twenty-foot crates atop the tallest stack snapped their cable restraints. When the next breaker came pounding in the crates slid off and smashed onto the floor, shattering the sturdy oak boards. The contents—two sixteen-inch-diameter steel pipes, marked with numbers and swastikas cast into the metal—began rolling back and forth in the walkway, alternately hammering against the bottom crate in the stack and then slamming against the hull.

Otto Klein and the two other Germans, Heinrich Stromer and Werner Hartkorn, were in the tiny mess, eating a dinner of pickled herring, cheese and flatbread—the best the cook could manage with the ship being tossed about like a cork. Otto was attempting to fork-stab a chunk of herring as his plate slid on the worn metal table when the bos'n burst through the cabin door, wild-eyed and breathless. He was drenched from the open deck and as his boots hit the waxed floor they lost traction and he slid-stumbled to a jolting stop against the table, rattling utensils and dishware, his hands flying out to grip the edge to keep from falling. A tin cup hit the floor and clattered off into the corner.

"The pipes," he gasped.

Otto reached out and grabbed the bos'n's arm to steady the man. "What about the pipes?"

The bos'n gulped down air, fighting to catch his wind.

Heinrich's eyes went razor cold when an immediate answer wasn't forthcoming. "Out with it! Tell us!"

Werner, practically a kid with blond peach fuzz still on his chin, held his silence.

On the first day out from the German port city of Wilhelmshaven the ocean was calm. But once they were well away and out of sight of the coastline the seas had risen as dawn broke. As they moved from the North Sea out into the Atlantic, the great ocean turned far rougher than any of them imagined possible. By evening, the little freighter was buried in an endless range of dark green canyons that crested in white spumes as gale force winds cherry-picked the peaks. It was impossible to turn and retreat to the safety of the port they had left, or even to struggle towards the Scottish coastline in the hope of finding temporary refuge in one of the infrequent harbors. The captain's choice was to plough directly into the waves and pray no rogue current spun them sideways to be rolled by the next great wall of water.

In the swaying cot in the tiny cabin Otto found little sleep. When it finally came there was a nightmare of seaweed entangling his body, twining through his hair, binding his feet, dragging him relentlessly toward the wreck-strewn seabed a thousand fathoms below.

The ship managed to survive through the second night and by morning it seemed the seas were dropping just a little. When it finally appeared they might survive this first great hurdle on the journey to America, the Germans decided to test their uncertain stomachs with a meal.

The bos'n finally regained his wind.

"A crate has come down. The pipes . . . two of them are loose!"

Heinrich was on his feet and out the door without waiting for the others. His footsteps echoed down the narrow corridor.

Otto jumped up. "Come!" he ordered the bos'n and Werner. They followed Heinrich down the pale gray corridor and out onto the heaving deck, through blasts of saltwater, sprinting toward the hold. The oval hatch was left open by the charging Heinrich and it was swinging wildly as the men entered. Once they were safely inside the bos'n secured the hatch to shut out the wind and spray.

Heinrich stood waiting for them at the top of the access ladder. "Come on!" he hollered.

All four men, dressed in heavy blue woolen coats, pants and knit caps, scrambled down into the gloom, clutching at the railing with numbed hands, deafened by the roar of waves against the outer hull, struggling to cling to wet rungs and keep from being thrown onto the floor.

"Over there!" Heinrich screamed as he dropped the last couple of feet onto the rough teak planking, pointing to three crewmen who were trying to stabilize the loose pipes with an anchor bar. Heinrich sway-stepped around the stacked crates to join them.

Otto paused in the safety of the open space at the bottom of the ladder. Almost immediately, the round wooden shaft the men were working with, wedged firmly against the outermost pipe and held in place by two of them, snapped like a twig as the ship pitched hard to port. The men were barely able to jump out of the way as the pipes once again slammed against the rusted outer hull.

Heinrich was surprised by the violence of the force. He grabbed a rope holding the stack of crates, pulled himself up, and the rolling pipes missed crushing his legs by inches.

As the ship righted itself Otto stepped up beside Heinrich, his eyes focused on the men now huddled at the end of the hold just beyond danger. "You!" he shouted at a gangly blond youngster with reddened cheeks. "Does the ship carry any manila rope and heavy timber? And pulleys . . . are there any pulleys!"

"Maybe!" The boy hollered above the din. "In the aft compartment there is rope and some deck skids! And maybe there are also pulleys." Relief flooded his face.

It was a rude confirmation. Aside from the captain and two or three officers, the ship's crew appeared to consist of a hasty collection of dockside hopefuls. With many still out of work, the wharf in this port city was littered with the

,

desperate, many of them unpopular minorities: Poles, Croats, Serbs, Russians, Jews. Men aplenty willing to work for a pittance even at the risk of their lives. Not so many sailors; but lots of common laborers, bartenders, carpenters, even farmers; men who would try a new and dangerous trade if it meant they could feed their families. Otto brushed the thought away. There was no time for it now.

The boy anxiously stood his ground, awaiting further directions, clearly relieved that someone with a capacity for command had arrived.

"Then hurry and bring them! Bring everything you can find! We will sort out what is useful when you get back!"

The boy gave a sharp head jerk to the two he was working with and together they picked their way around the mountain of crates, safely out of range of the rolling pipes.

They're just kids! Younger even than Otto!

The crewmen followed their cherry-cheeked leader like puppies and disappeared through the aft hatch.

The gaunt Danish captain arrived seconds later. He looked momentarily disoriented and clung to the railing above, a pockmarked face filled with concern beneath his black captain's hat, wearing a dark oilskin parka slickened by the rain and waves. He squinted in the dim light, searching out the movements of the men below. When he saw only the Germans his face contorted. Where was his crew? The louts! He cupped hands to his mouth he bellowed out a curse in crude German, followed by a more precise Danish expletive describing an impossible sexual act.

Otto ignored him. The fool had recruited an inadequate crew. Let him twist. Otto was fully occupied with survival. He'd finally seen a way to stabilize the pipes if the crew returned with usable wood and rope.

Realizing he was being ignored, the captain again cupped his hands and scalded down a rain of profanities so coarse that Otto spun around and glared up with utter frustration.

"Shut up you bastard!" he shouted, cutting the captain off mid-curse. "Better yet, come down here and make good use of that energy!"

Mercifully, the captain fell silent; his pebbly face a mask of unhappy, glowering at the Germans.

Otto returned his attention to the pipes. If they acted quickly, there was a chance. Still, he found a moment to regret what was happening to his precious cargo. As the two rollers banged and gashed each other, orange primer and raw steel were beginning to show through the dark blue paint. The flanges on the ends were already deeply scored and bent. Their structural integrity and ability to fit and seal was gone. The relentless pounding was rendering them into scrap.

Forget them! Save the ship!

Otto refocused on the condition of the outer crate at the bottom of the stack—still holding its own against the barrage of two-ton rollers. But cracks had begun to appear across its face. If it burst, the crates directly above would tumble down and dump their contents into the mix. And with more pipes in motion, the remaining crates would quickly disintegrate. Once the entire shipment was loose and banging around the expedition's fate would be sealed. The aging freighter wouldn't reach the coastline of the Americas, much less the Panama Canal and the Pacific.

The blonde kid and his mates finally returned with coils of rope and two large wood-and-steel pulleys plus armloads of skids. Otto began to direct them in an effort to block-and-tackle the rollers into submission.

Heinrich yielded completely and now took directions without question. Werner put his strong young back to the task. But even in the midst of the struggle, a corner of Otto's mind drifted back to the time when all of this might have been avoided.

⅄

There was heated debate over whether or not to leave the shipyard at Wilhelmshaven, nestled in a safe bay along the North Sea. Despite the threat of an Arctic gale in the forecast, the weather remained deceptively calm.

"The meteorologists cannot be right," young Werner insisted. "And don't forget that we have a contract and a schedule to keep. What if we are held up in the Panama Canal? What if we don't arrive on time?"

Heinrich had taken to calling him *The Worrier* for his obsession about keeping on schedule. Otto was more forgiving, attributing Werner's impatience to his youth. As he gained experience in life, the boy would become more charming, more able to see other's viewpoints. But at twenty he was still figuring things out, and one of those things was how to be part of a team.

"Worrier," Heinrich mumbled just loud enough to be heard.

Werner glared at Heinrich, unwilling to do more to challenge the older and tougher man who had already demonstrated a willingness to pick a fight for practically any reason.

Otto shrugged it off. Heinrich might be an unrelenting instigator, but except for when his temper got the better of him, he took orders and executed them with precision. In the few months they had all worked together on the project Heinrich repeatedly proved himself to be capable and fairly bright.

Otto had another reason to forgive Heinrich's mean streak. The pipe work for the American hydro project was originally Heinrich's full responsibility as head engineer. He'd overseen the design and casting of the pipes long before Otto was brought onto the team. But Heinrich spoke only a modest bit of English, and he now accepted that communicating with workers and engineers in distant America must be handled by someone fluent in English.

The good luck of how Otto became employed still amazed him. His mother emigrated from England before the start of the Great War to marry her German sweetheart. When her first son began to talk she taught him the King's English. This simple language skill now gave him a job at a time when good jobs were scarce, even for trained engineers.

But damn Heinrich! If only he could keep his mouth shut!

As they argued dockside about the weather, the captain stood on the bridge of the freighter, grinning while the Germans fought. Otto's patience with the captain had worn thin. The ship's crew should have been better supervised. Several times Otto had been required to give directions about how to stow crates. Not that he felt comfortable about it. He was an engineer, not a longshoreman. But the gaggle of youngsters and derelicts showed little initiative and even less competence. Underfunding had driven away the reputable shippers and professional dock workers. So they wound up with a dinosaur of a ship and a captain and crew to match.

He now hollered up at the captain, "What is your opinion on the weather?"

The captain scratched his salt-and-pepper beard and gazed up into the blue sky. "She may blow later on," he shouted in a voice graveled by years of pipe tobacco. "and this old girl," he pointed to the ancient freighter, which bore the disquieting name of *Gentle Sea*, "may not look like much, but she's capable of withstanding Neptune with a stiff one!" His broad smile of uneven nicotine stained teeth was purely a taunt.

Otto gave up and turned to Heinrich.

"Do you have any constructive thoughts?"

Heinrich cast a defiant look at young Warner. "Let the storm front move through. No use in taking risks. We should stay a few more days and enjoy the beer and the women!" He winked at Warner, who bristled and gave Heinrich the finger.

Otto refused to be drawn in. "I'll consider your suggestion," he said, turning away and walking down the pier to hide his frustration.

By the time the last crate was finally lowered into the hold and lashed into place, Otto's gut was in a knot. As he stood gazing up at the ship, trying to reconcile his fear of the predicted storm with the need to save money by proceeding with all possible haste, the captain came striding back out to the top of the gangplank, wearing a toady grin.

Driven by the pressure riding on him to make a decision, Otto's emotions got the better of him. He decided to put the captain in his place; to exact some small revenge.

"Alright," he barked, throwing the captain a vengeful look. "We wait for the storm front to pass."

The captain began to swear about exactly what he planned to do, and he seemed ready to come down the gangplank and make good on his threats.

Then, General Hermann Goering arrived and everything changed.

Chapter 3

Below the pale crescent of ankle, the foot still wore a low-heeled woman's dress shoe, a black pump, scuffed and dusty.

Jerry reflexively tossed aside his pole and creel and crouched defensively. When a quick look around revealed he was alone, his concentration shifted back to what lay at his feet.

Concealed by a massive clump of sagebrush was the body of a woman, lying on her side, just the one foot Jerry had nearly tripped on sticking out. Jerry pulled back a sage branch and saw the full awkwardness of her repose—fetal, with one leg bent severely beneath her body. There was no use in trying to rouse her.

He sidestepped around the bush and knelt to see her face, which lay with the right cheek against freshly disturbed dirt. There was still some hope the death was an accident. Had she'd gotten lost? Fallen and struck her head? Died of a sudden aneurism?

Not so lucky. A chunk of forehead was missing.

"Awwww shit!"

She had been pretty, with curly dark brown hair, probably in her late twenties or early thirties. He shifted to look at the back of her head, saw dried blood and a dimple—the bullet's entry point.

The indignity of her abandonment brought a flash of anger. It passed. Jerry stood and looked away from the body. His breathing slowed, his pulse rate returned to near normal. He began to consider his first option.

Catch the next bus out of Langston.

He'd need to be long gone before her body was found. It might be weeks or even months before some kid out hunting doves with a twenty-gauge discovered the corpse. But . . . the body might be discovered tomorrow. Or next week. Jerry remembered the two boys who'd seen him at his campsite. He assumed there were others who'd spotted his tent amongst the cottonwoods. Certainly there were locals living along the road leading out of town who watched him come and go over the past six weeks. If he disappeared—mysteriously—he would certainly become the prime suspect.

For a brief moment he considered digging a grave. But he'd have to buy a shovel. And he would have to dig. And if he were caught doing this . . .

There would be no fresh mound amongst the brush and wildflowers.

His disappearing act of last year now drove him to carefully weigh each fact for the equation of flight, whose result would always be measured in terms of survival. If he—the unknown transient who was camped near the body—was linked by proximity to the murder, and if the local authorities were able to produce a good enough artist's sketch—from the clerk at the supermarket who sold him groceries, the hardware man who supplied his fishing pole and lures, the barber where he got his hair cut—they might stumble upon his true identity. It wasn't difficult to imagine a composite being sent out on the wire and recognized by someone, somewhere, who would remember. And then *people really good at finding you* would come.

The Foreign Intervention Coordination Office . . . FICO.

Jerry took a long breath, looked up at the sky as if to accuse God of unfair play, and accepted that his departure would come only after any possible question of his involvement in this murder was erased. A conclusion which led to something he wasn't excited about. He chose to ignore it for a moment and shifted his attention back to the corpse.

The size and shape of the exit wound indicated a single shot fired close up from behind, execution style. His eyes wandered slowly over the body, and other clues began to emerge. A rope burn on her left wrist. A tiny scrap of blue plastic clinging to the golden buckle of her slacks. He almost reached to pick it off.

Stupid!

He stepped back and returned to the unpleasant reality of what needed to be done. He would have to call the sheriff. It risked a local cop making a connection with the black-and-white photo headlined in national papers a year ago.

But who looks for a dead man?

Are you sure?

Yes!

Trust your instincts.

Jerry turned from the body and yelled a single word.

"Shit!"

He took a wild swing at the air with his right fist. A catharsis of sorts. Even hardened killers need a moment.

He walked the last twenty yards through the brush and came out onto the access road. The blue sky and mountains and birds and summer flowers were forgotten. There was an emergency phone box at the intersection with Highway 97, a mile away. He set off down the road, moving with a nervous energy, the soles of his leather boots crunching double-time on the gritty surface, taking a kick at the occasional loose stone to vent his frustration. As he came down the winding road his mind was busy piecing together the murder, cataloguing the facts.

There was no pooled blood, so she had been killed someplace else, bundled in a blue nylon tarp, driven here and dumped. Her clothes were still on her body so the possibility of rape was small. She was dressed for the office, in a smart black suit and white blouse. She was almost certain to be a local. She might have even known her killer. A spurned lover? A jealous coworker? A neighbor harboring some awful grudge?

One other thought kept intruding. He hadn't heard the car. Sound carried a long way in this open country. Many times he'd heard cars come up the road; usually lost tourists, off-road yahoos, or young couples looking for a secluded place to make out. The sound of an engine powering up the steep grade was easy to hear. Jerry had passed the spot where the body now lay after yesterday's fishing and remained at his campsite since then. He didn't remember hearing anything come up the road during that time. Nevertheless, her body must have been moved by car or truck and dumped during the night.

Have my senses dulled so much that I would sleep through that much noise? Is that what jacked up my nightmare?

He finally came out at the highway and walked up to the call box. As he lifted the handset he half-hoped the line would be dead. But even before he pressed it to his ear he could hear a tone. He punched the button and waited. A woman's voice came on the line.

"Nine-one-one operator. What is your emergency?"

"I'm just downriver from the base of the gravel road near the Silver Falls Powerhouse." His voice was shaky. He didn't try to reel it in. Upset was good. You should sound shaken after finding a body.

"I've been camping up beyond the end of the old gorge road. This morning, as I was walking, I came across the body of a woman. I need you to send the police." Nice. Direct. Honest.

His pulse rate had rocketed.

Focus!

The woman's voice stiffened. "I'll dispatch a car immediately. Can you hold for a moment?"

"Sure."

The woman's voice was replaced by elevator music. Jerry had no doubt the nightmare would return tonight. And be even worse.

There was a click on the line and the music was gone.

"What is your name?"

Here we go.

"Jerry Wells," he replied evenly.

"I believe I've got your location on my computer. The phone you're using . . . is it the call box on Highway ninety-seven near the powerhouse junction?"

"I think so." Jerry looked up at the race of water surging from the base of a brick building set beside a power yard filled with huge gray electrical transformers.

Of course it's on your computer! Isn't the modern world wonderful? The demise of privacy is just a mouse click away.

"Mr. Wells, would you please stay where you are until the police arrive?"

"Certainly." He felt the pull of the vortex. His armpits were sweating. But there was no turning back.

"Thank you," she said with brisk efficiency. "Someone will be there shortly." There was a click and then the monotone of a disconnect.

He hung up and squeezed his eyes tight and took a deep breath. When he opened his eyes he gazed up the stream to where the tailrace waters surged from the powerhouse gates. Rising above the roiling water stood the three-story brick building, punctuated by window banks of old-fashioned plate glass. The overall impression was art deco, from an era when the Charleston was popular and Prohibition had finally ended. A style of architecture few masons were capable of today. In the sharp morning light, the pattern formed by the multicolored bricks resembled a Navajo blanket. It was poignantly beautiful. Jerry continued to stare at the lovely pattern, centering his thoughts in preparation for what was to come.

In less than five minutes the wail of a siren came drifting down the western bank of the Columbia.

Red strobes were blazing as the dark blue Taurus swerved onto the shoulder near the call box, throwing bits of gravel as it braked to a stop. *Cascade County Sheriff* reflected in bright gold letters on the side.

The doors banged open and two policemen—one tall, overweight with pasty skin and nearly bald; the other a skinny twenty-something kid with acne scars and a thick mat of curly blonde hair—jumped out. They wore neatly pressed blue uniforms with silver piping and black shoes buffed to a dull polish; each packed a Glock in a black leather holster. The big guy did all the talking.

"You Wells?" The cop demanded.

"Yes." He extended his hand to shake. "It's Jerry," he offered, continuing to hold out his hand. The cop ignored it.

"I'm Sergeant Danner. Where's the body you called in about?"

Jerry let his hand drop slowly to his side. He noted the young officer's brief embarrassment. Jerry was in high survival mode now. Adrenaline surging. A familiar rush. The exhilaration scared him—how much he had missed it over the past year.

"Up there," Jerry replied evenly, pointing toward the access road that wound up into the canyon, "At the end."

"Okay, let's go." Danner turned heel-and-toe and strode to the cruiser. He grabbed the passenger door handle and yanked it open, all without bothering to look and see if he was being obeyed. Jerry followed and climbed into the back seat, immediately surrounded by the vague but unmistakable odor of vomit. He settled reluctantly on the worn fabric. Danner slammed the door shut. There was no inside handle. There was no way to roll the window down.

Danner and the youngster climbed into the front seats and slammed their doors.

"Seatbelt!" Danner was staring at him in the rearview mirror. Jerry reached and pulled the worn buckle across his lap and clicked in the tab. He smiled at Danner in the mirror, but the cop shifted his eyes to the road and gunned the engine to life. Twin comets of gravel jetted as the car U-turned on the shoulder and angled for the access road.

The cruiser sped up into the brown hills, billowing a trail of dust that drifted out into the blossoming heat of the day. At one point they slewed around a hairpin turn and scared a covey of quail pecking along the roadside. How they missed having feathers in the grill was a miracle.

When they reached the end of the road Danner slammed on the brakes, slid to a stop, killed the engine. He was quick to open Jerry's door, standing tall, looking at him with unforgiving eyes, expectant, impatient.

Jerry remembered the Andy Griffith Show and the voice of Deputy Barney Fife echoed in his mind. *"We don't get many murders here in Maybury!"*

Death has a way of extinguishing humor, even for those familiar with the dance. "This way," Jerry said in a voice that carried not the tiniest shred of amusement.

You boys won't like this.

He crossed the turnaround and started into the brush. The two cops followed single file.

When they reached the spot, Danner bent down to see her face, and the aura of tough local cop vanished. There was now a glaze of horror spreading across his slackening face. His eyes glistened, and he blinked several times to forestall tears. Jerry wouldn't have thought the big man's skin could have paled further, but it had gone to parchment.

"Oh Christ!" Danner wiped away the sweat beading his brow.

The young officer crowded up to his sergeant's shoulder to see why Danner was so upset, and he now echoed the horror. He quietly said, "It's Her."

Danner gave a nervous cough that rattled in his throat. "Yeah . . . it's Fiona." He stepped back with his hands braced on his hips, as if he might fall over without this extra support, a quick wheezing breath, eyes unfocused into the distance. Then, in a shaky voice, "Billy, get the space blanket from the emergency kit. We'll put it over her." He turned to Jerry and his voice resumed some of its accusatory briskness.

"Did you move her at all . . . what was your name?"

"Jerry Wells."

"Did you move her, Mr. Wells?"

"No, sir."

"How close did you get to Fion—to the body?"

"Just close enough to know she'd been shot."

"How close was that?"

"I nearly tripped on her foot as I was walking out from my campsite. But after that, maybe two feet."

"Campsite?"

Jerry pointed to the thin trace of trail leading off through the brush. "Up there a ways."

Danner considered this for a moment before continuing in a skeptical tone, "And you were out for a walk?"

"I was heading down to the river to do some fishing."

Danner looked around and spotted something Jerry had entirely forgotten. "Is that your gear over there?" He pointed to the fishing pole and creel Jerry had flung away; the creel lay at the base of a large sage, the pole was tangled in another nearby.

"Yes, sir."

Does this tell him I was surprised? Shocked? Upset? Scared the killer might still be around?

Danner's head dipped slightly; he reached up and repeatedly squeezed his nose with his thumb and index finger as if it might help a thought process sucker punched to its knees. After a long moment the cop regained his composure and found his next question.

"Have you hiked through this way before?"

"As I said, I'm camped upriver. I've been there for six weeks and I've come down this way practically every day since I arrived."

"That would be?"

"Probably forty or fifty times."

"And when you came walking down the path this morning you didn't notice anything unusual until you, as you put it, 'nearly tripped on her foot'?"

"Correct."

"And you didn't touch her body?"

"Of course not!" Jerry left no doubt that he was upset at being grilled. He'd done the "right thing" and now he was being treated unfairly.

But does he believe me?

The sergeant briefly chewed his lower lip before giving a reluctant nod. His next breath came like a gust through a doorway crack.

The young cop returned with a folded sheet of silvery Mylar and began struggling to open it against the static cling. Danner went over and took two corners to help pull it apart, after which they spread it over the body—at least where the sage didn't prevent it—and settled it as best as possible in the brush, weighting the corners with rocks. Jerry watched and wondered if either cop had had much training in crime scene preservation.

Not my problem.

After radioing for an ambulance and an investigation team, Danner walked back to where Jerry stood. He let out another long sigh, looked away across the brown hills, slipped a pack of Marlboros from the breast pocket of his uniform. He tapped the pack, offering the first one up to Jerry.

"No thanks. I gave up years ago." Jerry had never smoked. But saying he once had might create some tiny bridge with the cop. It would say Jerry understood the need for a small routine, a comfortable habit with which to begin to reestablish normalcy.

"Good for you." The sergeant lit up and took a deep drag, making sure the match was cool before he sent it pin wheeling off into the brush with a practiced flick.

Jerry thought about the match, knowing the investigators—if they were good at their job—would find it and wonder if there was a connection to the murderer. It confirmed Danner's amateur status. He briefly considered mentioning this to the cop but decided against it.

Don't give him a reason to think you know his job better than he knows his job.

Through the smoke swirling around Danner's face he began to reappraise Jerry. "What brought you up this way?"

Be careful.

"Camping." He pointed beyond where the woman's body lay. "About a quarter mile up the gorge. Looks like there was a big campsite a long time ago. There's not much left to show for it now. I hope it was okay. Truth is I didn't ask anyone's permission before I set up my tent."

Danner took another deep drag, considering this. "That'd be what we locals call immigrant flats. It's where the Okie's and Arkie's jungled up during the Depression. Hell, I don't think anyone cares if someone wants to camp there. You come here to work the fruit?" It was more of an accusation than a question.

"No," Jerry replied evenly. "I came looking for a little laid back adventure in my retirement. I've been fishing, mostly. I've done a bit of hiking." He fell silent, keenly aware of the sergeant's attention. It would now fall to one side or the other.

The sergeant measured him again and seemed to find approval. "Guess you got a bit more than you bargained for." It came close to sounding like an apology. "Guess we all did, today."

"Yeah, I guess."

Danner continued in a more amiable tone. "Fishing, huh?" He glanced over to where the young cop stood with slack hands, half-listening, head hung low, depression suddenly aging his boyish features. "Go sit in the car if you want, Billy. Get out of the sun."

The kid shuffled off to the cruiser and methodically opened all four doors to let out the heat before climbing inside. Jerry and Oscar watched in silence.

After Billy was settled in the front seat the sergeant looked back at Jerry and abruptly stuck out his right hand. "Name's Oscar Danner," he said. "Call me Oscar. That's what my friends call me."

Jerry shook the proffered hand.

"I do a bit of fishing myself," Oscar continued in a softer—if not entirely happy—voice, slow and dreamy as if in his mind's eye he was somewhere else entirely. "Mostly bass, but sometimes I go for trout upstream from the lake. There's plenty of good fishing in these parts. Rainbows, cutthroat, even some ling cod down deep in the lake, but I'm not much for the fatty fish, 'cept for the salmon, that is. Give me a good salmon steak with crispy skin and that's good eating!" Feeling guilty for the sudden bit of enthusiasm, Oscar fell silent, working hard to look anywhere except at the body.

Jerry recognized the rambling. It was the kind of talk witnesses to tragedy make to keep their minds off what they've seen. A good sign. The cop was upset. His emotions were crackling hot and he was searching for a way to cool back down.

Jerry began to relax a little. "I caught a steelhead down in the Columbia last week," he volunteered.

Oscar looked grateful. He even smiled. "Steelhead?" he said. "I haven't seen many of them in the Columbia this year. You sure that's what it was?"

"I think so."

"Whatever it was, I'll bet it was good eating."

"Sure was."

Oscar fell silent again, unable to defuse the immensity of the situation. Jerry resisted the urge to say more. He seemed to have won the cop over. But it was now clear the woman was well known. The town would be a hornet's nest when the news broke. He briefly regretted not following his first impulse—to run.

In a few minutes sirens came drifting up from the direction of the Columbia. Two blue cruisers soon appeared over the crest of the road. Directly behind came an ambulance. Oscar greeted the new officers and the ambulance crew, pointed to where the body lay, told them who it was, which drew looks of shock. Then said, "Cruz is coming, so you boys better tape off the area and get ready." His mention of the name came with an edge.

Two cops took a roll of yellow crime scene tape and began stringing a barrier around the silvery Mylar.

Oscar walked back to Jerry. "Detective Cruz will have questions." He sounded apologetic. "He can be a handful . . . I'm sorry."

"That's okay. I don't have a lot to tell."

Oscar shrugged. "Cruz can piece it together. That's his job." He paused, as if coming to a final decision. "Fiona was well-liked in town. People will want to know what happened. Best thing is for you to come forward and let the locals know you've got nothing to hide. That way they won't—" He was suddenly embarrassed. "Sorry, Jerry. I didn't mean anything by that. It's just that gossip has a way of making the rounds in a place like Langston. Best not to give 'em a reason to wag their tongues."

"No offense taken." He smiled as if to agree, but Jerry was far from certain that Oscar's suggestion of thrusting himself into the public spotlight was a good idea.

As if to make up for it, Oscar offered, "Maybe we can go fishing sometime? Just you and me."

Jerry paused, as if to give it serious thought. "Can I have a rain check? I'm hard to get a hold of." He gestured in the direction of his campsite. "No phones out here, and I don't have a cell."

Oscar chuckled approvingly.

A minute later a red Mustang convertible crested the rise in the road and sped toward them. It slid to a stop behind the other vehicles.

"There's our boy," Oscar mumbled mostly to himself. He walked toward the Mustang and called greetings in a cheerier tone. A slender man in his early thirties stepped from the car, almost a flinty Clint Eastwood but with a face lightly scarred from childhood acne.

There was a woman with him in the car, late twenties, dressed in blue slacks with a matching blue blazer, white blouse, and a stylish red bow tie. Her hair was pulled back and tied up in a scarf. Professional yet charming. She stepped out, the body of an athlete but every inch a woman, following the detective with determination.

Oscar started hard at the woman and raised his hands as if in protest, but Cruz ignored the big cop and began walking directly toward the taped-off area. The woman followed close behind.

Oscar called out, "Detective!"

Cruz continued to ignore Oscar and reached the Mylar. Oscar stood his ground. An effort had been made. He now appeared almost pleased by what was about to happen.

When Cruz pulled back the space blanket and saw who lay under it, he gasped. But his reaction paled by comparison to the scream from the woman, who had moved in close behind to get a good first look. She stumbled back several steps, fell to her knees, buried her face in her hands, bent with her forehead nearly touching the ground, and began to sob uncontrollably.

For a few seconds no one seemed to know what to do. Cruz looked as if he was plugged into some cosmic electrical outlet, frozen, holding the corner of the blanket. The other cops' attentions were riveted upon Cruz, the body, and the sobbing woman kneeling on the ground.

Finally, Oscar walked over to the woman and reached down and helped her to her feet, then guided her to his patrol car. She collapsed into the right front seat, oblivious to the stares that followed her, tears coursing down her cheeks.

Oscar called out, "Hey, Billy!"

The young cop walked over.

Oscar spoke very softly, "Take her back into town."

Within seconds the rookie was behind the wheel and starting the engine. After the car disappeared down the road, Oscar walked back towards where Cruz now stood numbly staring at the space blanket. When he reached Jerry, he paused and shook his head slightly.

"Who was the woman?" Jerry asked.

"Holly Wells, our new deputy prosecuting attorney. And she was also the dead woman's best friend."

"What a nightmare for her," Jerry said.

"Yeah," Oscar agreed, offering in barely more than a whisper, "God damn, sometimes Cruz thinks he just knows fucking everything."

CHAPTER 4

As Manny Cruz directed the deputies to prepare the crime scene for the state patrol investigators, he couldn't shake the image of what he'd seen in that first instant when the silvery sheet was pulled back. Carrion flies. The vision of black dots around the open head wound burned in his brain, triggering bleak childhood memories of the tiny Mexican village in Jalisco province where he was born and spent the early years of his life . . . until the flood.

When Manny was four his family lived south of the border. Torrential summer rains thundered in from the west and struck his village on a hot and muggy July afternoon. Mudslides flushed down the ravines, uprooting trees and bundling them away like matchsticks. Churning brown water surged in the creek and cascaded over the banks, busting up stucco houses, obliterating timber huts, carrying away families huddled on roofs, sucking away screaming peasants and their farm animals, furniture, everything. Corpses choked up like cordwood on newly formed mud bars in the stifling monsoonal humidity.

Local emergency resources were overwhelmed. It took days for the police and the army to bypass washed out bridges and navigate muddy roads to help gather bodies and move them into makeshift morgues. Long before the bodies were safely stored the flies laid eggs and newly hatched maggots began their feast.

After the devastation of the cornfield and garden and the obliteration of their house, the Cruz family moved north to find agricultural work along the west coast, eventually settling on the outskirts of Langston where Manny was enrolled in school and became part of the first wave of Hispanics to be main-streamed into local white culture.

More than thirty years had passed since the family arrived, but for Manny, the vision of how black flies swarm to flesh had never faded. To see the flies again, and on someone he knew . . . it tore him up inside.

Even worse was Holly's gasp of horror and then her complete breakdown. He'd invited her to the murder scene on impulse, hoping to find favor. As a new assistant prosecutor she was routinely assigned the grunt cases: dependencies, misdemeanors, child support enforcement, DUI's. Manny figured if he gave her a taste of a capital felony, she might appreciate his effort, and maybe she would begin to see him as more than just another cop.

It had backfired.

Fiona had been Holly's closest friend. How could she ever forgive him?

Still, there was a job to do. He waved for the sergeant to come over; face to face Cruz stared hard and his voice cut like a knife. "I'm not going to forget this, Danner. You should have told me!"

"I tried . . ." Oscar began. But the rawness remained on Cruz's face and Oscar quickly gave up and fell silent.

Cruz continued in the tough cadence of someone who enjoys giving orders.

"Take Wells into Langston. Buy him lunch. Keep an eye on him until I return for the interview. It might be a while before the State Patrol arrives. Don't screw this up."

"Right," Oscar replied, happy to comply. With the heat and Fiona's body, the crime scene was the last place Oscar wanted to be.

Cruz continued, "Keep your ears open. I want a written report on every-thing he says on my desk first thing tomorrow morning."

Oscar absorbed the command with a straight face, but hating Cruz just the same. Writing detailed reports was his least favorite task, especially on a tight deadline. He imagined the pain of stiff fingers tapping at a computer keyboard.

Oscar shelved the anger as he walked to one of the deputies for a set of keys, then back to where Jerry leaned against a patrol car.

"Cruz wants me to take you into town. He expects to be at least a couple more hours down here. Sorry it'll take so long." He shrugged.

"Oh, well," Jerry spoke softly so only the big cop could hear. "Police work happens."

Oscar chuckled. "That it does, Jerry. That it does."

They climbed in and Oscar backed the cruiser, crunching rear tires in the dry grass. He drove at a leisurely pace on the winding road down to the main highway. Jerry noticed Oscar hadn't fastened his seat belt and hadn't asked him to fasten his, either. It was a small item, but the significance was not lost. Jerry gazed out the window to hide a grim smile of satisfaction.

After driving along the Columbia for two miles they turned left onto the East Valley Highway and made the steep climb from the river, passing through Turner's Notch, and began a gradual descent into the valley. In the distance Jerry saw the seven-mile-wide expanse of Lake Cascade; they passed a sign which read: *City of Langston – Pop. 9,582;* its last three digits on a removable plaque. An upscale housing tract with sprawling ranch-style homes soon gave way to gas stations and fast food restaurants and a car dealership.

Speed signs changed to twenty-five as the highway became the main drag through the heart of old Langston. The older buildings were mostly red brick, some partially covered with ivy. The middle divider held a line of stately maples with massive gnarled trunks and branches reaching over the sidewalks.

"You hungry?" Oscar asked.

"A little." Ordinarily, the apple he'd eaten for breakfast would have been followed by a lunch of pan fried trout with rice. The discovery of a body and the prospect of being interviewed by the detective had sidelined his appetite. Jerry would rather have sat in a quiet corner of the police station until it was time for the interview. But it would do no good to sour Oscar's favor by turning down a lunch offer.

"Me, I'm famished," Oscar rambled on. "There's a great cafe up ahead." Oscar pointed to the next block. "Best prime rib in town. All you can eat. It'll be my treat."

Jerry bit his lip. "Great," he said, trying to sound enthusiastic.

Oscar wheeled the cruiser into a parking space in front of a restaurant where an orange neon sign was raised against the bricks directly above a large plate glass window. The glowing letters read: *Sam's Place.*

The eatery was packed, but when the hostess saw Oscar she immediately led them to a corner table being wiped down by a skinny youngster in black pants and a black short sleeve shirt and wearing a white food-stained apron that screamed *minimum wage*. The kid finished a jerky mop-up of the table and headed towards the kitchen without ever having made eye contact with the hostess or the new customers.

A forty-something waitress with bleached blonde hair curled and frosted Texas large arrived and briefly scanned the table surface with a critical eye. Satisfied the kid had at least gotten the chunky stuff off the speckled Formica, she asked, "You boys want separate checks?" She reached into the pocket of her brown apron and pulled out a receipt pad and a ballpoint.

"No, Bess. Two full buffets, and put both on my ticket."

She raised a suspicious eyebrow. "Okay," she said in mild disbelief.

Oscar headed for the silvery steam tables at the back of the room. The waitress looked at Jerry. "Follow him," she said with what sounded like *Congratulations!*

By the time Jerry caught up at the line, Oscar had already piled on a slab of prime rib and generous scoops of potato and macaroni salad. Jerry asked the hair-netted server woman for a breast of roasted chicken, took a sourdough roll from the basket, and used plastic tongs at the end of the line to grab a helping of garden salad which he seasoned with oil and vinegar. Oscar waited patiently and then escorted him back to their table, eying Jerry's plate.

"Remember, it's all you can eat."

Jerry shrugged.

Oscar eyed his own plate with eager anticipation. "Dig in," he prompted, and immediately pinned the prime rib with his fork and started sawing at the fatty end with a serrated knife.

Jerry took a bite of chicken, chewed slowly, and watched Oscar become completely absorbed in his food. "Real shame about the girl," Jerry finally said.

"Yeah," Oscar mumbled around a mouthful of beef. "Cruz never should have brought her down in the first place. Prosecutor's not supposed to get involved 'till after we've got the evidence together for an evaluation."

Oscar had misunderstood. Jerry meant the dead woman. But this new information had its own value. The more he knew about Cruz, the better. He took a bite of salad, chewed for a moment, and hoped his next question would sound like small talk; just two guys who've had a long day and are glad to be off their feet.

"The two women knew each other?"

"Yeah," Oscar mumbled, pausing to swallow a mouthful of potato salad. "You always saw them jogging around courthouse park at noon. After work they went to that fancy gym in the old Anderson Warehouse." A mournful look filled his doughboy features. "That Fiona, she was a real gem. Did a helluva job with the museum."

"Oh?"

Oscar continued to work his fork and knife with a proficient ease, his eyes darting up occasionally to accent a point.

"Oh, yeah. Came here a few years ago, landed a job as museum director, and within two years she had that grungy old dump up to speed. Hell, there's stuff came up out of the basement nobody even suspected was down there. Indian baskets and arrowheads, old farming equipment, pictures of pioneer families, tons of historical junk. She talked some of the local merchants into donating money to put it in some fancy display cases. Even won an award from the state historical society." Oscar looked up, holding Jerry's gaze for a second. "Can't understand who'd want to do her in." He stood, picking up his empty plate. "I'm going for seconds. You ready for more?"

Jerry had barely eaten half of his food. "Go ahead," he said.

"Be right back," Oscar said. And he was, with another slab of prime rib and a slice of cherry pie with whipped cream.

Near the end of lunch, Oscar shared the gossip that Cruz had the hots for Holly. Gossip also said Holly had shown complete disinterest. Oscar leered as he shared this juicy tidbit. Then his face grew concerned. "Hey, don't tell Cruz I told you this, okay?"

"Sure, no problem. Our secret."

Oscar relaxed. "It's no big deal, anyways," he added. "She's from Seattle, and no one around here much likes the two-oh-sixers."

"The what?"

"That's for the area code. Phone numbers in Seattle have a two-oh-six area code. So people here in eastern Washington call them two-oh-sixers." He shrugged. "Besides, prosecuting's not a good line of work for a woman in a hick place like Langston." Oscar's tone became conspiratorial. "We're just a bunch of rednecks. Most locals figure a woman's place is in the home." He now sounded just a tiny bit apologetic. "Holly catches more shit than most. I'd bet a hundred bucks she moves back to the coast within a year. She'd be a lot happier over in Seattle."

Jerry let the judgmental comment slide.

Oscar seemed to realize he might have said something that wouldn't find universal agreement, especially from a non-local, and quickly switched to the safer subject of fishing.

He was near poetic in describing the annual runs of salmon in the Columbia. But he confessed that his favorite spot was the Big Cascade River, above the lake, where a lucky angler could pull in a limit of two- and three-pound rainbows if the conditions were right. "Caught me a six-pounder a few years back," he bragged. "But those days are gone. Too many fishermen. Not enough fish."

"I've always fished from the shore," Jerry said.

"Bet you'd change your mind if you saw my rig. I've got a sixteen-foot Alumaweld with a fifty-horse Johnson and an eight-horse Merc," Oscar shoveled in a mouthful of pie slathered with whipped cream. "A fisherman's boat, by God! I'll take you out and show you how to catch some real trout!"

"I'll think about it," Jerry said, trying to sound as though he actually was going to think about it.

"Whatever suits you is fine with me. It's there when you want it." Oscar seemed satisfied.

By the time they pulled into the courthouse parking lot Oscar was acting like he'd known Jerry for years, not just a couple of hours.

"Don't worry about Cruz," Oscar assured him as he led Jerry to a waiting area and then brought him a mug of coffee from the officers' pot in the tiny kitchen. "He's all bark, no bite." Then, as an afterthought, "He's not bad . . . for a Mexican." He winked.

Jerry settled back in the brown vinyl padded armchair to sip what turned out to be halfway decent coffee.

⅄

Manny was with the body for nearly an hour and it was beginning to weigh on his patience. He made one final note on the small pad and shoved the pad into his back pocket. The State Patrol's investigation team was en route from Spokane and would arrive around 6pm. That gave Manny enough time to get back to the courthouse, interview Wells, and return to meet the troopers.

As he stood beside his Mustang, an ancient red-and-white Ford Scout chugged over the hill and rambled up behind one of the county cruisers. As the relic wheezed to a stop, Manny walked over.

Cascade County's coroner was a physician named Saul Keegan who had retired at sixty-eight from a general practice and then decided to run for the one public office no one seemed too excited about holding. "Hi, Doc," Manny greeted the silver haired man who stepped from the Scout carrying a hard shell black suitcase. "Need a hand with that?"

"Nope," Saul Keegan replied in a brisk voice. "I'm not a fossil!" He made his point by hoisting the heavy case with one hand and walking over to where Manny stood. "What've we got?"

Manny liked Keegan. The doc filed his reports promptly, never gave you bullshit, and when it came to courtroom testimony Manny was convinced no juror could resist the grandfatherly image. Saul also had a knack for gently informing the next of kin, usually a spouse or a child, about the sudden death of a loved one. Manny had made some of those calls, and plain and simple it just sucked. He was quite happy to hand it off to Saul.

Manny now broke the bad news.

"Sorry to have to tell you this, Doc. It's Fiona Ross."

"Christ Almighty!" Saul shook his head. "Got any idea about the cause?"

Manny tried to keep the irony out of his voice and failed completely. "No offense, Doc," Manny replied, "but I think a first grader could make this call." Manny spread his hands wide in apology.

With the crime scene in the able hands of Keegan, Manny climbed into the Mustang. The brakes were dusted and they squealed as he eased the car down the graveled road.

As he turned onto the main highway along the Columbia, he remembered that Frank Brindleman, the operator at the Silver Falls Powerhouse, had recently called in to report a prowler. He'd not given much of a description to the deputy who took the call, and that irked Manny. Brindleman had served two tours of duty in Vietnam, and Manny had heard his nerves had been pretty much shattered in combat. Rumor was he had a purple heart and a bronze star. But it wouldn't have mattered if Frank had a dozen medals and wore them every day. To Manny, Frank was like Oscar. They were Good Old Boys. That was all it took to put you on a choice payroll like the county or the PUD.

White boys got it easy.

Manny tried to push the resentful thought aside. Hadn't the county also hired little ol' Manny Cruz? Wasn't he a genuine "Lucky Mexican?" But his employment came only because they needed someone fluent in Spanish who understood the gang-speak. Someone who knew the "brown-skinned, down-and-out" because he came from the same poor side of town.

Manny knew there might someday be another side to that coin. More and more Mexicans were settling in central Washington, starting their own businesses, enrolling kids in school, applying for US citizenship. A quiet flood of Hispanic voters loomed on the near horizon. Manny figured if he kept his head down and his mouth shut and did a first-class job, that maybe someday he might just have a chance at being elected sheriff.

He turned onto the narrow paved road that led to the powerhouse. If Frank Brindleman was available, this would be a good opportunity to take him up for a look through the interrogation room mirror. And wouldn't it be convenient if Frank recognized Wells as the mystery prowler!

CHAPTER 5

Frank Brindleman was having a shitty day. One of those fool engineers from the Chelan County PUD had been on the phone with him for an hour, grilling him for the history of maintenance practices on the original generators that had been running just fine since they were first brought on line in '34. Frank had several times nearly told the college educated know-it-all to take a flying leap into the penstock. Let him ride the tube and thread his ass through the turbines if he wanted to learn more about how they worked! Unfortunately, the engineer had more to say about how the powerhouse was run than did Frank, who'd been employed in that very same powerhouse since '73.

It hadn't always been this way. When Frank returned from Vietnam he had wrangled an entry level job with the Cascade County Public Utility District. After a couple years they sent him off for training and a bit of college at the local J.C. Frank continued to take a class here and a seminar there and eventually he worked himself up to operator level at the Silver Falls plant. By the 1980s Frank was the head cheese. He never quite mastered all of the math stuff, but the generators had been running more-or-less smoothly under his care for all those years, and if something weird happened there were plenty of consultants eager to charge a few grand to set things right.

Then the '90s arrived and running a single dam with just two generators and only sixty megawatts of power to sell became more and more of a problem for the three commissioners. Cascade County PUD had only one dam in its portfolio, and no promise of anything more, because when other dams were being built along the nearby Columbia River, the Cascade commissioners smugly passed up the opportunity of buying into more generation capacity. They was plenty of juice to service everyone in the valley, and a fair bit to sell in the open market.

But the world moved on and power generation and marketing became more technical and complex, and it got harder to find parts at decent prices when you were a pipsqueak in the greater scheme of power distribution in the Pacific Northwest. Even finding linemen to work the limited number of miles of distribution cable was problematic. And someday soon, those old generators would need to be replaced. And that was going to cost millions.

The commissioners finally voted in '96 to enter into a joint operating agreement with the nearby Chelan County PUD, which owned three dams and had several hundred employees and a great credit rating and would be able to carry the upstream utility on its back into the twenty-first century.

On the positive side, Frank kept his job, although his responsibilities shrunk to what amounted to making sure the lubricating oil was flowing and the gauges in the control room weren't swinging wildly into the red. On the downside, Frank became a step-'n-fetch-it for the highfalutin muckety-mucks of the Chelan County PUD which was sixty miles away in Wenatchee. And the hardest part was that Frank knew his own limitations, and realized his days were numbered. Eventually they would chuck him out, albeit with a nice little retirement that would at least not leave him working in the orchards like his old man.

But damn it all! There was something Frank hadn't yet accomplished. Something he'd worked on for years. And the specter of not being around long enough to finish this one thing was now starting to drive a wedge between Frank and the real world.

So Frank was pretty worked up when he heard the front door of the powerhouse thump open. As he walked along the hallway to find out who wanted to enter into his domain, Frank began to steam. In fact, Frank was so upended that a little corner of his mind was shouting caution.

Don't go too far! Not yet!

And then Frank saw the Mexican cop, and for an instant Frank hovered on the edge of rage. Stars exploded and the sky was shot with starbursts and crimson and napalm. And then the all-out blossom of madness checked itself.

Frank was still seething on the inside as he walked towards Detective Cruz, but on the outside he managed to throttle down and look a lot less *enraged* than he was *concerned*.

"Hello Detective," Frank said as he approached Manny. "To what do I owe the pleasure?"

Manny briefly shook the proffered hand, knowing Frank was being polite because it was the way you were supposed to act when the police showed up with no apparent reason. When they let go, both men momentarily thought how nice it would be to go and wash their hands with pumice stone soap.

"We've had a murder up the access road," Manny said.

Frank's reaction was exactly what Manny expected. "Holy crap!" Frank's head pitched a little forward and his mouth slack jawed for a second. "Do you know who it is?"

"Fiona Ross."

Frank shook his head in disbelief.

"Got any suspects?"

"Not really."

"When did it happen?"

"Last night. We're not sure of the exact time. Doc Keegan's up there now and he'll establish that." Manny waited for Frank to ask the next logical question.

"So . . . why are you down here?"

"Remember the intruder you reported?"

Frank did remember. He'd spoken to someone in the Sheriff's office just two days ago. It had been a delusion; something he later recognized as a flashback to a bad night patrol in 'Nam. But sure enough he'd said it, and now he was going to have to live with it. Sometimes the ghosts caught up with you at the exactly wrong moment. "Yeah," Frank said slowly.

"The body was found by some fellow who's been camped upriver from where the body was left."

"And you think it might be the same guy I saw?"

"It's possible. This guy made the call in to report finding her body, so it's a long shot. But in my business . . ."

"Understood," Frank said. "I didn't get a very good look at who was prowling around here. It was nighttime and this guy was mostly a shadow out on the edge of the parking lot. But if I can help, I'd be happy to oblige."

"Good," Cruz said. "We've got him up at the station house and I'll be interviewing him in an hour or so. Any chance you could come up and sit behind the mirror to see if he looks like your intruder?"

"Sure thing."

"Do you need a ride? I can have somebody bring you back down after you're through."

"No," Frank said quickly. *Calm down!* And when he continued Frank had slowed down just enough to sound normal. "I've got some chores to attend to in town and I'd just as soon drive my car."

"Okay," Manny said. "But could you please come soon so we can get you tucked out of sight?"

"You bet," Frank said. "I can leave here in fifteen minutes if that's soon enough."

"That will be fine. Check in with the receptionist at the front desk. I'll give her instructions so you don't stumble into the fellow in the hallway." Manny smiled and nodded like everything was just fine, but he didn't try for another handshake before he walked out.

When Frank heard Manny's Mustang fire to life out in the parking lot he finally allowed himself a sly smile. A new idea had blossomed. A truly great and wonderful idea. One single thought now pounded through his brain, over and over.

Fuckin' great luck!

Chapter 6

J erry was dozing by the time Manny appeared.

"Mr. Wells?"

Jerry's head snapped up from the back of the vinyl couch in the Sheriff's reception lounge. The detective was standing directly in front of him. His uniform was dusty and a cheat grass rider was stuck in the cuff of his pants.

"This way, please."

Manny led Jerry down a hallway through the middle of the building. The industrial linoleum beneath their feet was scuffed where the wood base had settled and warped. The walls were yellow.

The interrogation room waited behind a metal door near the end of the hallway. The door was secured by a deadbolt which Manny slammed back before pushing the door open. Inside were a wood table and two worn metal chairs. A mirror was framed into the back wall. Manny settled into the far chair, his back to the mirror, and waved for Jerry to sit opposite.

As Jerry sat he gave a quick glance at the mirror. It was impossible to tell if someone was behind. If there was a watcher, Jerry could do nothing about it. He pushed away the thought there might also be a camera, and concentrated upon the detective.

Manny reached inside his back pocket and pulled out a small spiral-wire-ring notepad with a ballpoint pen pushed into the wire. He opened the pad, extracted the pen, and flipped past several pages filled with scribbled notes until there was clean paper.

"You're not a suspect or a person of interest," he began bluntly, jotting down a note as he spoke. "I want you to know that right up front. There might be some who'd think it a smart way to cover up a murder by reporting it themselves. Like the pyro who starts a fire and then calls it in so he can watch the engines arrive. But—" Manny looked through him like a hot poker, "you don't strike me as that type."

The statement may have been calculated to set him at ease, but it had the opposite effect. Jerry dismissed Oscar's lukewarm assessment of the detective. Oscar might be a creampuff. Manny was not.

Manny Cruz reminded him of a Mexican operative he'd worked with in Guadalajara. Raul Gomez had little DEA training, but he possessed awesome street savvy. Time and again he reported with exactly where the drug runners would show up, "Got it straight from the homies," Gomez would say. "Only cost me half an ounce this time!" And then he'd laugh in a braying voice that sounded like a mad donkey.

Raul's connection to, as he put it, "his people," exposed a weakness. He was always stopping along the road to pick up a struggling senior or some flat-out-busted peon, whether he knew them or not. It earned him the moniker of "Mister Charitable" with the locals, but this was always said in a kind way. The habit of being overly helpful eventually got him killed. He was ambushed when an old woman named Rosa flagged him down. The men who came running from the jungle paid her well. Raul Gomez had died from the short burst of a Kalashnikov. The fact that Rosa was later "cleaned" was of no consolation to Jerry. He'd lost not only his best native operative, but also a good friend. And in that line of work there weren't many people you thought of as "good friend." Hell, there was hardly anyone you could even trust.

"How long have you been camping on the river?"

Jerry came back to the moment.

"Six weeks, give or take."

Manny gave him a long look. "That's a fair bit of camping."

Jerry shrugged. "It's free, and I got to like the place."

"And where exactly is your campsite?"

"About a quarter of a mile from the end of the road where I found the body."

"Had you camped anywhere else in the valley?"

"No."

Manny paused to make notes in his little spiral pad.

"And before that?"

"I retired from the government last year. Left my apartment back east to do some driving around. I wanted to see the some of the Southeast so I drove the back roads down the coast and into the Florida Keys." Jerry decided to test the detective, to see if he would engage in more of a give-and-take. "Have you ever been down through the Keys?"

Manny answered politely. "No."

"Too bad. You should check it out some day."

Manny gave a disinterested shrug. "And after Florida?"

So much for being sociable.

Jerry needed to begin inventing a story that drew closer and closer to Langston. He could feel the pull of the vortex. The detective was jaded and bright—a dangerous combination. All he could truly hope for was not to spike Manny's interest by saying something stupid, or inconsistent.

I should have run.

Trust your instincts! Get on with it!

"I enjoyed the freedom of traveling, so I came back up across the Florida panhandle and drove to New Orleans. Then up through Louisiana, Oklahoma. I pulled an all-nighter across Kansas and eastern Colorado, headed north through Wyoming and Montana, and then spent a few days camping near Yellowstone and Glacier."

Manny focused on Jerry's story and for the moment was ignoring his notepad. Nothing was being taken for granted, nothing was unimportant to the detective. Jerry reminded himself to stay loose. He was supposed to be describing the rambling retirement of a carefree fellow with no specific plans beyond whatever new adventure came along.

"I'd never seen Washington State, so I headed up this way. Then my car broke down. I took it into a shop and they said the block was cracked and it would cost two grand to fix. The old clunker wasn't worth much, so I sold it to the mechanic for a few bucks and caught the bus for Seattle. When the

Greyhound passed through Langston I saw how beautiful this part of the country was and decided to spend a few days. It was early May and the weather turned nice. I was in no hurry to get anywhere, the fishing was good, and, well, that's about all there is to it."

The reality was that after crossing back into the US from Mexico, he'd lived for eleven nervous months in a battered singlewide, set inconspicuously amongst dozens of similarly distressed mobile homes in a seedy west Texas mobile home court. He rarely left the trailer, usually just to buy food, and then only late at night when the swing shift clerk at the neighborhood grocery was too tired to take much of an interest in anything except getting home and prying the shoes off her swollen feet. Jerry gained weight, and was starting to go stir crazy.

When he thought enough time had finally passed to dim the memories people of who'd seen his black-and-white photo in the national papers, he worked up the nerve to leave, hoping for a new hiding place that was close enough to Canada for a wild stab at political asylum if he was discovered by the U.S. authorities. A Trailways bus eventually brought him to Langston. The one solid truth in the story was that he did think the area was beautiful. But the area's remoteness was of far greater importance.

His story would stand up to moderate scrutiny. What could the detective do? Any trail Jerry might have left was by now cold.

Manny kept plugging away.

"You said you worked for the government?"

"Yes. I had a desk job with the Army in Virginia." The Army released no information without a federal subpoena, and Manny had about as much chance of obtaining one of those as he had of being nominated for a Nobel Prize. And without Jerry's real surname, any inquiry would be useless.

"I retired after thirty years of pushing paper."

"So you get a pension check?"

A gold star for effort! Jerry's assessment of the cop notched one peg higher. Checks would be deposited. Tracing bank records was easy for the police. But Jerry had a perfectly reasonable explanation for why he had no banking records.

"I took a lump sum. An old pal of mine had a private investment advisor in Switzerland. It all went into a foreign mutual fund. Whenever I need money

I just call and they wire me some dough. I'm strictly cash these days. It doesn't take much to make ends meet when you're camping." *And no one but a fool would try prying banking information out of the Swiss!* Jerry waited to see if the detective would challenge him on any of this. His luck held.

Manny jotted another note, and then asked a series of questions about where Jerry had been and what he'd been doing in the hours before the murder. These Jerry answered fully and honestly. There was nothing to hide.

It was nearly an hour before Manny said, "Okay, that's all for now."

"So I'm free to go?"

Manny gave him a calculating look.

"If by 'go' you mean back to your camp . . . sure. But you were planning on sticking around the area, weren't you?"

"I hadn't thought much about it. It's summer. The living is easy." Jerry laughed, and Manny gave a brief smile before his mouth firmed up. The subject had cooperated so he wasn't going to be impolite. But there was no reason to get chummy, either.

"Like I said earlier, you're not a target of our investigation. But you might be an important witness, provided we catch whoever did this. I want you to remain in the area for now, and keep in touch with our office."

"Okay," Jerry said reluctantly. The detective's eyes studied him. Wheels were turning. Jerry felt his palms grow warm. Had he given some clue that things were not quite right? Had Manny spotted something with his inquisitor's radar?

Manny shifted direction. "It might be a good idea for you to move into town. No telling who did this. They might have seen you."

Jerry doubted that. If the killer had spotted him and been concerned, either Jerry would already be dead, or he would have killed whoever came after him. Odds favored the latter.

"Okay," he replied, slowly. "I'll give it some thought. But I'm partial to camping right now."

"Suit yourself," Manny said, as if it were of minor importance. As if he'd only been trying to do Jerry a favor. But clearly, it wasn't minor, and doing Jerry a favor was the furthest thing from Manny's mind. "Of course, if you were here in Langston it would make it easier for us to contact you if we need to. But I suppose we can always send someone down to find you." It was pressure, and both men knew it. Jerry let the wave of resentment wash through him without any visible reaction.

Manny now seemed to remember something. "Could you wait a minute?"

"Sure."

Jerry sat alone in the room for what seemed entirely too long, finding it increasingly difficult not to stare into the one-way mirror. Cruz was doing something other than the bathroom. Was he taking pictures? Were others being brought in to take a look? It began to play on his nerves, to the point where he was glad to see the interrogation room door swing open again. The detective was alone. Jerry half expected to be finger printed and booked, although he knew the thought was irrational. Still . . .

Manny offered no explanation for his long absence. He said, "Thanks for waiting. Can we give you a lift down to your camp?"

Jerry had endured more than enough contact with the police. He smiled as he declined the offer. "No thanks. I'll catch the bus. It's a nice day."

"Suit yourself."

Manny escorted him down the hallway and out to the reception area.

"Sure you don't want a ride?" he again offered.

"Positive."

"Okay. Don't forget to call and check in. Tomorrow would be good."

"Where do I call?"

Manny reached into his shirt pocket, withdrew a business card. He handed the card to Jerry. "Call and ask the operator to ring extension twenty-three. If I'm not in you'll get my voice mail. Just leave a message to let me know where you are."

The two men shook hands like neighbors who've agreed not to squabble over a community fence.

Jerry felt better the second he exited through the front door. He walked down the cement path that cut across the vast lawn of the courthouse/police station complex, looking forward to getting out of Langston. He was standing at the bus stop, waiting for a ride to the highway where he could hike back up the access road, when a stranger walked up.

"Excuse me," the man said. He looked to be in his fifties, five-foot-seven, with a middling beer gut. He wore faded jeans and a long-sleeved gray shirt and he smelled of machine oil. His sparse brown hair was cropped short in a cut that might have been performed at home in front of a mirror. Dark rings shadowed his eyes. Jerry expected him to ask for spare change. What came next took him completely by surprise.

"Lieutenant Dockins?"

Jerry couldn't mask his shock.

The stranger gave a wry smile. "I thought so," he said triumphantly.

Jerry hadn't used *Dockins* since 1973 in Vietnam, on a short term deployment with I-Corp's Special Ops out of Danang. He'd never expected to hear it again.

The stranger gave him a crisp salute and then stuck out his hand. "PFC Frank Brindleman, One Hundred and First Airborne," he said proudly. "My friends call me Frank."

Numbly, Jerry shook Frank's hand. "Jerry," he said, wondering exactly how many people called this man "friend."

"Wells," Frank added conspiratorially. "The detective said you're last name is 'Wells.' Of course, they don't know your real name, do they?" Frank saw concern flash across Jerry's face, and continued reassuringly, "Don't worry. I didn't tell." Frank grinned, and behind the joy Jerry knew unpleasant things were scuttling around.

"Do we know each other from 'Nam?"

"You wouldn't remember me," Frank conceded. "I was just a grunt. But for a couple days they assigned me to make sure nobody bothered your room while you were out on a mission."

Jerry nodded, still not able to pull up a memory of the man. Doubting they ever had a conversation.

Frank's glee faded. "We need to talk." He glanced around nervously, first at a nearby oak and then over at concrete blockhouse public restrooms. Neither satisfied Frank. "I've got a car," he said, pointing to a vintage blue Chevy II parallel parked. "I'll give you a ride back to your camp. C'mon." He began walking away, as if there could be no question about Jerry's accepting the offer. Jerry followed, his mind screaming.

He knows things about my past!

Jerry tried to convince himself everything was still all right. Cruz remained in the dark. This was just an unexpected bump that he would find a way to handle. After all, the *nom de guerre* of "Dockins" was three decades old. Even if Frank told the detective, the Army would have no record of a "Lieutenant Jerry Dockins." At least none that would ever see the light of day.

Still, it wouldn't be good for Cruz to know. Jerry might be able to explain it away by saying it was classified; but the clean cut image of a government employee would be eroded. Manny might begin to puzzle out other things once he knew Jerry lied about what he'd done for a living. Not a "desk job", but active military service that required the use of an alias. And Cruz would want to know which was his real name, "Dockins" or "Wells." And once that door of inquiry was open . . .

Of all the shitty luck!

There was no alternative except to follow Frank and hope for the best.

⅄

Manny took Frank behind the one-way glass, saw Frank's flash of recognition as he looked through at the man seated at the interrogation table, and challenged Frank for an explanation.

"Well?"

There was too long of a pause before Frank answered.

"He's not the one I saw prowling around the Powerhouse."

"Are you sure?"

"Absolutely," Frank replied evenly. "This guy's taller, and maybe stockier."

"Maybe?"

"He's definitely stockier. I'm certain of it." Frank looked one more time, to confirm. "Yup," he said. "For sure."

Manny prodded. "You seemed to recognize Mr. Wells, I thought, maybe just for a second."

Frank scrunched his face in concentration before giving a cautious answer.

"He looks like a guy I knew a long time ago. But just a little. It's not him. I'm certain."

Manny let it slide. It was possible the flash of recognition was an innocent confusion with someone else.

But a couple minutes later, as Manny chanced to glance out his office window, he saw Frank crossing the lawn tracking after Jerry like a bloodhound. He watched as Frank caught up at the bus stop; a salute from Frank, the two spoke, and shook hands. Then, Frank led Jerry to his car.

He lied! But why?

It didn't transform Jerry into a suspect in Fiona's murder. But the connection between the two—which Frank had so adamantly denied—was disquieting. Why had Frank not told him that he knew Jerry Wells?

The answer to that question would have to wait. There were more important things for now. The team from Spokane hadn't yet reached the murder scene, so searching Fiona's house was now on the top of Frank's to-do list. The cop he'd sent an hour ago had radioed to report everything looked normal; the doors were locked and he'd secured the front and back with crime scene tape.

Gaining entry wouldn't require a warrant, but Frank didn't want to bust the door down either.

No reason to give a reporter from the local rag a free shot.

Manny knew Holly and Fiona had been best friends. She might know if Fiona kept a key hidden outside the house. He picked up the phone and punched the number. One ring . . . two. And on a sudden inspiration he jammed the handset back into its cradle.

He jogged down the hallway to the kitchen. The mug Jerry had drunk from, a coral-colored ceramic with a brown teddy bear glazed onto the side, still lay on the counter. Manny lifted it, fingers on the inside, and carried it upside down back to his office.

He got out his kit, dusted and lifted two full prints—a ring finger and a thumb. Once these were safe he picked up the phone and hit the redial button. "Prosecutor's office, Marge speaking," came the voice on the line.

"Hi, Margie. It's Manny."

"What can I do you for, Manny?"

"Is Holly in?"

"No. She never came back this afternoon. I think she went home. Hey, it's a damned shame what happened to Fiona. Got any suspects yet?"

The gossip mill's already in gear.

"No, Margie. But you folks will be the first ones to know. And I promise we'll catch whoever it was."

"You better."

"Yeah." *No shit.*

"I can give you her home number if you want."

He pictured a devastated Holly at home. *Bad idea.*

"No thanks, Margie. I'll catch up with her later." He hung up, reached for the Rolodex, flipped through until he found what he wanted. He punched the numbers and waited.

A voice gone rough from hard living answered after the fourth ring. "Jake's Lock and Key."

"Hey, Jake. It's Manny. Have you got a few minutes to open a door for me?"

"Sure, Manny. Is this a warrant job, or just regular?"

"Just regular." Manny felt like saying this was definitely not "regular," but knew the irony would be lost on Jake. The guy had the sensitivity of a pickup fender.

"Where's it at?"

Manny realized he had no idea where Fiona's house was. "Just a minute." He reached for the phone book, flipped through the pages, and there was *Fiona Ross* with a street address.

"Two-forty-two Fairview," he said. "Meet me there in ten minutes?"

"Yup."

Manny hung up and walked out of his office and into the staff room. Roy Otis and Barney Feldenberg were sitting at their desks.

"Roy, Barney!"

Their heads came up.

"Saddle up."

Both pushed away from their desks and grabbed their hats, glad to escape the stifling office air that a wheezing compressor on the roof never quite managed to cool to a comfortable level.

Fiona's place was a two minute drive from the courthouse. They arrived in two separate cars, Manny in his Mustang and the deputies in a cruiser.

The single story white house was located near Waterfront Park, built in the late fifties when the town was flush with cash and local builders took extra pride in their work. A white picket fence enclosed the well kept yard. The hip-and-valley roof was of cedar shakes; the dormer windows had cut glass panes with milled frames and wide sills. Three brick steps ran up to the porch.

Jake Trotter's white Ford van was parked out front and Jake, dressed in shop coveralls and wearing a black baseball cap rally-style, was standing beside the fence, a lock pick set in a rolled leather sheath held firmly in his right hand.

"This the Ross house?" Jake hollered as Manny stepped from his car, followed closely by Roy and Barney.

Manny walked up to Jake before answering. "Yes," Manny replied quietly.

"Heard about it on the scanner." Jake sounded both pleased and excited. When he saw Manny's grim reaction, Jake's demeanor darkened. "Damned shame," he continued with a slow shake of his head.

Manny's anger blossomed in a tight little spiral directed at his dispatcher. They were supposed to keep things private at least until the next of kin could be informed. When Manny found out who was blabbing on an open channel he'd kick their butt. But for now, he needed inside the house. He spoke in an even tone; no sense in letting the locksmith get him started.

"Get her open, would you Jake?"

"Sure thing, Manny."

As they pushed through the gate, Manny warned, "And Jake, let's try not to disturb any prints on the doorknob." He handed Jake a pair of latex gloves, which the locksmith snapped on before going to work. Manny watched to make sure Jake didn't rub anything off, but Jake handled it like a pro. Within a minute the lock was jimmied and the door stood slightly ajar. He stepped aside with a grin.

Manny pulled on a pair of gloves before he pushed the door wide. He looked back at Roy and Barney. And then he stepped inside.

In the small living room were a sofa, a leather recliner, a television, and several framed prints hung on the walls. A yellow sweatshirt with *Cannon Beach* printed in big block letters was lying on the back of the recliner. Otherwise, the room was neat as a pin.

Manny walked into the kitchen, which opened off the living room. A single plate and a fork and knife had been rinsed and left in the sink. Otherwise the kitchen was neat and clean.

He retraced his steps through the living room and turned down the short hallway. He entered the front bedroom. Here was a queen bed and a large antique oak dresser. A hand stitched quilt with a star pattern of cream and lavender was neatly spread and tucked, with two pillows in matching slipcovers at the head. Again, nothing seemed out of place, and Manny began to feel an edge of disappointment.

He walked down the hallway, into a small back room which had been converted into a study. An oak roll top desk with a matching filing cabinet stood against the far wall. The slatted roll was up and a few papers lay in a neat pile. Manny walked over and carefully lifted the corner of the top paper, a billing statement from the telephone company. Beneath it were two more statements, one for a credit card and one for city water and sewer.

He returned to the hallway and entered the bathroom. Clean as clean, the white porcelain tub dry, the chrome handles shining like new. Even the towels were folded and put away, with just one pink hand towel and one wash rag neatly arranged on the towel rack beside the sink.

A woman's place.

Answers wouldn't come from here. Not unless the state crime lab people found something. But Manny doubted there was anything to be found. Fiona left the house that morning and expected to return.

He walked back through the house and out to the front door, pulled off the rubber gloves and handed them to Roy who took them despite a look that said he hadn't been hired as maid service.

"Well?" Roy asked, eyebrows raised.

"Nada," Manny replied tiredly. "Zero, zip, zilch."

Jake had hung around to see what came of the search.

"Jake," Manny said evenly as he turned on the locksmith. "You keep your big trap shut about this. If I hear rumors that trace back in your direction it'll be a cold day in hell before you do any more work for the sheriff. Comprende?"

"Sure thing, Manny," Jake wheedled. "Yo Comprende! Mum's the word."

Manny realized the warning was pointless. Jake would almost certainly tell his wife, after making her swear to keep it a secret. But she'd go ahead and tell everyone down at the hair salon and then at the grocery store and probably everyone on her bowling team so they wouldn't feel left out or offended. And before long everyone in Langston would know that Fiona's house had been searched and Manny found the inside undisturbed. With frustration, Manny looked Jake straight in the face and said, "I mean this Jake. Keep a lid on it!"

Jake nodded furiously. "I will," he replied, matching Manny's ardor. "Not a word!"

"Okay," Manny said tiredly. "Get out of here."

Jake walked briskly to his van. After the locksmith drove off, Manny turned to Roy and Barney.

"The state patrol's investigators will be along soon, so we'll leave the front door unlocked. Roy, do you mind sticking around?"

Roy took this as a cue to dispose of the gloves, which he handed over to Barney with a smirk. "No problem. How long do you think they'll be?"

Barney took the gloves as if he'd been handed a soiled diaper but he kept his mouth shut. Manny watched the quick exchange and then answered Roy's question.

"An hour or two. However long it takes. You be here when they arrive. I'll make sure they get up here before dark."

Roy sat down on the edge of the porch to wait.

CHAPTER 7

*N*umb.

Billy led Holly to the patrol car and held the door while she collapsed into the back seat. Her heart was hammering and her body was one enormous bruise.

Fiona!

She tried to take a deep breath but her chest was shivering so violently it was nearly impossible to breathe at all. And now her hands began to tremble. Holly intertwined her fingers and squeezed as hard as she could, but when she tried to relax, her hands were still twitching at marionette speed.

Not fair!

It was just last month . . . Fiona's thirtieth birthday, the trip to Seattle they took to celebrate, the gathering of a few friends at a bistro in the Green Lake District, a single red candle on the chocolate layer cake. What had Fiona said as she blew it out?

"I never want more than one candle on my birthday cakes. That way I'll remember to celebrate the coming year as if it were my last."

Holly's rage began to blossom. She began talking to herself, unaware of her surroundings, unaware that she was not alone.

"You can't be dead."

Billy gripped the steering wheel of the cruiser just a little tighter and nearly said something, thought better of it, and pushed the accelerator to move just a little faster down the gravel road towards Highway 97.

Why?

She had to answer that one question. Above all else she had to know why this happened. Because if left unanswered, the unknowing would haunt her for all of her life. And at the moment Holly didn't care how long she had left to live. Life itself seemed so uncertain, so unfair, so undependable.

Fiona!

The vision of the body came suddenly and rolled over her and into her and through her like a hurricane and without volition Holly was shivering back there in the brush, standing over Cruz's shoulder, seeing the horror of—

She tried to block the image. In its place came the face of Manny Cruz, turning with wide eyes to see her standing behind him, speechless and rocked by the moment. As she replayed that instant Holly realized Manny had not been so stunned by the discovery that it was Fiona who lay dead on the dry earth, but in seeing Holly and realizing the damage he had caused to her.

You bastard! You were more concerned about hurting me than you were for the death of my friend!

"Son of a bitch!"

Billy assumed Holly was cursing the murderer. The urge to say something finally overcame his good sense. "No doubt," he said in a solemn and focused voice that he hoped sounded sincere.

Holly hadn't even heard what Billy said.

Billy took this for agreement and felt better. They crested the hill and were descending toward the lake and Langston and the moment seemed ripe for the question he needed to ask.

"Holly . . . do you want me to take you back to your office?" It didn't seem the office was the right place to take her. But where? To her house? Maybe to a friend's home?

Holly was still intent upon her rage at Manny Cruz when she realized the young officer had said something. What was his name? Did she really care? He was one of Cruz's underlings. Didn't that make him somehow complicit?

"What?" Holly blurted out.

Billy heard the anger, the confusion. He wished that he had simply taken her back to the county courthouse and dropped her at the front and driven safely away. But there was no pulling back now.

"Where should I take you?" Billy said slowly, trying to sound as if it were the most important task ever undertaken in his entire life. But he suspected it came off sounding more like a cabbie pushing a drunk for a quick ride.

Holly tried to process the question and found she had to replay the words several times before they made sense. The young cop was trying to be polite. Maybe even sensitive. She weighed the question and shifted uncomfortably on the seat. The office? *Hell no!* She felt like she'd been run over, and she probably looked like shit. Her house? No. Not yet. A single lonely thought came swimming up.

I'm in shock.

And following that came another realization.

I'm in survival mode. And I need to stay *in survival mode.*

She needed to live at least long enough to see Fiona's killer caught. And then she would find some way, even if it meant doing the task herself, of ending his life. Holly was certain it was a "he" and not a "she." Because no woman would brutalize another woman the way Fiona had been brutalized.

To survive, at least for the next few days, she would need drugs. Valium. Maybe something stronger. "The clinic," Holly said.

"Right." Billy felt relieved to have a destination. He was coincidentally also thinking how nice it would be to have a drug to take the edge off. A double shot of whiskey would do just fine.

Chapter 8

A s Otto finished informing everyone—and in particular the *Gentle Sea's* captain—
of his decision to delay the ship's departure, he saw both Werner and Heinrich
were no longer looking at him but were instead staring intently down the long
pier. As he followed their gaze he saw what had captured their attention.

Where the main road emptied onto the waterfront, about a quarter of a
kilometer from where the ship was moored, a black Mercedes-Benz Pullman
Limousine with lustrous red side panels and brilliantly polished chrome trim, escorted front and rear by four motorcycles, had turned onto the pier. The throaty
chatter of two-cycle engines punctuated the gentle lapping of waves against the
pilings, and a few seconds later came the powerful rev of acceleration from the
limo's engine.

As the motorcade drew near and began to slow, Otto could see the stony
faces of the young SS troopers who rode the cycles, with chin-strapped helmets
polished and perfectly aligned, their eyes riveted straight ahead to the task of
delivering the massive limo and its important occupant to its destination. Their
uniforms were crisply clean; oil glistened off the sub-machine guns slung from
their shoulders on thick black leather straps.

The flag of the Third Reich fluttered from the right front fender of the limo
and a general's pennant fluttered from the left.

The limo pulled to a smooth stop near the bottom of the freighter's gangplank, and Otto's apprehension blossomed as he finally spotted the single occupant. General Hermann Goering sat with royal splendor inside the passenger bay.

He remained unmoving until his chauffeur came around from the front, grasped the chrome handle, and opened the door. And then he looked out through the opening with a distracted recognition, as though he had been lost in some distant and extremely important thought and was just now realizing where he was.

As the chauffeur stood attentively, Goering swung his feet across the doorsill, slid over, and planted his boots firmly on the running board, then took a brisk and determined step to the ground.

The SS troopers had dismounted from their cycles. They now snapped to attention, with their arms raised in the angled salute. "Heil Hitler!" they chanted in almost perfect unison.

As Goering completed his grand exit his pudgy face broke into a satisfied grin; he returned their salutes with a casual flip of his right hand, and a soft almost reluctant, "Heil Hitler." He gave the captain in charge a quick nod of approval. The captain, who stood at rigid attention beside the limousine, allowed himself a faint smile. The soldiers let their arms fall to their sides, secure in the great man's acknowledgment of their existence.

Goering wore a cream-colored uniform with black piping and high-top leather boots burnished to the luster of polished ebony. Hardly standard issue, even for generals. Otto dismissed the notion that Goering had overstepped the bounds of military dress etiquette. Even thoughts could be dangerous.

Goering ignored the three engineers and instead walked down the pier, carefully surveying the freighter from stern to bow. When he returned, his chubby face was full of happy approval. Otto, Heinrich and Werner formed up at attention to greet him.

For Otto, it was the second time. The first meeting was a brief introduction at a New Year's celebration thrown by the Party in Berlin—a gathering attended not just by Goering but also by Hitler and Goebbels and most of the Nazi elite. Otto was quite content to remain in the background. But he was encouraged by the director of Goering's manufacturing company to join the line that formed to meet the Great Men. Otto reluctantly went up and was introduced to Goering; he even shook Hitler's cold and bony hand. The fire in Der Fuhrer's dark and merciless eyes sliced through Otto to his very bones, but he doubted Hitler would have remembered his face five minutes later.

Otto's palms were sweating and his heart pounded as he faced the man second only to Adolph Hitler in the new German politics.

"Gentlemen," Goering said generously, purposefully reaching out to shake each of their hands. Otto felt the corpulent fingers close around his and was reminded of the plump sausages his father made on the farm. He was now shaking hands with breakfast sausages. Goering continued to squeeze Otto's hand, speaking directly to him and for a moment ignoring the others.

"How is our little project going?" His jaunty voice was full of springtime and power. And just beneath, the perfectly honed edge of a hunter's gutting knife.

Sweat broke out in Otto's armpits. "Fine, Herr General." His voice cracked with fear. Goering seemed pleased. Otto felt like he stood before some great troll, the heavy scent of cologne, the black silk cravat around Goering's neck, the enormous gold ring with the broken cross on his right pinkie. Goering's excesses were made mention of by someone in the rank and file only at lethal risk. Otto continued without pause, forcing the words to sound objective despite the enormous lump that had formed in his throat.

"The cargo is loaded, Herr General, and the ship is prepared to sail." And here it got sticky, because Otto was left with no alternative but to confess his declaration of just a few minutes before. Nervousness fractured every word.

"Herr General . . . we have a small problem. They say there is a storm coming from the north. We are advised to consider a delay of a day or two, to make certain of a safe crossing." The words practically stumbled out and Otto fell silent, embarrassed. Would Goering think him scared? There was no room for weakness in the rebuilding of the motherland; Party propaganda had made that explicitly clear.

Goering frowned. "The weather, the weather," he mused, throwing a skeptical glance at the cloudless skies. "You know, we have the same problem with our Luftwaffe. Always the weather." A great laugh boomed up from deep in his chest. Everyone on the dock joined in, laughing nervously, even the Danish captain who remained at the top of the gangplank.

Goering now looked over to Werner, his face suddenly serious. "Is this true, cousin? Is the weather going to delay our little adventure?"

Otto was stunned! Werner had never mentioned a special connection with Goering. Much less a blood tie! He instantly regretted everything he ever said about Goering or the Party in Werner's presence. There was no telling how an off-the-cuff comment might have been reported. Not that he felt like a traitor, or even a doubter. Otto generally approved of what had been done to ease the country out of the vast depression it had wallowed in since the end of the Great War. He was proud to be employed by a company headed by so important an individual—a world war flying ace, and recently elected president of the Reichstag. Even so, an occasional grumble came naturally, wise or not. His cheeks flushed as he remembered that he had made the choice not to formally pledge himself to join the Nazi Party.

Werner replied with unease, knowing the disclosure was a surprise. And to Otto's amazement, Werner did not take the opportunity to voice his previous displeasure at the prospect of a delay. Instead, he did a complete about face.

"Yes, sir. We considered delaying for a few days. It would be a shame to see such fine German craftsmanship sink to the bottom of the ocean."

Otto's opinion of Werner skyrocketed.

Goering gave Werner a secretive smile, and it returned Otto to the moment with a chill down his spine.

Goering clasped his hands behind his back, having the effect of emphasizing the clustered medals and decorations on his chest. He again gazed up at the unbroken blue sky, then across the wharf at the flag, which hung limp atop the pole on the peaked roof of the maritime customs building.

"Do any of you see bad weather moving in?" he asked mildly. Goering paused a moment to emphasize his point, and when no one spoke up he appeared vastly pleased that none of them dared. "Let us be sure," he concluded in a generous voice. He turned to one of the SS who stood nearby and in a tersely clipped voice said, "Corporal, get the weather center on the radio."

The officer obediently trotted to his motorcycle and flipped a toggle to warm up the tubes in the box radio bolted above the rear fender. He unlatched the whip antenna and began speaking into the handheld black Bakelite microphone.

"Soon, we will have the real answer!" Goering proclaimed. "Until then," he put his arm collegially around Werner's shoulder, "A few words, cousin." And to Otto's amazement, Goering led Werner off down the pier, talking to him in a low voice. When the duo reached the far end of the ship they stood at dockside, Goering's arm still protectively draped over Werner's shoulder.

Heinrich hand rolled a cigarette and smoked, with an occasional nervous glance at the troops standing beside their motorcycles. Otto stared at the SS corporal who had completed the call to the weather center; but the corporal, who had received whatever information was available, studiously ignored him. His information was only for the Great Man.

Goering and Werner finally returned, and the young man looked sheepish when his eyes met Otto's.

Goering addressed the SS corporal crisply. "What is the report?"

"Herr General," the corporal replied in a brisk voice. "There is a storm but," and here he glanced condescendingly at Otto, "the winds are forecast to be no more than modestly strong."

Goering turned to face Otto, Heinrich and Werner. "So!" Goering proclaimed.

And that was that.

CHAPTER 9

No matter how hard she tried, Holly Curtis could no longer picture Fiona's face in her mind. Not just the face lying in the dirt with a portion of her forehead missing. Thank God that image was blocked! But everything else that was a visual of Fiona seemed to be gone.

Please! Not the beautiful face!

Holly sat at her dining table staring at the yellow plastic pill bottle. The tamper proof cap was off. Inside were just four yellow tablets.

As if I couldn't be trusted.

She argued with the doctor that she would need more. Maybe a lot more.

"Then call me when you run out and I'll have the pharmacist fill your prescription again."

"I don't want to go outside for a while. I don't want to have to go to the pharmacy again. I don't want people to see me."

"Then we will have someone bring the refill to your house."

And now, thinking of that exchange, Holly realized she was pleading with the doctor for two separate things. Not having to return to face the pharmacy staff. And . . . maybe not having to face anyone ever again.

For what seemed like the hundredth time Holly shifted in the chair to get up and go into her bedroom to retrieve the scrapbook that held pictures of Fiona. To be able to see that beautiful face again. The face that her mind's eye now denied her. Hiking in the mountains. Down at the beach volunteering to teach swim lessons to first and second graders. At the museum, all dressed up for the

Christmas fundraising gala. And for the hundredth time Holly settled back in her chair, knowing that opening the scrapbook would be Pandora's Box. If she visited the visual memories she might be upset enough to drive to the liquor store and buy a bottle of scotch and together with the four valiums that might just do the job and then her pain would be—

STOP IT! WOULD FIONA WANT YOU THINKING LIKE THIS?

And the answer she would hear from her late friend, if she could now speak, was most certainly, "No. I would not want you to end your life because my life has ended. So take one of the valiums and crawl up into a ball in your bed, cry for as long as you need to cry, and then try to sleep."

"Not yet," Holly said to the little yellow bottle. First, she would determine how far she was prepared to go. The answer came swiftly and with complete certainty.

My life is now a mission to find whoever killed Fiona. And there are no limits to what I will do.

And what if she did come across an opportunity to inflict revenge? What form might that take? There were infinite possibilities. Given the opportunity, it might involve something like a hot iron, and be very, very slow.

Please take the valium!

"In a minute."

The real problem wasn't deciding what to do if she got an opportunity for revenge. The real problem was finding a way to be involved in finding Fiona's killer. And here Holly saw only problems. She was a deputy prosecutor. And prosecutors didn't *investigate* murders. They *prosecuted* murderers. In a courtroom. Holly couldn't even hope to be assigned to handle any part of that prosecution. She was the lowest deputy prosecutor on the totem pole in the Cascade County's prosecutor's office. More importantly, she had been Fiona's friend. Personal involvement with a case was an automatic conflict of interest. There was no way she would be assigned to the trial, even in an auxiliary role.

The valium, Holly. It's time for you to get some sleep.

"Of course . . . you're right."

Holly went into the kitchen and ran a glass of water before returning to the table. She picked up the pill bottle and dumped two of the valiums into the palm of her hand. It was tempting to take all four but she knew the voice in her head would disagree.

You would have to explain to the doctor.

"Right." Holly swallowed two tablets and went into her bedroom, pulled back the white quilted cotton summer blanket and the pink sheet, and crawled in.

CHAPTER 10

Frank talked in a nonstop banter from the moment Jerry stepped into the Chevy. He rambled on about Vietnam; the PUD and his work at the powerhouse; the weather; what the apple crop looked like. And what did Jerry think about the war in the Middle East? A veritable Turret's of small talk. But no mention of the murder. As they came to the final crest before pulling into sight at the end of the access road Frank suddenly became nervous, slowed the Chevy and pulled to an abrupt stop.

"Maybe I'd better drop you off here." Frank was fidgeting behind the wheel.

"Is anything wrong?"

"No," Frank replied. Then, "Remember, I didn't tell Detective Cruz I knew you. If I was to drop you off and the cops spotted who I was . . ."

"Oh! Right." Jerry grabbed the door handle, glad to be rid of Frank so easily. As he stepped out of the Chevy, Frank leaned across.

"Maybe I could swing by later, after they're gone?"

Jerry hesitated. "Probably not a good idea today." Jerry rolled his eyes suggestively toward where the investigation would be in progress, probably for a good while longer.

Frank was quick to agree. "Right."

Jerry shut the door and Frank backed the Chevy several yards to where there was a wide enough spot to turn around. Jerry watched the Chevy disappear down the hill.

There were now four vehicles parked in the turnaround: a sheriff's cruiser, a white-and-black state patrol car, an ancient red-and-white Scout, and a yellow-and-black ambulance. It was ninety-eight degrees and Jerry felt a moment of pity for the officers who were forced to work close to a body.

He was far more concerned about Frank's behavior. Jerry had seen enough veterans with post-traumatic stress syndrome to recognize the signs. It was hard to predict what would set them off, but rejection was certainly on the list. Frank also seemed to believe that since they shared a Vietnam experience, they should automatically be, as Frank put it, "Buds." It would be difficult to convince him otherwise. He seemed incapable of shutting up long enough to listen. It would be wise to handle him gently.

He was exhausted and all he wanted to do was get back to his campsite and take a dip in the river.

Tired people make mistakes.

Where Fiona's body still lay, five cops, and an old fellow wearing a yellow straw fedora who Jerry presumed was the coroner, were focused upon their work. The space blanket was gone and the brush cleared away. Above the body stood a white canvas canopy, raised on aluminum rods. A state patrolman dressed in a natty blue uniform and wearing a blue skimmer was aiming a tripod-mounted survey laser, pointing it at a monopod reflecting unit several yards away held by a deputy sheriff. The last thing Jerry wanted was a conversation, but the deputy saw and recognized him, waived a greeting, and hollered, "Don't forget your fishing tackle!" The deputy pointed to where the pole and creel were laid up beside a patrol car.

Jerry went over and picked up his gear and waived back to the deputy and hollered, "Thanks!"

The deputy returned his attention to the state patrolman after the briefest of waves. Jerry made a wide detour around the crime scene before joining the faded track that led back to his campsite.

He was relieved to find his gear undisturbed. He grabbed the towel and a plastic jug he used to carry water and walked down to the river. He looked out across the stream and back up towards the hills to make sure he was alone before stripping. The air was hot and the icy bite of the deep pool felt wonderful.

When he climbed out, the terrycloth towel felt like sandpaper against his skin. He slipped back into his jeans and pulled on a white T-shirt and again checked to make certain he was alone. Satisfied, he walked over to the flat expanse of bedrock and began to limber up, shaking out arms and hands, rolling his head side to side, taking deep breaths, letting his gaze wander into the irregular shapes of the gorge rocks and the slow moving water.

And then it got tough. His thoughts kept returning to the woman, lying in the brush, so vulnerable in death. Shards of image came and went. The way the dust clung to the cuff of her pants. How her fingers curled, just below where the rope had blistered her wrist. Skin beginning to peel from her lips.

He fought to push the dark visions away, but after several frustrating minutes it proved impossible. He stared down into the waterhole, as if it, too, might contain a body in some dark corner of its depth.

A bird's sharp cry pierced this morbid thought. He looked up. A flock of seagulls was riding the warm updrafts, sailing blissfully against the blue sky. He watched, envying their freedom, until they glided out of sight beyond the northern lip of the gorge.

Now fully distracted from his attempt at finding some degree of calm, he gave up. He pulled on his sneakers and laced them, dunked the plastic jug in the flow just upstream from the pool, and scrambled back up the bank.

After a long nap, he warmed a can of chicken soup on the small kerosene camp stove. It settled uneasily in his stomach.

As the campfire burned to a low bed of gray ash, spotted by an occasional orange wink from a dying coal, he felt grateful for the isolation. The pressure of loneliness had eased by the time he reached his fiftieth year, and he felt no urgent need to share the stars that began to pop into existence. A crescent moon rose above the hills.

He checked his sleeping bag for rattlesnakes. With the last of the water from the jug he doused the campfire, sending up a small white plume. He crawled inside the tent, hoping that for a few hours he would find escape in sleep. But as his eyelids closed and his breathing evened out, the nightmare was all too familiar.

CHAPTER 11

On those nights when it came it was brutal, and he would wake up drenched in sweat, the smells and sounds and sights of the jungle ripe in his mind, with a fresh feeling of horror about having his world dissolve. He always tried to convince himself that this night was the last. But it never was.

The phone call came while Jerry was staying at his ranch in Montana. He took his golden retriever Hobbes to the kennel and unplugged his computer and television. He didn't bother to empty the refrigerator, except for an opened quart of milk that he drained into the sink, and a partial head of lettuce which he chucked into the compost bin in the back yard. The carrots and celery and the block of cheddar cheese and the slab of maple cured ham would keep just fine. He'd be back in two or three days.

He drove sixty miles to Bozeman where a Citation jet was waiting. He boarded and flew to Miami. In the dream this was compressed into a few seconds.

He knew in his dreamscape that everything was about to go wrong. He tried to scream at his other self and tell him to stop. But his mouth made no sound and his other self kept moving toward destiny.

He saw himself greeting DEA agents Al and Mike at the opened hatch of the jet, its engines spooling with a turbine whine. Inside the cabin sat the gray high-impact-plastic suitcase containing a disassembled .50-caliber Windrunner rifle with a Carbon One graphite barrel and a Leupold 24X optical scope.

Some nameless face was there to fill them in on the details.

The Mexican authorities tipped off the DEA that Fernando Alfredo Manzuella, otherwise known as the "Coco Man," was having a family gathering at a private compound near the city of Champoton on the Yucatan Peninsula. The DEA, in turn, called the Foreign Intervention Coordination Office—a fancy title for a small group of ex-military assassins. A retired Special Ops colonel named Art Fields ran FICO's tight shop with a sterling reputation for completing missions.

They took off and flew straight across the Gulf of Mexico, almost nicking Cuban air space, reviewing satellite maps, checking the communications gear, going over contingency plans. In the dreamscape this time flashed by, except the part where he felt the cool weight of the graphite barrel as he slid it through his hands and checked to make sure the bore was clean. That part seemed to spin out forever.

Ten hours from the time he was summoned, the team was unpacking at the Champoton airport. If anyone asked, the cover story was they were there to hunt puma.

No one asked.

Two drug Special Forces members from the national police met them at the strip and provided specifics on where Manzuella would be arriving for the family fiesta the following morning.

The Coco Man ran the largest cocaine smuggling operation on the Gulf. Most of his shipments crossed into the U.S. in turbine-powered V-hulled super cats capable of open ocean speeds in excess of one hundred miles per hour. It was a smooth operation that frustrated law enforcement on both sides of the border. After more legitimate strategies for discouraging the smuggling operation repeatedly failed, they waited for a different kind of opportunity. It now came down to Jerry.

The two Mexican officers arrived in separate vehicles, one of them a gray Land Rover. Jerry took the keys to the Rover and followed the police in their Jeep up into the jungle. His team stayed with the jet. If Jerry were caught, the jet would leave and he would be on his own.

It took an hour to reach the staging area. The local police sped away, leaving Jerry to his mission.

In the dreamscape he again tried to scream out the danger. But he was again unable to make a sound.

Jerry put on a ghillie suit, made from strips of earth- and plant-colored silk pulled from FICO's extensive stocks to exactly match the colors of the Champoton jungle. He wore his jeans and crewneck shirt beneath.

He hoisted the components of the disassembled Windrunner in a shoulder-slung drag bag, picked up the daypack holding the rest of his gear, and hiked off into the dark green canopy at dusk. Within seconds, the camouflage of the ghillie suit blended with the tropical foliage and he disappeared into the backdrop of the rain forest.

With a GPS unit, he spent the next three hours trekking through the darkness of a new moon night, surrounded by the sounds of birds and insects and the occasional howls of monkeys. When the tiny illuminated screen told him he was near, he found a huge banyan tree and began to climb, settling into position high up in the crotch of its spreading limbs.

At dawn he moved for a better view across the jungle. Over a mile away, armed men in black were patrolling the perimeter of the hacienda grounds. A few ventured short distances into the jungle, but none came close to discovering Jerry far away in his tree.

The sprawling adobe ranch house gradually came fully to life. A nearby bunkhouse began to disgorge more men to join the existing patrols, all of them toting machine pistols or shotguns. They fanned out, searching the corral and horse barn area, the outbuildings, the near jungle, appearing to leave nothing to chance.

By mid-morning, the compound was dotted with gaily-dressed señors and señoritas who came from the hacienda to enjoy the morning air. Children were pestering an old woman in charge of four long wooden tables on the hacienda's portico, hoping for an early treat from the many bowls of food that were set out.

Jerry rested the rifle's bipod on a twelve-inch-thick limb and sighted down the laser range finder. The tiny red numerals said it was 1946 yards to the front porch railing. A check of the GPS told him he was 490 feet above sea level. After checking the barometric pressure and the relative humidity, he began to tweak the Leupold scope to compensate for the conditions. He was glad to have chosen the Windrunner. It was the only rifle in FICO's arsenal capable of killing from this far away.

More people arrived in cars and on motorcycles, each of them first being stopped and carefully searched by the men guarding the gate before being allowed to pass. The guards were methodical and careful in their searches, using long-handled mirrors to check for explosives underneath each car or truck, and having a German Shepherd sniff around every vehicle. Identification was demanded and checked against pages in a large spiral binder. Jerry admired the thoroughness, wondering if he would have done it any different, cataloguing that thought in case it became handy for a future mission.

Around 10:30am, a black Mercedes came barreling up the road and was waived through by the guards. Jerry was certain it held his man. But a look through the rifle's scope revealed a surprise. Jose Fernando, the godfather of the heroin trade, stepped out, dressed in a black jacket and black cotton pants, with a pink shirt unbuttoned to reveal a thick gold chain that hung down into his matted chest hair. Incredible luck! He'd been on the DEA's short list for years.

Jerry had no authorization to take out this target, and FICO's world was one where authorization mattered a great deal. Still . . . when the opportunity presented itself, it was no less of an opportunity. Jerry transmitted the surprise discovery on the tiny keypad of his satellite unit. Authorization came back within seconds: *Duck Soup.*

As he prepared for the shot, no longer expecting the king of cocaine, a turbine helicopter came screaming in low over the saddleback hills to the west. Jerry's finger eased on the trigger. The helicopter quickly touched down near the limo. Jerry inched the rifle to his left, focusing the scope on the darkened canopy of the copter. The door popped open, and out stepped the Coco Man, wearing a white ice cream two-piece suit and a black fedora with a snakeskin band. He smiled as he strode toward Fernando.

Double bonus!

The helicopter was a definite problem. The first shell was already in the chamber, but there was still time to change the next shell. Jerry pulled the magazine from the rifle and reached into a side pocket of his vest and pulled out a bullet that carried an incendiary charge and pushed it into the magazine. He shouldered the rifle and settled his finger on the trigger, bracing for the solid kick.

Everyone pulled back to give the two leaders room to greet. The drug lords hugged each other like loving brothers in a long embrace.

Jerry softly squeezed the trigger and the gun butt slammed against his shoulder. The bullet left the barrel at over twice the speed of sound. No one in the compound would hear the distant *crack* of the discharge for five seconds. The bullet would cover that distance in just over two. Jerry edged the barrel until the Leupold's cross hairs were centered on the nearest fuel tank of the helicopter. Jerry squeezed and the second bullet screamed away.

He moved the scope back and saw the two men crumple while still locked together in their greeting embrace. The bullet was designed to tumble and mushroom when it hit flesh, delivering an enormous body shock. But just to be certain, small channels within the bullet contained a half gram dose of ricin, a poison so lethal it was capable of bringing down an elephant. Maybe a dozen elephants. With the body shot there was no doubt about the outcome. Even before the two drug lords had fallen all the way to the ground, Jerry was twisting the barrel to break the Windrunner down, and at that moment the helicopter erupted into a massive ball of flame. Jerry slid the pieces into the drag bag, stashed the GPS into a pocket, slung the bag over his shoulder, slid down the rope to the ground, and sprinted off into the jungle, thinking he had left nothing to chance.

In the full light of day and knowing the path back through the jungle it took Jerry just half an hour to reach the Rover. When he reached the air strip, Al ran up to him, anxious and angry.

"Oh, Man! Why'd you have to do that?"

"Huh?" Jerry had expected congratulations. At least a solid high five. Had he gotten the confirmation wrong? Was he *not* supposed to have taken out Fernando? Had there been something wrong with taking out the helicopter as a distraction for his getaway?

"The girl. Why'd you have to kill the little girl?"

In his dreaming world everything went cold.

"What girl?"

Al looked confused. "Didn't you know?"

"Know what?"

"Your bullet caught a six-year-old girl."

Jerry's mind spun and he was back in the tree and looking through the scope and there was no girl anywhere near the drug lords.

There was no girl!

"I didn't see a girl anywhere near the two men!"

"Well there was one. And she just happened to be the niece of a cabinet minister in the Mexican government."

"Just happened?!"

"Yeah, she just happened! You killed her, along with the two bastards you were supposed to take out. Not to mention the pilot of the bird."

"Oh, shit!"

"A fragment must have spooned off a bone. It caught the poor kid in the head. Killed her instantly. The Mexican government has been all over our Ambassador's ass for the last fifteen minutes. It's a huge shitting mess."

Then the oddness of it struck Jerry. "What in the hell was the niece of someone in the Mexican government doing there in the first place? I thought these were supposed to be the bad guys!"

Al remained focused. "Beats the crap out of me. But the bottom line is we're on our own until we get back on U.S. soil. They've shut down all communication because they're afraid the Mexicans are monitoring our frequencies."

Jerry had a nasty premonition.

Trust your instincts!

He'd taken out a little girl! Someone would be looking for a scapegoat. It didn't take an active imagination to think Congress would want a stooge to blame it on.

"Look, guys," he said, as the jet's turbines began to whine. "Some serious shit is going to come down the pike. Maybe I should hang out here for a while. Just till it quiets down a little."

"Like hell," Al said. "Get your ass on board."

So I'm your scapegoat too!

"Sorry, amigo. But I've decided to stay."

88

Al turned on him. "We'll see what Fields has to say about this!"

Mike stepped protectively between them. "Al, we can't call Fields. Remember? Radio silence."

"Shit."

Both DEA agents now stared at Jerry, measuring their chances. Al wasn't carrying a piece. Neither was Mike. Everything was already aboard the jet except for the gear in the Rover. No one was going to easily win a race to the nearest weapon.

"You won't get away with this," Al said.

"Shit, Al. What would you do?"

It was a standoff, and Mike finally became the voice of reason.

"Al, if he wants to stay, he can stay."

"But—"

"He's right. If he goes back, he's screwed." Mike turned to Jerry, reached out and shook his hand. "Good luck. And don't stay a stranger for too long." But the words rang hollow.

The jet left.

Jerry took the Rover and drove until he found a farm house with a clothesline full of drying laundry. He took the items he needed to blend in on the street and left a 500 peso note clipped to the line. He wrapped his jeans and crewneck around his waist so that he would now seem to have a paunch and pulled on the chinos and the loose brown peasant shirt. He was dirty from the jungle but that was good. He would look like a fair-skinned local down on his luck. He spoke Spanish fluently enough to pass for Mexican unless someone questioned him closely, and had a Mexican passport and local identity papers as part of the contingency planning. The money belt he always wore on missions was his own special precaution. There was enough to carry him for months if it became necessary. He didn't think it would, but the security of several thousand slotted into the elastic waistband was reassuring.

He came to a bridge, pulled off the highway, and tracked along the muddy bank until he saw no one around. He got out of the Rover and took the components of the Windrunner and his satellite communication equipment and tossed everything piece by piece into the swirling brown water.

Jerry considered driving the Rover north towards the U.S. border, but there was too much risk in being stopped in a vehicle with government plates. He finally ditched it two miles outside the city, down a ravine where it looked like an accident and was likely to be stripped before the police found it. Jerry walked back along the road and into the downtown.

He slept in an alleyway that night and caught a bus north the next morning. Two days later he crossed into Texas. Later that day he picked up a *USA Today*, and there on the front page was a story about the Citation, shot down by a Cuban MiG over the Gulf. The US government claimed the jet was a private charter. The Cubans claimed the jet was inside their territorial waters and was a spy plane. The higher echelons of both governments knew the Mexicans had asked the Cubans for a favor. Both the Cubans and the Americans had cruisers out near the 60-mile international boundary, searching for bodies. The Cubans found the bodies of the two agents fairly quickly. A day later the Americans found the last piece of the pilot the sharks hadn't disposed of.

As events unfolded in the press, most of the truth came out. Someone inside the Mexican Ministry of Defense leaked a summary of events. After two days, the US press was using the ugliest of words: *KID ASSASSIN*. And when Jerry's grainy black-and-white photo, together with those of Al and Mike and the pilot—all supplied to the international press by the outraged Mexican government—appeared in the newspapers, Jerry knew it was prudent to quietly fade from existence. He rented a cheap trailer in a small town out in the Texas panhandle and went to ground.

$$\lambda$$

Jerry awoke in a cold sweat.

A six-year-old girl!

He lay in his bag as the wave of guilt shuddered through him. After months anger at his carelessness, he now allowed himself only a few minutes of feeling like pure shit when he awoke. And then it was time to move forward. There would be no redemption for what he had done. Inside his mind a brand was seared and there was no way to remove it.

A few minutes often seemed like forever.

Outside, the first rays from the sun were painting the hilltops. Light filtered through the tent flap. He pushed back the sleeping bag, pulled on his jeans, and went to bathe. Once back in camp he made coffee in the small aluminum pot. Sitting on a folding canvas chair, he watched a golden sunrise crown the nearby hills.

He still had no clear idea about what to do. Leaving the valley was tempting, but a subpoena could bring him back in the Sheriff's custody, and a warrant for his arrest was likely. He had to plan against the worst. They would catch him if he fled. Fingerprints would be taken. His prints were still on record somewhere. And even if they weren't, he might not be able to ditch his dog tags before they took him into custody, in which case fingerprints would be superfluous. The cops would call the military, and then it would be over. A black van would pick him up, ostensibly to be taken into federal custody, but Jerry would instead end up buried deep, either in the ground, or in a third world country where his constitutional rights would be just the scribbling of some old guy named Jefferson on a piece of crinkly paper under a glass case in the Smithsonian.

Even if he lost his tags, and the fingerprints drew no alarm from the feds, the sheriff would demand his social security number, and he couldn't produce one that would hold up. The fake one for emergencies belonged to an accountant who had lived in Maryland. If they called to confirm his identity, they would discover a dead man named Conrad Schultz who had been employed in a small firm that did tax work.

Likewise for the fake passports. They looked nice. But run one through the system and what would you get? Caught. They only worked when the INS had a *Don't Intercept* order on file. And that was certainly ancient history by now. Jerry hadn't even tried using a passport to get back across the border. He'd instead done what Mexicans had done for decades: he'd waded the Rio Grande, and dodged the border patrol until he could ditch the stolen clothes and put on his own jeans and T-shirt and hold his head high in the daylight as someone obviously American.

For the umpteenth time Jerry considered taking the dog tags and dropping them into the river. And for the umpteenth time he rejected the idea. They had been a part of him for too long. If someone caught up with him and found the tags? So be it!

So what to do? Move into town, as the detective suggested? That raised a different set of problems.

His cash was limited, most of it spent while living in the trailer in Texas. Renting an apartment would chew up the rest in a hurry. He had a bank account in Argentina, but accessing it was a last resort. He'd have to transfer money out by wire. Since the funds in Argentina were under one of his fake passport names, he'd have to use that name for the Langston bank. Argentina was a known haven for money laundering, so if he transferred more than a few thousand, certain government agencies would become curious. The dominos would begin to fall.

Moving into Langston also meant people could more easily find him. Would the local newspaper want to interview the man who found the body of their beloved Fiona? Some alert reporter might even remember the AP photo from the previous year. Even worse, they might want to publish his photo with the article! Hundreds of people would have the opportunity to remember where they'd seen that face before.

With no clear solution, he decided to go fishing. He would let things settle out for a few hours, and the answer would maybe eventually come a little clearer.

Jerry gathered his tackle and left the cottonwood thicket, walking through the brush toward the access road. As he came into sight of the road he was surprised to discover a white Toyota sedan parked at the turnaround.

He saw a woman, kneeling near where Fiona's body had lain just hours before. Her head was down and her hands were clasped in what looked like prayer. Jerry was uncertain whether to creep back into the brush, or to come forward. He stood still for a moment, and lost the opportunity to make a choice.

Sensing his presence, her head came up with fear; then she recognized him. Embarrassed, she stood, brushing away the dirt and twigs that clung to the knees of her pantsuit.

It was Holly Curtis.

Jerry saw a bouquet of roses on the parched ground, a mix of perhaps two dozen pink and red blooms.

She feigned a smile, the corners of her mouth barely turning up. "I just . . . wanted to leave some flowers for. . ." She couldn't bring herself to say the name. There was moistness in her eyes.

Jerry took a few steps and when he was close he glanced from Holly to the bouquet. "They're very nice," he said softly. "I'm sure she would have liked them very much."

She fought back tears. "You're the one who . . . found her, aren't you?"

"Yes."

"Thank you for being so decent in calling the police. If you hadn't—"

"It was the right thing to do," Jerry said, giving her the dignity of not having to imagine what might have happened if the body had been left for scavengers and the sun. "I hardly deserve thanks."

"Thank you just the same. Is there anything I can do for you? Do you need something? Food? Money?"

Jerry felt embarrassed. "No," he said abruptly. And realized how defensive that sounded. Her offer was heartfelt. "Thanks," he continued. "I appreciate the offer, but there's nothing I need. Really." Just the same, he tucked away the thought that here might be a source of cash. If things got real desperate. And then he felt like a cheap bit of filth for even having such a thought.

She was having trouble processing his reply. Jerry imagined that Holly might be having trouble processing a lot of things. He could empathize. He'd lost so many associates—a few of them even friends—over the years. Death has a way of dissolving the fabric of reality. A need to comfort welled up and Jerry was surprised by its strength. Without giving it the thought it deserved, Jerry blurted out words he would later regret.

"Is there anything I can do for you?"

She looked surprised. And then she looked at him again, as if for the first time. An awkward silence held the moment. And then she let him off the hook.

"I don't think so." Fiddling with empty hands as if they held something, she said, "I suppose I should be going. It's nearly eight, and I should get in to the office."

Jerry wished he'd crept back into the brush before he was seen. "You don't have to leave," he insisted. "I was headed down to the river to do some fishing." He held out the fishing rod and creel as confirmation. "I'll leave right now and give you more time—"

"No," she insisted. "I've spent enough time here already. Maybe I'll come back tomorrow. Bring more flowers. It helps . . ."

"I am so sorry." His cheeks flushed.

"Well," she said, renewing her earlier offer. "If there's anything I can do, please let me know. I feel I owe you something."

"Thank you. But really, there's nothing."

"Well . . . okay." She found the courage for a brief smile before she turned away.

As the Celica disappeared down the road Jerry realized he couldn't remain at the campsite. Others would be curious. Locals would naturally wonder about the transient who found the body. They might make the short hike to meet him. And there was always Frank, who would probably show up later that very same day. Like it or not, his cherished isolation was gone. Even if no one came, he'd still have to live with the continual fear of an unannounced visitor.

Possibly even the killer.

Coupled with Manny's admonition to "remain available" this left Jerry with only one option. He returned to his campsite and began to pack. Later that morning he hiked down the access road to the main highway and caught the bus up to Langston. He asked the driver if he knew of any cheap places where he might rent a room for a few days. "The Belvedere," the driver said. "I can drop you off right in front if you want."

CHAPTER 12

Two crewmen were holding back the pipes with wood poles while Werner tried to loop a length of thick hemp rope underneath and around when the death wave slammed against the hull. It pitched the ship, tossing the pipes. Everyone except Werner managed to scramble out of the way. The flying steel pinned the youngster's legs against the plating of the hull. Everyone heard the *snap* and *crunch* of shattering bone as Werner went down.

Werner screamed. Otto lunged in behind the pipes, futilely trying to pull them off from Werner's mangled lower body.

"Get back!" a crewman shouted. Otto ignored him, desperate to free his fallen comrade. A crewman grabbed Otto's arm and yanked him to safety as the ship floundered over a mountainous sea swell. The pipes rolled back, slamming bottom crate and sending wood splinters flying. For a moment Werner was free, but helpless, passed out from the pain.

Two crewmen jumped down and blocked the pipes with a chunk of wood and their own straining arms and bodies while two others lifted Werner's limp form up to Heinrich and Otto.

Three more crewmen scrambled to join the effort to secure the pipe, while Otto and Heinrich carried Werner to his cabin. He lay unconscious in the bunk, his legs now swollen like balloons. No doctor was aboard to perform the necessary amputations. Otto's and Heinrich's eyes met in the dim light of the tiny cabin; there was no need for words to confirm what both knew; the injuries were too severe for there to be any hope.

"You go back," Otto told Heinrich. "Help the others save the ship. I'll stay with him."

Heinrich hesitated, his eyes shifting anxiously between the dying man and Otto. Then he clapped Otto on the shoulder. "Right," he said, and sprinted for the hold.

Otto sank to the floor beside the bunk and braced his knees against the rolling of the ship.

In a few minutes Werner regained partial consciousness. He writhed and moaned in the narrow bunk, barely aware of his surroundings. Otto spread a wool blanket over Werner to keep him warm and tucked it tightly under the edges of the thin mattress to hold him in the bunk. He felt utterly lost and numb and hugely angry with Hermann Goering. He wanted to scream and run from the room and imagine it was just a bad dream. But he steeled himself to sit back down on the floor beside the bed, clenching his fists and teeth each time Werner cried out.

The captain soon appeared and stood silently in the open cabin doorway, hands pressed firmly against the doorframe to form a sort of human cross, watching and listening. He left abruptly, only to reappear shortly carrying a small vial and a well-used syringe. He entered the cabin without a word, calmly drew the clear liquid into the glass tube, and expertly injected it into Werner's arm. He left without an explanation.

Within seconds Werner was blissfully drifting along. Otto realized the captain had used his personal supply of morphine.

Otto held a bunk-side vigil for the next hour, hoping Werner would give him some words of farewell to pass on to his family. In the morphine haze Werner remained oblivious to Otto at his side.

There came a time when Werner began a wild and lonely rambling, a conversation between him and his mother, asking his imaginary mom hovering over him for a bedtime cookie and a glass of warm milk, and wanting to be told one more time the story of Hansel and Gretel. For just a moment Werner's eyes seemed to focus, and Otto thought the last words for the family might be on his lips. But as quickly as the moment came, it slipped away. Werner continued in his imaginary world and began to babble about a hike in the Black Forest when he was a boy.

When a crewman came to report to Otto that the pipes were finally secured, Werner smiled and surfaced briefly into the real world. "Looks like you will see America," he said dreamily.

"You will, too," Otto said.

But Werner looked away and the smile faded from his lips. "No," he said. That flat declaration ended the conversation. Otto settled in to await the inevitable.

Near the end Werner grew absolutely calm, as if the pain had entirely lifted. He beckoned Otto to lean close. Otto bent his ear near the dying man's lips. At last he would receive words to convey to a grieving family.

"The briefcase," Werner whispered secretively. "Must call Goering for instructions about the briefcase." And then he lapsed into unconsciousness.

Otto knew of no briefcase. Goering had given Werner a box that was certainly large enough to contain one. But he'd made a point of saying in front of all three that it was, "The new wool suit you asked me to pick out for you." A deception?

A violent spasm arched Werner's body. The blanket ripped free from under the mattress and Otto wrapped his arms around Werner's body to keep him from jackknifing onto the floor. Werner relaxed as suddenly as the spasm had come. A last rattle of air brushed past his lips. The lines of pain contorting his face settled and smoothed. Otto unwrapped his arms from around the body, brushed shut the eyes, and went for the captain.

"A burial at sea," the Dane said. "There is no possibility of returning to port. The risk is too great."

Otto and Heinrich discussed it. Should they insist on turning back? Or, should they continue the voyage west? In the end they agreed that neither wanted to face Goering any sooner than was absolutely necessary. And so their choice became easy. They asked the captain to arrange a ceremony. They wrapped the body in an oiled tarp and placed it in a lifeboat on deck where it would be cool and out of sight. The ceremony would be held as soon as they entered calmer waters.

Otto now told Heinrich about Werner's puzzling last words, and they returned together to Werner's cabin. A search revealed two dog-eared engineering texts, a few toiletry items, some shirts and pants hung in the tiny closet, and undergarments folded in the one drawer at the closet's bottom.

They turned their attention to the trunk beneath the bunk. A heavy steel padlock secured it. The family was already going to be upset, and there was no point in inflaming them further by bashing apart the man's luggage. They looked at each other, knowing what was necessary. "I'll go," Otto finally said.

Reluctantly, he went topside, wary of the occasional wave that came crashing across the deck; he climbed inside the lifeboat and unwrapped the greasy canvas from the body. He felt like a criminal. The flesh was already cool to the touch. Rigor mortis was setting in. But there had to be a key somewhere.

He slid his hand inside the shirt pockets and then the pants pockets. All empty. He finally found the key on a chain around the neck. He broke the chain and slipped the key off. He again patted down the clothing, just to make certain there were no other keys hidden in the fabric, knowing he would be unable to stomach returning to the lifeboat for another search. Satisfied and relieved, he re-wrapped the body in the tarp and slipped over the lifeboat gunwale.

Back in the cabin, with Heinrich by his side, he tried the key in the padlock. It turned easily.

CHAPTER 13

When Oscar got the call from Cruz shortly after 11am, asking if he could come to the courthouse conference room for a meeting, he didn't think it would be anything special. All Cruz told him was that it concerned Fiona's murder. The written report Cruz demanded the previous day was already delivered. He was certain Cruz just wanted to confirm a few details.

So when he entered the small conference room on the third floor of the courthouse and found both police chief Pete VanWeiss and prosecuting attorney Len Handley present, he began to sweat.

Handley stood and waived one hand toward a chair on the opposite side of the oval table. "Thank you for coming, Sergeant." Oscar's stomach churned as he sat down next to Van Weiss. Handley sat down across the table. He was a tall man with an aura of authority. Len Handley grew up in Langston, played on the '64 state championship basketball team, and had held the prosecutor's job since first being elected in 1986.

Oscar looked to his right, at Van Weiss, who nodded back and said, "Sergeant," in a pleasant but noncommittal tone. Cruz sat at the end of the table in silence, deferring to Handley.

"Sergeant Danner," Handley began after everyone was settled. "You spent a bit of time with Jerry Wells the other day." It was a statement, not a question; a lawyer's habit of confirming something already known. Once he stated the obvious to reinforce its importance, he continued with, "What's your read on him?"

My read? What in the hell is he looking for?

If there was one thing Oscar had learned over the years it was to keep his head down in situations like this. "Well, sir . . . he doesn't talk a lot. He likes to go fishing. Says he's retired—"

Handley raised a hand to stop him. "We already have the routine information from Cruz's interview and from your written report, Sergeant." He continued in a more encouraging tone. "What we want is the *feel* you have for him. What does your gut tell you? Is the man hiding something?"

All his gut was saying was that he wanted out of this meeting. Wasn't it Cruz's job to do the second guessing? Confused and wary, Oscar took a stab in the dark, hoping it was what they wanted to hear.

"He seems okay. I don't get the creeps when I talk to him."

Oscar looked at the faces, hoping for some clue that he'd said the right thing. VanWeiss smiled politely. Cruz was cold as stone.

Handley waited to see if there was more. When Oscar remained silent, he leaned forward intently. "You were the first one to arrive when he called in to report the body. You had lunch with him afterwards, so he's familiar with you. We'd like you make some additional contact. Keep an eye on him. Ask him if he'd like to go to the funeral. Everyone will be there and someone might recognize him. You could even invite him on a fishing trip if you're comfortable with that."

"Okay," Oscar replied, wondering why Jerry would want to attend the funeral of a woman he hadn't known. But if that was what they wanted, he'd give it a try. Then it occurred to him that if Wells accepted an offer to go fishing, maybe the department would pay for the time spent in the boat. Suddenly, the prospect of babysitting Wells seemed just a little bit rosier.

Handley was satisfied. "That's all, Sergeant. Thanks for your cooperation. Please pass anything you learn on to Detective Cruz. You may go."

Oscar walked down the hallway to the elevator, took it to the basement where the snack shop was located, got a glass of milk to settle his stomach, sank into one of the padded chairs, and began to consider his new assignment.

He was a nuts and bolts cop. Drunks and speeding tickets and the occasional domestic squabble. And he preferred it that way. It left plenty of time and energy for the more important things in life, like hunting and fishing. Now he would have to deal with something at an entirely new level. The trench coat image of Columbo flitted briefly through his mind.

But I ain't no Columbo!

Slowly, carefully, he recollected the lunch conversation at Sam's. And the more he thought about it, the more he realized that Jerry Wells let him do the talking. He felt foolish for having been such a blabbermouth and glanced around to see if anyone was looking. The line cook, Myrtle Conway, her gray hair caught up in a fishnet cap, was busy dishing up a plate of spaghetti. Three dowdy middle-aged women wearing juror badges were intensely discussing what was on sale at Kmart. The only others in the room were two attorneys, one absorbed in reading a *National Geographic*, the other studying a legal paper. No one was looking in his direction. He felt relieved.

He finished his milk and headed to the police station across the square. With a stack of speeding citations waiting to be processed, he could justify putting off contacting Wells for a bit. And then Oscar remembered Jerry was camped down by the river with no cell phone. *So how in the hell am I supposed to get a hold of him? Do I have to hike up to his campsite?* Oscar began to think this "special assignment" was going to turn into a massive pain in the butt.

⚹

As Oscar tackled the speeding paperwork, Jerry was choosing a room. The Belvedere was an older three-story building constructed of slowly disintegrating concrete painted a dying shade of pink. In a larger city, the Belvedere might have become a focal point for drugs, but Langston was too conservative to tolerate a slum. Surrounding houses had modest but clean yards where you found tire swings and hopscotch squares chalked on sidewalks. Old elms lined the street and spread a green canopy for a welcome shade. Three blocks away was a school, now closed for the summer, where you could usually find a group of boys hotly contesting a game of pick-up at one of the three basketball hoops, or playing flag football or soccer on the grassy field.

Jerry had lived with cockroaches before, so the fact that one skittered between his feet as he was being shown around made little difference. This was short term. A few days at best. A few weeks at worst. The manager, a Hispanic in her thirties in brown slacks and a yellow blouse, made an errant stomp at the insect as it scurried underfoot. Rosa smiled apologetically after she missed.

Most of the thirty-four apartments were single bedroom. Jerry chose one on the third floor because it had decent basic furnishings: a double bed, Formica table and two wooden chairs, mustard-colored vinyl recliner, two brown throw rugs only just beginning to unravel at the edges, an ancient color TV with a rabbit-ear antenna wrapped in aluminum foil, and a hodge-podge of utensils and cookware.

When they returned to the small office on the first floor a boy was waiting. "Mama," he asked in Spanish. "May I go out to play?"

Rosa scolded him softly in Spanish, "Pablo, I have told you before not to come in while there is a customer."

She turned to Jerry. "I am sorry, Señor. My son is twelve and he knows he is not supposed come here when I am with a customer."

She turned back to Pablo and said in English, "Pablo, this is Mister Wells. He is a new tenant."

"Hello, Mister Wells," Pablo said politely in an English that suddenly held no trace of Spanish inflection.

"Hello, Pablo," Jerry replied. "It's nice to meet you."

Pablo looked back to his mother with expectant eyes.

"Okay, you may go," she said in English, shooing him lovingly with both hands toward the door.

The retreating *slap* of Pablo's tennis shoes echoed down the hallway, followed by the thump of the front door shoved open.

Rosa pulled out a rental form and smiled. "He is good boy."

"Yes," Jerry agreed. And felt a tug in his heart. *The boy isn't much older than the girl I—.* Jerry deflected the thought and instead pictured the flat rock in the gorge. Being around people again would take some getting used to. *There are always going to be children.* He slowly penciled in the blanks on the form and the pain began to subside.

Around noon Jerry walked to the police station. He asked for Cruz, intending to check in as requested. The thirty-something receptionist, with her hair in a bun and fireplug-red lipstick, told him the detective was out. He left a note saying he was rooming at the Belvedere and giving the manager's phone number.

𝄞

Oscar just missed Jerry in the hallway, having gone to tell Beulah he would be out for at least two hours and maybe more, headed off in search of "that Wells fellow who found Fiona."

"He was just here," she told him brightly.

"Aw, shit!" Oscar said. "Do you know which direction he went?"

"No," she said. "But he left an address for Cruz."

"Let me see it, Beulah."

It wasn't protocol to share notes intended for other officers, but Beulah wasn't a strict protocol kind of gal. She lifted the note from her desk with thumb and forefinger and daintily handed it over to Manny.

"I owe you," Manny said, as he scanned the note and realized he wouldn't have to go for a hot hike down by the river after all.

"I know," Beulah replied as she took the note back from Oscar. "I'm partial to those vanilla lattes from the Flying Saucer." She gave Oscar a hard wink.

Oscar sighed, knowing he was totally on the hook until he delivered at least a grande-sized beverage. "Iced or hot," he conceded.

"In a brick oven summer like the one we're having you have to ask that question?"

"Iced then."

Beulah gave a little victory smile as the phone rang and she turned to answer the call.

𝄞

Glad to be back outside, Jerry walked the few blocks down to the waterfront where he found the city park crowded with kids. A teen volleyball game was in progress. Dozens of boys and girls were out swimming inside a roped-off area. A few energetic kids were running and jumping off a short pier and making cannonball splashes. Several parents sat on benches or on towels, most of them keeping track of young children playing in a small concrete-walled wading area.

Jerry watched the little ones for a moment and had the same queasy feeling as back at the Belvedere.

Give it a rest.

He turned away and walked back through the downtown, stopping at a Safeway to buy groceries.

Back at the Belvedere around 1pm, he found a note thumb tacked to his door. It read: *Stopped by to see how you were doing. Please give me a call at 771-3424. Oscar.*

Jerry put the perishables in the ancient refrigerator and sat the bag holding the rest of his groceries on the kitchen table, locked the door, and descended three flights, wondering what the big cop wanted. He plugged thirty-five cents into the payphone bolted to the wall outside the manager's office and dialed.

"Danner," came a steady voice at the other end of the line.

"It's Jerry Wells. I found your note."

The sergeant's voice brightened. "Hi, Jerry. Hey, I'm sorry I missed you. I stopped by with some stuff I thought you might need. Towels, detergent, some silverware. It's just extra I had lying around. Didn't feel safe leaving it, you know, out in the hallway." Oscar sounded embarrassed.

Jerry cared nothing about embarrassment, but more about what his intuition said: there was more here than Christian charity. Still, it was hard to imagine a dark motive. Maybe Oscar was genuinely trying to be helpful? A year of life on the sly made everyone seem suspicious. This was a town where nice folks did nice things, even for strangers.

Just getting used to people. It'll take some time. Go easy.

"Thanks," Jerry replied. "I stopped at the Safeway and picked up the necessities so I'm okay for now."

"Oh." There was an awkward pause. Then, "I also wanted to let you know about the funeral tomorrow."

"Fiona?"

"Yeah. It's a big deal. Everyone will be there. I thought you might like to . . . well, maybe you would want to go. I could pick you up."

It seemed a weird offer. But as he thought about it, it began to make some sense. Oscar said people would be curious about who found the body. Now he was going to make it easy for a cameo appearance, and in the tow of a local cop that would look good. He still wasn't excited about being seen, but better to come out and let them all get a good look and then everyone could go on with their lives not wondering who the stranger was that found the body. The possibility of being recognized from a black-and-white picture that appeared in national newspapers a year ago was low. He had a buzz cut in that fuzzy print, and the articles reported him dead. His hair was now much longer, and the black and white was a poor image to start with. Had the *Langston Courier* even run the story? A local paper would be more inclined to report city council meetings or electric rates going up. The national news was left to big papers like the *Seattle Times* or the *Spokesman Review*. Showing up for the funeral would also be a solid step in convincing Cruz that he was harmless. Refusing the offer might actually draw more interest.

"Where and when?"

"It's at the Methodist Church at ten. When should I come and get you?" Oscar sounded relieved.

"How about nine-thirty?"

"Good. Want me to come up to your room?"

Jerry pictured the overweight cop laboring up the steep concrete steps. "No, I'll be downstairs. Just pull up out front."

"Great." There was clear relief in Oscar's voice. "See you tomorrow."

As he hung up, Jerry realized he had no suitable clothing for a funeral. Jeans and a cotton shirt wouldn't pass. He'd seen a St. Vincent de Paul on his walk into town. He still had time to get there before the store closed.

He was sweating by the time he arrived, but it was mercifully cool inside St. Vinney's. He found a pair of black slacks, a serviceable pair of black oxfords, a blue long-sleeved cotton shirt, and a navy sports jacket. He passed on the paisley and herringbone ties.

When he got back to the apartment he hung the clothes so the wrinkles would fall out and took a cold shower. After several minutes of standing under the bracing water, the warm breeze blowing through the window felt good. He turned on the television for the news, dressed in his jockeys. A jet had gone down in Egypt, and some nutcase had shot up a fast-food restaurant in the

Midwest. After listening to how the drought in Texas was forcing farmers to slaughter their cattle because the price of feed was so high he turned the TV off.

Same old, same old, he thought, as he opened a can of ravioli and emptied it into a battered aluminum frying pan.

CHAPTER 14

Pablo pushed open his bedroom window to let in a whisper of cool night air; it ruffled the loose curtains hung from a plain wooden dowel. Slivers of sodium-yellow light from the streetlamps in front of the Belvedere cast shadows that danced on the wall where a poster hung, of the great Brazilian footballer Ronaldo in his yellow and green jersey, his hands outstretched in triumph.

His two best friends, Roberto and Marguerito, met him at the city park that afternoon. After a swim the three spotted a game of pick-up at the half-court and they walked over and sat down on the wooden bench to watch, hoping to be asked to join in. But the boys playing were older and taller than even Roberto. More importantly, they were non-Hispanic, and showed no interest in Pablo and his buddies. After a while the three boys stood and left the park.

As they came up the sidewalk towards the center of town Pablo said, "I want to check out the library and see if my book has come in."

"Boring," Roberto said. "It's too hot for indoors. I'm heading back to the park for another swim."

"Me, too," Marguerito said. "And maybe we'll find some girls."

"See you later then," Pablo said, feeling a little discomfort at the mention of girls. Both Roberto and Marguerito had traces of a mustache, but Pablo's lip was still smooth. He could run faster than either of the boys and everyone said he would be the best athlete when they were all in high school, but an interest in girls had not yet arrived. He called after his friends as they traced their steps back down the sidewalk, "Are we still on for practice tomorrow?"

"You bet! We'll be there early!" Roberto hollered back. "Before the heat comes. And this time I'm going to show you a few moves you haven't seen!"

Marguerito nodded in agreement.

"Yeah, sure," Pablo shouted. "Do either of you want to make a bet who's going to score more goals?"

Roberto shook his head and turned away. Even with the advantage of a year and four inches of height, he knew victory would fall to Pablo. It had always been that way, and Pablo was only getting better. His sports ability was the main reason they hung out with him. He was going to be good, real good. And that mattered. Roberto turned to Marguerito. "Come on," he said. "Let's get going." And to goad Pablo he added, "There's bound to be some hot chicks, maybe even some tourist girls!"

Pablo turned away and smiled. His friends might be a year older and have a bit of facial hair, but they were still only twelve years old!

Now, as he lay in bed thinking about that conversation, he looked at the door frame where marks in black grease pen charted his height each month since he had turned eleven. The last was *4' 10"*.

So short!

"Pablo, you are normal," his mom kept telling him. But Pablo didn't want to be normal. Not at anything! Especially sports. He looked at the poster of Romero, hoping, praying that he would one day be the same height and maybe, just maybe, have a hero's skills on the soccer field.

He lay back in bed with his fingers laced behind his head, staring at the ceiling, his thoughts turning to the new tenant. Mr. Wells was certainly as tall as Romero. And strong. He looked like he might work out at a gym. But how likely was that? A tenant who showed up to rent a room at the Belvedere was usually poor or Hispanic or both. Belvedere tenants often worked in the orchards or lived a rough life. Sometimes it was drugs. But his mom was tough when it came to dopers. If she so much as suspected that someone was using or dealing they were out the door in a big hurry, often with sheriff deputies on either arm.

His mom's attitude towards drug use and crime came at a price. Pablo knew to be careful and watch out for those who were denied a room or evicted. They might be angry and try to take some kind of revenge. Part of the price was the shotgun his mom kept in the apartment. She took Pablo out to the gun club last year and taught him the basics of how to load and shoot. And after that she told him that if she ever caught him using the gun for anything other than defending the apartment he would be spending the next month doing nothing but homework and chores. The shotgun was for emergencies. Not play. Never play.

So who was this mysterious Mr. Wells? Pablo's imagination took hold. This guy came from far away. Maybe so far away that people from Mexico weren't considered second class citizens. Pablo knew of countries like Australia and Switzerland where being a Mexican was okay. Someday, he would visit such places. He would be a soccer star and people would stand up in stadiums and cheer.

Yes . . . I will be accepted, and even loved.

With the pleasant thought of victory on a field of grass, Pablo drifted off into a young boy's dreams of glory.

Chapter 15

Otto and Heinrich sat in Werner's cabin, staring at the black briefcase inside the opened steamer trunk. It was solidly made, with a fine leather handle attached by thick brass ringlets. A swastika was tooled into the flap and a small steel padlock secured it. The key which opened the trunk did not fit the padlock.

"You found no other keys on the body?" Heinrich had already asked this twice, with stubborn disbelief.

Otto bristled. "I told you I checked everywhere. His pockets, the linings of his shirt and pants. There was nothing. If there were, I'd have found it."

"It doesn't make sense he wouldn't have another key. Are you certain?"

"I'm positive," Otto said bluntly. He would not revisit the corpse. Heinrich could go and paw through the dead man's clothing if he wanted. But he suspected Heinrich's tough act was just that: an act. Heinrich didn't have the stomach for something as ugly as frisking a corpse. During the time they worked together, Otto noticed Heinrich was quick to point out others' faults, but never seemed to find any fault with his own actions. Besides, another reason occurred to Otto why such a search was likely to prove useless.

"I think we have to consider," Otto began carefully, "what may be inside the briefcase, and why there isn't a key."

Heinrich might be a bully on occasion, but he wasn't stupid. Comprehension dawned on his face.

Everyone was aware of the disintegrating relations between the Reich and the American president, Mr. Roosevelt. The need for knowledge about what the

Americans might be doing to prepare for war was a frequent topic of conversation among the educated and the politically savvy.

"He was a spy?" Heinrich whispered, stunned and fearful.

Otto nodded slowly. "It's a possibility. And if he was, then the briefcase was meant for someone in Seattle. That's who has the key. The lock is to keep nosy people out. People like us."

Otto stared at Heinrich to make certain he fully understood. They had been hired to do the installation work at the American powerhouse. That job still lay ahead. But it would take only a few weeks, and then they would return to Germany, to Goering, and to whatever consequences flowed from how they handled the briefcase.

Finally, Heinrich spoke. "What do we do?"

Otto now wished he'd never been hired. But like it or not, he had to deal with it. There seemed only one reasonable action to take—or more appropriately—one reasonable *inaction*.

"We do nothing. We tell Goering we couldn't get into the trunk and didn't want to break it open. He doesn't have to know that Werner told me about the briefcase. We wait until we reach Seattle and send a telegram. For now, we put the briefcase back into the trunk. It leaves Goering with options that don't involve us."

Heinrich nodded slowly. "Yes. I agree." He buried his face in his hands, rubbing his eyes hard. "Good Lord, Otto. How did we ever get ourselves into such a mess? It seemed like so much fun, coming to America."

"We'll survive," Otto encouraged. "We'll do our job. And then we'll go home."

But it was hard to believe things would turn out fine. What if an American customs agent discovered the briefcase and demanded that it be opened? What if it contained spy equipment? Secret codes? Would they spend the rest of their lives in prison? Might they be shot? They couldn't get rid of the briefcase, for fear of what might happen when they returned home; but keeping it raised the peril of arrest and punishment in Seattle.

For all the desire Otto had to lead them out of this mess, to get the pipes safely installed and the work completed, he felt utterly lost. He again remembered his choice not to enroll as a Party member. Everyone knew about the new secret police, the Gestapo. Who had not heard rumors about hard men in trench coats who came in the night and took away people who were never seen again?

Every terrible rumor about Hitler's secret police now welled up in his dark imagination. For the rest of the voyage Otto would get little sleep.

CHAPTER 16

Jerry sat on the boarding house steps, waiting for Oscar to pick him up for Fiona's service, happy for the distraction of watching the boys play in the alley. They were hollering to each other in Spanish, pretending it was a soccer field and not oiled dirt with cardboard box goals, pretending it was a soccer ball and not a battered tin can. Rosa's son, a whip-thin kid with a winning grin, was easily the best at guiding the can with deft feet and feigns the other two boys had no answers for. None of the boys acknowledged their one spectator who now sat on the far right side of the steps to watch. They remained oblivious to everything but their game until a police cruiser rounded the corner.

The washed-and-waxed Taurus pulled to the curb, sunlight heliographing off its clean trim. A few drops of water from the carwash still clung to the undersides of the bumpers. Checking his watch, Jerry saw Oscar was exactly on time.

The boys now drifted a few nervous paces up the alley, watching the cruiser and the cop inside. Pablo held the can protectively, as though he'd been caught doing something wrong. The joyous banter of their play was replaced by an apprehensive silence.

Jerry stood and walked down the steps. Oscar leaned over and pushed the passenger door open.

"Morning, Oscar," Jerry said, glancing back over his shoulder. He gave the boys a wink, and it did the trick. The can was tossed back onto the ground, and Pablo began working it toward the farthest cardboard box goal.

Jerry missed the curious look Pablo gave him—just for an instant—before returning his full attention to the can.

Oscar had the air conditioner blasting; the radio was playing *Windy* by The Association. Wedged between the seats was a flimsy cardboard box filled with maple bars and jelly doughnuts. "Thought you might want a snack," Oscar said, nodding at the box as Jerry pulled the door shut. As Jerry settled in Oscar handed across a Styrofoam cup of coffee and again nodded at the pastries. "Help yourself."

Jerry leaned against the seat and picked a doughnut with a raspberry center and took a bite, carefully cradling the steaming cup as Oscar pulled from the curb. "Thanks," he said, licking away a dab of jelly that squirted onto his lower lip.

"Bakery gives cops a good deal. The day-olds are free. Of course," he added quickly, "these are fresh. They came out of the oven this morning."

"Where's the church?"

Oscar pointed to the small hill that rose near center of the city. "Other side of Pine Butte," he replied. "A mile as the crow flies, but we'll need to drive around." He settled comfortably, both hands on the steering wheel. No seat belts.

Pine Butte stood between the central district of Langston and the south end of town. At two hundred feet the Butte was a mound of glacial till dumped fourteen thousand years ago when the ice sheet from the last ice age retreated northward. Memorial Cemetery, on top, commanded a sweeping view of the lake and mountains.

Oscar took the West Lake Road Bridge over the Little Cascade River and exited onto a side street that led through a residential neighborhood. Beyond the canopy of maples Jerry caught glimpses of a gleaming silver cross on the peak of a cedar shaked steeple. Both sides of the lane leading up to the church were lined with cars, all washed and gleaming.

At the church there was a crowd stretching out into the lawn, easing its way through open double doors. Two young women in green and gold choir robes handed out programs as the mourners entered.

Oscar circled the block and pulled the cruiser in alongside several police vehicles parked at the back of the church.

"That was quite a group out front," Jerry said as Oscar killed the engine. Oscar seemed reluctantly excited. "Yeah. It'll probably be the biggest funeral of the decade. Let's get inside before it gets too packed."

A single deputy stood at the back door. Oscar said, "Nate," and the man said, "Oscar." Nate nodded politely to Jerry, and he nodded politely back.

They passed through a kitchen where middle-aged women were shuttling plates of baked goods and pots of coffee out into the reception hall. Oscar grabbed a chocolate chip cookie from a passing platter. The dumpling cheeked matron in a red and white checked apron carrying the tray scolded, "Shame on you, Deputy!" But her eyes twinkled.

The reception line wound toward the chapel entrance past the official greeters. Jerry touched Oscar's arm and pointed to the four men who were busy shaking hands and speaking a few words to the newly arrived. "Who are they?"

Oscar said, "The tall fellow with the sloping shoulders who looks like a bear is Judge Tucker Holman. Second guy is my boss, Chief Len Handley. The greasy fellow with the toupee is Mayor Fred Cannaday." Oscar looked to see if Jerry thought his comment was funny. Jerry was in no mood for funny. Not today. Oscar continued quickly, embarrassed by his attempt at humor.

"The last guy is Tom Burton. He's president of the historical museum's board of directors." Jerry studied Burton for a moment, a tall, gaunt man senior who reminded him of Jimmy Stewart's character in the '50s movie *Mr. Smith Goes to Washington*. Burton was older than Stewart had been in the movie, with wispy white hair the texture of cotton candy.

"No relatives?"

"Nope," Oscar replied. "And everyone thinks that's strange. Cruz said the coroner was able to contact two brothers and her father, all on the east coast. None of them had an interest in flying out for the service. Scuttlebutt is there was a big rift between her and the family, but I haven't heard anything specific. The father gave permission for her to be buried and left it up to the reverend to decide the particulars." He shook his head sadly. "God knows what could have pissed them off that much."

Jerry glanced around the room for the one person he'd expected to see. Not able to locate her, he finally turned back to Oscar. "Where's Holly?"

Oscar scanned the room. "I don't know. Maybe she's already in the chapel?" He shrugged. "Let's get in before they start."

Oscar jostled through the crowd with Jerry in tow. At one point Jerry heard someone in the crowd say, "That's him." The skin on his neck prickled but he kept moving. Looking to see who it was would only draw more attention. The speaker's words were swallowed up in the mass of soft voices and occasional sniffles.

Oscar introduced Jerry to each of the greeters, who in turn smiled politely and shook his hand.

The judge gave Jerry a firmer handshake and a steady look. "Glad you did the right thing by Fiona. Someone in your shoes might have headed out of town. We're happy to have you here this afternoon." Impressing the judge was a bonus he hadn't expected and it settled him somewhere close to comfortable.

It was a closed casket. The white oak box with brass rail handles lay just below the podium. Jerry and Oscar found seats at the back, and as they settled in Jerry finally spotted Holly. She sat alone in the front pew with her head bowed. She wore a black suit and a pillbox hat with a veil. The judge and the mayor walked to the front of the chapel after the reception line broke, but as they settled into the front pew neither sat too close to the grieving woman.

By the time Reverend Mason was ready to start, the chapel was packed and a line of people stood at the back, with dozens listening on speakers in the reception hall.

The eulogy focused on Fiona's work for the museum, and touched upon her other community involvements. Throughout the service, hankies were blown into, sleeves raised to muffle sobs, and tears knuckled away.

Above all the grieving Jerry sensed a wave of violation coursing through the crowd. It had been a good idea to come. To be seen. To visibly appear interested in right and justice. Because if this group of folks had their fondest and ugliest wish granted, the killer would be swinging at the end of a rope beneath one of those huge maples that dotted the courthouse square, and the lynching would happen right soon. They wanted the killer corralled and punished, and would look unkindly upon any delay. And no mistaking, the mayor and the chief and the prosecutor understood their political futures were at risk if the job wasn't done quickly.

Jerry hoped the spotlight would now focus anywhere but upon the kind stranger who found—and reported—the body. The fellow who came to the funeral of someone he didn't even know because it was the right thing to do.

At the end, the reverend suggested that only those who were invited should come up to the cemetery for the burial. The rest were welcome to cookies and coffee in the reception area, and to share memories of Fiona. He encouraged them to visit the gravesite later, to leave flowers, or to spend a moment in prayer. A book in the foyer was available for anyone wanting to write a few lines. Finally, he said there was a box at the front door for donations to benefit the museum.

"Let's scoot out of here," Oscar said to Jerry when the last "amen" echoed through the congregation. They headed for the kitchen and a quick exit to the patrol car, and everything was fine until Jerry heard someone say loudly over the din of conversation in the room:

"Excuse me Mr. Wells!"

Jerry turned and saw the reverend hurrying towards him through the mingling crowd. Jerry looked to Oscar who returned a "Beats Me?" look.

Reverend Mason worked his way past one last clutch of people, dispensing a brief word of thanks and a quick handshake, and finally reached Jerry and Oscar at the doorway to the kitchen. "I'm sorry to bother you Mr. Wells, but Holly asked me to ask you if you would please attend the burial."

It had all gone so well, so easily, up to that point. Jerry's look of surprise was quickly replaced by a slight tug of fear. It must have shown on his face because the reverend rushed to explain.

"Holly wants to thank you in person, privately, for what you did. She didn't think here at the church it was possible with all of these people around. She's hurting right now. And it would mean a great deal to her if you could join us up on the hill."

Jerry searched for a reason. Had she forgotten to say something when she'd come to lay the flowers and he'd surprised her? What else was there to say? Growing nervous, Jerry realized he was stuck. But . . . better to put a good face on it. Jerry smiled and tried to look humble. "Of course." He turned to Oscar. "Could you drive me up to the cemetery?"

"Sure," Oscar said, curious, and thinking it might even be worthy of reporting to Cruz.

"Thank you," the reverend said, reaching out and pumping Jerry's hand. "If you'll please excuse me I've got to get up there myself." And with that he began dodging his way back through the crowd to the front of the church where the hearse was parked.

Jerry and Oscar headed for the back door, and when they reached the patrol car Jerry turned to Oscar.

"Do you have any idea why she would ask?"

"Nope," Oscar said. "Seems strange, but if it makes her feel better, what's the harm?"

And that was the question Jerry was asking himself. What is the possible harm? But with no alternative, the question was pointless. Holly had asked the reverend to ask him to go to the burial. And Jerry had no good reason to say no.

Oscar drove around to the front of the church and pulled into the line of cars that formed up behind the hearse. After the casket was loaded, the procession drove a quarter of a mile before starting up the narrow winding road. When they reached the top the hearse passed through a massive wrought iron gate and eased along between the neat ranks of headstones punctuating newly mown grass.

The line of cars came to a stop near the middle, where a new grave was dug on the left. A marker of salt-and-pepper granite was already in place: *FIONA ELLEN ROSS – May 12, 1972 – June 19, 2002 – Now in the Hands of Our Lord.* A mound of dark earth was piled on a canvas tarp beside the rectangular hole. Nearby lay a stack of green turf.

It was a short ceremony, attended by around thirty people. The reverend commended Fiona's soul to God. A few folks came forward to grab up handfuls of earth to drop onto the burnished wood. Holly remained off to one side, alone in a world of hurt. After a final moment of silence the mourners began to leave.

Jerry hoped Holly would change her mind, but when the condolences from the final departing mourners ended she turned, looked at him, and began walking back. He stood with Oscar, not knowing what to expect.

She lifted her veil to reveal dark circles under her eyes, and a look of determination he hadn't expected.

"Mr. Wells," she said formally. The stiffness in her voice intended for Oscar's benefit. Only he and Holly knew of their impromptu meeting . . . unless she had told someone. And from the way she was acting, he doubted that.

"Miss Curtis," he replied, matching her formality. "I was touched by what I heard about Fiona today. I'm certain she would have appreciated the love people have shown. I'm very sorry."

There was an awkward moment; she took a shaky breath and after a few seconds regained her composure.

"Thank you. I'm certain she would have." A flash of decision—or was it commitment?—crossed her face.

What is it she wants?

"Could I please have a few private words with you? Maybe over there?" Holly nodded toward a rock outcropping twenty yards away; a solid spread of granite swelled twenty feet across; too large to move, so it had been transformed into a rock garden with bluebells and lady slippers in the cracks and a small arbor alongside crowded with wild pink climbing roses. A white marble cherub poured water from a pitcher into a bird bath, and a wooden bench was placed for visitors to sit and appreciate the beauty and reflect upon their loss.

Jerry looked at Oscar, who shrugged. Jerry looked back to Holly.

"Of course."

Oscar said, "I'll be over by the car." He walked back toward the cruiser.

Jerry and Holly were silent until they reached the bench.

She sat down and looked up and patted the bench beside her. "Would you mind? The sky is bright when I look up at you."

He sat.

"I want to thank you again for what you did. It took guts, especially for someone new to the area."

"It was the right thing to do."

"It's easy to say that. But people don't always follow through on what they think is right. So, again, thank you. I truly mean it."

"You're welcome."

Holly took a moment to work up the nerve to continue.

"I haven't been here in Langston so long myself. I came over from Seattle just last year. If it hadn't been for Fiona, I wouldn't have stayed."

He continued to be attentive, looking like he cared. And he did. But his intuition said there was danger here.

"You're well traveled and experienced, aren't you Mr. Wells?"

"I suppose so."

"This is a conservative town."

"I've noticed."

Holly began to blush. Jerry waited.

"Did you really mean it when you asked if there was anything you might do for me?"

It had been one of those innocent remarks to make someone feel better at a difficult moment. Jerry wanted to say, "No." But instead, he found himself saying, "Of course."

"Then I have a favor to ask. It's going to sound presumptuous, but please understand that I don't have close friends here. It's a hard town for me. Fiona was good at fitting in. I'm not." She hesitated as if still uncertain, and then continued as if it were her only option.

"I don't know why, but I feel I can trust you."

"Miss Curtis—"

"Holly. Please call me Holly."

"Holly, I'm not sure where you're headed with this. And I don't know what I could possibly help you with. But if it is possible, then I'll try. But I'm not in a position to do much." And there . . . he'd said it. What could a transient possibly offer, especially to someone in the prosecutor's office, a lawyer for Heaven's sake!

Her brown eyes closed for a long moment. "All right," she began slowly, carefully, now looking straight and unflinching directly into Jerry's face. "I want to be involved in tracking down Fiona's killer. Len Handley has made it clear that since I was her friend I have to steer clear of the case entirely."

"Maybe it's not such a bad idea—"

"I don't accept that!" She was embarrassed at her outburst. But it wasn't going to stop her. She began again, slowly, in a firm and determined voice.

"I'm not willing to sit quietly on the sidelines. The only option I've come up with is to hire a private investigator. Langston has none. The closest are in Wenatchee, sixty miles away. Even so, Handley would find out. I could do my own investigating but I wouldn't have a clue where to start, or how to go about it." She stopped, flustered. "Oh hell! What I'm trying to get at is I'd like to hire you. I don't know who else to turn to, and you seem . . . capable, God I don't know why I think you are, but you just seem to be."

Hire me as an investigator? It was utterly crazy. Didn't she know that? It took several seconds before he found the words.

"I'm honored. Really. But I don't know Langston and its people. I'm a short timer. I'll move on as soon as Cruz says it's okay. Which shouldn't be more than a few days. And I've never done any type of investigating." Which was a bit of a lie.

Holly grimaced at the mention of Cruz. Jerry knew the stakes and continued his protest.

"There's got to be someone better."

Holly leaned forward. "Let me tell you the truth, Mr. Wells—"

"Jerry."

"Jerry. Thank you. As I was saying, the truth. Can you please keep this a secret?"

Did she know something the cops didn't? And if so, why hadn't she told them? But that was his rational mind searching for an explanation. His intuition said it was nothing rational that drove her to ask this desperate thing. "Okay," he finally conceded. "I promise."

A deep breath from Holly, and, "Fiona and I were lovers."

That was one I didn't see coming!

He tried not to look surprised and failed. She continued as if he had shown no reaction. Nothing would slow her down now, or change her mind.

"There must be some here in town who already suspect we were involved as more than friends, but everyone is so damned polite they wouldn't dare mention it to my face. If I hire someone professional, someone known to the authorities, to start my own investigation, they'll have a reason to use it against me. I could endure it. But it would tarnish Fiona's image. And I don't want that to happen."

He nodded.

"Fiona and I talked about everything, Jerry. And just before she was murdered, she told me she was scared of someone who had contacted her from Russia. Fiona thought I might be in danger. She gave me a gun. I've now got a loaded gun in my kitchen drawer." She began to shake and the corners of her eyes glistened. She looked hard at Jerry. "I've got a fucking *gun* in my kitchen!" She looked away in frustration, fighting back the tears.

It took a full minute before she regained her composure and was able to continue.

"Fiona uncovered something that happened a long time ago. Something to do with the Nazis. She was trying to figure it out just before she got . . . before someone got to her." A tear streaked her cheek. "Jerry, will you please help me?"

Nazis? He wanted to say it sounded too crazy. And to tell her no, he would not get tangled up in something so strange. But a corner of his heart was breaking for this woman. She was a long way out on the wire. And Jerry had a debt to pay, somehow, for the little girl he'd accidentally killed. And also, just maybe, for the others he had very intentionally killed over the past thirty years. The image of Fiona, lying alone in the brush, the flies buzzing around her head. How many times had he left someone the same way?

Another thought came. Maybe there was some advantage to be gained. He was in deep enough with Cruz demanding that he stick around; and it might get deeper; he could plunge to the bottom in a hurry. Any edge was worth exploring.

"Okay," he agreed, slowly, cautiously. "But on these conditions. First, if Cruz says I can go, I split—no questions asked."

"Agreed." But she didn't sound happy about the prospect.

"Second, you come clean on everything you know. Not now. Later, when I can ask you detailed questions. You hold nothing back."

"Fine."

"Third, if you learn of something that affects me, you get in touch immediately."

"Meaning?"

"You work in the prosecuting attorney's office. You would know—"

"Of course. Agreed."

"And finally, you don't hire me. I do this for free." *Unless I decide to ask you for money, and I know you'll say "Yes" if I ask.*

"I can pay." She was offended.

Jerry pressed his point home. "I know you can pay. But if someone catches you giving me money, it's going to look awfully strange. And there's a selfish reason. If I'm not taking money I'll feel more inclined to leave when the time comes."

Attorneys are used to getting their way, especially prosecuting attorneys. It was hard for her to accept conditions, but there was acceptance in her face nonetheless. She slowly said, "All right."

Jerry glanced across the field of gravestones to where Oscar leaned with his back against the cruiser, his arms crossed. He was doing his best not to stare in their direction but he couldn't help an occasional glance and these were becoming more frequent.

"I've got to go now. I'll give you a call at the office on Monday. In the meantime, I want you to write down everything you think is important."

"I can do that."

"Good." He stood up. "I'll be in touch."

She rose from the bench, and for a moment it seemed as if she might hug him. But she appeared to reconsider, and instead shook his hand, and said, "Thanks. I didn't know who else to turn to."

Jerry walked to where Oscar stood.

"That sure took a while," Oscar said. "What did she want?"

"Oscar, you wouldn't believe me if I told you. And don't ask. It was personal." He looked at the cop, and then shook his head in disbelief.

Oscar seemed satisfied and tired in the same instant. "Okay," he said. "Let's get out of here."

On the way back to the Belvedere, Oscar asked if Jerry would like to go fishing on Monday. It was Oscar's next day off, two days away, and he intended to take his boat upriver. Jerry realized it would be a chance to gently pump Oscar for details about the investigation. He accepted.

During their banter about fishing, only one thought was going through Jerry's head.

What kind of hole have I dug for myself?

CHAPTER 17

Frank wanted to search out Jerry's campsite late on Friday but that plan went out the window when a senior administrator, accompanied by a woman who was the public relations officer for the PUD, arrived to discuss "the situation." When Frank asked, "What situation?" in a tone that was half serious and half sarcastic, the woman rather pointedly replied, "The body they found at the end of our access road."

"Oh, that situation," Frank said deadpan. "I actually didn't think it was a situation that involved us."

"It shouldn't," she said. "And we don't want it to accidentally start involving us, if you get my drift."

Frank nodded vigorously. "Completely agree on that," he said.

Her direction on what Frank was to do to keep the PUD uninvolved was clear and unequivocal. Frank was to simply say: "I don't know anything."

"And don't go off embellishing what you mean when you say, 'I don't know anything.' Don't say how terrible it is. Don't say what a shock it was. Don't tell them it's a mystery. Just keep your mouth shut. You can't imagine how easy it is to get in trouble trying to convince the press you're in the dark. It comes off like you're covering something up. So just shut up. Understand?"

"Gotcha," Frank kept saying as she belabored the point. He hated being treated like he was five years old. Finally, after continued reassurances that he would hold to the four word script and keep his trap shut, she finally let up and she and the administrator left.

Frank still wanted to make the hike to Jerry. But leaving the powerhouse unattended and driving up the access road raised the possibility that someone from the PUD might show up to check in on him. And if he were caught near the murder site there was no way he would be able to explain. He might even get fired.

A long afternoon wound down to quitting time. Outside it was hot, and with the specter of a PUD observer dogging him if he went up the access road, Frank decided to delay his jaunt into the brush until the next morning, which was conveniently a Saturday and his day off. In the cool of morning he would drive to the end of the access road and trek to the campsite he'd heard Jerry describe in the interrogation room.

But the next morning, as Frank stood in front of the clump of cottonwoods, looking at cold ashes inside a small fire ring, and the flattened area where the small dome tent had been staked down, he regretted the delay. His gut churned. Had Jerry flown the coop? But then he remembered Detective Cruz's admonition to Jerry about sticking around until the investigation was wrapped up. There was really only one like place where Jerry had gone. He must have moved into town. That meant a short term rental. And there were only a few options in Langston. So when Frank got back to his house, he picked up the phone book and began making calls to all of the places that rented by the week.

Chapter 18

The nightmare returned, this time with a nasty twist. The drug lords were now surrounded by hundreds of kids. Jerry kept shooting and missing the bad guys, and the kids kept falling. The two men were laughing and pointing at Jerry in his tree, and the guards were rushing through the jungle towards him and he was glued to the branch and couldn't move. And then, instead of guards swarming through the jungle, there came a tidal wave of blood sweeping toward his treetop vantage, and in the blood floated the faces of people he had killed, and children . . . thousands of children.

Jerry awoke and discovered his bed sheets were soaked with sweat. The window was open a few inches and sounds from below drifted up and soothed him fully awake; the bark of a dog, an occasional car rumbling along the avenue at a sleepy Sunday morning pace, the laughter of boys at play in the alley beside the Belvedere with the dull tinny sound of a can being kicked.

As he lay in bed Jerry imagined how nice it would be to remain in Langston and fade into obscurity in a backwater where murders were once-in-a-decade events. Where people say "Hello" to you in the grocery store. Where kids kick cans in the alley and no one thinks less them for it. To remain invisible. To not have fear rule your life.

He indulged the fantasy a bit longer, before pushing aside the sheet and taking a shower to wash away the sweat that had begun to dry on his body.

This morning the room seemed more of a prison than a sanctuary, so rather than scramble his own eggs Jerry set out on foot to find breakfast. He passed several fast food joints and walked into the center of Langston until he found a restaurant with tables that spilled out onto the sidewalk. There was a line, but it moved quickly and within minutes Jerry was being served at a small round table by a twentyish girl in a tank top and jeans and wearing a forest green apron with COUSINS RESTAURANT in white across the front.

"Is there anything else?" she asked as she presented a plateful of cheese omelet, thick sausage links and whole wheat toast.

"Could I please have a refill on my coffee?" Jerry asked, followed by what he now wanted to do with part of his Sunday. "And, do you know if the historical museum is open today?"

The girl thought a moment. "I think so."

"Where is it?"

"Not far," she said, pointing down the street. "Three blocks, and then a block over from the courthouse."

The idea had come as he pondered the predicament of his commitment to Holly. By checking out the museum he would at least appear to Holly to have taken his commitment seriously. And who knew? Maybe something helpful would turn up.

After breakfast, Jerry headed in the direction the waitress had pointed and finally came to an imposing building constructed of rough-faced granite that looked almost like a fortress. LANGSTON HISTORICAL MUSEUM was frosted onto a second-story window. At some point it was decided to paint the granite a shade of red somewhere between burgundy and dried blood. It stood out—you could say that with certainty. The front door was oak, inset with four small panes of thick beveled glass. Jerry grabbed the brass handle and pulled.

On this Sunday morning the museum was empty of people except for one man sitting at a small desk in the far corner of the room. His eyes came up as Jerry entered, and Jerry immediately recognized him from the funeral as the chairman of the historical society. The man stood and walked towards Jerry and then held out his hand and said, "It's Mr. Wells, isn't it?"

Jerry felt both nervous and pleased. Nervous because someone recognized him so easily. Pleased because there was an enormous and enveloping smile behind the hand.

"Yes," he said, shaking Tom Burton's hand and feeling the bony warmth of the old man's fingers as they closed gently around his own.

"To what do I owe the pleasure, Mr. Wells?"

"I wanted to see where Fiona worked. Learn a little about the good things she did with her life. I thought if I could see the things she accomplished, maybe it would—"

"Make it easier to accept that she hadn't died in vain?" Burton finished.

"Yes," Jerry said, happy that Burton had reached the conclusion without much prompting.

"I think you'll find that Fiona accomplished a lot of good in the few years she was with us." Burton's countenance darkened for a moment, the pain of her death still fresh. "Let's start with the upstairs." His smile gradually returned as he proudly showed off the collection.

Burton said the building was originally a bank, but was converted into a museum in the 1950s. Prior to then, the collection was housed in a smaller building on the outskirts of town. Much of what was donated during the earlier years was boxed up at the old museum because there was insufficient display space. With the move to the new building many of those boxes were carried downstairs and stacked against the basement walls, the contents soon forgotten.

"When Fiona came to us four years ago and found that trove of history piled up in the basement she was like a child on Christmas morning. She spent the first year going through all of those boxes and cataloguing everything on the computer. And then she went to work raising money for display cases. For instance," Burton said as he led Jerry to a long line of new oak-framed displays, "here is a collection we received from an estate that never got properly laid out until after Fiona arrived."

Inside the case, arrowheads and spear points were arranged in fan-shaped groupings. One set of leaf-shaped points was chipped from caramel colored agate. A set of spear blades had been flaked from green flint. At the end, a set of long and delicate arrowheads with razor edges were of black obsidian.

"Those are some of the finest Clovis points in the world," Burton said of the arrowheads. Jerry was thinking that in the ancient world these would have been the equivalent of his own long range rifles. Different age, same purpose: killing from a distance.

As Jerry backed away from the case Tom Burton said, "Would you like to see what she was working on just before she died?"

Jerry nodded as if he were curious, but not too curious.

"It's in the basement," Burton said, leading to a door that opened onto a stairwell.

When they reached the bottom Burton found a switch and lights came on to reveal three large tables. One held a collection of blueprints laid side by side to form the larger pattern of a building project.

But it wasn't the blueprints that caught Jerry's breath. It was the black leather briefcase. Tooled into the burnished leather just below the handle was a swastika about the size of a silver dollar, raised with well defined edges. Holly's words from the day before leapt to mind.

"Fiona uncovered something that happened a long time ago. Something to do with the Nazis."

Jerry began, "That's—"

"Yes," Burton said. "Fiona and I talked quite a bit about this particular project. And where it came from."

"You knew about it?"

"I knew the man. But I had no idea the briefcase was down here in the basement until Fiona dug it out and started asking me questions."

"So who was he?"

Burton chuckled. "One of the good things about being my age—I'm eighty-nine—is that by the time you get this far along you've met all kinds of folks over the years, many of them no longer around. So when I saw the Nazi mark on the briefcase, and the swastikas on those blueprints, I knew it must have come from Otto Klein."

"Who was he?"

"An engineer who came over from Germany in nineteen thirty-four to help with installation of the pipe work for the Silver Falls hydro project. The PUD commissioners saved a small fortune by having a German manufacturing firm handle the subcontract for the pipes inside the powerhouse. It was all high tech, and the Germans had terrific engineering expertise. Germany was still emerging from a terrible depression, so their engineering firms were eager to submit highly competitive bids. When the pipes arrived, they had these swastikas cast into them. Nobody thought much about it at the time because it was still five years before Hitler invaded Poland. And later on, when the war started, the PUD put a clamp on anyone knowing the pipes in the powerhouse came from a firm with Nazi connections."

"And you knew Otto Klein?"

"I did. In fact, he was a good friend. We were on the same bowling team and we skied together up at Kearny Ridge. When I first met him in nineteen forty-seven he'd been a U.S. citizen for twelve years. He finished up the legal process in nineteen thirty-five. If he'd waited much longer, he used to tell me, he would have ended up in a detention camp, on the possibility that he was a German sympathizer, or even a spy. But Otto finished the naturalization process and was a citizen well before the war came. He spoke English well, though he still had a German accent."

Tom Burton paused a moment, remembering how Otto had told the story.

"He was grilled by FBI agents shortly after Pearl Harbor. But he was so well liked and had so many good references from everyone from the superior court judge on down to the school custodian that the FBI finally gave the okay and left him alone."

"Did Otto ever talk about this," Jerry said, waving at the documents and briefcase on the table.

"Not that I'm aware of. I think it caused him a great deal of pain to even remember that he'd come from Germany."

"What did he do for a living?"

"After the PUD installation, he joined the office of a civil engineer here in Langston and worked on a variety of projects over the years, mostly buildings."

"What happened to him?"

"He died back in seventy-eight of lung cancer. Funny thing is he never even smoked. He remained unmarried and as far as I know he had no relatives in America. In his Will he left everything, and it wasn't very much—a small house on the edge of town and a jalopy of a car that had over a hundred thousand miles on it—to the historical society. These blueprints and the brief case must have come to us directly from his estate, because if the PUD had gotten hold of them they would still be in their filing system and not in our basement."

"Was there anything else in the bag?"

Tom Burton shrugged. "Other than the blueprints? Maybe. But if there was, Fiona never mentioned it to me."

Burton shut off the lights and led Jerry back up the stairs, pausing once as they neared the top and making a comment about his arthritis and growing old not being for sissies.

As Jerry was getting ready to leave the old man put a hand on Jerry's shoulder and said, "Fiona was a good girl and it's a damned shame she died like she did. It's nice to know that you cared to ask after her."

"Thanks," Jerry said. "I was just curious."

"Sure," Tom Burton said, and then he shook Jerry's hand again and wished him well.

Jerry left the museum and walked in the direction of the lake and when he reached the shoreline he sat down on a grassy spot and gazed out across the water, awed by what he'd just seen.

He now found himself missing his golden retriever. That dog would chase and retrieve a stick you threw into the water until your arm was sore. When Jerry hunted ducks, Hobbes always retrieved with a soft mouth. How long had it been since he'd left the dog at the kennel? Had more than a year already passed since that ill fated flight to the Yucatan? Jerry wondered if Hobbes still missed his old master. If he were to show up, suddenly, where Hobbes now lived, would the dog come running to him with that happy bark? Would he lick Jerry's hand in gratitude for having finally returned?

Jerry sat at the far end of the beach, tossing little pebbles into the clear water, watching them wobble back and forth as they settled towards the sandy bottom.

Later on he found a BBQ place called *Country Boys* and ate a rack of baby back ribs with a mess of coleslaw and beans and cornbread with butter and honey dribbling down the sides. He again thought of Hobbes, and how the dog would be in the car, the windows rolled down, waiting for his master and a nice piece of pork with no sauce but with a sliver of fat to gobble up. Hobbes would then lick the hand that fed him on the off chance that rib grease might still be on the fingers.

When Jerry finally arrived back at the Belvedere the boys were nowhere to be seen and the street was Sunday evening small town quiet. Jerry slowly climbed the stairs with a feeling of dread. The last nightmare had been a notch up in the terror department. He wasn't sure if he could tolerate much more. Maybe being discovered wasn't the worst thing he faced. Maybe his nightmares were the supreme punishment.

CHAPTER 19

Oscar arrived at the Belvedere on Monday morning driving a green Ford F-150 and towing a sixteen-foot Alumaweld fishing boat with a big Evinrude outboard beside a small black Mercury trolling motor. The pickup had a full canopy and extension mirrors. Everything was cherry, right down to the custom mud flaps and chromed rims. Jerry was waiting on the steps. As he climbed into the cab he saw a vintage Remington over-under shotgun in a rack above the back window. *Only in a place like Langston,* Jerry thought as he greeted Oscar with a smile.

"Doughnuts 'n coffee," Oscar said as Jerry settled in. A flimsy pink cardboard box sat between the seats and a large Styrofoam cup occupied the dashboard holder.

Jerry selected a maple bar as Oscar pulled away from the curb. "So how's the investigation coming?"

"Same ol' crapola," Oscar said. "Nothing new. I think Cruz is over at her house today, looking for more evidence." He gave a snort of disgust. "Didn't find anything the first time around, so what's the chance he'll find something on a second pass? Besides, the staties sent a couple investigators to check it out so I doubt there's a square inch that hasn't been under the magnifying glass. Sounds like busy work to me."

Jerry didn't react to the implicit racism. The Mexicans he'd known were as hard working and honest as anyone else. He pictured the Belvedere's manager, Rosa Fernandez. Her son Pablo's clothes were always clean, his hair always washed and combed. She was polite, kept the hallways swept, garbage wasn't allowed to accumulate in the alleyway; and for this he imagined she made minimum wage. Jerry wanted to correct Oscar; to tell him it was the white folks you had to watch out for. The real crooks wore expensive suits and silk ties, not chinos from Walmart. But he kept silent. In a world filled with complicated people, it was always good to know where someone fell. Even if it was the wrong side of political correctness.

They drove through Langston and took a right onto Fuller Avenue, which soon became the East Lake Road. Oscar held the pickup just under the posted speed limit of forty. Within a few minutes they were nearing Portage.

Jerry had never had a reason to travel up lake beyond Langston, so it was his first time seeing the trellised rows that stretched up the gently sloping hills above the small town.

"Grapes," Jerry observed.

"Yeah," Oscar said. "Quite a wine industry up this way."

"You a wine drinker?"

"Beer," Oscar said flatly. "Doc says I shouldn't drink at all, so I limit myself to a can or two when I fire up the barbecue." Oscar looked over at Jerry. "Maybe three on a hot day." He smiled as he looked back to the road. "How about you?"

"I have a glass of champagne on my birthday. If I go to an event like a baseball game, I might have a beer. But I've never been very keen on alcohol."

What Jerry couldn't say was that FICO took an extremely dim view of booze in any form. Even becoming a little tipsy isn't a bright move when you need to keep a low profile. People under the influence sometimes say the wrong things. The agency kept close track of its people. You never knew who might be watching.

Oscar slowed as they entered the main business district—one long block of low commercial buildings—mostly restaurants and gift shops and a western-styled bar.

Oscar casually confessed, "Back in my younger days I hit the bottle pretty hard. I could polish off a twelve-pack on a hot evening and chase it all down with Tequila. My liver must be a sponge by now." He laughed, but then his face took on a shadowy hardness as some distant thought intruded. Within seconds his face softened. "The piss hasn't changed color and it doesn't stink so I guess I'm okay for now."

Both men laughed, and Jerry felt better about the day. More than a year had passed since he'd been social one-on-one with another person. It felt surprisingly good.

λ

As Oscar eased along the main street, they passed the historic three-story Bosecker Mansion, which had been converted into a bed and breakfast during the mid-eighties. Inside, Viktor Anchevsky was getting ready to leave on a winery tour.

Getting this far hadn't been simple for the Russian, but Viktor was patient and relentless in the same way that made him an effective KGB officer before the fall of the Soviet Union in 1990.

When he arrived in the U.S. he first visited the California vineyards. After listening to hype about how California wines were superior to those from anywhere else—even France and Italy—Viktor was finally able to beg a few days off. His hosts thought he was in Carmel to relax and enjoy the beach. Instead he flew to Seattle and caught a commuter flight inland.

Viktor had previously contacted vintners from Cascade County, telling them he wanted to explore the possibilities for a small and exclusive market in Russia for their premium wines. His business cards showed him to be the president of *Anchevsky Wines, LTD.* It looked impressive. But the company was nothing more than paper.

The boutique wineries in Cascade County had long felt snubbed by the Washington Wine Commission. Their annual tonnage was too small to merit serious advertising dollars from the state organization, and they now hoped a Russian wine importer would finally help generate the attention they deserved. He was met at the Wenatchee airport with a bit of fanfare and driven up to Portage, where they reserved him a room at the B&B. They even rented him a white Hyundai Accent from Avis when he asked if a rental car might be available.

Americans!

Viktor's imaginary import company got him in the door, but he was now politely grilled about whether he thought his fellow countrymen could afford imported wine. His reply went down well with the Cascadian Wine Cooperative.

"There are many newly wealthy Russians who prefer a crisp white wine like your Rieslings. Russians love an exclusive product, so your small output becomes an advantage. For the oligarchs and their close friends, being able to pay a high price is a sign of success. I'm certain we can negotiate a substantial contract once I have taken back samples for my customers to try." The pitch was delivered with poise and certainty. Here was a businessman very much in need of their product and willing to pump up the price! They were delighted.

In reality, they needed him desperately, and Viktor understood this. He had a keen grasp of the sophisticated swindle. Viktor worked his audience to perfection. Each of the cooperative's members readily offered free cases from their best vintage years. When he was ready to leave they even agreed to rent a truck to take the wine to Seattle for transport by air cargo back to Russia.

Viktor, however, intended a far more precious commodity to be loaded in the truck when he left the valley. And his destination was Canada, not Seattle. A KGB comrade who immigrated in 1991 and was now living in Edmonton would help him fence the gold. Viktor would then be able to repay the money loaned by a friend of a friend who had a reputation for making people disappear if they came up short in repaying their obligation with hefty interest.

The plan seemed foolproof, but shortly after his arrival something went terribly wrong.

λ

The boat ramp was on Stanford Point at the Fields Lodge. Built on thirty acres of peninsula jutting into the lake, the original lodge was constructed in the Roaring Twenties with cedar logs cut from local forests. A geothermal spa was added shortly after WWII; tennis courts were laid during the fifties. Extensions to the lodge and updated wiring and plumbing came along as the tourism industry grew throughout the eighties and nineties. By the end of the century, most of the rooms were priced at hundreds per night in the summer season.

As they pulled into the paved parking area, Oscar said, "I grew up with the fellow who manages this place. When we were kids we used to go down to the Columbia and shoot pigeons off the power lines with pellet guns. He tells his staff to look the other way when I put the boat in and park my pickup."

Oscar edged the trailer down the concrete ramp and held the brake pedal to the floor while Jerry got out and flipped the lock on the winch. The boat slid smoothly into the water. Jerry held the mooring rope so it wouldn't escape, pulling the craft alongside the dock. Oscar drove the pickup and trailer to the parking area and locked up and then walked back to the water.

The big man now carried a small red cooler in one hand and a large green one in the other. The boat was gently bobbing against the dock. Oscar was winded and straining at the weight. "Too many cheeseburgers," he said, struggling to catch his breath as he set the coolers on the wood planking. Jerry wondered if it might be more than just cheeseburgers. He stood, waiting as Oscar caught his breath, and it seemed to take a bit too long.

"Oscar . . . do you still want to go?"

"Just give me a minute." Oscar walked to a bench and sat down heavily, sucking in air. "I need a smoke," he grumbled, but then he reconsidered. "Maybe after we're done." He smiled. "Doc says I should give that up too. Before you know it I won't have any decent vices left!" He tried to make it sound funny but it fell short. He took a couple more deep breaths.

"We really don't have to go out," Jerry insisted.

"Oh, no! I'm not going to miss a day like this." Oscar waved toward the mouth of the river where it fanned into the mirrored lake, finally seeming to catch his breath. "There's trout out there for the taking. I'm fine. Really!" To prove it he put his hands on his knees, boosted himself up, and walked to where Jerry had loosely tied the yellow nylon cord to a cleat. "C'mon," he insisted, stooping down to untie the slip knot. "Hop in and I'll shove off."

Jerry stepped into the boat. Oscar threw the rope into the open bow and pushed with one foot as he stepped aboard, giving the boat a shove away from the dock. He tottered across the ribbed hull, and Jerry was ready to grab him if he fell, but Oscar made it safely to the seat, sat down, and turned the ignition key. The big outboard sputtered and then revved smoothly as a cloud of oily smoke rose from the stern. Oscar brought her around and headed slowly out into the lake, leaving barely a ripple on the surface.

Jerry watched buildings slide by. First came the old lodge—a long three-story building of real logs. Then came two newer sections, still with a log facade but Jerry suspected the framing underneath was two-by-six and plywood. A lawn sloped gently to a wide sandy beach for two hundred yards. Scattered upon the sand and grass were fancy padded recliners occupied by tourists in search of a tan, some enjoying paperback thrillers, some keeping an eye on children in the water.

Oscar kept the speed slow. "No one wants to run over a tourist," he observed at one point, but a mischievous smile conveyed an entirely different message.

Once they cleared the resort, Oscar pushed the speed up a bit. They were soon past the river's mouth and then under a highway bridge and motoring upstream. After a couple minutes the river began to narrow and the current picked up pace. Oscar throttled back and Jerry stepped into the open bow and threw out the anchor. It dragged briefly along the bottom before catching hold. Oscar cut the engine and the boat swung into a stationary position roughly fifteen yards from either bank.

"Here," Oscar said, handing Jerry a fiberglass rod with a casting reel. He then held out four coppery lures in his open palm. "I've been having some luck with these flashers."

Jerry took one of the nickel-sized lures, careful not to prick a finger on the three-pronged hook. He threaded the leader through the pole guides, squinting to get it through the tiny eyelet of the swivel. He hadn't gone fishing since he was a kid and found himself enjoying the day more and more.

Oscar began casting from the port side, plopping his lure neatly beside the rocky shore and reeling it back with a jerking motion.

Jerry took the starboard side and, careful not to hook Oscar or get their lines tangled, pulled back his rod and cast into the current. The lure landed just shy of a cluster of yellow Japanese iris rooted along the bank.

Oscar glanced over his shoulder. "Nice one," he said as Jerry's lure splashed into the clear-running water with a *kerplunk!* It shimmered just beneath the surface as Jerry reeled it in. Oscar's eyes fixed upon the iris for a few seconds before he turned back to his own line.

There were fluffy clouds spotting the sky, but none seemed inclined to drift between them and the sun. The temperature had risen into the low eighties, but down on the water it felt cool. The scent of woody moss filled the air.

Finally, a silvery trout rose and took Jerry's lure. It fought hard, jumping out of the water several times, flashing in the bright sun, but soon lost the struggle. When Jerry pulled it alongside, Oscar scooped it up with a hand net. Jerry removed the hook with a pair of needle nose pliers while Oscar removed the lid from the green cooler and scooped several gallons of water from the river. He struggled the cooler back onto the floor of the boat and Jerry dropped his fish in. The trout slowly righted itself, sloshed around a bit, and then settled on the bottom, its gills fluttering as it fought for oxygen. Oscar replaced the lid. He was winded and took a couple of deep breaths. Finally, Oscar said, "We'll gut 'em back at the resort. They've got a fish-cleaning table near the dock."

Half an hour passed with no more strikes. Oscar finally put his pole down, wiped a thin sheen of sweat from his brow with the back of his hand. "Want a sandwich?"

"Sure."

Jerry laid his pole on the bottom of the boat as Oscar reached into the red cooler and sorted through four cellophane-wrapped sandwiches. "I've got ham and cheese, or peanut butter and raspberry jam."

"Peanut butter and jam," Jerry replied.

"Orange soda or root beer?"

"No beer?"

"Nope. The open container law applies to boats. It's a bad way to lose your job as a cop getting caught drinking while driving . . . even if it is a boat!"

"Makes sense. A root beer, please."

Oscar handed him a sandwich and a can.

"Just another day in paradise," Oscar observed. He swung his chair around to face the stern and put one foot up onto the gunwale and leaned back comfortably.

"Agreed," Jerry said, taking a bite of sandwich. "Doesn't get any better than this."

"Yup," Oscar said. "Sometimes, I wonder how I got so lucky as to be born in a place like Langston."

"You're from here?"

"Yup," Oscar confirmed. "I've got a row of ancestors buried up there on the Butte, going back to the 1890s."

"That's special."

"How 'bout you, Jerry? Where do you hail from?" It seemed an innocent question and Jerry didn't feel like inventing too much "new" personal history. After a moment he decided there was no harm in telling mostly the truth.

"Barstow."

"California?"

"Yes."

Oscar smiled. "I drove down that way once to see the Mojave Desert. It reached a hundred and fourteen. A local dude in the tavern called it dry heat. I told that guy, I got dry heat like that in my oven and I don't go in there, either!" Oscar chuckled. "Couldn't say I'd want to live in a place that gets so hot in the summer."

"That's why I left," Jerry said. But that was hardly the truth. Jerry had been happy to split from a desert town with little to offer for a bright kid. By the time he was ready to graduate in 1972 his mind was made up. He'd seen the Uncle Sam poster, mounted in the window of a main street office that had been vacant until the army rented it to drum up recruits for the Vietnam War. He spoke to a sergeant, left the office with a brochure describing how wonderful military life was, and how great the college benefits were when you got out.

After he enlisted they discovered he possessed a natural talent. After basic training he was sent to a jungle compound in Nicaragua for advanced training. He wound up stationed in 'Nam as part of a unit with six specialists. You went out on solo missions, and there was no chit chat about what had happened after you got back. You filed your report, talked to a Colonel who choppered in from Saigon, and in a week or two you got another sealed packet and shouldered your sniper rifle and headed back out into the bush.

Oscar had been watching him. "Wool gathering?" he finally asked.

"Yeah, I suppose. It's been a long time. Haven't thought much about it recently."

"Still have relatives down in California?"

"My folks both died of cancer in the late sixties. I always wondered if it had anything to do with the nuclear tests in Nevada."

"Government sure has a way of fucking things up," Oscar observed.

"You got that right," Jerry replied. *And you're sitting beside one of the big time fuckers!*

"Any brothers or sisters?"

"Nope."

"Ever been married?"

It was now Jerry who looked out of sorts. How do you marry someone when your job is to disappear for extended periods of time to kill other human beings? Do you really want to spend the rest of your life dodging the question of why the government sends you a check each month? Jerry never found a way around the problem. Any girlfriends who came his way were brief flings. It was impossible to explain any of this to Oscar, so Jerry settled for what he'd always said when someone asked if marriage had been a part of his life.

"I never found anybody who was willing to put up with me!"

This brought a smile from Oscar, and a wistful look. Jerry returned the focus to Oscar. "Have you got any brothers or sisters?"

Oscar's smile faded. "I've got an older sister who lives in upstate New York. At least I think she still lives there. She got real heavy into the anti-war movement and moved out east. One day she hitched a ride with a busload of hippies up to Woodstock for the weekend and ended up living on some commune. We had quite a fight on the phone and she slammed the receiver down. She was nineteen and we thought she must have gotten pregnant or into drugs. But I never heard anything about a baby, and the police never called to tell us she was in jail. It broke our parents' hearts when she stopped writing."

Oscar drew a reluctant breath before he continued.

"I had an older brother. He got drafted in sixty-seven and went to Vietnam. He was just an ordinary grunt. He survived till three months before his discharge, when his patrol got caught in firefight. Joey came home in a box.

"That's what really cut the family ties with my sister. See, Nellie—that's my sis—she called him a traitor to true liberty and freedom just before he left. Hell, Joey never had a choice about going to 'Nam. If he'd had one I'm sure he wouldn't have gone. But we were all good American kids here in Langston. If you got drafted you never considered going up to Canada or claiming you were a conscientious objector and going to work for the Peace Corps. But Nellie kept nagging Joey to go up to B.C. and wait out the war, or go feed starving kids in Africa. Well, anyways, when Joey got killed it was too late for her to apologize. There was a lot of shouting. She left not long after that." Oscar fell silent.

There was nothing for Jerry to say. The circumstances of life trap people. Shit just happens.

Oscar stirred from his reverie. "Our parents both died in seventy-four. I sent funeral announcements to the last address I had for Nellie. I don't know if she received them. She didn't show up. Didn't bother to send flowers or even make a quick phone call. For all I know she's dead." There was a pause. "You got any other relatives?"

"The only one I know of is my dad's brother who lives down in Galveston. But I haven't spoken to Uncle Bob in over five years." A bit of misdirection. He had no living blood relatives. Uncle Bob was long since dead. Jerry's immediate kin simply hadn't chosen to breed. FICO loved that! Jerry was someone who wouldn't be missed.

One last question seemed an innocent way to move on. So when he asked Oscar, "You ever been married or had kids?" he expected Oscar to say "No." Everything about Oscar shouted he was a lifelong bachelor. Men with grown kids usually talk about them, their accomplishments, and the grandkids. So it seemed one of those "No Never Mind" questions. An easy segue into another topic, like the weather or "Do you think your team will make the playoffs?" To Jerry's surprise, tears traced Oscar's cheeks before he replied.

"Sorry about that," Oscar finally said.

"It's okay. There's no need to say if you don't want to."

Oscar looked off across the water to the yellow irises and finally said, "That was her favorite color."

Jerry looked to where Oscar was now staring at the flowers clumped along the bank. "The irises?"

"Yes," Oscar said. "She loved yellow. The last time I saw her she was wearing a yellow dress just about exactly that color."

"Your daughter?"

"No." Oscar said flatly. "The girl I got pregnant."

He'd held it bottled up for so long. Now it tumbled out of its own accord, like an avalanche down a mountain chute after a heavy wet snow.

"When I was sixteen I was dating a local girl. We were both in the tenth grade, and she was my sweetheart. She was pretty and got good grades, and her dad even liked me." Oscar looked at Jerry with a rueful smile. "But he told me if I went any further than a kiss that he'd beat the crap out of me. And I knew he meant it."

Oscar's voice trailed off.

"And she loved yellow?" Jerry finally prompted.

"Not her." Oscar sounded wounded, but he finally had a chance to confess.

"I was sixteen and when you're that age you do stupid things. You let your hormones do the talking. I wanted to get laid for the first time. Real bad. And I wanted this girl to be the one, but she was a good girl and I knew her dad would put a hurt on me if I went all the way with his daughter. So one day I was messing around in study hall and there was this Mexican girl who'd come up to Washington with her family following the harvest and they put her in school that fall. She had long dark hair and full lips and big brown innocent eyes. What we used to call a "Real Looker." The day I met her she was wearing a yellow dress that was old and worn but clean and I guess her mother had probably sewn it for her because it didn't look store bought. We were in study hall and sitting next to each other and we started talking and she was real friendly, and she looked real sexy."

Oscar paused. He looked at Jerry as if a string had been pulled up inside his guts.

"I asked her out to a drive-in movie at the Vue-Dale in Wenatchee. After the movie started we climbed into the back seat and started making out. And before long, her panties were down and we were doing it there in the back seat." Oscar paused again and took a long breath. He looked at Jerry from a world of sadness. "It was her first time. There was blood. I drove her home and I felt pretty damned important about having lost my virginity. But I was also scared. I hadn't used a rubber. I kept telling myself the same thing I had told myself when we really got going, that it was safe, since she was a virgin and all. Guys I talked to who were older had said a virgin couldn't get pregnant the first time. Only that was wrong. A few weeks later she came to me and told me she was expecting. She was wearing that same yellow dress."

Oscar looked off towards the bank to where the irises were swaying in a slight breeze. "I asked her if she wanted to go to a doctor. To get an abortion. And she got angry. She screamed, said she didn't want an abortion, she wanted to get married. That scared the shit out of me. I was only sixteen. I couldn't imagine getting married. And I knew what my parents would say. They would have told me I wasn't going to marry a Mexican. No way in hell. And my old man would have probably beaten the crap out of me if he'd found out."

Oscar was watching Jerry closely. A calculating look said he knew he'd gone too far. But there was no way back. Oscar looked off across the river towards the bank.

"Her name was Dulce. That means 'sweet' in Spanish. Did you know that?"

"Yes," Jerry said.

"Well," Oscar continued, "she was a sweet girl and not just because of her name. I acted like a real shit. I ignored her at school. When all the apples were picked that year the family left for Mexico, and I was off the hook."

"What about the other girl? The one with the protective father?"

"Oh . . . well, you know how easily rumors get around. Before long everyone at school knew I'd knocked up a Mexican. The girl I'd been seeing, she had fallen in love with me, and she didn't understand why I'd cheated on her and she had every right to get mad and she told me to go to hell and never talk to her again. And I never did talk to her again. For the next three years we never said so much as 'boo' to each other. We would just look the other way when we passed in the halls. I figured out how not to be in the classes she took. I guess she figured out how not to be in mine." Oscar's face held the wistful look of old tragedy. "You know what the worst thing is?"

Jerry waited.

"I've got a kid out there, maybe even grandkids, and there's no way I'll ever know their names or how they turned out in life."

"Have you thought about trying to find her?"

Oscar smiled. "A million times over. But every time I start to work up the nerve I remember that I was the one who told her to get an abortion. She was a Catholic. How could she ever forgive me for asking her to commit that sin? She left here and must have put her life together, somehow, and moved on. The last thing she and her husband and her kids and grandkids need is a fat middle-aged white guy showing up to make life difficult."

This sealed it for Oscar. Telling Jerry had taken a weight off, and Oscar was ready to move on. He sighed and relief played across his face.

"Well," Oscar said, "We better get back to fishing, maybe move the boat upriver where there's a deeper hole I've had success in. By the way . . . would you like to come over for a barbecue this evening?"

Jerry would have declined if Oscar had asked earlier. But after the hard luck story, he didn't have the heart to say no.

"Sure."

"Great." Oscar began to stand up. He froze halfway, put his hands heavily upon his knees, as if bracing against a fall. Then he slumped back into the chair and grabbed at his left side. "Shit," he said quietly.

"Oscar?" The cop's skin was turning blue. Jerry stood up and put a hand on the big man's shoulder to steady him. "You okay?"

Oscar took two hard, anguished gulps of air. He looked up and his face was torn with fear. "I'm not sure," he said, grimacing from another burst of pain. "But I don't think so. In fact, I think I'm having a heart attack."

And then he slumped over like a sack of potatoes.

Chapter 20

The Seattle skyline materialized though low clouds as the tugboat nudged the Danish freighter towards a long wooden pier. Otto stared from the deck at what seemed a magical vision of modern buildings, rail yards and docklands. On the skyline just beyond the Pioneer Square waterfront district stood the colossal forty-two story Smith Tower with its pyramidal white crown and wide-windowed offices; a stunning exclamation point of modern architecture. The city was vibrant and alive, in stark contrast to Europe, still firmly rooted in its medieval past.

A southwest wind was blowing occasional fat raindrops. Otto tightened his greatcoat collar and snugged the wool cap over his ears. The local pilot said blustery weather was typical of early May, but it could rapidly change. Just yesterday the sky had been blue and the temperature seventy-one.

The tugboat nosed the freighter against the pilings and mooring lines were thrown. Otto wanted to leap onto the wharf and run through the city's streets, talk to people, breathe every new scent, listen to every new sound, sample every new food. He was giddy at the prospect.

He'd heard so many tales about the American West. Gold rushes in California and Alaska. Trees with names like Sitka Spruce, Douglas Fir and Red Cedar; so immense you could build a house from a single trunk. Streams filled with salmon you could spear by the basketful. Land given away by the government if you would only cut the trees and till the soil. Wheat, apples, row crops; all easy to grow in freshly turned virgin earth. Men with calloused hands who made a living by working land they themselves owned. Imagine! For someone who came from a place where the aristocracy did everything possible to hold the common man down it seemed like a fairy tale come true.

And Indians! Otto yearned to see just one buckskin clad brave, a single eagle feather stuck in his braided ponytail, face painted in bright red and sullen black, at full gallop on a spotted Appaloosa. That would be a story to tell in the beer halls of Munich!

Thoughts of Nazi Germany and his job brought him crashing back to reality. Two months of work in this new land, and then a return to Goering and having to relate the gory details of the death to Werner's family. Otto's cheerful mood vanished. There would be no leaping and running today.

Heinrich strolled on deck, the glowing ember of a hand-rolled cigarette cupped in one hand. He took a long drag and offered it to Otto, who waved it off. Heinrich knew he didn't smoke. But that was Heinrich, wasn't it? Always looking for a way to poke and irritate even if it accomplished nothing more than to exercise a mean streak.

Heinrich chuckled darkly, took another drag, gazed at the buildings that ran up the hills. "Do you think they make good beer here?"

"I suppose," Otto said. "With all these people they should have good beer." But his thoughts were not of saloons. Goering had the power to do whatever he pleased. And if the family wanted to blame someone, Otto was a likely candidate. He'd been in charge when the accident occurred. Sending a considerate and respectful message might improve his chances for getting off with a mild rebuke. A poorly composed telegram could easily make things worse.

Heinrich seemed to read his mind. "Don't worry," he chided, mimicking the general's grandiose manner of speech. "It will not bring down the Third Reich!"

Easy for you to say. You can treat it like a game. You weren't the one in charge.

Heinrich continued trying to cheer him. "It wasn't your fault! Goering will know that. Come into town with me and drink some beer. We'll find you a woman. One with big tits!"

Otto stared at Heinrich. How could he possibly imagine liquor and a whore would make him feel better?

Heinrich persisted. "Come on, Otto. Don't be such a Prussian!"

Otto bristled. One of his grandfathers came from Prussia. "I've got to get over to the Western Union office," he said bluntly.

Otto had been working on the wording of the telegram since the ship passed through the Panama Canal. As they moved through the American controlled waterway, Otto focused upon the telegram's wording, praying for a piece of luck. The briefcase was still in Werner's empty room, inside the re-locked trunk. If it were a German controlled waterway, the authorities would have certainly gone through the ship with great care, found the briefcase, and demanded that it be opened.

But the American inspector just glanced through their papers and made a cursory inspection of the crates in the hold, not even bothering to pry up a lid. It was easy to see what the cargo was with two of the pipes damaged and already rusting. He asked what had happened. After hearing the captain out, he concluded his inspection. The Germans had suffered enough.

Otto now lived with the fear that the U. S. Customs Service in Seattle would be more inquisitive and find the briefcase and demand that it be opened. When he couldn't produce a key, they would cut the leather, revealing whatever terrible secrets Werner had carried. And then would come questions about their project and whether it might be a clever cover-up for something more sinister. After that, who knew? Maybe prison. Maybe worse.

Heinrich finished his cigarette, pitched it into the salt water, and stood with his hands jammed into his pockets, waiting for an answer. "Well," he finally demanded. "Is it beer, or the telegraph?"

"The telegraph," Otto said in a steady voice. "But I'll join you later."

"There's a good man!" Heinrich slapped him on the back. "Take your time. I'll even buy your first stein if you don't take all day!"

人

Otto found the Western Union office in the core of the business district, three blocks up from the waterfront. A man in a bill cap and wearing a crisply pressed long-sleeved white linen shirt beneath a black vest stood behind the slim iron bars protecting the marble counter. He took the half page of handwritten script

Otto passed across, looked at it skeptically, and handed it back. "What language is that?" he asked accusingly.

"German," Otto said.

"You'll have to translate it," the clerk said bluntly. "This office only sends messages in English." Another customer entered and was standing behind Otto. As if to make his point, the clerk called out, "Next!"

Otto hadn't expected a telegram would need to be in English. He stepped aside and looked at the nine carefully penned lines he would have to re-draft.

I can't rewrite this in English in just a few minutes. What if I make a mistake? What if the words come out wrong!

He folded the paper and angrily stuffed it into his pocket, pushed open the door and stomped off toward the Kaiserkeller where he had agreed to meet Heinrich.

As Otto disappeared down the boardwalk, a man concealed in a vestibule across the street left his hiding place and hurried through the busy traffic, dodging a black Model A that refused to slow down for a jaywalking pedestrian, and stepped inside the Western Union office.

The clerk gave the newcomer the same requirement as he'd just given to the other German. "All messages must be in English!" he insisted in a frustrated voice.

Heinrich considered the unexpected rebuke for a moment, reached into his pocket and pulled out a twenty dollar bill. As he slid the bill onto the counter he said in his rough English, "Is difficult for me to write in English. Can you do Deutsch for me please?"

The telegraph operator eyed the twenty. He looked around; there was no one else in the office. "Now that might just be possible," he said slowly. He slipped on a pair of bifocals and scrutinized the handwriting, then glanced at the twenty that lay beside it on the counter.

Had the message been translated into English it would have read: *Werner died in crossing. Stop. Cargo safe. Stop. Will proceed to remove material shortly and find suitable place for storage. Stop.*

The operator stared over the tops of his glasses at the German. "And you want it sent to this Goering fella all the way over in Germany?"

"Yes."

The clerk's distrust did not keep him from discharging his duty once his palm was greased. He was, after all, an employee of a private business. If he were a G-man he might have some pointed questions. But he wasn't a G-man, was he? Besides, his feet hurt and he'd spent enough time on Germans for one day. He saw no harm in the peculiar message since it was quite short and didn't have any funny dots above any of the letters like the first message he'd rejected. No real reason occurred to the clerk not to send it. Not when Andy Jackson was staring up at him! He looked at the German.

"And you want that signed *Heinrich Stromer?*"

"Yes."

The operator reached out and took the bill and pushed it into his pocket. "Okay. I'll get it right off." He paused to add up the company's cost for such a telegram. "That'll be three-fifty." Heinrich reached into his pocket and counted out three ones and two quarters. He laid the money on the counter and the operator picked up the paper bills and scooped the coins and put them in the cash box before walking over to the telegraph set, where he began tapping in Morse Code.

Heinrich stepped back from the counter, satisfied. He had avoided Otto, and if he hurried, he could arrive at the *Kaiserkeller* quickly enough to make it seem as though he'd been there all along. Absentmindedly, he reached into his pants pocket and fingered the small key Goering had given him before the cargo was loaded and the briefcase given over to that dolt of a cousin who'd recklessly gotten himself killed. He would now have to complete the removal work without Werner. Tonight he would take the templates from the brief case and hide them in his luggage. With the templates in hand it was simply a matter of finding the right pipe sections by matching the numbers on the templates against the numbers raised on the pipes. Once a template was fit against the end of its designated pipe, all one had to do was drill through an inch of cast steel and the gold slugs would come sliding out! He would have his chance after they reached the powerhouse and the pipes were removed from their wooden packing cases. He could figure the exact timing later. With Werner out of the picture and unable to assist, he might now have to tell Otto, whose help in drilling out the channels and removing the gold slugs might be necessary. Of course, Otto would then have to die.

But first, the beer! And titties!

SS Leutnant Heinrich Stromer, perfectly happy with the way his day had turned out, exited the Western Union and jogged down the boardwalk toward Pioneer Square.

Chapter 21

Funding for FICO appeared officially as a single line item in the thick Drug Enforcement Agency budget. No mention was made of what the group actually did. And if you asked anyone at the DEA what FICO's functions were, you were going to get, "FICO? Never heard of it." For the majority of low level DEA staff that would be the truth. And for the more elite who were aware of what FICO was all about, none were going to talk.

Not that the DEA was FICO's only client. Several of the more clandestine agencies of the U.S. government could access FICO's unique services if they came with the right reason and high level authorization. The CIA and the NSA were no strangers to FICO for dealing with matters outside the U.S. On the other hand, the FBI was excluded, and this exclusion created an unpleasant political division within the U.S. government; a division that would hopefully never see the light of day or gain attention from the press. At least that was what the Congressional Oversight Committee had counted on for nearly thirty years.

Without knowing precisely where to look it was impossible to find the small office suite that housed FICO. First came a solid wood door in a long hallway in a nondescript office building in a Virginia suburb. The door to FICO's domain had no number. Someone walking down the hallway might mistake it for a storage room.

If you were one of those random persons who each year confusedly pushed open the door, you came face-to-face with a matronly woman seated behind a tall counter who would ask in a rather bored voice what you wanted. If you were lost, she would politely try to help with directions. But just to be on the safe side, while she gave instructions on how to find your way she would be shifting one hand beneath the counter so that it was easy for her to grab the magnum-loaded Colt .45.

If you came with a less than innocent motive, and somehow managed to get past the woman and her weapon, you encountered the next hurdle.

Behind the desk was a mahogany door. Beneath the lovely polished wood veneer was half an inch of tempered plate steel. If you somehow got past that barrier—no one ever had, but FICO took no chances—you came into corridor that was lined on one side with doorways for the offices of the special agents who performed support work for the assassins. On the other side were open cubicles for secretaries and support staff. Each staffer was trained to use deadly force should someone intrude this deep into FICO's sanctuary. Each had a load-ed handgun in a desk drawer. Two staffers near the end had pistol grip shotguns slid into long holsters bolted to the undersides of their desks. At the far end was a well-armored mahogany door led to the office of FICO's director.

There were no offices for the assassins. If an assassin needed to visit head-quarters, they temporarily worked out of a large room which held a worktable and ten locked cabinets containing weapons and other equipment.

Special Agent Denny Nevler had spent most of the morning trying to deter-mine if a Mexican cartel had helped to finance the recent construction of a pri-vate airstrip in northern Arizona. His dark blue tie was comfortably loosened; his white shirt sleeves were rolled up. On his desk sat a mug with *"MOM"* on the side. Next to the coffee was an article clipped from the *Lake Havasu City Morning Star*, which reported the construction details for the airstrip and the dedication ceremony with local dignitaries. Denny was in the process of cross referencing names which appeared in the article with the Agency's list of bad guys known to be operating in or near to Arizona, when his phone rang. He absentmindedly stabbed the intercom button and answered, "Nevler."

"Denny?" It was Director Fields.

When he heard the boss's voice Denny unconsciously straightened in his chair.

"Yes, sir?"

"Have you got a couple minutes to take a look at something?"

"I'm working on the Arizona airstrip issue, sir. Should I finish up before I come down?"

"Right now if you don't mind." Fields sounded put out.

"Be right there, sir." Denny straightened his tie and rolled down and buttoned his sleeves and went out into the corridor, saying to his secretary, "Boss wants me."

Fields' secretary was standing beside the mahogany door. "He said you should go in without knocking."

Denny turned the knob and pushed.

Art Fields was seated behind a massive oak desk. Behind him, three large tinted windows looked out from six stories into a canopy of summer-green oaks. From the outside, these windows reflected silvery light in the same way as several dozen other windows on that side of the building. But the tempered glass in FICO's windows was nearly an inch thick and was designed to stop a .50 caliber full metal jacket bullet.

Fields was balding and with a hefty build resembled the late Telly Savalas, earning him the nickname *Kojak*. He enjoyed the moniker. Even more so because no one ever dared say it to his face.

His desk was normally awash with paperwork, arranged in stacks of varying height, closer or further depending upon the importance of each project. Today, everything was moved onto a credenza except for a single sheet of paper lying dead center on the desk. Denny recognized it as an FBI fingerprint request. Someone had filled it in by hand.

Fields waved to one of two black leather armchairs. Denny settled uncomfortably, sitting forward so that his back wasn't touching the leather.

"You did the wrap-up on Champoton?" It was an accusation, not a question. Denny sat up a little straighter.

"Yes, sir."

"Turned in the report four months ago?"

"Yes, sir." Compiling the report took nine months from the time the Cubans shot down the Citation. Penetrating the internal workings of the Mexican government was the first barrier. Getting reliable information out of Cuba proved more difficult. Denny was quite pleased he'd been able to finish up in such short order.

Fields reached back to the credenza and grabbed a gray-jacketed file stamped with bold red letters: *CLASSIFIED – NEED TO KNOW AUTHORIZATION REQUIRED.*

"And one of your conclusions," he continued, folding it open on his desk and thumbing to the back of the file, "was that, *"All team members died when the Cubans shot down our aircraft."* He looked up for confirmation. "Correct?"

"Yes, sir, that is correct." The skin on the back of Denny's neck began to crawl. What had Fields discovered? Denny knew an unpleasant answer was coming. Fields had a flair for the melodramatic, but it rarely lasted for long. He used it to command attention. And this morning it was working quite well. Denny was scared to even blink as he waited for the hammer to fall.

"I've been reviewing your report," Fields continued. "The Cubans recovered two bodies, and we found an arm. We obtained copies of their photos and positively identified DEA agents Al Eberle and Mike Dell. The pilot, a fellow named John Card, we confirmed from DNA taken from that single arm. There was no mention of any physical evidence to identify our man, Jerry Dearborn, in your report. Does that square with your recollection?"

"Yes, sir, that is correct."

"Did you ever come across anything to prove Dearborn was on the plane?"

Denny's gut grumbled in a way that said he'd be skipping lunch. "I suppose . . ."

"What?"

"I suppose Dearborn might have stayed. But why? It would have placed him in danger. And he never reported back. If he stayed, why didn't he contact us?" *What does Fields know?* Denny's mind began freewheeling with the possibilities.

"Unless he didn't make it to the plane and the Mexicans picked him up. But if they did then why didn't they make a show of it? Wouldn't they have done that? Unless they've got him squirreled away somewhere. Jesus, I hope they don't." He fell silent and wished he were hiking in the Catskills. Better yet, the Himalayas.

Fields slowly pushed the FBI fingerprint report across the desk with the tip of his right index finger.

Denny picked up the single sheet and read the name written in by hand: *Jerry Wells*. The signature at the bottom of the form—in the same handwriting—was for a detective named *Manuel Cruz*. There were two finger prints; not perfect prints, but enough for identification. In Field's clean and flowing script directly below the subject's name was added: *aka: Jerry Allen Dearborn*.

Denny's hand holding the sheet began to tremble. He looked up.

"They match?"

"Ninety-nine-point-nine-nine-eight percent likelihood."

"Good Lord!"

"Yeah," Fields mused, momentarily lost in the irony. He'd been mulling it over and much of his initial anger had faded into acceptance that the impossible had likely happened. And if it were true? And if their supposedly deceased agent now surfaced and the press got hold of it? Dearborn would make headline news. The Mexicans would issue a murder indictment and file for extradition. Castro would have a heyday. And everyone at FICO—Fields in particular—would be in the shit.

Denny was still having difficulty believing. "Are you sure this isn't someone pulling our leg?"

A chimerical grin flitted across Field's face. It quickly disappeared.

"It came through regular channels. When the FBI ran their standard check a red flag came up with directions that I be contacted, personally. It's the standard ID routine we have in place for our assassins. We apparently forgot to remove Jerry's data. Good thing, that. Dumb luck has its place."

"Does the FBI know who—"

"*Christ no!*"

Denny flinched. Fields returned to calm, like flipping a switch. "The FBI has nothing more than a number to identify the file. We're the only ones who know he's alive. Except, of course, Dearborn himself. And we're going to keep it right here in our little family. At least until we confirm it is Dearborn. I'm thinking our man is alive and well, although I'm damned if I can guess how he got out there to Washington State. I'm sending you west this afternoon. You'll catch a flight out of National in two hours. Once you've reach Seattle there's a commuter flight into some place called Wenatchee. You'll pick up a rental car and drive up to Langston, about sixty miles north. Find him, get a digital photo, and please don't let him spot you. Send me a photo of this guy by secure email."

"What about the fingerprint request? What's the FBI going to tell Cruz?"

"That's been handled. Cruz gets zip."

Denny settled back in his chair, staring at the fingerprint form.

Fields chuckled maliciously. "Of all the crazy things I've seen, this takes first prize. The man outshines Houdini."

Denny barely listened. If Dearborn surfaced, it would be years before the Congressional hearings concluded. The conservatives would fight the extradition request by the Mexican government, but the liberals would scream about jack-booted thugs running around killing children with high powered rifles. There would be protests and violence in the Spanish communities from Miami's Little Havana to East L.A., plus all along the California, Arizona and Texas borders with Mexico. The media would swarm like piranha. And FICO would emerge into the public spotlight, likely accompanied by cartoon caricatures in the liberal press. Denny pictured sniper scope crosshairs X-ing a black eye on Uncle Sam's leering face.

The logical solution was not a happy one, but the boss's level stare left no doubt. Still, he had to ask the question.

"What are we going to do?"

"Do?" Fields said. "We're going to take this one step at a time, that's what we're going to 'do.' We're not going to rush to conclusions. We're going to get a positive ID. And then we're going to consider the next step. Is that clear?"

"Yes, sir."

"Good. Dolores has your tickets. Any more questions?"

"No, sir."

"Then get out of here."

"Yes, sir!"

⅄

A few miles away and in a far more prestigious office building inside the D.C. beltway, FBI Assistant Director Pete Cross was having an ordinary and somewhat boring morning until the phone chimed. He picked up the receiver. "Yes, Marci?"

"It's Jim Wheeler, sir. Line six."

Wheeler worked for Cross, and was, among other things, the FBI's direct link to Senator Axton Correll's Military Oversight Committee.

Pete punched the button. "What's up, Jimmy?"

"We've got a possible lead on Art Fields."

"Tell me."

"A fingerprint request came in from Washington State. It was red-flagged in the computer and automatically transferred to Fields."

"Have we got a name?"

"Jerry Wells."

"And?"

"No matches so far. The info on this guy may have been erased from our database, or maybe it never existed. I've spoken to Tom Furbeck and he's working on it from the senator's side. Don't worry boss. We'll find out who he is."

"Good work." Cross replaced the receiver in its cradle. Fields and his bunch of thugs had been one of the FBI's quiet targets for a long time. The possibility of catching that bastard up to one of his tricks positively turned the day around. He punched the intercom.

"Marci?"

"Yes, sir?"

"Call the Seven-oh-one and see if you can get us a reservation."

"Is it a special occasion, sir?"

"Marci . . . there's hope!"

CHAPTER 22

Cascade Valley General Hospital stood just off the East Valley Highway near the Langston city limits. Built on a small rise, it commanded a sweeping view of Lake Cascade and the sharp peaks of the Sawtooths along the western horizon.

Jerry sat on a worn couch, staring out the waiting room windows. On a TV in the corner Oprah was touting a book written by a paraplegic who had traveled solo around the world. A young boy was playing with a red plastic fire truck on the gray carpet while his mother spoke anxiously to the admitting nurse about her husband who had come in with his hand wrapped in a blood-soaked cloth. Jerry heard something about a lawnmower, glanced at the thirty-something woman, then zoned out, thinking instead about Oscar.

When the big guy keeled over in the boat Jerry felt his neck and found only a faint pulse. Oscar's breathing was shallow and fast.

Jerry's first thought was CPR. His next thought was that CPR was going to be damned difficult with a guy Oscar's size lying in the bottom of a boat. So instead of attempting to roll Oscar onto his back, Jerry pulled out his pocketknife and ran to the bow and slashed the anchor rope. The boat came free in the slow current.

He stepped back from the bow, sat in the pilot's seat and twisted the ignition key, gunned the engine, and spun the boat in a tight circle until it was aimed toward the lake. He pushed the throttle full open and the boat shot downstream.

He was tempted to try for the seven-mile run straight across the lake to Langston. But Oscar needed immediate help. He might be dead by the time they reached the far shore. Even if he survived, his brain might wind up being not much better than tapioca pudding. So as soon as Jerry cleared the sand spit along the river's mouth he turned for the resort.

As he sped past the beach the roaring outboard brought tourists' heads up with concern. A man with children in the water yelled at him to slow down, but Jerry was too busy trying to figure how to bring the boat in as fast as possible.

He blew along the dock, barely missed three moored boats, and killed the engine at the last second. The boat shot up the ramp, the aluminum hull scream-ing as the skeg scraped across the dry concrete throwing a shower of golden sparks. The propeller ripped off and pin wheeled across the lawn. For a moment the boat threatened to roll, but it straightened and slid to a stop thirty feet from the water's edge.

Two men who were putting gear in a boat moored near the end of the dock came running. Jerry yelled, "This man's had a heart attack! Call nine-one-one. Do either of you know CPR?"

Looks of anger vanished. The stockier of the two said, "I'm a fireman." He looked inside the boat and said, "Oh shit! That's Oscar Danner." He turned to his friend. "Clayton, my cell's in the gym bag. Call for an ambulance." He turned back to Jerry and as he climbed into the boat he said, "Let's get him onto the grass."

The boat lay with one side low to the concrete. Together they lifted Oscar, with Jerry under his arms and the fireman holding his feet. It was a struggle but they finally hefted the unmoving body over the gunwale and laid him on his back on the grass. The fireman straddled Oscar. "You ready?"

Jerry was on his hands and knees at Oscar's head. "Go!"

The fireman began pushing on Oscar's chest, alternating with Jerry giv-ing mouth-to-mouth. They kept performing CPR until the ambulance came screaming up.

By the time two medics jumped from the cab both Jerry and the fireman were nearing exhaustion. The fireman knew the medics, and as he broke off performing CPR he said, "Jack," with relief.

"Alan," the medic replied. "Heart attack?"

"Yeah. Have you got a defibrillator?"

"Yes. Let's get him on the board."

They lifted Oscar onto a stretcher and Jack ripped open Oscar's shirt. The other medic carried a defibrillator from the ambulance and snapped open the case, turned it on, jelled the paddles, all in one nearly fluid motion. He handed the paddles to Jack who took them and pressed one above the heart and the other low on the chest. "Clear!" he yelled, and there was a large *Thump!* Oscar's body jerked as the current passed through. The second medic listened briefly with a stethoscope. Satisfied with the rhythm he said, "Got it!"

The medics lifted the stretcher into the ambulance.

"Can I come?" Jerry asked.

"Inside with me," Jack said as he climbed into the back of the truck. "Ralph!" he hollered to the other medic who was already in the driver's seat. "Let's go!"

That was over an hour ago.

Jerry now sat in the waiting room, the smells of antiseptic and floor wax jarring another set of memories; visions of the first time he visited a hospital for an emergency. He was young, and recently graduated from high school, and—

—Jerry was rocketing across the Mojave at 110 miles an hour in a cherry '67 red Mustang convertible with the top down, absolutely loving how the suspension and radials held the road. The rush of air made it feel like he was inside a tornado. He glanced down at the dashboard and the odometer was in the process of rolling over from 25777 to 25778. He smiled wide as the hot night air pushed against his face, and then a bug hit his teeth. He spit the bug out, now grinning with his lips pressed tight.

He had just spent three glorious days in Las Vegas—gambling, boozing, and hiring a hooker to erase his virginity. It was unlikely behavior for a kid who graduated with honors and was lauded by his teachers as someone destined for success. "The world is your oyster," his guidance counselor pronounced during their final meeting.

Jerry surprised everyone when he chose to enter the Army. It was an idea he'd had for quite a while but kept quiet about, knowing everyone—especially his teachers—would try to talk him out of it. It was none of their business, as far as Jerry was concerned. Sure, there would be college later, and maybe the professional degree everyone expected. But there'd been enough book study.

Jerry wanted a piece of the real world. He wanted action. And the military seemed like a good ticket. The teenage confidence of *I'm gonna live forever* still burned strong.

He came out of basic training, and then advanced training in the jungles of Nicaragua, and by the time all of that was over he lost much of his sense of invulnerability. The reality of what he was doing finally hit: he was shipping out for Vietnam in less than two weeks. The fledgling fear that he might not come back alive made a bit of complete irresponsibility seem right. Vegas was the logical place and it was just a few hours' drive from his hometown.

A sports car was icing on the cake. The financing agency found it quite workable for a corporal in the Army, especially when he agreed to purchase life insurance to pay off the loan in the event—as the policy put it—of his "untimely demise."

Now in the process of returning from "Lost Wages," he decided to set the *Dearborn Family World Land Speed Record* for the Vegas-to-Barstow run. This peculiar honor currently belonged to his renegade uncle, Bob. Or, as Bob preferred: *Bob the Fabulous!* Every Thanksgiving, Uncle Bob worked his way through a half case of Schlitz stubbies, and when he was well and fairly blitzed he would start to brag about how he'd "done the run" in one hour and forty-five minutes in a '56 Chevy. Jerry figured he could shave twenty minutes off that figure. Maybe even twenty-five.

Piece of cake in a street rod like the 'stang.

It being 3am on a Tuesday morning in late May made the record dash easier. The road was empty. Darkness allowed him to see headlights coming for miles. And the night was invigorating, but not chilly, even at warp speed.

He came over a rise at a hundred and fifteen, feeling like Captain Kirk, and nearly pissed his pants when he saw the dark outline of a smashed car lying upside down, dead center in the middle of the road, two hundred yards ahead. The Mustang's headlights flashed past the exploded carcass of an antelope lying alongside the road.

He slammed on the brakes and the Mustang began laying twin stripes of smoking rubber on the faded asphalt. At first the car arrowed straight for the wreck like a great red metal dart. Then it began to drift slightly to the right. He pumped the brakes, fighting the wheel to keep her on the road. Mario Andretti couldn't have worked it better.

He came to a stop thirty feet short of disaster, hazy blue tendrils of burnt rubber settling across the highway and drifting into scattered roadside brush and grass like dissolving ghosts.

The wreck hadn't been there long because the twisted radiator protruding from the front was still venting steam. The air was flush with the smell of gasoline leaking onto the road's surface, spreading in a dark pool and slowly soaking into the ditch.

He punched the Mustang's emergency flashers and left his headlights on high. Grabbing a flashlight from the glove box, he hopped out without bothering to open the door, adrenaline surging as he ran toward the wreck. It was a white, hard-topped, sixty-four Impala. Beach Boys' lyrics echoed in his head.

"She's so fine my four-o-nine."

A dead boy, still belted in and hanging upside down like some cruel *Twilight Zone* victim, occupied the driver's seat. His forehead was gone.

Jerry felt sick and wanted to throw up.

Not yet.

Looking around, he spotted another body about forty feet back, just off the right shoulder of the road where the pavement ended in gravel. He walked over and shined his flashlight down. The girl had long curly brown hair. It was hard to tell if she had been pretty.

He again felt sick and now emptied the contents of his stomach on the gravel. As he took a deep breath to clear his head he heard someone moaning back up the road.

He sprinted toward the sound and discovered another girl, lying on a small sand dune about thirty feet off the highway. He knelt down. Her legs were twisted in a very wrong way. He reached to straighten them. She screamed before she passed out. At first he thought he might have killed her. But when he checked by holding two fingers against her neck—just like they'd taught him in basic training—he found a pulse.

He finished straightening her legs. She now lay on her back, arms at her sides, making little gurgling sounds as she breathed. Her clothing was torn up—a white blouse with a bra underneath, partially shredded brown corduroy slacks. She wore short nylon socks but her shoes were nowhere to be seen.

He sat with her for what seemed like an eternity, waiting for another car to come down the highway. When none appeared, the emptiness of the open desert became frightening.

In the stark light of a full moon he saw that her soft curls were soaked with blood. The arch of her cheekbone and the curve of her chin were still intact, but there was a wound somewhere in her hair. She was still pretty. That would leave beauty for the coffin if he didn't do something soon.

He stood up and looked off into the distance, down the road in both directions, and still there were no oncoming headlights. It was forty miles to Barstow and the closest hospital.

He again glanced down the road in each direction. Still no lights. He squatted down and reached under her in the soft sand; cradling her head against his left shoulder, he lifted. The smells of perfume, vomit and blood nearly overwhelmed him. He fought back the gorge, concentrating upon his footsteps in the heartless moonlight. She moaned as he carried her onto the highway and to the Mustang.

When he reached the car he swung his right leg up over the door and managed to get his rear up onto the edge—holding her in balance—then swung his left leg over and in. He laid her across the back seat. There was a nasty clicking sound in her busted right leg as he folded it to make her fit; she cried out but did not regain consciousness.

Standing over the girl he scanned the horizon for car headlights and came up empty. He climbed into the front seat and started the engine, pushed the shift lever into first, and edged past the Impala. When he was safely beyond the gasoline pool he shifted the Mustang through the gears and shot off into the night. Within a few seconds the speedometer was pegged out.

Uncle Bob would have been proud. Even after stopping at the wreck, Jerry beat the old record by five minutes.

He came screaming into Barstow at ninety and was pursued by a traffic cop who was cruising the main drag. Jerry beat him to the emergency entrance by a full block.

As the cop pulled up behind, Jerry was already running for the door. One look in the Mustang's back seat told the officer everything he needed to know.

The doctor arrived at the hospital shortly after they moved the girl into the operating room. Jerry sat in the empty waiting area, staring at the yellow wall, depressed and feeling helpless.

She was eighteen years old and on the verge of graduating from high school in San Bernardino. She died half an hour into surgery. The doctor came out and tried to console Jerry. He said Jerry had done everything possible. But he couldn't explain away the brutal and pointless waste of a life for no reason beyond a fast ride in the desert. One unassailable fact kept coming back to Jerry: she died for no good reason. It seemed completely unfair.

In a strange way, the wreck in the desert and the girl's death became the perfect experience for a sniper headed to Vietnam. Jerry now understood death up close and personal. The girl's death would now cause him to decline any mission where the target was a civilian. If the target he was offered hadn't chosen to enter the North Vietnamese Army, Jerry was willing to spend time in a stockade rather than take him out. He'd been recruited to kill soldiers and he was willing to do that. But not civilians. Non-military folk hadn't chosen to risk their lives in combat, just like the girl in the car hadn't been the driver and chosen to risk her life with reckless speed. In Jerry's mind, there was no meaningful difference between the two.

An Army shrink spent a considerable amount of time with him trying to work out the problem. But the girl's death had given him a permanent dose of free will.

Oddly, this made him the most effective sniper in his unit, for when Jerry went out on a mission it was with a true conviction that the killing was justified. Army Intelligence decided to test his resolve. If Jerry wouldn't take every assignment, then by God he'd get the worst of the worst—the supposedly invulnerable Vietcong top brass. They would see exactly what this principled young man could accomplish, or they would destroy him in the process.

Jerry kept coming back, surviving two of the harshest years *in country* any soldier ever served. But not without cost. By the time he returned stateside, Jerry knew he was too good to quit. He had unwittingly found his life's calling.

⅄

A woman's voice broke his reverie.

"Sir?"

Jerry brushed away the memories of the girl and of Vietnam. He looked up at the woman in nurse's whites who stood before him.

"Mr. Wells?"

"Yes."

"The doctor would like to speak with you."

He followed her along a tiled hallway until they reached a small consulting room with a door slightly ajar. She knocked softly. A man's voice said, "Come." She pushed the door open and stood aside.

Inside were a small desk and two chairs, a filing cabinet; a framed diploma and several certificates hung on one wall. A doctor in an exam coat stood looking at an X-ray clipped to a light box. He extended his hand as the nurse softly closed the door behind Jerry. "I'm Bert Wilson, Oscar's doctor."

Jerry shook the doctor's hand. "Nice to meet you, Dr. Wilson. I'm Jerry Wells."

"Ordinarily," Dr. Wilson began, "I would be talking with a family member, Mr. Wells. But since Oscar has no immediate family he's asked me to talk with you about the options that might be available. Oscar intends to make you his power of attorney if you're comfortable with it."

It came as a surprise. He'd expected just a few words about Oscar's condition. "Okay," he said, wondering what this might require. "But I'd like to know the situation first, before I make any commitment."

"Fair enough. Oscar's had a myocardial infarction—a heart attack, in layman's terms. That's not too dramatic. People have them and survive them all the time. Oscar's seems to have been mild. We're running tests to see if there was significant damage to the heart muscle. If not, he'll be able to walk out of here in a day or two. A bypass procedure is the indicated treatment."

He now pointed to white blotches on the illuminated X-ray. "Except, we've also found these. They're lesions in his lungs. I'm not an oncologist or a radiologist, but I'll be surprised if this isn't cancer. We've taken a biopsy and we're doing a blood work-up for an oncologist. He'll be able to give a more definite diagnosis by tomorrow morning."

Jerry studied the film. The white patches looked like watermarks. There were a lot of them.

The doctor walked to a stiff-backed vinyl chair in back of the desk and sat down. He waived for Jerry to be seated on the opposite side and Jerry settled tiredly.

"So where do we go from here?" Jerry asked, expecting to now hear something positive.

The doctor interlaced his fingers on the desk. "I wish it were simple," he said. "Oscar's heart problem is treatable under ordinary circumstances. A multiple bypass is available in Spokane or Seattle. But the cancer—presuming it is cancer—affects his ability to survive an open heart procedure."

"So you treat the cancer first?"

"His heart may be too weak for chemotherapy or radiation."

"So what's the bottom line?

"This is all conditioned upon what the specialist says. But my prognosis is that Oscar has no attractive treatment options. He probably has anywhere from a few weeks to a few months." He unfolded his hands and withdrew them from the middle of the desk with a sense of finality.

"Does he know?"

"I told him we'd have to wait for the oncologist's report. But he pressed me to level with him. I believe a patient is entitled to know from the start what he's facing. I gave him the simple version."

"Is there anything else I should know?"

"Not really."

"Okay." *Shit happens.* The thought brought a feeling of disgust. *Am I really that jaded?*

"Oscar asked if he could talk to you."

"Is he in good enough shape?"

"He's been given a mild sedative but he's awake. There's no reason why you can't see him. But keep it short."

When Jerry reached the third floor he found Oscar with an IV butterfly needle taped to his forearm. Wires led from beneath his blue hospital gown to an oscilloscope behind the bed. A series of regular peaks and valleys were being traced across the small screen.

A young nurse was taking Oscar's temperature. Oscar gave Jerry a wink and nodded toward a chair beside the bed. Jerry sat and waited.

The nurse pulled the probe from Oscar's mouth, studied the number on the instrument, made a notation on the chart, smiled and left.

Oscar reached for the controls and toggled the bed into an upright position. "I hope you've got that fish on ice," he said deadpan.

Jerry had entirely forgotten the catch. Caught off guard, he began to apologize.

"Jeez, Oscar, I—"

"Jerry!" Oscar's sudden, wide smile betrayed the joke.

Jerry was chagrinned. *This guy almost died and he still has a sense of humor! Would I?* Jerry's respect for Oscar jumped to a new level.

As quickly as it came, Oscar's joy retreated. With curiosity, he asked, "By the way, how'd you get me back from the river?"

Jerry described the mad dash to the resort, driving the boat up the ramp, giving CPR, the paramedics. He finished with, "Oscar, I'm really sorry about the boat. I know how much it means to you."

Oscar waved it off. "I owe you my life. Last thing I'm going to bitch about is how you did it. Besides, from what the doc says, I won't be doing much more fishing."

"Doctors don't know everything."

Oscar fixed him with a skeptical look. "Let's talk straight. I heard enough from the doc to know the score. Besides, I saw it coming. I drank like a toilet and smoked like a chimney ever since I was fifteen. My body is burned out. I'm not happy about it, but what's there to do? I've had chest pains since the first of the year and I've been hacking up greenish crud since March. I tried to convince myself it was just a virus, or the first stages of emphysema. Now it looks like I'll die in short order. And frankly, I don't give a rat's ass."

Jerry was stunned by the casual acceptance of what amounted to a death warrant. Oscar took it as a cue to continue.

"I'm fifty-five and I've had some fun along the way. But I haven't had sex in five years and I'm not sure I even want to any longer. I'm tired of being a cop. There's so much ugliness you deal with and no one seems to appreciate what you do. But even if I were healthy I wouldn't have the guts to switch to another job. So there's not much for me to look forward to. A bit more fishing and maybe another whitetail deer come hunting season. But I sure as hell wasn't looking forward to retirement. Nowadays they make you retire if you can't pass a physical. Last time I took it I cheated. The chief looked the other way. That option's gone now. I never thought I'd be any good at sitting around watching the grass grow. Hell . . . I'm a grouchy old fart. I'd only get worse."

There was a brief silence, like standing on the edge of a cliff, before Oscar continued.

"I owe you for giving me the chance to wrap up the loose ends before I check out."

"Oscar, you don't—"

"No. I owe you," he insisted. "And there's something I can do to repay you. In fact, I'm certain you'll be interested."

"What?"

Oscar grew embarrassed. "I was supposed to keep an eye on you. To make friends with you and to report back."

Jerry couldn't have hidden his surprise.

"Who?"

"Manny Cruz. But it's at the direction of Van Weiss and Handley. It was their idea that I take you to the funeral and fishing." The regret was clear in his voice. "Hey, I really enjoyed fishing with you. Don't take it wrong. I wasn't just following orders. I'd have taken you even if no one asked."

What do they know? Jerry felt the vortex rising from the darkness.

Oscar's tone brightened. "So while I'm still around, I thought I'd keep you posted on what they're doing. If something comes up I'll give you a call. How's that sound?" He grinned. For the first time in his life Oscar was going to be a snitch. One last great act of defiance!

Jerry sat in silence. Oscar took this as agreement. But Jerry was still considering the possibility that someone knew far too much about his past to make sticking around a safe thing.

"Jerry, I can smell 'bad' a long ways off. And you don't have that stench. Maybe you screwed up somewhere along the line, maybe you didn't . . ." Oscar was thoughtful for a moment before continuing. "But you're a good person. You did the right thing by Fiona. And the Bible says, *'Do unto others'* . . ." Oscar let the reference hang for a moment. "Unless you feel you have some burning need to confide in me?"

"No," Jerry said. "I'd just complicate your life more than you can possibly imagine."

"Okay."

And that was where they left it . . . until things completely fell apart.

CHAPTER 23

On Monday morning Manny received a preliminary report from the State Patrol's chief investigator. It wasn't promising. The pathologist found no evidence of sexual molestation. They found only a scrap of blue tarp clinging to the belt buckle but it was of a type commonly available at most hardware and building supply outlets. More importantly, there were no hairs, no skin under the finger-nails, no odd fibers. Swabs for DNA traces from the skin and clothing would take weeks to process. But even if they found genetic material from a third person, they would first need a suspect to attempt a match. There still were no suspects to test, other than Jerry Wells, who remained an unlikely candidate.

The FBI hadn't replied to his fingerprint request on Wells, and he took that as a negative. If there were a match to a known criminal they called right away to arrange for a warrant.

The house yielded fingerprints from doorknobs, furniture and appliances. But these could easily be from innocent sources—friends; pizza delivery; even door-to-door weekend evangelists, of which Langston had its fair share. Manny held just a small hope that anything collected from the house would prove of fruitful.

As he returned to the house mid-morning he was now interested in devel-oping a clearer picture of who this woman had been and how she had lived her life. Because over the weekend he'd discovered that no one in Langston seemed to know much about the deeper personal life of someone who at first glance had been on a social fast track. Fiona Ross was proving to be somewhat of an enigma.

When he arrived, yellow crime scene tape still blocked the front door. For this visit there was no particular need to open the door with the spare key the State Patrol investigator gave him, so Manny walked around to the back yard, intent upon learning more about what Fiona did outside. The inside shades along the side of the house were still drawn shut as he trod the narrow cobbled path, between lilac bushes fronting the neighbor's fence and Fiona's white-painted siding.

In the back yard he found a small vegetable garden with radishes and sugar peas ready to pick. The tomatoes were still green. A small patch of herbs included basil, parsley, sage, rosemary and chives. Manny jotted in his notebook that Fiona had liked to garden and probably also to cook.

As he turned to go back to the front something caught his attention. The back door had been taped, just the same as the front. But Manny now saw that the yellow tape was torn. It had been carefully Scotch-taped back together near the middle. No police officer would have left it this way; new tape would have been put in place.

Manny walked up to the door. He reached into his jacket pocket and pulled out a latex glove, pulled it on, tried the knob. It was still locked. Through the small rectangle of glass in the door he could see into the hallway that led through the house. And midway down the hallway was something that shouldn't have been there. A bath towel lay on the hardwood, as if casually dropped by the last person to take a shower.

Manny pulled the key from his pocket and tried the lock. No luck. He jogged around to the front, inserted the key, turned the knob, slowly pushed the door open, and lifted the yellow crime scene tape so he could slip inside.

Everything had changed. *Devastation* was the word that came to mind. Furniture was disassembled, and not in a nice way. Sticks of wood, swatches of fabric, springs and padding, lay strewn across the floor. Framed prints were pulled from the walls and their backings torn away, the glass shattered. Some of the room's light oak paneling had been ripped off, exposing sheet rock beneath.

Several large irregular pieces were leaned against one wall. Smaller pieces were thrown into a corner.

Who did this? And what were they looking for?

His initial shock was turning to anger. After jotting notes on his pad Manny walked down the hallway and into to the main bedroom.

The drawers of the antique oak dresser had been emptied and thrown into a corner. The mattress was sliced open; the wooden handle of a carving knife protruded from the wall above the head of the bed with barely two inches of blade showing. A full-length mirror had been trashed. All of the clothing from the closet was thrown onto the floor. Parts of the drywall inside the closet were punched in. He jotted notes and moved across the hallway, his heart pounding.

The medicine cabinet in the bathroom had been wrenched off and thrown into the tub. Towels from the recessed shelving had been tossed into the tub, except for the one which lay in the middle of the hallway. The top of the toilet tank had been removed and it too was in the tub.

He went back out into the hallway.

Manny cautiously pushed open the door to the bedroom-turned-study and discovered the antique oak roll top desk had been stripped. The slatted roll leaned precariously against one wall; the drawers had been thrown into a corner.

The contents had been removed from the oak filing cabinet, and here the intruder had taken some degree of care. There were several neat stacks of paper on the cabinet and on the floor beside the cabinet, segregated according to type. Billing statements in one. Personal correspondence in another. Documents pertaining to the museum in a third. And so on. It was going to be impossible to determine if any paperwork had been removed from the house. But if the intruder had been careless, there might be fingerprints.

It was now that he glanced back to the stacked drawers, and noticed that the bottommost—which looked like the middle drawer because it was thinner than the others—had a partition. He remembered pulling open the middle drawer on his first inspection and it had not come out as far as the others. Manny had attributed this to the desk builder taking into account someone sitting at the desk and installing a block to keep the drawer from coming out further. Now he knew the real reason.

The secret compartment was nothing fancy. Just a false back and then eight inches of space where anything could have been hidden.

Anything!

Manny would never know what had been in that compartment. *Damn!* He stepped carefully out of the room so as not to disturb anything.

After a quick look around the back porch and the kitchen, Manny pulled out his cell phone.

This time it took just over an hour for the State Patrol investigators to arrive. They flew into the small local strip in a Cessna Centurion. He picked them up and drove them to the house.

After leaving the house Manny took a break for lunch, not wanting an immediate confrontation with the chief. He thought about what he'd seen, wondered if he could have done something to prevent it, and concluded there was nothing that could have been done. Someone who was very committed to searching Fiona's house had found the right time to enter, a time when everyone was not likely to be around. When? *The funeral!* It would have been the perfect time for a break-in. And that would rule out Jerry Wells, who was at the church and the burial afterwards.

Manny finished his meal and picked up his hat and reconciled himself to what would happen next.

When he arrived back at the office, shortly before two, the receptionist greeted him with, "Boss wants to see you ASAP." She fixed him with a deadpan look that confirmed his fears. "The cat's in the microwave, Manny. Keep your head down. And good luck."

"Thanks, Beulah." Manny slid past the counter and slapped a little smiley face magnet onto the day board next to his name. He angled across the expanse of the common area, toward his own office, and heard the Beulah's distant words as she spoke into the phone headset, "He's here."

He tossed his hat through the open door of his office, landing it neatly on his desk, and continued straight on to the chief's office. Van Weiss's door was open, but he knocked just the same.

"Come."

Manny entered.

Van Weiss was sitting behind his desk, studying new photographs of the recent destruction at Fiona's house. He glanced up and then pointed to a chair. "Sit," he said, and went back to the photographs.

Manny sat. The chief ignored him.

Shortly, there was a knock. Manny turned to see Len Handley standing in the doorway; directly behind him came Mayor Cannaday. The chief laid down a photograph he had been scrutinizing. "Gentlemen," he said. "Please have a seat." They entered and sat on either side of Cruz.

Van Weiss got up, closed the door, went back behind his desk and slumped tiredly against the high backed brown leather.

Investigations were usually purely police matters. Occasionally, someone from the prosecutor's office became involved if there was an unusual point of law or a search warrant was required. Cruz had never seen the mayor invited to participate. Which led him to conclude that this was political. They were interested in damage control. And this led him to further conclude that he was going to be the excuse, if it came to that. He settled back in his chair, expecting the worst.

CHAPTER 24

After a few days in Cascade County, Viktor Anchevsky was sick of visiting wine production facilities, sipping white wine, and talking (endlessly) with vintners. His frustration grew with each passing day that brought no new development in his search for the templates. He felt the trail growing cold.

To prevent an emotional meltdown and the disastrous blow-up that would inevitably follow, he resorted to a trick he'd learned during his years with the KGB. He looked for the most strenuous form of exercise he could find. He found it on the steep slopes above the vineyards.

After finishing breakfast, he went on a forced hike in the brilliant morning sunshine. By the time he reached the top of a hill far above the valley floor, his shirt was soaked with sweat, his temples were pounding, muscles ached, and his lungs were screaming. But it turned the trick. His rage was gone; replaced by a settled determination to see this through to the end.

He stood on a small rise, knee-deep in cheat grass, surveying the patchwork of vineyards spread out below, and beyond to where the lake was ruffled by a wandering breeze, reflecting upon how it had all started.

The unlikely odyssey began in a huge document storage warehouse, cryptically named "Block 23," one of many such anonymous depositories scattered across Moscow and its suburbs. This network of drab concrete buildings formed the archives for the old communist state. Block 23 was devoted mostly to documents spirited out of Berlin at the end of WWII.

He arrived for work on a frigid February morning, intent upon starting to catalogue the contents of room 328. Igor Ivanoff already had a pot of coffee perking as Viktor walked into the small break room, kicking the last few chunks of snow from the soles of his boots. He grabbed his chipped mug from its peg and sat down at the simple wood table across from his comrade.

Despite the rundown condition of the building—the green paint in the break room had faded until it was hardly green anymore—there were a few token amenities. The room was warmer than Viktor's apartment. The coffee was strong, and two hundred grams of raw brown sugar came each month to sweeten the brew. A wall calendar featured a bare-breasted woman astride a large chopper motorcycle. You took what you could get in these hard times.

They sat, sipping coffee, smoking strong Cuban cigarettes, gossiping about a colonel who had recently been caught by the Moscow police in a black market sting. Around nine, both men headed out into the vast building to tackle their tasks for the day.

The warehouse was crisscrossed with hallways lined with doors spaced twenty feet apart. Each of the storage rooms was roughly five hundred square feet in size, with file boxes packed against the walls and on shelves down the middle.

The Soviet government had been so obsessed with secrecy that no windows punctuated the walls. Viktor climbed the dusty cement staircase in the pale light thrown by infrequent bulbs dangling from ceiling cords.

When he reached the third floor, he turned down the main hallway running through the middle of the building, continuing until he reached the last hallway branching to his right. He walked down until he reached the last door on the left, his boots recording a path in the dust on the floorboards. He jangled a tarnished brass key from the ring on his belt, checked the number against the one etched on the padlock, and jammed it into the keyhole. With one hard twist it broke the rust and the lock popped open.

The musty smell of mildew swelled into the corridor. He reached inside and flipped the light switch, bathing the room in yellow. It had been years, if not decades, since someone had come in here. He put on his dust mask and began to towel away the thick blanket of dust, gradually exposing labels on the crates.

After finishing the first row of small wooden crates stacked along the far wall, he left the room for several minutes so the dust he stirred up could settle. Standing in the hallway he drank a cup of coffee from the thermos and smoked a cigarette down to the last puff. He carefully crushed the tiny butt on the sole of his boot until the ash was cold. Everything in the building was brittle dry, and Viktor wasn't about to risk starting a fire. If there was one kind of death he feared, it was by flame. When the butt was safely out he pitched it down the hallway and went back into the room.

He had seen swastikas on several of the nailed-down lids of the second row of crates and was curious. Sometimes there was interesting stuff in these German crates, like the nude photos of women prisoners he found last spring. Igor and he enjoyed the sorting and indexing of those, even where there were signs of torture. Maybe something equally titillating would emerge from this new room?

He pushed the pry bar under the boards of the first crate at the end of the row, and soon discovered that it contained five years of meteorological reports from the Luftwaffe's weather service. Boring. He nailed the cover back in place, made a note on his clipboard, and moved on.

The next crate contained what appeared to be personal mementos from Goering himself. There were typed speeches, neatly folded and stored in envelopes. There was correspondence between the general and his staff. There was a packet of menus from various restaurants, all in French. The first bonus was a collection of medals and other military decorations in a green silk pouch. Viktor slipped an Iron Cross into his pocket. The guard stationed at the front door, who received a fair share of last year's nude photos, would not bother to search him when he left because of the occasional treasure Viktor bestowed for his cooperation. Viktor's black market contact would love the medal, and proceeds from its sale would easily pay for a month of electricity for Viktor's apartment.

It was in the third crate that he found the second—and much greater—bonus in a brown folder, several inches thick, labeled "Industrial Records." He untied the string binding the folder, pulled open the flap, and extracted a thick sheaf of papers. When he saw a reference to America he became more interested. He continued to flip through the pages, and soon realized these were no ordinary records. They contained schematics and other documentation for a pipe system for a hydroelectric project, dated 1933-34. It wasn't long before he found the account of how gold slugs were to be inserted into holes bored into three of the pipes, afterwards to be welded shut and painted over to complete the disguise.

Viktor's heart began to hammer. Why had records of a gold cache been abandoned? He concluded it must have something to do with the struggle for control of Berlin in May of 1945. The Germans had been near starvation and there was panic and looting. The political troika with the British and Americans was collapsing. General Patton was boasting about turning his tanks to go after the Communists. In the resulting chaos, Russian military intelligence gathered up everything they could put their hands on and dumped them into railcars and trucks for a hurried trip to safety in the East. These records must have been lost in the shuffle—buried beneath a landslide of documents, forgotten until he stumbled across them more than half a century later!

Shaking with excitement he carried the documents out into the hallway. He slumped with his back against a wall under one of the hallway bulbs. With the sheaf of papers propped on his knees, he went back to the first page and began to read more carefully, blessing the time he studied German in school.

Over the next hour the story emerged. A contract was purposefully under-bid for manufacturing hydroelectric power plant pipes for a generating station being built in the American west. Three of the pipes were cast with extra-thick walls. Twenty-eight holes were drilled into the pipes from each end and gold slugs were inserted. Three heavy paper templates, keyed to fit over the connecting bolts at the pipe ends, mapped where to drill out the gold-bearing channels.

Three tons of gold were smuggled into America. Goering intended it as a nest egg in case things fell apart for him politically—a brilliant bit of foresight that had proved utterly worthless.

The templates traveled to America with three engineers. Apparently there was only one set because Viktor found no second set in the file. Each pipe had a serial number, and Viktor guessed that somewhere there was a record of which ones contained the gold. But there was no clue in this set of documents about which of the numbered pipes held the treasure.

The records were clear on one point: the gold had never been extracted. It wasn't entirely clear *why* it hadn't been removed. There was a telegram from an SS officer named Heinrich Stromer which reported the ship had arrived in Seattle. There was a later telegram from an engineer named Klein which detailed how the pipe installation was proceeding. The final notation, in what appeared to be Goering's handwriting, stated that the gold's removal would have to be delayed until Germany won the war.

Viktor rocked back, rapping his head against the wall, overwhelmed. Three metric tons of gold must still be inside the pipe-work at the Silver Falls Powerhouse!

For the next few days he searched through every box in Room 328 for a second set of templates and the serial numbers—anything to positively identify which pipes contained the gold. He found nothing.

Viktor turned his attention to the other side of the Atlantic. Using the Internet he began to research the town of Langston, hoping to find some clue about why the gold was apparently never recovered.

One of his inquiries was an email to the local historical museum. He invented a story about a relative who had fled the Nazis, settling in Langston during the thirties. He gave the name of *Klein* to the woman, Fiona Ross, saying the man had been Viktor's great uncle. She agreed to research the name and to get back to him.

Two weeks later she emailed that she had possession of a black leather briefcase with a swastika tooled into the leather. It had been squirreled away in a corner of the basement, with a handwritten tag bearing the name of Otto Klein. When the locksmith picked it open, Fiona found schematics for what appeared to be an engineering project, plus three other rather peculiar documents. Did Viktor know anything about the circular pieces of paper with holes punched in their perimeters?

Back in Moscow, Viktor screamed in triumph.

He embellished his story in the next email, telling her that his uncle Otto had been an engineer, and maybe the documents concerned some mechanical device he worked on. Would she mind hanging onto them? He planned a trip to the U.S. in the near future and could look at them when he visited Langston.

He would also like to talk with her about anything else she learned about his dear lost uncle.

Yes, she replied in her email. *I'll be happy to hold them for you.*

For a while, Viktor was a very happy man. Anxious . . . but happy.

While awaiting the issuance of a visa, Viktor considered asking her to mail him the templates. But anything coming into Russia by regular post ran the risk of being intercepted. And everyone knew the Internet was closely monitored by intelligence agencies worldwide, so sending copies of the templates by a large and curious PDF file heightened the risk of discovery. A Russian bureaucrat who sniffed financial opportunity could cause havoc, possibly the loss of Viktor's job, or even his arrest. Requesting copies of the templates might also cause Fiona to become overly curious and start thinking they were valuable and worthy of further research. So he steeled himself to await the visa.

During the slow weeks of waiting for the bureaucracy to grind out his travel permit, he worked out a plan for after he had the templates. He would enter the powerhouse late in the evening when everyone had gone home, and disable the alarm system. If there was a night guard, Viktor was prepared to kill. It would take too long to disconnect all three of the pipes and load them into a rental truck. He'd have just enough time to unbolt and remove one pipe. One ton of yellow metal, around twelve million on the current market, would have to do.

His visa finally came through. Viktor arrived in the US, ostensibly to investigate importing wine to Russia. He made a two-week survey of California vineyards—long enough to confirm that the CIA and FBI weren't following his movements. When he thought it safe, he headed north.

Everything seemed perfect. And then . . . disaster. Fiona died the day before he arrived. Even worse, her body had been discovered almost immediately, because some transient happened to be camping nearby and stumbled across the corpse! Had Viktor believed in God, he would have been certain that He was toying with him.

With police swarming all over Fiona's house, Viktor was forced to lay low and wait for an opportunity. It finally came on a Saturday when everyone was at Fiona's funeral. He parked his rental car in the alleyway and picked the back door lock. He searched carefully at first, but came up empty. He then tore the place apart and still found no templates.

He did find Fiona's personal journal in a secret compartment in the roll top desk. It mentioned the templates, but not their hiding place. He took it when he left, and after he studied it and found it contained no useful information he tore it into tiny pieces and threw the confetti into the burn barrel out back of the B&B.

There was also a bundle of love letters from another woman stashed away with the journal. Viktor was intrigued. This Holly Curtis might know something about the templates. He kept the letters just in case they became useful.

After he left the house he broke into the museum. He found the briefcase and schematics in the basement, but no templates. In Fiona's house he made a mess. In the museum Viktor was careful to leave no clue he'd been there. Fiona's devastated house would be a puzzle to the police. If both the house and the museum were torn up the cops might begin putting the pieces together and bring their focus to bear upon the powerhouse.

What did she do with them?

After two frustrating hours he left the museum and returned to the B&B. He went to bed that night puzzled and angry but determined not to give up.

The next morning was Sunday. Viktor mulled over the possibility of using explosives to blow apart the pipes. He might get lucky. But then again he might not. There were dozens of pipes in the powerhouse, and the rational part of his mind said explosives were far more likely to result in his arrest than in his enrichment. Just buying dynamite presented a problem. Stealing some was nearly as risky. And even if he managed to acquire a few sticks, there remained the danger of a pressurized release of what was inside the pipes, or a fire from the blast. He'd probably have to destroy several pipes before he found one containing gold. This would take time. With nothing flowing through the system the generators would shut down automatically. The plant would drop off the distribution grid; alarms would sound in the main control center. An emergency crew would be dispatched, possibly accompanied by police.

Viktor was stymied. As he stewed about what to do his rage blossomed.

As he stood on the hilltop he finally accepted that there might be no solution. He might have to return to Russia empty-handed. And the Russian Mafia would be awaiting his return; wanting their loan and the double-digit interest repaid immediately.

He sat down and began to pick cheat grass from his socks, gazing southward across the hills toward Langston, pondering the big question.

Does the person holding the templates know what they have?

CHAPTER 25

The Kaiserkeller was a working man's place to relax and let go of the day's struggles. Less than a year after the end of Prohibition, the rowdy saloon located in the core of Seattle's ocean port district was a huge success. It sported a long bar of finely crafted Philippine mahogany, a floor covered daily with fresh pine sawdust, and a huge mirror fronted by a back-bar of three long shelves filled with bottles of booze. Clusters of oak tables and chairs checkered the floor. A sweeping staircase led to a veranda and four upper floors.

A variety of local beers were on tap, which the proprietor advertised as: *Authentic Bavarian Ales, Genuine German Lagers,* and *Classic Austrian Stouts*. No one really cared about the accuracy of these representations. A man needed relief after a long day of hard labor on the docks, sawing lumber from old-growth trees, or laying bricks for one of the many buildings rising on the city's hills. As long as the suds were tasty, who cared where they were made!

There was another compelling reason for the establishment's popularity. The buxom server girls wore low-cut peasant style blouses; they didn't seem to mind a pat on the derrière as they passed; and several plied the world's oldest trade in flophouse rooms on the top floor.

The food was in keeping with a European flair. Included on the menu were a variety of sausages made by a recently immigrated German butcher who was expert at his craft. Prices were reasonable. You could have a bratwurst with sauerkraut and a schooner of suds for six bits.

As luck would have it, on the evening that Otto and Heinrich arrived at the Kaiserkeller a birthday celebration was in progress for one Benjamin Goldstein. Ben emigrated from Austria shortly after the end of WWI. The term "payday loans" was not yet invented. The en vogue term was "shylock." Simply put: Ben lent money to those who couldn't get a regular bank advance. This made him a rich man, and a respected citizen among his Jewish peers. He lived in a mansion on Queen Anne Hill and was an elder in Seattle's synagogue. His grown daughters married well, one to a rabbi in Portland, the other to a lumber baron in British Columbia.

Ben could be generous given the right circumstance. And now that Prohibition was dead and alcohol could be freely served, he decided for his birthday to invite those whom he dealt with during the previous year to the Kaiserkeller for as many free rounds of beer as they could put away. If a few freeloaders snuck in, they were treated with equal largesse. Ben knew the value of advertising. He had learned very early that you remained popular, even if your collection agents twisted a few arms or busted a few heads, if you occasionally threw a wingding of a party. And this year's alcohol giveaway promised to be a real beauty.

Unknown to Ben's "guests," the night seemed more expensive than it actually was. Ben cut a special deal with the proprietor. He bought the beer wholesale, paid a ten percent carriage charge, and promised to replace anything broken if fighting erupted.

One reason for the possibility of fisticuffs was Ben's varied customer base. He loaned to Jews and non-Jews alike. There wasn't a prejudicial bone in Ben Goldstein's body when it came to business. A buck was a buck, whether it came from a Wasserman's pocket, an O'Reilly's billfold, or a Yakamoto's silk coin purse. In fact, some of his customers were expatriated Germans who held Hitler and his National Socialist Party in high regard. The Aryans in particular resented the Jew's hefty profits, garnered from their financial misfortunes, but it didn't stop them from asking for a loan when things got tight. And most of them planned to show up for Ben's shindig. Free beer was, after all, *free beer.*

Otto spotted a bathhouse on his trek to Pioneer Square and decided to bathe and get a razor shave. He smelled of lilac water as he pushed through the batwing doors of the Kaiserkeller. The smoky room was filled with the chatter of a ragtime piano; the aromatic mélange of beer, cigars and pine assaulted and thrilled the nostrils.

He spotted Heinrich near the back, engaged in close conversation with a voluptuous blonde wearing a swishy red skirt. Otto wound his way through the crowd. Practically everyone seemed to be swearing or bragging or laughing, and generally having a grand time.

Maybe this wasn't such a bad idea.

"Heinrich!" he hollered above the din. Heinrich looked up and saw Otto pushing toward him.

"Otto!" he shouted back, lifting his mug in happy salute. "Is a good night. The beer is on some old Jew. Lucky for us it's his birthday!"

A few patrons cast a dour glance toward Heinrich upon hearing the slur, but none stepped forward to challenge him. Ben was, after all, both *old* and a *Jew*. Conversations resumed with barely a hitch.

Heinrich said, "Get a stein." With a grand sweep of his arm he added, "And meet Fräulein Helga."

The woman's red lips parted and her irregular teeth emerged in a predatory smile. Otto forced a polite nod before turning towards the bar to fetch his first free schooner.

Heinrich bellowed out from behind, "And she is no kike!"

The bartender sullenly shoved Otto a mug, cautioning in a low voice, "You'd better tell your friend to keep his yap shut or someone's going to rearrange his teeth."

A man standing nearby, sporting a salt-and-pepper beard, a beer gut and a bulbous nose, echoed this sentiment more vociferously. "Yeah," he said ruggedly. "Tell your fucking kraut friend to keep his fucking kraut mouth shut!"

Heinrich somehow heard this above the din of conversation. He stood abruptly, abandoning Helga, and strode toward the bar. As he walked up to the mouthy stranger he said, "Sorry," in a mocking voice. "I thought here a man could make free speech. Is this a mistake? You can call me kraut but I can't call a Jew a kike?"

The man slammed his mug down on the bar and glared at Heinrich, who in turn straightened with his chest jutting out a bit further.

Otto stepped up and put a restraining hand on his compatriot's right arm—an arm that now ended in a bunched fist. Behind the counter the bartender studied every movement of the three men. Jocular patrons who heard the threatening exchange ended conversations and refocused upon the promise of rowdy entertainment.

The stranger stiffened to Heinrich's accusation. "You started it," he blurted, squaring up to Heinrich, who was six inches taller and obviously fitter. "And you shouldn't start something you can't finish."

The two eyed each other with stony faces as Otto tried to worm in between. "Now just a moment—"

"No," Heinrich cut Otto short, pushing him aside and into the suddenly restraining arms of onlookers who were now eagerly clearing a space. Without looking away from his opponent Heinrich continued speaking, this time in German, but easily loud enough for anyone to hear. "If this kike lover wants a fight, he picked the right German."

Several in the crowd grumbled. Those who understood German were irked because the arrogant foreigner was making a prick of himself. Those who did not understand German were ticked off because, well, what right did this kraut have badmouthing someone in a language they couldn't understand!

Otto tried to break free. More hands materialized from the crowd, this time clenching him as tightly as if he were laced up in a straightjacket.

The spectators had by now pushed tables and chairs back to form a rough ring. Behind the counter the bartender signaled to the bouncer at the door, who was cut off from the action by the spectators. Instead of trying push through to the bar the bouncer exited out the batwing doors and rushed off down the cobbled street in search of a policeman.

People in the back began climbing onto chairs and tables to see the action. Those in front were squeezed together like bees in a hive. Men began shouting encouragement and their yells and jeers became an angry roar filling the room. Cheers erupted, and even though none were for Heinrich, he did have a few not-so-vocal supporters. Wagers were placed, with fisted money offered and passed.

"C'mon, Bert. Kick his ass!"

"Show him we don't take shit from krauts!"

"Bust his face, Bert!"

Bert was enjoying the chorus falling squarely on his side. He cast a smile around the room as Heinrich assumed a boxer's stance. Bert continued to accept the admiration, more or less ignoring his opponent.

Heinrich resented this and became even more determined, moving in closer. As Bert turned and faced off, Otto's right fist lanced out and struck Bert's nose straight on. Bert stumbled back two steps, stunned. A trickle of blood dribbled through his whiskers.

The crowd booed and hooted, but Heinrich was undeterred. His response was to flash a vicious grin at the crowd and then at Bert, triumphant and unrepentant.

Bert, off balance, saw Otto coming toward him again. He was expecting another right jab and raised his hands in defense, but Heinrich's left hand came in a looping undercut that sank deep into the round gut. There was a *whoof* from Bert as he went down onto one knee, the wind knocked out of him. Shocked as he realized he was clearly outmatched.

Heinrich strutted around the edge of the impromptu ring, giving his best Max Schmeling impression, his chest puffed out and his chin jutting, fists held high. This was answered by boos and catcalls, but the angry enthusiasm for the local boy was now muted. The mob sensed a winner and was fickle enough to switch sides if a victory was assured.

Bert scrambled up and lunged, planting his head squarely in Heinrich's midsection. The crowd cheered as the two went down in a tangle, throwing scrappy punches that did no real damage. They rolled around on the floor, first one man on top, then the other. Their clothes and hair became peppered with sawdust. Blood streamed from both fighters' noses. The crowd screamed encouragement for their local boy.

Heinrich finally broke free and stood up. He wiped blood from his nose with one thumb, inspecting the red drops before flicking them into the sawdust. Bert still lay on the floor as Heinrich's words, this time in clear and unmistakable English, rang sharply above the hullabaloo of the crowd.

"Come on you cunt Jew lover!"

Enraged, Bert stumbled to his feet and made a reckless torpedo lunge. Heinrich neatly sidestepped him matador-style and landed a hard shot to the ribcage as Bert flew past. Bert went down like a sack of oats, splayed on the sawdust, coughing bloody mucus and moaning as pain lanced through his chest.

Heinrich resumed his gaudy parade, strutting like a rooster, not caring what the onlookers thought. Blood still leaked from one nostril and dribbled down his cheek but he didn't care. He lifted his arms skyward. "Deutschland!" he shouted. Several men in the crowd cussed, but a few couldn't fully suppress smiles.

Behind him, Bert wheezed as he labored to regain his wind. He clambered onto his hands and knees and tried unsuccessfully to stand up, tottering for a moment before falling back onto his rear.

"Stay down, Bert!" someone yelled.

"Yeah," another agreed. "You lost, Bert. Fair and square."

Bert looked up at unsympathetic faces and tears streaked down his cheeks. His face contorted in anger. Grabbing the brass rail that ran along the front of the bar he struggled to his feet. Heinrich ignored him, his back turned as if Bert no longer counted for beans, continuing to play the crowd, taunting those who still favored his thrashed opponent. Behind him, Bert swayed in pain. His fists came up, but he resembled a punching bag more than a fighter. Heinrich whirled around, faking surprise at the sight of Bert's revival.

"Da kommt er ja!" he announced in a voice laced with ridicule and amazement. Bert was infuriated at again being mocked in German. He raised his balled fists higher, ignoring the pain of a bruised ribs.

"Der schwein!" Heinrich continued.

Bert understood this. His face filled with rage. It was one thing to be beaten by a kraut. It was something entirely worse to be called a pig by this foreign bastard.

Bert stumbled forward.

Heinrich moved in for the kill.

Bert's right hand flashed down, as if to fend off an imagined body blow. But the hand instead darted under his loose shirt. There was a hidden sheath strapped to his waist. The hand emerged, gripping a short knife with a bright blade made for skinning animals. Bert drove the steel home in one fluid motion.

Heinrich's eyes filled with surprise, and then with horror, as he looked down and saw the carved bone haft, still gripped by Bert, protruding from his gut.

There was a shocked, "*Ooh!*" from the crowd. Those who hadn't seen the knife now surged forward to see what had happened. Word spread and a nervous energy filled the room. The tight knot of spectators dissolved; men shuffled toward the exit.

Bert released his grip on the knife, almost as shocked as his victim. Heinrich went down onto his knees, still staring in disbelief at the weapon's handle. He now reached for it and with a hard tug pulled it free. Blood gushed from the wound, soaking his shirt and splashing onto the sawdust.

Hands that restrained Otto now released him. He rushed forward, kneeling beside Heinrich, who opened his mouth to speak and instead spit out a mouthful of blood. The steel had penetrated his stomach. "Someone get a doctor!" Otto screamed.

Through the batwing doors came a man in a blue uniform with a silver badge. He pushed through what was left of the crowd, towards the bar.

Someone shouted, "It's the coppers, Bert. Run for it!"

Bert, standing dumbly above the two Germans, made a mad dash toward the alley door. The policeman took one look, saw blood squirting from the injured man and knew nothing could be done. He saw Bert making good his escape, lifted a whistle that hung from a chain around his neck, blew a shrill blast and charged off in pursuit.

Otto gently rolled Heinrich onto his back. Heinrich repeatedly tried to speak but each time he coughed a spume of blood. The essence of his life bubbled indelicately from his lips. His panicked eyes were turning glassy.

The barkeep brought a linen towel. Otto folded it and pressed it against the wound but Heinrich was already fading. The sawdust beneath him was now caked dark red.

In fifteen minutes, and without having said anything intelligible, Heinrich Stromer died.

Λ

Otto met the man from the Cascade County PUD the next day. Eddie Verellen was bright enough to have been a Wily Post or a Mark Twain if he'd chosen to write. But Eddie loved building things more than he loved words, so engineering school was the direction he took.

During the first three decades of the twentieth century many of the counties in the Pacific Northwest formed their own public utility districts. The electrification cooperatives were organized for building power generating dams along the Columbia and its tributaries. After college, Eddie went straight to work on the dam and power plant in Cascade County. That was in 1931, when the project was still just initial surveys and a hopeful dream.

By 1934 the magnificent little dam and powerhouse were nearing completion. Some of the work requiring advanced engineering was subbed out to a German company, not only because the Germans were fine engineers, but also because the post WWI German economy was depressed and desperate for work and bargains were to be had. Throwing the Germans a bone wasn't thought to be such a bad idea. Many Germans had immigrated to American, and there was sympathy for the National Socialist's efforts to rebuild the homeland.

Eddie thought the pipes should have been cast in the USA and had suggested a foundry in California. But the PUD couldn't ignore a bid twenty percent below the nearest competitor, especially when it came from one of Germany's preeminent engineering firms. And when the Germans threw in the offer of engineers to make a custom installation, well, what other responsible alternative was there? It was the Depression. Money was dear. The contract was let out to *Goering Ingenieurwesen Maschinenfabrik.*

Eddie had been eagerly awaiting delivery of the German pipes. Once these were installed he could raise the penstock gates, rev up the generators, and begin throwing relay switches. The PUD would be in business at last.

It came as a shock when Eddie learned that two of the German engineers had recently come to tragic ends. "I am so sorry," Eddie kept telling Otto, as he helped supervise the unloading of the Danish freighter. But he nevertheless felt a thrill at seeing the crates laid upon the planks of the pier. As the crane swung each box across, Eddie imagined the joy of fitting the pipes together and then turning the valves so the lubricant and coolant could begin to flow to the generators. With the two Germans dead, he would get to do more of the work, and that suited him fine. Put a wrench in Eddie's hand and he became a happy man.

Only when the two damaged sections came out of the hold did his enthusiasm sour.

"What happened?" he asked, dismayed by the scored and rusted steel.

Otto's head nodded weakly forward as he explained. "There was a storm. They broke free and we were trying to secure them when the ship pitched, throwing them against Werner's legs."

The rough-and-tumble storm had scraped off paint down to the metal. In the short span of four weeks the raw steel had begun to rust in the salty marine air. The flanges were of even more concern.

"Gee," Eddie said, as he ran a finger along the twisted metal. "It'll be impossible to get a seal."

"I know. And we don't know the strength where it is bent."

There was concern in Otto's voice and Eddie felt a sudden liking for the German. His next words were kind and reassuring.

"Don't worry. We'll figure something out." As he said this Eddie saw it as just another engineering problem to solve. Another wonderful challenge!

Otto had dreaded the moment. In his worst nightmare the PUD man rejected the entire shipment, sending him back to Germany and Goering's wrath. "Thank you," he barely managed to say, overcome by Eddie's generosity.

Eddie reached out and put a gentle hand on Otto's shoulder. "C'mon," he said. "Let's get these onto the railcar."

A flatbed was waiting on the Union Pacific spur that served the docks. Standing beside the rolling stock was the U.S. Customs inspector.

Eddie told the inspector about the tragic deaths. After a cursory walk-about the inspector signed the form without asking if there was anything else to declare. "All cleared," he said crisply, handing Eddie a receipt. To Otto it was a miracle. There would be no questions about the briefcase.

After the railcar was loaded and the pipes secured, Eddie led Otto to a black Ford Model-A truck with *CASCADE COUNTY P.U.D.* stenciled in white letters on the door. They drove to a nearby funeral home so Otto could make burial arrangements for Heinrich.

The next day they made the long winding drive into central Washington, cutting through the Cascades. Otto was stunned by the vast stretches of raw mountain wilderness. When they reached Snoqualmie Pass he saw something he hadn't expected. Although it was late April, the snow pack was still heavy and the mountains carried a thick white mantle. On the steep slopes, people were skiing. A rope tow was in place to pull skiers back up the mountain.

"Look!" he shouted to Eddie. "I did not know you skied here in America!"

"Oh, yes. We even have a ski hill back in Langston. Mind you, it's nothing fancy. I never had much interest in the sport myself. Do you ski?"

"Oh yes." Otto was enthralled. "I have skied ever since I was a boy."

Otto's nose pressed against the glass for as long as the ski hill was visible. He finally settled back in his seat, overcome by the wondrous thing he'd seen.

Chapter 26

Jerry visited with Oscar in his room until the cop dozed off, then went out to the nurse's station and left the manager's number where he could be reached.

He arrived mid-afternoon at the Belvedere with the sun beating against the pink concrete. As he entered the lobby and reached the stairwell, imagining a cold shower, Rosa poked her head out from the office.

"Señor?" She looked agitated. He momentarily shelved the idea of a shower.

"A man came looking for you. He gave me this." She thrust a folded note into his hands then nervously shifted from foot to foot.

Jerry unfolded the pencil scrawled sheet of lined notebook paper, signed *Frank* at the bottom. He refolded the note and looked at Rosa.

"When did he come?"

"Maybe one hour ago. I think he was upset."

"Thank you, Rosa," he said calmly, guessing she was right about Frank Brindleman's emotional state. He smiled as if to say he understood and everything was okay. He would handle whatever had Frank all riled up.

Satisfied that her duty was discharged, Rosa turned and went back into the office, pulling the door shut with relief.

Jerry climbed three flights of stairs and found his apartment hot as a furnace with the window shut. He pushed the wood frame fully open so a draft could move through, all the while mulling over the note he'd read while climbing the stairs.

I must meet with you as soon as possible. There is a story you must hear. Can you come to the powerhouse tomorrow morning at nine?

There were phone numbers for office and home, but no clue as to why a meeting was urgent.

He laid the note on the kitchen table, stripped off jeans and shirt and headed for the shower. After ten minutes beneath a cold jet of water he felt better. Frank could be managed. He should have done what was necessary when he'd first been approached. Frank was a nuisance and would continue to be one until he was firmly told to stay away.

But how did he find me?

He toweled off, pulled on a pair of boxers, went out to the kitchen and opened a can of tuna. As he mixed in mayonnaise and spooned the spread across a slice of bread, he considered how best to put an end to Frank's pestering. The more he thought about it, the more certain he was that a short visit to the powerhouse held the answer. He would tell Frank there was no reason for them to meet again. He would insist there be no further contact for any reason.

He weighed the likelihood of Frank telling Cruz about his *Dockins* identity. But the more he considered the impact of such a revelation, the less important it seemed.

Why would Cruz care? If he asks, I'll tell him it was for a classified mission. If I don't act like it's important, how excited is he going to get? And is Brindleman really going to tattle on me? If he does, he paints himself out as a liar for having denied he knew me in the first place.

Having made the decision, he picked up a McCulloch paperback and stretched out on the bed, determined to put the "Brindleman Problem" in perspective. It was no big deal and he wasn't going to turn it into one. Frank was a harmless, burned out GI, whom nobody would seriously listen to. After reading for a while he fell into a light and dreamless sleep.

He awoke shortly after sunset. The night air was cool and the apartment was now comfortable. He pulled on jeans and sneakers, foregoing a shirt, and went downstairs and plugged a quarter and a dime into the payphone. He was relieved when an answering machine came on. He left a short message.

"This is Jerry Wells calling to confirm I'll be there for a meeting with you tomorrow morning at nine." He hung up before Frank would have a chance to grab up the receiver if he was listening.

He climbed the stairs and dove back into the McCulloch novel.

⅄

Jerry awoke early the next morning and wound up with an extra half hour before the 8:30 bus. He went downstairs to sit at the top of the Belvedere's steps and enjoy the morning air. He was pleased to discover the three boys were back at play in the alleyway, this time with a cheap red rubber ball for their soccer. They all wore jeans with holes in the knees. Rosa's son showed obvious talent as he repeatedly passed his playmates and scored cardboard box goals.

After a few minutes of watching and listening to them pretend they were in a World Cup final, he shouted out, "*Ola, Muchachos! Como ustedes?*"

The kids paused. The biggest kid answered after a moment of hesitation.

"We're okay." Caution underscored his curiosity. "You are new to the building, sir?" There was no inflection in the way he spoke, so Jerry dropped his attempt at a conversation in Spanish.

"Yes, since Friday."

The other two boys formed up behind the first, sizing up the man on the steps. Jerry now confirmed what he'd first seen in Rosa's son when renting the apartment. The restless intelligence was like looking at himself in a mirror. The boy's face was browner, younger, and more elfin; but the eyes told everything.

"Where do you come from?" the first boy challenged.

"California."

"Los Angeles?"

"No, Barstow."

"Oh." There was disappointment.

The third boy, with a pug nose and straight black hair, took a step forward. "I've been to Barstow," he said proudly.

Jerry smiled politely before turning his focus to Pablo. "Do you like to play soccer?" he asked.

"Yes," came the hesitant reply.

The first boy cut in rudely. "When we grow up, we will be professional players on the Mexican team!"

Jerry glanced at him. "Really?"

"Oh yes! They are the best in the whole world."

Pablo gave a snort of disgust. The two boys cast hopeless glances at him. "Pablo likes Brazil," the first boy said, as if Pablo might be suffering some dreadful mental confusion.

"Is that true Pablo?"

The first cut in again. "My name is Roberto."

"I'm Marguerito," the third volunteered.

Jerry ignored the intrusions, wanting to establish something—but he wasn't yet exactly certain what—with Rosa's son.

"Pablo?"

Pablo beamed, pleased to be singled out.

"You like Brazil?"

A smile to cure the hurt of the world blossomed on his face. "They have Romero and he is the best player in the world!"

Roberto crossed his arms in disgust. Marguerito shook his head.

Pablo turned on both. "They have won the World Cup five times!"

Roberto taunted, "Mexico will whip them in the next one!"

"Will not!"

"Will too!"

"Boys!" Jerry interrupted. The kids ceased arguing. Jerry used the truce to ask what had been on his mind since he'd first seen them kicking the can in the alley.

"Don't you boys have a real soccer ball to play with?"

"They are too expensive," Pablo said.

"How expensive?"

"Maybe fifty dollars."

Jerry now surprised himself.

"What if I were to buy you a real soccer ball? Would you like that?"

All three faces lit up with amazement.

"Really?" Pablo said.

Roberto was suspicious. "Why would you do this?"

Jerry understood the fear and tried to set his intentions straight.

"When I was a boy there were many things my parents couldn't afford. I remember wanting to be a drummer, but my dad didn't make enough money to buy a drum set. I never got to join a rock group my friends formed. If you have a real soccer ball, maybe you'll get to practice enough so you can have a chance at becoming professional soccer players."

That's a great fabrication!

Who cares?

The little girl in Champoton?

I've already paid that price.

Really?

He shoved the pain back into a far corner of his mind.

"Okay," Roberto agreed, not wanting to endanger the gift, yet still suspicious of some unspoken catch.

"Good. Then I need you to go to a store where they sell soccer balls and find the one you want. Bring me the price and the model of the ball and I'll buy it for you. Be sure you choose a good one that will last."

They looked at each other, speechless at this incredible piece of luck.

Jerry glanced at his watch, realizing his bus would arrive soon. He stood up. "I've got to leave now, but when I'm back this afternoon I expect you to have the name and price of a ball written down for me. And a store where I can pick one up."

Pablo's face was luminous. "Thank you," he said politely.

A lump came up in Jerry's throat.

"Yeah!" Roberto said.

"Thank you, Mister," Marguerito agreed.

All the way to the end of the block he could hear the boys hollering with joy over the prospect of a real soccer ball. Jerry held a faint smile until the bus dropped him off along the Columbia.

It took five minutes to walk the quarter mile to the big brick building; while he walked he replayed what had happened on the steps of the Belvedere. Had it not been for the meeting with Frank, Jerry would have called it a perfect day.

As he strode across the powerhouse parking lot, the heavy metal door swung open. Frank came skipping down the front steps. He extended a hand and furiously pumped Jerry's in a shake that threatened never to end.

"I'm glad you came! I was worried you changed your mind. Please, come inside!"

Jerry almost stopped right there. His gut told him to walk back to the highway, and damn the consequences of what Frank thought. But then he remembered his purpose in coming: he was going to convince Frank to leave him alone.

I'm four inches taller and forty pounds heavier and in far better shape. Things are going to be fine. I'll be out of here in fifteen minutes.

Oh really?

Leave me alone!

He followed Frank up the steps.

Frank first led him through an arched hallway and out onto a balcony edging fifty feet of a chamber nearly two hundred feet long. High above, a massive bridge crane hung from rails running the length of the building. Two stories below, buried in the concrete floor, were two forty-foot-wide dynamos. They reminded Jerry of washing machine motors he'd scavenged from the dump as a kid, only these were immensely larger. The massive gray casings were embellished with a stylized *GE* in eighteen-inch brass. A gentle but powerful vibration filled the room. The tang of ozone and the sweetness of oil completed the sensation of being in a place where a great amount of electricity was born. Frank stopped mid-way along the railing and looked out across the main floor.

"Most of the water in the river is diverted through a ten-foot pipe that passes through rotors a hundred feet below us. It drives the turbines at three hundred revolutions per minute. Each generator delivers thirty megawatts.

"That," Frank continued, pointing to a dark blue eighteen-inch pipe which ran from near the wall out toward the first generator until it turned back down into the concrete floor, "carries coolant. I'll want to show you something really neat about it," he said mysteriously, "but that's for later. C'mon. First you should see the control room."

Frank led him back the way they had come, turning down a hallway and then into a room dominated by a long control console. Along the walls were several large rectangular gray breaker panels and two instrument cabinets. Exterior windows gave a view onto the parking lot and the access road and the Columbia and the hills on the far side of the river.

Most of the equipment Jerry saw was modern digital, but one of the cabinets contained vintage round glass gauges.

"Central control," Frank said proudly. "You run the whole shebang from here." He pulled a swivel chair away from the console and offered it to Jerry. "Impressed?"

"Sure," Jerry said as he sat down, beginning to realize that dealing with Frank was going to be simpler than he had imagined. Frank wasn't crazy. He was lonely. A burned out veteran. Someone easy for people to ignore. Jerry resolved to politely listen to whatever it was Frank wanted to say. And then he would tell Frank to leave him alone. Nicely, if possible. But it *would* end here.

"They couldn't build something like this today," Frank bragged, pulling up a chair just a little too close. He sat down and grinned at his now captive audience. "Not with all the environmental laws and the unions. They lost two men on the project when it was built in the early thirties. Rumor has it one of them is still in the concrete! OSHA would shut a job down these days for a whole lot less." He appeared ready to carry on and on, now that he had cornered a listener.

"I can only stay for a few minutes," Jerry interrupted, as Frank paused to catch his breath. "So let's hear the story." And then he remembered to ask the question that had been on his mind since Rosa handed him the note.

"By the way, Frank. How did you find out I moved to the Belvedere?"

Frank flashed a mischievous grin. "When I was behind the glass during your interview with Cruz I heard him tell you not to leave the valley, and then he pretty much insisted you move into town." Frank shrugged. "I hiked up to find you on Saturday morning and saw your campsite was abandoned. Now, there aren't many places in Langston where someone can rent by the week. So I made a few calls . . ." Frank held up his hands as if to beg forgiveness but he couldn't help the smirky grin.

Jerry could feel the vortex. If it were that simple for Frank to locate him, how easy would it be for anyone else to find where he was?

Frank's small effort at levity vanished. He settled back in his chair, crossed his arms, his mouth hardened to a thin line.

"Can you keep a secret?"

"Sure." Jerry felt silly agreeing. What could Frank possibly know that would merit it remaining a secret?

"I mean *really* keep a secret?"

"I promise not to tell a soul, Frank." Jerry made it sound as if he really meant it.

Frank's demeanor brightened; a great burden seemed to lift; his words resumed their earlier excitement. "Good. I think you'll be amazed."

And Frank was right.

Chapter 27

June 1969

Eighteen-year-old Frankie Brindleman hadn't meant to drop the wrench. It was, after all, only his first week on the job. And in that languid summer of 1969, with the Vietnam War awaiting a kid who'd had the bad luck to draw number eleven in the draft lottery, Frankie should have been doing everything possible to ensure the security of his position as the summer kid at the local powerhouse. He desperately needed money for college tuition and board and room that his folks didn't have. Mom was a housewife and Dad was laid off from his orchard foreman job. It was hard enough to put food on the table and clothes on their backs, so the option of college rested squarely upon Frankie's new job.

Frankie might have planned during his earlier high school years to work summers and put money aside. Except he'd never planned on an education after high school. He'd hoped to get a job pumping gas at the Texaco and eventually work his way up to mechanic. So during high school he'd spent his money on other things. A four-barrel carburetor and a fancy dash-mounted tachometer for his prized fifty-six Chevy. A Honda 90 cc trail bike with a blown engine that he rebuilt in Mr. Brown's shop class. Smokes and beer, bought for him by winos anxious to make an easy buck.

And then there were the chicks. A girl, no matter how hot to trot, required flowers or a box of candy before she'd even begin to think about letting you get to first base, much less go all the way.

Frankie got the bad news from the army lottery office and found himself desperately needing a good summer job. It turned out his mom had a connection. She and Bob Sidel, who worked for the Cascade County PUD, attended high school together. She kept saying that Bob owed her a favor; it sounded a little nasty and Frankie knew well enough not to ask for details. For a short while he resisted his mom's urgings to apply, thinking he had a snowball's chance in hell at the position; but the last thing Frankie wanted was to go off to war, so he finally agreed to let her introduce him to Mr. Sidel.

The powerhouse summer job was a legend for helping Langston kids. It paid over four bucks an hour, which was more than twice the prevailing teenage wage. The goal was helping kids get through college. But it always went to the sons of union men and state employees.

Surprisingly, the interview had gone better than a carton of cigarettes in back of the football bleachers at homecoming. Frankie was hired on the spot, and told to report for training the next morning. And then Sidel asked, "Would you and your mother like a tour?"

His mom gave Bob a *favor repaid* smile as he began to usher them around the imposing building.

From the balcony Sidel pointed proudly to the glowing red bulbs atop each of the two turbines, signifying they were "puttin' out the watts." He showed them circuit breakers in the control room that controlled the flow of the "juice" to electrical transformers out in the yard. And everywhere there was brass. Sidel said it would be Frankie's responsibility to polish it until he could see himself looking back.

Finally, Sidel took them down a long black metal staircase and out onto the generator floor. He pointed to a section of eighteen-inch pipe with a heavy coat of blue paint. "Come 'round the back side," he said mysteriously.

When they were on the far side, Sidel pointed silently at something raised in the metal.

"Jeez," Frankie said. "Isn't that a—"

"Nazi swastika," Sidel said smoothly, with mingled disgust and reverence. "The guys who built this place back in the thirties bought the pipes from the krauts. There are more of these on the other pipes."

To celebrate that evening Frankie was allowed a glass of the Gallo wine his parents drank at dinner. When he crawled between the sheets, still a bit looped from the sweet burgundy, it was nearly impossible to fall asleep. He felt so much like a man, proud of the fact that tomorrow he would start his first real job. It was midnight before he finally drifted off.

He reported for work the next morning and Sidel started him out cleaning brass rails near one of the turbines, scouring segments one at a time with a rag saturated with polishing compound and then buffing the brass to a high luster with a cotton polishing cloth. He was enjoying the effort until the trouble started.

Around mid-morning, Gary Porter, who worked under Sidel as an electrician, broke off from splicing cable on a control panel at the far generator, lit up a cigarette, and strolled over to where Frankie was bending his elbows to the railing.

"Lookin' good, kid," Porter sniggered, as if Frankie could have polished till you could see the cracks between your teeth and it wouldn't have made the Earth spin one damned second faster. "You're a born natural."

Frankie caught plenty of crap from adults and knew meanness when it came his way. *Like being sent to the principal by a teacher who wants to jerk you around. Or the gym coach making you run extra laps because you aren't a jock. So keep the head down. It'll pass.* Frankie doubled down on his polishing while a nervous sweat began to darken the armpits of his blue chambray shirt.

Porter continued to stare at him, taking an occasional drag on the unfiltered Marlboro. The tobacco aroma made Frankie's mouth water. He considered pausing to stretch his arms, testing to see if Porter would offer him one. But the meanness in the man's voice said he was dreaming if he thought Porter was going to be friendly.

Porter took a long final drag on the cigarette, dropped the butt onto the concrete floor, ground it into the cement with the heel of his boot. "Don't miss that one, kiddo." He smiled malevolently at the smoldering black smudge.

The following morning Porter approached him again. "Making progress?" he sneered. And then he strolled around the generator to where they had had their confrontation the previous day. Out of the corner of his eye Frankie saw

Porter scrutinize the spot where he snuffed the cigarette, and Frankie bit his lip to keep from smiling. He'd taken extra special care to remove the burn mark as soon as he'd arrived that morning. Porter could examine the floor with a magnifying glass and he wouldn't find a trace.

This perturbed Porter. He walked back to where Frankie was hard at work with his polishing cloth and stood still as granite for two minutes, watching.

"Heard your old man's in orchard work," Porter finally said.

That cut deep. If his father owned the orchard where he worked things would be different. If you owned even a few acres you were your own boss, and driving a spray rig, setting sprinkler pipe, even thinning or picking were proud duties. But a hired hand was lumped together with Mexicans and the fruit tramps. Frankie had been called white trash too many times to count.

"Yep," Porter pressed on, seeing he'd finally gotten under Frankie's skin. "Bet your old man's a real whiz with pruning shears."

Frankie bore down on the brass, shoulders bunched, flat anger churning up inside. *You need this job. You don't want to go to 'Nam. You need to go to college. So whatever his problem is, just ignore this fuck-head.*

By some miracle, he kept his composure and continued to polish without so much as a twitch of hesitation.

A quiver went through Porter's body. He began to pace nervously, a tight little weave, seeming confused.

This gave Frankie a chill. *What's wrong with him? Why does he want me worse than a twelve-point buck on opening day?* As he pondered this, Frankie became even more determined not to respond to Porter's taunts. Maybe his dad did work the apples. What of it? Frankie was still beating this son of a bitch. And for the first time in his life, Frankie realized that anger was a pale candle when compared to dignity.

Eventually, Porter walked away, burning with frustration, grumbling to himself.

With that fine start Frankie might have lasted the entire summer, and drove his freshly waxed Chevy off to college in September looking like Joe College and feeling like a king.

Except for the wrench.

Porter hounded him on the third day. As he spliced wire near the second generator he was muttering loudly about the shit-ass piss-ant snot-nosed know-it-all bastard orchard tramp's brat who didn't belong here. This wasn't the kind of kid they were supposed to hire. They should have given the job to a kid who'd earned it with a high grade point, or whose father had earned it for him by belonging to the union. The verbal barrage got so bad by late afternoon that it caused Sidel to come down onto the generator floor and confront Porter. "Gary," he said flatly. "I need a word with you."

Porter looked up innocently from his wiring. "Sure, Bob. What about?"

Sidel glanced sideways in Frankie's direction. "In private," he said, jerking a thumb toward his office. As they walked away Porter threw an accusatory glance at Frankie, who returned a defiant glare of his own.

For the next fifteen minutes Frankie worked with a merciless focus. He would have given anything to hear the reaming Porter was receiving. But the thrumming of the turbines and the distance to the office made it impossible to hear anything being said.

When the men returned it took every iota of his willpower not to look up. So when he heard Bob Sidel's voice behind him Frankie practically jumped.

"Son?"

As he turned around it felt like a loaded gun was pointed straight at his chest. Bob Sidel had a pained look. He said in a low, frustrated tone, "I need to talk with you." It seemed like the voice of doom.

Frankie's voice cracked as he replied, "Sure, Mr. Sidel."

Now it was he who followed Sidel upstairs, ears burning and heart pounding. Out of the corner of his eye he saw Porter sullenly return to his wiring job. To make matters worse, Porter began to whistle a low and malicious tune.

Sweet Jesus! I didn't do anything to deserve this!

When the office door swung shut Frankie felt more alone than he ever had in his entire life.

"Please sit," Sidel said, motioning toward a metal chair. Frankie numbly sank onto the hard seat as Sidel leaned his rear against the front of the battered desk and gave a tired, frustrated sigh.

Frankie's eyes focused on the floor like a beaten dog, afraid to look up and incur the wrath of its master.

"I guess you know we've got a problem," Sidel began reluctantly.

"Yes, sir."

Sidel sighed deeply. *Here it comes,* Frankie thought. *Here it comes.*

"You deserve an explanation, Frankie. So I'm going to give you the straight up truth. Gary has a boy starting his third year of college this fall. It's tough going since the Porters have two other kids at home and the wife doesn't work. Gary was hoping he could get his Bobby your job."

Sidel didn't seem to notice the redness that flushed Frankie's neck and crept across his face. Or, maybe he just chose to ignore it.

"When I told Gary you were going to be our summer boy, well, he hit the roof. He even threatened to go to the commissioners and make a big stink. But I stuck firm. I told him you were a poor kid from a poor family—no offense kid, but that's God's honest truth—and you'd end up over in Vietnam if you didn't get this job, whereas his kid would go to college and get a military deferment either way."

Sidel now surprised Frankie.

"I'm going to keep you on, Frankie. I'll adjust your schedule so you come in at noon and work 'till eight. That way you'll see less of Porter, and more importantly he'll see less of you." Sidel's voice picked up speed, as if he were inventing a solution moment to moment. "His schedule runs from seven to four so there will only be a few hours of overlap. You'll get an hour for lunch so that brings it down to only three hours we have to worry about. I'll put you on jobs at opposite ends of the powerhouse so there's less chance of contact. Hell, if I need to I'll send you on errands outside the powerhouse."

Sidel paused, took a deep breath. Frankie wanted to pinch himself to make sure it wasn't a dream.

"Of course," Sidel cautioned, "you and Gary are going to cross each other's paths from time to time. If he baits you, then like it says in the Bible, you've got to turn the other cheek. Because if you take a swing or even get into an argument there's probably nothing I can do to keep the commissioners from giving you the boot, and maybe giving me the boot, too."

Frankie surprised himself, replying in a calm and even voice, "Sir, you can count on me." Frankie meant it. And more importantly, he *knew* it. This was the proudest moment of his life. And he knew *that* as well. *This is what it means to grow up!*

"Well then," Sidel said, happy and relieved. "Let's get you off the main floor and up onto the balcony. That'll keep you busy for a solid week. Maybe Gary will cool down by then."

So Frankie moved up to the balcony railing. With Porter far away on the generator floor the confrontations ceased.

By 4:30pm, Gary Porter had gone home. As Sidel left for the day he hollered, "Be sure to lock up!" Frankie listened as Sidel backed his battered Dodge pickup, spun the tires, and drove off down the access road. And then he returned to the new problem.

The balcony had three-inch brass rails. They had been neglected over the years and grease had accumulated in the joint crevices, hardening into a sticky black sludge nearly a quarter of an inch thick. It would take forever to get it out with just a rag and polish. Using a knife or wire brush would scratch the brass. He figured the pipes might be easier to clean if he disassembled them first. He could then take each piece to the motorized buffer in the shop and do a proper job. He also figured this would show he was capable of something special. He'd prove to the boss that he'd been right in keeping Frankie on.

And that was where the wrench came into the picture.

One room halfway down the middle hallway on the lower floor was reserved for tools. One wall of the tool room was filled with wrenches of every imaginable kind. Frankie now stood before that grand assortment, considering which one was best for the job.

Not one of the really big ones. That would be like hunting chipmunks with a ten-gauge.

A couple of the wrenches were nearly as long as Frankie was tall. He finally eased a thirty-inch red-handled crescent off its peg.

Oh yeah! A true nut buster!

Actually, the wrench was oversized for the job, with a jaw capable of handling seven inches. But to Frankie, the wrench was power, and besides, there was no one around to question his choice. All he could see was how easy it was going to be to turn those brass nuts with this giant-killer.

And it turned out to be *easy peasey* when Frankie got going. He slipped the big crescent over the first nut on the top rail and pulled the handle of the wrench up, then over the top, then out toward the powerhouse floor, careful to keep a grip so it wouldn't fall. Up, over, down, slip it off, up, over, down, slip it off. In two minutes he'd fully exposed the joint crack where the pipe abutted the tee. He left it loose in the hole and moved to the other end of the eight-foot pipe.

The second nut gave the same smooth and predictable resistance for the first three turns. But when Frankie came over the top on the fourth, the nut unexpectedly came loose. Frankie watched with horror as his gentle push on the handle seemed to magically accelerate the wrench. It slipped from his fingers in an eye-blink and continued around, striking the lower rail with a dull *clank*.

The wrench quivered and the jaw slipped from the nut. Too late, Frankie made a grab for it. But his fingers weren't nearly strong enough to hold twenty pounds of metal chasing gravity.

He watched the wrench slip away, and was horrified to see that its trajectory was directly for the pipe with the Nazi swastika that he'd been shown on that first visit with Mom. It plummeted like a lead arrow and couldn't have scored a truer bull's eye if a bombardier had dropped it using a Norden Bombsite.

Thunk! A direct hit dead center on that long blue pipe.

Then it fell to the concrete with a hard clatter.

Frankie waited for the explosion; for a gusher to shoot towards the ceiling. An ugly vision danced through his head, of telling Mom how he'd messed up.

Only . . . the metal wall of the pipe held. There was no sudden geyser.

He began to breathe again. The acrid smell of sweat poured from his armpits. There was a sudden urge to pee.

After he relieved himself in the bathroom he climbed down the stairs. He was too chicken to look at the pipe right away so he looked at where the wrench struck the concrete. A fifty-cent-sized chip was missing from the floor, but he soon found the dislodged piece and it fit back into the tiny crater as neat as a jigsaw piece. A little glue and you'd never know the difference.

Screwing up his courage he walked over to the pipe. The wrench had actually punched a small hole in the metal, and it seemed like there should be water or oil squirting out. But when he looked more closely at the fracture Frankie saw the wrench hadn't punched all the way through the pipe. And even more incredible, there were two colors inside the hole. Around the edge the color was steel. But at the bottom of the dime-sized hole was a glint that was the same color as the thin band of his mom's wedding ring.

Gold.

"Holy Shit!" He ran a fingertip across the different textures: the rough steel, the smooth gold. It was hard to tell for sure but it looked like the gold might run all the way through the pipe in some kind of channel. For a moment he wondered if pipe of this kind was manufactured with gold inside. And then he realized how completely ridiculous that was.

Then the problem dawned. *How am I going to cover this up?* As he thought about it, an idea came. There were cans of Bondo in the paint room. He'd worked with epoxy when he fixed up his Chevy. Frankie could smooth a dented car body with Bondo so as you'd never even know it had been damaged. He could do the same with the pipe! He'd just putty it up and then paint it over.

He ran upstairs to retrieve the epoxy. Within minutes he was spreading resin into the gash. It hardened fast and after a little sanding to match the contour of the pipe he opened a can of paint, stirred it, and got ready to brush it onto the hard red putty.

There are moments when lives change, irrevocably, dramatically, unpredictably. This was Frankie's moment.

"Hey, kid," came Gary Porter's soft, snarky voice, "yah doing a little engineering?"

Frankie's head jerked up. Porter seemed to have materialized from thin air. He stood above him on the balcony with a triumphant grin. Frankie froze. Porter would have no trouble getting him fired. Even Sidel couldn't justify keeping a kid who, after only three days on the job, drops a wrench and damages a pipe, then tries to fix it without reporting the incident. The gold suddenly seemed unimportant.

"Thing I can't figure out," Porter continued, gleeful but puzzled, "is how you thought you'd get away with it." And Gary Porter's curiosity now sealed his fate. He put his hands down and leaned against the rail Frankie had been working on to get a better look.

Frankie realized the danger too late. "Look out!" he screamed. But by then the ends of the rail had popped free. Porter wasn't expecting the railing to give way. With a startled look he fell.

Frankie dove.

A fall from twenty feet wasn't impossible to survive, even onto concrete. Porter could have broken a leg, an arm, or shattered a hip. But he managed exactly one half revolution on his journey to the powerhouse floor, and even though he braced with his arms, the sound of his skull striking the concrete was like that of a pumpkin being hit with a baseball bat.

Frankie slowly drew himself up on hands and knees, staring in horror at Gary Porter's spasming and soon-to-be lifeless body just a few feet away. And then he turned his head and threw up.

It took a while before the urge to puke his guts was over. And then a desperate idea came.

He quickly finished the paint job. When it was done it looked like the rest of the pipe unless you looked real close. It was still tacky to the touch but he doubted anyone would take much time to scrutinize the pipe, not with Gary Porter's body lying just a few feet away. By the time anyone thought to examine it the paint would be dry.

Frankie shook as he dialed the office phone. When Sidel answered, Frankie cried his way through the story, nearly choking as sobs broke up his words. Sidel told him to hang tight, he'd be right down.

The police and Sidel arrived at nearly the same moment. They found Frankie huddled near the front door, as far from Porter's body as he could get and still be inside the building.

The police questioned him. He told the story of how he'd been working on the railing, dropped the wrench and gone down to retrieve it, and Porter seemingly appeared from nowhere and leaned against the rail and began to cuss at Frankie before he could warn him the rail was loose. Frankie said nothing about the wrench striking the pipe or the discovery of the gold, praying no one would notice the small patch of new paint.

The divot in the concrete floor was still there and the police examined it and it seemed to confirm Frankie's story. No one bothered to look at the pipe. Frankie felt a huge weight lift when the officer finally told him that what happened was an accident and he shouldn't worry; adults would handle the matter from here on out.

Frankie was sent home.

When he arrived, his father had left for the bar. Frankie didn't know whether to be relieved or scared. If his father went on a binge there'd be a beating with the belt for sure.

After his mother convinced herself he was uninjured, she lapsed into an unsettled quiet, puttering around in the kitchen before telling Frankie she was going to bed and so should he.

Frankie crawled between the sheets, lay his head on the pillow, and found it impossible to sleep. The image of Porter's smashed head and crumpled body wouldn't go away. He cried for a little while and then buried his face in the pillow and closed his eyes but his mind raced and his breathing came fast. Frankie finally gave up, got dressed, and slipped quietly out the front door. Dad's car was still not in the driveway.

He wandered the streets of Langston and tried to imagine what the following day would bring. Would his father beat the crap out of him? He could survive that. More important: would Sidel find a way to make it okay? After all, he hadn't done anything wrong, had he? It was Porter who had been somewhere he wasn't supposed to be, right? But in his gut, Frankie knew a reckoning was coming. He wasn't sure what it would be, but he knew the situation was too big to simply go away.

⅄

Shortly before noon the following day Sidel called Frankie into his office, sat him down, and gave him the bad news.

"I'm going to have to let you go, Frankie. I'm sorry."

"Why?" He felt weak.

"Remember what I told you about Porter's boy?"

"Yes."

"Mrs. Porter says he now needs the job to afford college this fall. She threatened to raise hell with the commissioners and the newspapers. She says that when she gets through with me I'm going to wish I fell and broke my neck. Unless . . . I get rid of you and hire her Bobby. I'm sorry, son. I have to let you go."

The story took half an hour. After he was finished, Frank gazed off at the banks of switches and dials, letting Jerry digest what he'd heard. Finally, the questions came.

"How long were you in 'Nam?"

"Two tours. Nearly four years."

"What about the gold?"

"When I got home I applied for a job with the PUD. I figured the gold was still in the pipe. All I needed to do was figure a way to get it out."

"And?"

"It took me a year and a half to get hired, and another three months before I got a chance to drill for the gold when we were doing maintenance and the generators were shut down." He had a frozen, angry look. "It was, of course, not there. The epoxy patch I'd put on was still in place, so the pipe itself hadn't been changed out. I drilled a few holes partway into the pipe. But inside, where I'd seen the gold, there was nothing but empty channels."

"So what happened to the gold?"

Frank's face turned even colder. "That bastard Sidel retired early, while I was still in 'Nam. They said he moved to Arizona, but he wasn't listed in any of the Arizona phonebooks, and the operator said there wasn't even an unlisted number. He must have removed the gold and gone a lot further than Arizona."

A determined frustration came to Frank's face. "I spent the next year checking out the rest of the pipes as best I could. I did a lot of tapping with a hammer to see if I could find another section of pipe that sounded like the one I'd seen the gold in. I found nothing."

"Do you have any idea how the gold got there in the first place?"

"I've got a theory."

Jerry nodded for Frank to continue.

"I did some research at the newspaper office. They have all the old papers on microfiche. Most of the pipe was imported from Germany in nineteen thirty-four. There was a German engineer named Otto Klein who supervised the installation. It was manufactured by a company owned by Herman Goering."

"*The* Herman Goering?"

"Yup." Frank gave a smug smile. "Same bastard who ran the Luftwaffe for Hitler."

"And you think—"

"That Goering used the pipe to smuggle gold out of Germany? You bet that's what I think."

Jerry nodded. Suddenly, everything he'd been told by the man at the museum made complete sense.

Frank tied up the loose ends of his theory.

"Old Herman sent a fortune across the Atlantic, all packed up inside pipe. Only something went wrong."

"What?"

"I'm not sure. After the pipes were installed, Otto apparently decided to immigrate. He applied for a permanent U.S. visa, eventually got his citizenship, settled down in Portage, did a little engineering for a local firm."

"Doesn't sound like he had access to a fortune in gold bullion."

"Nope."

"Is the engineer still alive?"

"No," Frank said. "He died in seventy-eight."

"And you never got to talk with him?"

"Nope. By the time I had the chance he was senile. I only met him once up in the nursing home but he was drooling by then."

As Jerry mulled over the story one question leapt to mind.

"You aren't afraid I'll tell someone?"

"We're Army, aren't we?" Frank realized how naive this sounded. He straightened in his chair; resuming the plucky confidence of someone who's certain he's thought of everything. "The statute of limitations for anything short of first degree murder passed a long time ago. I didn't murder Gary Porter so I've got nothing to fear. And you've got nothing to gain by repeating what I just told you." He paused, as if going over a mental checklist. "Besides, I need your help. And I can't think of anyone else to ask."

"Help?"

"A few weeks ago Fiona Ross called and asked if I knew anything about German engineers working on the power plant when it was built. She said a fellow from Russia contacted her and told her about an uncle of his from Germany who settled in the area back in the thirties. She called me the day before she died and said the Russian was about to arrive. She sounded scared. And then she turned up dead."

The answer to Frank's problem seemed simple. "Can't you just tell the police?"

"I'd have to tell them the whole story of what happened back in the sixties."

"Why?"

Frank looked perturbed. "Because none of it makes any sense unless you know about the gold! That's the motive for the Russian killing Fiona. I'd have to tell how I discovered gold in the pipe. People around here have long memories. There are plenty who still think of me as white trash, just an orchard worker's kid who got lucky with a PUD job he never really deserved. They'll turn on you in a second if you give them a reason. They'd call me a liar and have me fired. I'd be tossing my whole life down the drain if I called the police. And I'm not willing to do that. Fiona's dead and nothing's going to bring her back. I'm sorry about it, but I'm not going to lose my job over it."

"Are you certain the Russian knows about the gold?"

"Why else would he be asking Fiona those questions?"

"But how could he know?"

"I don't know!"

"Calm down. I'm just trying to understand."

Frank relaxed. "Sorry. I've been going crazy since her death. It feels like I'm next in line and there's nothing I can do about it." He gave Jerry a searching look. "Will you please help me?"

Jerry's opinion of Frank bottomed out. He wasn't just a lonely man. He'd been searching for over thirty years to find a Nazi treasure trove that probably no longer existed, and was now certain he was being stalked by a Russian who somehow learned—seven decades after the fact—that tons of gold had been smuggled out of pre-war Nazi Germany hidden inside pipes. *This guy eventually winds up in a jacket laced from the back. But he won't take kindly to me saying, "No."*

"Okay. I'll try."

"Good," Frank said, relieved. "I knew I could count on you." He reached out and clapped Jerry on the shoulder.

Chapter 28

When Jerry returned to the Belvedere, Rosa came to the open office door, eyes wide with concern.

"Ah! Señor," she said apologetically. "Los Niños, they bother you?"

What was she was talking about? And then he remembered his promise.

"You mean the boys this morning?"

"I tell them to leave you alone."

"No," Jerry insisted. "It's alright."

"But Señor! They asked you to buy something? It is not right!"

His generosity had been misinterpreted. He hoped Pablo hadn't already been punished.

"It was my idea to start with. I offered to buy them a soccer ball," he explained, watching her reaction turn from concern to puzzlement. "I *want* to buy them a soccer ball. Boys should have good equipment to play with."

"You offered?" she said, head slightly cocked as if this didn't quite square with the reality of the world.

"Yes. It was my idea." *And my guilt.* But for Jerry there was more to it than guilt. He'd grown up with Hispanic kids who never had a real chance in life. It would take a good deal more than a soccer ball to put boys on the road to a serious education and good jobs. But you never knew what might spark a kid to achieve. Maybe one stranger's kind act would make the difference in how a boy viewed life. The soccer ball was a vote of confidence from a white guy in a white guy's world.

Rosa's brow furrowed in calculation. Then she reluctantly dug into the right pocket of her slacks and pulled out a wrinkled piece of grocery sack paper. She handed it to him. "This is not necessary," she said, but her resistance was fading. On the torn brown scrap someone had written in pencil: *LANGSTON SPORTS, WILSON OPTIMA SOCCER BALL.*

"Thank you," he said, folding the note and slipping it into his jeans pocket.

"Are you sure?" she said.

"It is as much for me as it is for the boys," he said.

This brought a smile. Rosa understood.

Jerry smiled back and nodded.

"Thank you, Mr. Wells. You are a good man." She backed through the doorway as if to protect the moment, the gift. "Muchas gracias!" The door closed.

Jerry bounded up the stairwell, slowing only as he reached the top, absurdly pleased with himself as he walked down the hallway to his room.

He pushed up his window to let in fresh air, made a peanut butter sandwich, poured a glass of milk, and sat at the table to mull over Frank's story. It seemed so incredible. What was the old adage? *Truth is sometimes stranger than fiction.*

He washed down the final bite of sandwich with the last swig of milk and went downstairs to the pay phone. It was time to set up a meeting with Holly. When the call went through her secretary said she wasn't available. Jerry left a message that he would try to get in touch with her the following morning.

He left the Belvedere, having looked up the address for Langston Sports in the Yellow Pages. He pictured Pablo's excitement when he was handed the tooled-leather ball. He would rush off to the field at the school. Other kids would ask to join in when they saw the new ball. Not just Hispanic kids; local white boys might also ask when they saw that beautiful ball.

And that is how you begin to fit in.

⊼

Denny Nevler was finishing lunch at the hotel coffee shop when the pager began vibrating. He pulled it from his pocket and checked the number, paid his bill, and returned to his room.

He placed his call through a portable scrambler. When the bleating on the line ceased, Arthur Fields' voice came sharply.

"Denny?"

"Yes."

"There's a new development."

"What?"

"We ran the town of Langston through the computer and there may be another player. A Russian named Viktor Anchevsky. NSA's tracking software says he booked a room in Langston a few days ago. We checked with Immigration and they say Anchevsky's here on a business visa. But he's got a history. Justice expelled him several years ago when he was working in the Soviet embassy. It was a tit-for-tat thing; they caught some of our boys, so we sent an equal number of theirs packing."

"And?"

"They never pinned anything specific on Anchevsky. He was just on the list." Fields paused. "We can't be certain, but it's possible the Russians are in contact with Dearborn. We can't risk them sneaking him out of the U.S. I've brought in Tom Delacorte."

Delacorte was a shooter. Denny bit his lip, reined in the urge to say anything that might sound like disapproval, and calmly said, "Do we have anything current on Anchevsky?"

"No. He could be legit. We just don't know." Fields sounded concerned. "Denny, we're hamstrung. I can't request specific info from the FBI on Anchevsky without stirring up a hornet's nest. Christ! All we need is those bastards poking around. We're playing dumb for now; telling the NSA we ran the town's name for a standard background check on someone we're thinking of hiring and hoping they don't share our request with the FBI."

Denny had never heard Fields frustrated. He shut up and listened.

"Track down Anchevsky. He's staying at a local bed and breakfast. We'll send you a secure file with his most recent picture."

"And then?"

"Look for a connection between Dearborn and Anchevsky. If you come across anything, call me immediately. Clear?"

"Loud and clear."

"Oh, and Denny . . ."

"Yeah?"

"Keep an eye out for anyone who looks like FBI."

⚔

Langston Sports was housed in a red brick warehouse with metal-framed windows angling out from a glass door. When Jerry entered it smelled of leather and new clothing. There were chromed wire shelves holding everything from roller blades to baseball gloves, and hangers filled with name brand jerseys and sweat pants. As he wandered past a wall of shelves displaying running shoes, a teenage girl with short dark hair and wearing a numbered sports jersey came from the back of the store. "Do you need some help?" she asked.

Jerry handed over the scrap of paper. "I need one of these, please."

She took it, read it, and nodded her approval. "Good choice. It's the same model the high school team uses." She led him to a barrel-sized wire basket filled with balls near the back of the store, reached in, selected one and handed it over.

Jerry bounced it experimentally on the floor. It said *poing* on the oak parquet and came lightly back into his hands. "Feels good," he said.

"Is it for your son?" There was a bit of curiosity.

"No, just a friend's kid."

"Oh." Her interest evaporated. The handsome older man had no son she might be interested in. It was just another sale; a few minutes chewed up at minimum wage.

"How much?"

"Forty-nine ninety-five plus tax."

They walked back to the counter and Jerry pulled out a hundred dollar bill from his wallet and handed it across. He briefly riffed through the few remaining bills.

She rang up the sale on the register.

"You want it wrapped?"

"No. I'll take it like it is." But his mind was now occupied with money. Or, more precisely, with the lack of money.

She didn't notice, busying herself with breaking the hundred. She handed him a receipt and his change and said, "If anything goes wrong, we have a full refund return policy."

"I don't think that'll be necessary," he said.

"Have a good day."

As he exited the store it was hard to resist the urge to bounce the ball. Harder still not to put it on the ground and move it along with his feet. Not wanting to scuff it up, or run it across a blob of chewing gum on the hot sidewalk, he reluctantly tucked the ball under his arm and headed for the Belvedere.

As he walked up the sidewalk Jerry wouldn't have noticed he was passing a bank except for his concern back in the store as he'd counted his money. Now the gold lettering in the window: *NATIONAL BANK OF LANGSTON*, caught his eye. Through the glass he saw a long oak counter. Three women stood behind it; only one was helping a customer; the other two were trying not to look bored.

How much longer before I leave? Two days? Three? A week? Why let it get down to the wire?

He stopped, thought about it for a few seconds, made up his mind, and pulled open the heavy glass door. There was a small black-lettered sign at the last teller cage which read: *New Accounts.*

The young woman behind the counter had curly red hair cut just above her shoulders and a white peach complexion. "May I help you?"

"I'd like to open an account."

"Fine." She reached for a card and pushed it across to him. "Will you want checking?"

"No, just savings."

She rattled off more options. "We offer a credit card if you deposit at least a thousand dollars. And if you deposit two thousand you can rent a bank box for a yearly rate of just twenty-five dollars." She waited to see if he was interested in the promotions.

"No, just a savings account, thank you."

"Okay." She sounded mildly disappointed.

He took the form, lifted the pen on its beaded chain, and began filling in the blanks. Where it said *Name* he almost wrote *Jerry Wells.* He'd lived with it for so long it was now second nature. That was good. But he'd need to wire money in from Argentina. And that account, which he'd established six years ago, was under a different name. Carefully, he spelled out *Jerry Allen Sikes*, giving the Belvedere as his current address. The birth date and social security number would eventually bring a report from the IRS that the person reported was not currently in their records. But by that time Jerry would be long gone. He pushed the card back across the counter, noticing the woman's name tag.

"Thank you, Michelle."

"Thank you—" she paused, looked down at the card for his name. Her eyes fixed on his handwriting for a long moment before she flashed a perfunctory smile. "—Mr. Sikes. This will just take a couple minutes." She made a notation on the card he'd just filled in and looked up again. "I'll need to see some picture ID."

Jerry pulled the Sikes passport from his back pocket and handed it across. She scanned it briefly and then folded it and pushed it back.

"How much will you be depositing to open the account?"

"I want to wire money in from another bank. Can I open it now with just a hundred?"

"Certainly." But again there was disappointment. This wouldn't make an impression during the annual salary review. She wrote down *one hundred dollars*. He pulled out his wallet and withdrew a hundred dollar bill and pushed it across the countertop. She picked it up, filled out a receipt, neatly stapled it to the customer copy of the deposit agreement and handed it to Jerry.

"You'll need our routing number so the other bank can send a wire." She pulled a business card from a holder at the side of the window and wrote a number on it before laying it on the counter. "If you need anything else, just call."

"Thanks." He picked it up.

As he left the bank he felt better. It was now past the close of business in Argentina. He'd call the *Banco de la Nación Argentina* tomorrow morning to make the necessary arrangements. Five thousand should be enough, but not so much as to stir up interest with the Feds.

He would have felt far less comfortable if he'd spotted the dark blue sedan with an *Avis* bumper sticker parked across the street. A thirty-something man with short hair sat behind the wheel, trying to act nonchalant. He'd just taken a digital photo with a telephoto lens and was watching Jerry through the sharply angled rearview mirror as he walked back up the street toward the Belvedere.

After the new customer left the bank, Michelle grabbed the phone and dialed. After two rings a voice came on the other end of the line.

"Langston Courier, Jocelyn speaking."

"Can I speak to Marni?"

"Certainly. Who should I say is calling?"

"Michelle Rhodes."

There was a brief pause as her call was transferred.

"Hi, Michelle. What's up?"

Michelle suddenly had cold feet. She'd been with the bank for three years, and in all of that time, whenever there was an issue, she'd always gone to her manager. But this was too strange. And besides, she and Marni Long were best friends, and they shared a fascination—Michelle would have called it a "sincere concern"—about Fiona's death. They attended her memorial service at the Methodist Church and just before the ceremony began Marni had pointed out the man who found the body. "That's him," she said just a bit too loudly. The stranger paused but hadn't glanced in their direction and both girls were certain he had no idea who had spoken. After he moved on, Michelle continued in an urgent whisper. "His name is Jerry Wells. He's a homeless guy who was camping near where Fiona's body was dumped. If you ask me, he seems pretty suspicious."

Suspicious indeed! The same man who was now claiming to be *Jerry Allen Sikes!*

Michelle made up her mind. "Marni," she said softly, careful not to let the other tellers overhear. "You'll never guess who just opened an account."

⅄

The boys were waiting on the front steps. As soon as they spotted him, all three jumped up and hurried out onto the sidewalk, their eyes riveted on the ball he carried under his right arm. Roberto spoke first.

"Is that one ours?"

"It's the right one, isn't it?"

"Oh yes!" Roberto's eyes were wide with excitement and he reached out expectantly.

"Just a minute," Jerry said, and Roberto instantly deflated, again suspecting there was some sort of catch. "One of you needs to be the boss. If I give it to all of you there will be arguments."

The boys looked at each other, then at Jerry.

"So . . . I'm officially giving the ball to Pablo." Upon hearing this, Pablo glanced defiantly at the other two. "But," Jerry continued sternly, "you must be fair and share, Pablo. Can you promise to do that?"

"Oh, yes!" Pablo agreed, ecstatic at the prospect of being *The One.*

"Have fun." He tossed the ball to Pablo.

Pablo caught it as if it were a religious object, turning it slowly, while his two friends stood looking on in awe. Then, without a word, all three turned and sprinted off toward the school playfield.

Jerry watched them dash up the street, Pablo carefully carrying the ball in both hands, the other two running just behind.

After they turned the corner, Jerry climbed the front steps with a spring in his step.

That evening, he heard a knock on his door. When he opened it the hallway was empty. There were footfalls descending the stairs. On the worn green hallway runner sat two foil-covered plates; one salad-sized, one dinner-sized. Condensation beaded the surface of the foil. He peeled back the cover on the large plate and discovered two *chilies rellenos,* yellow rice, and a pool of refried beans. The small plate held a stack of warm flour tortillas.

CHAPTER 29

When Assistant FBI Director Cross walked through the door at 8am, special agent Wheeler was waiting with copies of the documents he'd obtained over the past twenty-four hours. There were three complete sets laid on the round table in the conference room.

Cross glanced at the documents and smiled. "Got to like a man who gets things done early."

"Good morning, sir."

"Morning, Jim. How's it going for you today?"

"Ready to fight the battles, sir."

"Good man."

The formality would have led an outsider to believe the two men had a stiff working relationship. Hardly. It was simply what suited two ex-marines. At sixty-four, Pete Cross was just three years older than Jim Wheeler, but he was still the boss. The protocol came hand-in-hand with polished Oxfords, white shirts, conservative ties, and navy blue wool suits.

Cross leafed through one of the stacks. "Is this everything?"

"I think it's all we're going to need, sir."

He paused at a photo. "The Russian's image must be dated."

"Yes."

"By how much?"

"Seven years. I couldn't find anything more recent."

"Can we age it on the computer?"

"Already being done."

"Good."

They were interrupted by the intercom.

"Director Cross?"

"Yes?"

"Mr. Furbeck is here."

"Thank you, Nancy. I'll send Agent Wheeler to escort the senator's aide in."

"Back in a flash," Jim said, as he headed toward the front desk. He took a visitor's badge from the receptionist and extended his hand to the man who stood waiting. "Tom," he said warmly, giving the badge to the younger man, who clipped it onto his suit coat lapel. Jim escorted Tom Furbeck through the checkpoint and back to the conference room.

Furbeck visited the FBI building often. As a senior aide to Senator Axton Correll, the ruddy-skinned youngster had a calm efficiency that always seemed to produce the right answer in the shortest possible time. When Jim learned Furbeck had graduated cum laude from Harvard he was not surprised.

They sat down around the small conference table and Cross said, "Okay, let's get started. Agent Wheeler, please fill us in on what you've learned. Then we'll hear from Mr. Furbeck."

"You each have a set of documents," Jim began. "The first is a map of Langston. The second contains basic information on the town and the immediate area. Briefly, Langston sits at the southern end of a lake on the eastern slopes of Washington's Cascade Mountains. The lake doubles as a reservoir for a small hydroelectric project built in the nineteen-thirties, and is a popular place for summer recreation. Langston has a population of nearly ten thousand. There are two smaller communities on the lake; Portage has a population of three hundred, and Dartmouth Village has a population of one hundred. The primary industries in the valley are tourism and agriculture, the latter consisting mostly of apples, pears and wine grapes. Langston is the seat for Cascade County, which is bordered by Canada to the north and the Columbia River to the south. The sheriff's department has nineteen officers." He shifted the first two pages to the bottom of his stack.

"The third sheet is a photo of FICO agent Denny Nevler."

They all studied the photo of a man with short brown hair. He was strong in the face, a go-to guy.

"Nevler's bio, which is the fourth sheet, says he's thirty-eight, six-foot-one, weighs roughly two hundred pounds. He has bachelors and masters degrees from Michigan State in police science. He's worked for FICO for the past nine years as an information specialist. He flew to Seattle yesterday morning and caught a commuter flight into a town called Wenatchee, where he rented a car for the sixty-mile drive to Langston." Jim waited until Cross looked up from the bio and nodded for him to continue.

"Next, we have Tom Delacorte." The photo showed a man with angular features and straight black hair of medium length, parted on the left. A thin scar ran along his jaw line below the right cheek. The face had a clock spring intensity. Pete Cross studied the photo. It was easy to imagine what Delacorte did for a living. The eyes told the story. Hard, cold, serial.

"Delacorte was a Navy Seal who served in Desert Storm where he won a Silver Star. He holds a BA in philosophy from Columbia, and has been with FICO for eleven months. He's the newest of their trigger men, having been hired after they lost Dearborn."

Cross frowned as Dearborn's name was mentioned. The death of a child at Dearborn's hands was the major reason the Senator and Cross had become allies. Pete Cross believed the days of foreign assassinations should come to an end. Senator Correll shared this conviction. The Champoton debacle finally provided decent leverage to wage the battle in Congress, where it presently seethed behind the closed doors of the Military Oversight Committee.

Cross said, "Tell Mr. Furbeck why we've included Delacorte."

"We keep track of everyone at FICO these days, from the secretaries on up to Art Fields. As the bio reveals, Delacorte lives in Sarasota, Florida. The assassins never come into town unless there's a high profile job. Delacorte flew into D.C. yesterday. He met with Fields, and later made an interagency request for information about Langston. Someone at the NSA gave him access and then realized something odd was happening. They gave us a call. We must assume he has everything we have."

"Do you think this involves Anchevsky?" Tom interjected.

"Maybe. At this time we cannot confirm it."

"Could Anchevsky's presence be a coincidence?"

"Maybe." Jim looked at his boss, who now turned over Nevler's photo so he could look at the next document, glancing up briefly to signal that Jim should continue.

"And speak of the devil, here's our wild card . . . Viktor Anchevsky. A former KGB agent expelled while serving as an attaché at the Russian Embassy, ostensibly for spying, but in reality to punish the Soviets for outing some of our people in Moscow. After he was sent packing he dropped out of sight. Rumor has it he was demoted, but we've never confirmed this. After the Soviet Union broke up he apparently remained in the Moscow area. We believe he does something for the current government, but from everything we have, and what we have is very sketchy, it appears his job is low level. You never know with the Russians. His business visa has to do with importing wine. He's supposed to be in California. We traced him to Washington State through his airline tickets. The next sheet is a bio."

Cross studied the photo and the bio and then asked, "What would be of interest to a Russian agent in this backwater town?"

This had also puzzled Wheeler. But after a discrete call to someone who knew someone who was a Langston vintner, he'd arrived at a plausible conclusion.

"It could actually be a legitimate interest in importing wine," Wheeler said. "He's been talking to the local growers about exporting to Russia. I'm damned if I can see any other reason. The area has nothing of military interest. There is no high-tech industry within a hundred mile radius. It's possible he's simply up there trying to piecemeal something together on the business side. He might even be running a scam. It's all guesswork at this point."

Cross cut in. "And then there's FICO, also with someone up in Langston for no apparent reason. Is there a connection?"

"More likely they showed up in the same place at the same time by pure coincidence."

Cross said, "And there's a tooth fairy." No one laughed. "What about the messages we've intercepted?"

"They were encrypted. I've got Bob Rider in the cipher department working to crack it. He says maybe this afternoon, tomorrow morning at the latest."

Cross thought for a moment about the name. "That's the new man?"

"Yes, sir. The youngster we hired out of Reed College. Graduated top of his class with a major in math and a thesis in cryptology. We're lucky he didn't go straight to Silicon Valley. But he got married, and government benefits plus the challenge of cracking sophisticated codes were enough to pull him in. He'll find out what we need to know."

"Good. How many messages have been sent so far?"

"Two phone calls and one email from Nevler, one email from FICO to him. Attachments to the emails must be images judging from the file sizes."

Cross turned to Furbeck. "Any questions?"

Tom had just one. "Isn't FICO supposed to operate entirely outside the US?"

Cross's reply was sardonic. "That's what their charter says."

"Then what are they doing up in Washington State?"

Cross smiled. "I'd wager that if find the answer, we can finally shut down Art Fields and his little troupe of killers for good!"

There were grins all around the table.

After Tom Furbeck left, Cross sat at the table, troubled, contemplating the question Furbeck had asked. Why did FICO sent one of its agents to the Pacific Northwest? They knew Correll's committee was debating their future. So why take the risk? What could be so important? His instincts told him it was big. And his gut told him it involved the Russian.

"Jim," he finally said, tapping at one corner of the Nevler photo with his pinky finger. "I'm sending you to Langston. We need someone on the ground. Keep a low profile. Don't let Nevler spot you. See if you can figure out what the devil they're up to. I'll call the Spokane office and have a team assembled to back you up."

Jim nodded, and Cross completed his thought.

"They've done something bad; they've messed up big time; and Nevler's been sent for damage control."

"And Delacorte?"

"Five bucks says he's on a jet within the next six hours." Cross clapped his hands together. "Something's rotten. Something to do with the Russian."

"Something they can't afford to let get out," Jim added, catching his boss's fever.

"Right! And if we're lucky, it's treasonable. Or at least a felony. And if we catch them red handed—"

"It'll short-cut the Congressional hearings."

"Precisely. So get up there and get to the bottom of it, Jim. And maybe we'll get a chance to do some old fashioned butt kicking!"

CHAPTER 30

Jerry was sorting through his camp gear on Wednesday morning, deciding what to take, what to leave, when he was interrupted by a brief rapping on his apartment door. He waited to see if it would come again. It did.

He considered not answering. The mystery visitor would eventually go away. But that would only leave a nervous uncertainty about who it had been.

On bare feet he crossed the room and stood cautiously to one side of the door.

"Yes?"

"Señor Wells?"

The tension vanished. Jerry reached for the deadbolt, slid it back, turned the knob.

Pablo stood in the hallway holding the soccer ball; dressed in black gym shorts and a dark green T-shirt with a white Nike swoosh. His face expectant.

"Good morning, Pablo."

"Good morning, Señor Wells—"

"*Jerry*, Pablo. Please call me Jerry."

There was a shy uneasiness as the boy remembered his mission.

"Señor Jerry, we are going to have a game at the school. There are enough boys for two teams, but there is no referee. Can you be our referee?"

The word "yes" formed and then disappeared from Jerry's lips. The Argentine bank and the money transfer. Buenos Aires was four hours ahead of Pacific Time. He needed to call soon. The words came surprisingly hard.

"Pablo, I wouldn't be a very good referee. I'm not really up on the rules for soccer."

"I could teach you! The rules are easy to learn!" The boy's enthusiasm was undeniable, and catching.

Jerry reconsidered. Did he really need to make that bank call today? What was the urgency? He could certainly call tomorrow. A small voice echoed in the back of his brain.

When was the last time you had fun?

Can I count Oscar and the aborted fishing trip?

Do you want to?

Maybe . . .

Well?

"All right. Let me put some shoes on."

"Great!"

They left the Belvedere and walked toward the school and Pablo explained the basics of soccer.

"On a full team, there are eleven players. But there are usually less for our games."

"Okay."

"You play the game on a 'pitch' that can be any size as long as it is a rectangle. We use the football field. The goal posts at the school are wrong, but Roberto has found some wood sticks to put below the ends of the crossbars. You score a goal when you kick the ball between the other team's posts and below the bar. But you can't kick it unless you are on side."

"On side?"

"Yes, on side."

"I don't understand what that means."

"No one can pass a ball to a player attacking the goal unless there is at least one defending player ahead of him."

"What if one player is faster than the others? Can't he run ahead, like a football receiver, and get a pass from behind?"

Pablo shook his head. "No. That would be an off side and it would be a turnover. The other team would get a free kick."

"A free kick?"

"They would get to kick the ball in the other direction and no one could try to stop them."

"Oh."

"Don't worry, Jerry. You will see when we start. And we will help if you make a mistake."

In the end Jerry grasped the basics. Calling fouls was the referee's most important duty. Kicking, pushing, grabbing or tripping another player were the most common fouls. After a foul, the referee gave the other team the ball. He could also penalize the offender with a yellow card for a bad foul. Any violent foul earned a red card and the offender was ejected from the game.

When they reached the field only seven other boys were there. Pablo ran to join them. They formed a circle and began to toss around a small beanbag using just their feet.

Other boys finally arrived and two teams were chosen and a one-hour match agreed upon.

Play went smoothly. The boys were intent upon fair combat. By the end, Jerry only found it necessary to give out two yellow cards (he had no actual card, but raised his hand and then said it was a yellow card.)

Pablo's side won five goals to two. Pablo scored a goal on his own and made two assists leading to goals by other boys, both times deftly guiding the ball between defenders to a teammate who then kicked it past the goalie. His talent was obvious. What Jerry liked most was that Pablo didn't hog the ball; he readily passed to other players, making the win a true team effort.

Several more boys showed up during the match and they pleaded for another game. Jerry was tired from chasing up and down the field, and with no other adult to serve as referee the boys reluctantly agreed to another day later in the week.

Pablo took names and phone numbers so he could call to schedule the game. The boys were satisfied and left, mostly in the direction of the city park, some on bicycles, the rest on foot.

"Pablo," Jerry called out, after the name gathering was finished. "Would you like to go for a hamburger and a milkshake?"

Pablo's playmates eyed him jealously.

"Okay," he called back. When he came over he was clutching the soccer ball—now fully ordained with grass stains and scuffmarks.

They walked four blocks to where the East Valley Highway cut through the outskirts of Langston, not far from the Belvedere. Along the town's fast-food strip they chose a local joint—*EZ's*—which had survived the chain invasion.

Pablo practically inhaled a double cheeseburger, fries and a vanilla shake. Jerry watched him eat, so full of energy and promise, still capable of believing anything was possible, even becoming a professional soccer player. He found himself wanting to do more than just buy Pablo a soccer ball. But what could he do? Perhaps one day in the not too distant future one of Pablo's friends would be doing a school research paper and would find an article with the AP photo of Jerry. Suddenly, there would be police knocking on Jerry's door. What Pablo really needed was a father figure who was always there. Even if Jerry had possessed enough money to stick around, it seemed impossible. He finally let the idea drop.

The thought of money reminded him of the Argentine bank. He glanced at the wall clock above the service counter and realized the bank was already closed. It would have to be tomorrow.

Pablo was gobbling down the last of his fries, dipping them in ketchup and pushing them one after another into his mouth. As the last crispy brown shoestring disappeared between his lips he looked at Jerry with vast appreciation.

"That was great!"

"I'm glad you liked it, Pablo."

"We don't come here—" Pablo fell silent, embarrassed.

Jerry finished the thought. "Your mother must have a hard enough time just paying the bills."

Pablo's embarrassment deepened.

Jerry felt stupid, and now compounded his error by asking, "Is your father able to help her out?"

The boy's joy disappeared entirely; the wonderful, imaginative spark extinguished. "He's dead," Pablo said blankly. He continued with a child's calm acceptance of tragedy, as if he'd already explained it a hundred times.

"Mom says it was when I was two. He died in a car crash."

"Pablo, I'm sorry. I didn't mean—"

"It's okay." Tiny words.

And it wasn't okay.

Jerry wanted to give the boy a hug and tell him that everything would work out in his life. But he didn't believe it. Finally he offered, "Would you like to stop by Safeway and pick up a carton of ice cream to take home?"

The boy saw the diversion for what it was. "Okay," he said, but with little enthusiasm.

After Jerry bought a half-gallon of Breyers Rocky Road, Pablo's mood lightened a bit.

Rosa was in the office and saw the ice cream. She thanked Jerry before taking it to the refrigerator. As she returned from inside her apartment, she said, "Señor, a lady come and leave something for you. I put it under your door."

Jerry calmly thanked her while his insides churned.

What lady?

He found a large brown manila envelope slid under his apartment door and tore it open. Inside were a short note and three quarter-folded pieces of stiff paper.

Sorry I missed you. Please take a look at these and let me know what you think. Holly Curtis.

He unfolded the circles and spread them out on the kitchen table. In the center of each was a small black swastika. Three-digit numbers were penciled near each swastika. *204, 225, 261.* Two different sizes of holes were punched around the perimeters. Why hadn't Holly mentioned these earlier?

He decided to walk over to her house that evening and ask. And he would also tell her of his decision to leave in a day or two.

Chapter 31

Marni Long scrunched down in the front seat of her Nissan Sentra, parked half a block from the Belvedere. She held a Nikon, into which was screwed the biggest lens the *Langston Courier* owned—an 800 mm f2.0 that cost two grand. The pricey lens was used sparingly, mostly for action shots at high school football and basketball games. Marni hadn't asked for permission to use the camera and lens; that would have required explaining to her boss why she needed them, and in particular why she needed the lens. And there was no way Marni was going to share what had come her way. At least not until she had the photo. And then, if managing editor "Chislin'" Chet Freebourg wasn't willing to give Marni the bonus she had been denied for the past six months, plus a full and exclusive byline for the article—hell, the series of articles—well, there was always the AP. And the people at Fox News would undoubtedly drool at the opportunity.

Marni was still finding it difficult to believe her luck. She'd happened upon the biggest story ever to hit the valley. The words *Pulitzer Prize* now occupied much of her thinking.

When Michelle called the day before and told her that Jerry Wells had come into the bank claiming to be Jerry Allen Sikes, it sounded weird. Why would this guy have an alias? If Chislin' Chet hadn't put the deadline thumbscrews to her earlier that day, Marni might have dumped the bowling report right off her computer screen and gone straight to the Internet to do a bit of research. But with the five o'clock submission cutoff looming, her thoughts were consumed by Cascade Lanes trivia. Like who had won the frozen turkey for the highest game; Mrs. Boyd going into labor in the eighth frame but still bowling out all ten frames; and eight-year-old Kenny Watters posting his first hundred-plus score.

Marni hated the bowling report. It wasn't even close to the lofty journalism she studied at Northern Dakota State. But Chislin' Chet assured her, "You've got a real knack for that one, missy." Small town newspapers churned out the grist of small town life, and for towns like Langston, bowling was an integral part of local culture.

And wasn't that just too sweet! Four years and forty grand for a journalism degree, and here she was, struggling to pen an electrifying description of how Tom Oden managed to fight off a dry patch between the boards and hook his ball to pick up a vicious 8-10 split and win this month's beer stein trophy.

Whoopie!

Whenever she got into this kind of a funk, and it happened regularly, Marni would remind herself it was her own fault. Born and raised in nearby Wenatchee, she yearned for high-peaked mountains, winter skiing, clean air, and no rush hour traffic. But returning to the social, cultural, intellectual wasteland of rural Washington also meant she was stuck with slim job pickings in the news business. There were only a few dailies scattered across the center of the state. Almost no reporter jobs came open each year, and the competition was fierce. The *Wenatchee World*, *Tri-City Herald*, *Ellensburg Daily Record* and *Yakima Herald-Republic* all turned her down. So it seemed infinite good fortune to land a job with the *Langston Courier*. Since then, Marni suffered dark moments, wondering how fortunate landing the job had truly been.

Within a few months reality set in that the best story she could hope for was a drowning or a fatality car wreck. True investigative reporting was left to regional and national newspapers.

She accepted her fate. But it didn't make the accursed bowling report any more enjoyable. To the contrary. It became a millstone.

When she finally finished at 4:52, Marni was tempted to call it quits. She'd been at her desk for over ten hours and there was no reason to stay. Except . . . what Michelle had told her nibbled at the edge of her imagination. So when she finally transferred the completed bowling report into the central computer, she logged onto the Internet and Googled *Jerry Allen Sikes*, uncertain what to expect.

It turned out there were hundreds of listings for *Jerry Allen Sikes* or *Jerry Allen* or *Jerry Sikes.* Marni dutifully paged through the hits. There was a dentist in Des Moines. An attorney in Miami. A car thief in Montana (but he was in his twenties so it couldn't be the same guy.)

Marni reached the end of the *Sikes* combinations and was about to log off when she saw another *Jerry Allen* listing, but this time with the last name *Dearborn.* And she sure remembered that guy.

The "Kid Assassin" story had riveted the nation's attention early last year. The US government denied everything. No politician granted an interview, not even a comment off the record. After a while, rumor said the whole mess was contrived by the Mexican government as a ploy to enhance their position in trade negotiations. The story crept to the back pages when the next big tragedy came along. The public's interest faded.

On a whim, Marni pulled up the article, written in the *Washington Post,* and there was a black and white photo, originally furnished courtesy of the Mexican Federal Directorate of National Security. As Marni studied the photo it sure looked like the guy she had seen at the funeral. Her imagination began to tell her that it looked a *lot* like the man who called himself Jerry Wells.

She spent the next hour reading article after article, trying to convince herself that this Jerry Allen Wells/Sikes wasn't the same man as that Jerry Allen Dearborn. The real Jerry Allen Dearborn was dead. Right? But jeez . . . they looked so damned much alike!

She found an article where the quality of the image was better and blew it up two hundred percent and then printed it. The black-and-white Dearborn in the Mexican photo had a buzz haircut. The Jerry she'd seen had a head full of hair. Marni took a marker pen and scribbled in the hair. And wow! Maybe the two men were the same person! But for proof she needed something current to compare the old photo to.

Marni retrieved the *Courier's* photo file on Fiona's funeral and ran through the images on the screen, looking for a picture with Dearborn in it, but found nothing. It was then she got the idea of taking one herself.

The *Courier* had two staff photographers, but Marni wouldn't risk another person discovering this story. That would run the risk of someone coming between her and glory. So she went into the photo equipment room and lifted the 800 mm lens from the lens drawer, then snatched up a Nikon body with a high res memory chip.

She went back to her desk and called Michelle at home.

"Mich', it's Marni. Have you told anyone else about this guy Wells, or Sikes, whatever?"

"No. Should I?"

"Don't mention a word of it to anybody!"

"What's up? Who is he?"

"I can't tell you yet. I need to find out where he lives. Did he give you a local address?"

"The Belvedere."

"The one everybody calls the 'Pink Palace'?"

"That's the place."

"Thanks, Mich'. I owe you."

"Hey," Michelle said warily. "I'm not going to get into trouble for telling you this, am I?"

Marni knew Michelle would catch bucketful's of trouble if this guy turned out to be the guy from a year ago, and she might even lose her job. The FBI would contact Langston National's management within hours of the story breaking. And banks, run mostly by cruel bastards, don't tolerate employees calling the press about a new customer who seems suspicious. No way. Not even if he turns out to be a notorious dead guy! Marni assured herself she would find a way to make it up to Michelle. Somehow. So in her most sincere voice Marni said, "Of course not Michelle. I promise I won't mention you in the story."

"You're going to do a story?!"

"Maybe. I don't know yet. Look, Michelle. Just keep quiet about this. Please!"

"Okay. But you've *got* to tell me what's going on."

"In a couple of days. Okay?"

"Deal."

After she hung up, Marni danced a little jig around the empty newsroom while singing, "I'm gonna be famous! I'm gonna be famous!" And if she was wrong? Well, it was at least a great fantasy to have for an hour or two!

Now, as she hunkered behind her steering wheel, balancing the camera on the dash, Wells/Sikes came down the front steps of the Pink Palace.

Bzzzzp, Bzzzzp, Bzzzzp. The Nikon with its honker lens captured Jerry's face. Marni pulled the camera from the dash and scrunched out of sight until Jerry disappeared down the opposite side of the street.

She sat back up, paged through the images on the camera's little screen, chose the best one, transformed the image into black and white, and compared it to the photo from the papers.

Wow!

She whispered to the camera, "I'm gonna be famous!" before she turned the ignition key and drove away.

⅄

After a long nap, Jerry awoke at seven with an uneasy feeling about missing the bank transfer. He pushed the thought aside, shifted his thoughts to Holly. What information would she have for him about the strange pieces of paper?

He laced up his shoes and glanced at the circles on his kitchen table. He almost picked them up.

How would I carry them?

He left them in plain view, locking the door as he left.

Holly's house was on Trow Street. The route he walked took him through residential neighborhoods. The warm evening had brought people out. Kids played on sidewalks; men mowed lawns; dogs barked from the protective sanctity of their yards but quickly lost interest as he passed.

He arrived shortly before 7:30, the sun cutting shadows through a large maple in her front yard. He pushed open the gate in the fence and walked up the short brick pathway to the front door, fingered the buzzer, heard its distant ringing, and waited.

Half a minute later he pushed the buzzer again and still there was no response. He pulled open the screen and knocked sharply. For a moment he considered going around the side to see if she was in the back yard. But he'd already gotten sharp glances from a woman who was weeding in a petunia bed across the street. It would do no good for some neighborhood watch type to call the police.

After a final hard knock with no response, he closed the screen and retraced his steps. As he closed the gate, he paused, looked across the street at the woman kneeling in her flowerbed. She returned his gaze, and he smiled. She smiled back. It made up his mind. He walked across the hot asphalt, doing his best to look friendly and innocently perplexed by Holly's absence.

"Hello," he said.

She brushed the leaves and twigs that clung to her apron as she stood. "Hello," she replied, properly polite. "Are you looking for Miss Curtis?"

"Yes. I left a message earlier at her office but we missed each other so I thought I'd drop by." The mention of Holly's office appeared to put the woman more at ease. He continued, "Has she been home yet?"

"Oh yes. She came home just after five. She had another visitor about half an hour ago. They left in his car."

"Do you think it would be okay if I left a note on her door?"

"Of course. I'll tell her you stopped by, Mister—"

"Wells. The name's Jerry Wells."

"I'm Alice Jensen, Mr. Wells. I'll make sure Holly knows you came by. And that you left a note."

He had neither paper nor pencil, and asked if he could borrow some. She went inside and returned with a tablet and a pen, waiting while he wrote.

Jerry's note was short and to the point. He informed Holly that he intended to leave soon, and asked that she call the apartment manager's number, or drop by his room at her earliest convenience. He thanked Alice and walked back across the street, folded the paper, and slipped it behind the screen.

He left, headed toward the lake. A long walk along the shore would be his reward for following through on this detail. As he strolled down Trow Street, the presence of a blue Taurus parked halfway up the block didn't register. The man behind the wheel watched until Jerry was out of sight. Then he got out and walked purposefully toward the woman working in her petunias.

Alice Jensen was fifty-five. She had been pretty when she was young but had only ever loved one man. The relationship had never materialized. Since then, Alice hadn't developed an interest in another man. After graduating from high school she settled into a job at the library, acquired a series of cats (one at a time), bought the house she would end up living in—alone—for the rest of her life, and now devoted most of her time to gardening, the hospital guild, and the Catholic Church.

Holly Curtis became a fascination for Alice shortly after she moved in a year ago. Here was a bright and pretty girl who never brought men home. But there was Fiona Ross, who came often and sometimes stayed overnight. Alice concluded there was more than a platonic friendship between the two. Many times she peeped through her curtains, observing Fiona's arrival or departure, sometimes just before sunrise when the street was quiet and the neighbors (except Alice) were still in bed.

Alice wasn't a gossip. And to her further credit, neither was she particularly upset that a "woman who liked women" lived across the street. In fact, Alice rather admired Holly's gumption for taking such a risk in conservative Langston. She made a point of establishing a neighborly friendship with the younger woman, and everything she observed about Holly seemed to confirm Alice's suspicions.

So when the first man arrived that sweltering Wednesday afternoon, speaking only briefly to Holly through the screen door before she let him inside, Alice was intrigued. She moved outside to work in her petunias. In a few minutes, Holly and the man came out and got into his car and left. Alice was careful to go inside and write down the license plate number.

It was odder still when the fellow who called himself Jerry Wells showed up. After a year of no men coming to call on Holly, now there were two in the space of one hour!

The third and final visitor was the proverbial straw that broke the camel's back. He was tall, in his thirties, and flashed an ID that identified him as a DEA agent. He walked straight up to Alice, who was still working in her petunias, and asked about the man who had just left. Once she saw the badge she readily shared the stranger's name. He never bothered to ask if there had been any other visitors that evening, and Alice decided not to volunteer.

"What did he leave inside the screen door?"

Alice dutifully related what she knew about the note. As he turned away, Alice was surprised he hadn't given her a card with his number. It didn't seem quite right. On the TV shows they always gave you a card!

He walked across the street, opened the screen door, and without so much as a pause he took the note and slipped it into his shirt pocket. Did he have a warrant for search and seizure? Not likely. He'd brazenly stolen it!

Her late mother's favorite saying, one that Alice wholeheartedly believed in, now came to mind. *Don't poke your nose in other people's business.*

So Alice went into the kitchen and brewed a cup of chamomile tea, took it into the living room, and plunked down in the beige recliner. Her orange tabby sprang into her lap. She stroked the cat, sipping her tea from a bone china cup, replaying in her mind everything that had happened. But as hard as she puzzled, she came nowhere near a solution to the strange series of arrivals.

After a while she shooed the tabby onto the floor and went to find the mystery novel she was reading. She read for two hours. Afterward, she went into the living room and worked on the 1000-piece crossword puzzle laid out on the card table. None of this calmed her down. If anything, she became more agitated. Something was wrong.

"Damn!" Alice finally declared to the walls.

She finally worked up the courage to sit back in the recliner, reach to the burnished oak end table, lift the telephone receiver, and dial a number. She hated to bother him this late at night. But he was the only person she knew who might be able to help her piece it all together.

CHAPTER 32

The American West of 1934 that Otto Klein discovered was a country in the process of inventing itself. With population growth and fledgling industry came a demand for more and cheaper electricity.

Dam construction was one of the brightest job opportunities. Hopeful husbands and sons, with dog-eared hats and re-soled leather boots, from as far away as Maine and Florida, stood in long lines for the chance to ride a jackhammer or just to work with a shovel. Construction jobs meant long shifts six days a week for a few dollars a day, but a few bucks ensured survival during the Great Depression. Into the great rivers—Snake, Columbia, Colorado—were were poured millions of tons of concrete to build dams. Hydroelectric miracles soon made deserts bloom and cities glimmer.

Langston stood at the forefront of this vast wave of progress. Tax dollars financed the construction of the Silver Falls Dam and Power House. The Porridge Creek Mine was practically bleeding silver. Production of apples and pears doubled almost yearly.

When Eddie Verellen's Ford truck crested Turner's Notch, the view took Otto's breath away. The pristine lake and jagged western Sawtooth peaks were the icing. The cake was the bustling commercial hub of Langston. Shiny cars moved upon freshly paved streets lined with new buildings, driven by well-dressed people whose faces glowed with optimism.

It was the opposite of Germany, a country mired in a social catastrophe unmatched since the Romans conquered the tribes two millennia before. In the few minutes it took the truck to ease down the hill into town, Otto knew he wanted to stay.

He delayed sending Goering a telegram. The pipe installation was going smoothly. Replacements for the two damaged sections were ordered from a Seattle foundry and arrived by rail. How could Goering help but be pleased with his ingenuity and perseverance? Especially if he could report that the project was successfully completed!

At the same time, he was learning the intricacies of immigration law. His new friend, Eddie Verellen, referred him to an attorney to help with the application. Three months after his arrival in Langston, his resident green card came back from the immigration office. Filing to become a full citizen would follow.

After three months, Otto sat down and composed a long letter to Goering, explaining his decision to remain in America. He also penned two separate letters, one each for Frank's and Heinrich's families, relating the stories of their deaths. Except in Heinrich's case he left out the particulars of how Heinrich instigated the fight.

As he dropped all three envelopes into the slot at the post office, Otto knew this was the right move. He would begin a new life. As Americans liked to say, the future looked rosy.

CHAPTER 33

Art Fields lay in bed, deep in thought beside his snoring wife, when the phone rang. He reached in the darkness for the handset and picked it up before it could ring twice.

"Mr. Fields?"

Denny Nevler's voice brought Fields into a sitting position and he reached to switch on the bedside lamp.

"Yes?"

"Dearborn went for a walk to see someone this afternoon, but she wasn't there. He talked to the woman across the street. After he was gone I went over and identified myself. She wasn't much help, but Dearborn also put a note inside the door. I've got it."

"And?"

"It says he's leaving."

Fields glanced at the bedside clock and saw it was nearly midnight. "I'm going to wake up Tom and have him meet me at the office. Can you be in your hotel room in an hour?"

"Sure."

"I'll call you at nine-thirty your time."

"I'll be waiting."

Fields hung up. As he rolled out of bed his wife barely hitched in her snoring. It wasn't the first time her husband had been called to work in the middle of the night. Selma Fields was accustomed and oblivious.

After calling Tom Delacorte, Art showered and dressed. Time was now the enemy. It was still possible to lose Dearborn, and Fields was determined not to let that happen.

Chapter 34

Holly floated toward consciousness like rising smoke. At first, it seemed she must be lying in the darkness of her bedroom, but that couldn't be right. For one thing, the surface she lay upon felt much too hard. And the smell was wrong— the air reeked of oil. A gentle thrumming vibration surrounded her, as if she were inside a huge machine.

She tried to focus, but it proved to be as impossible as pinning a shadow to a wall. Finally, she relaxed and let her thoughts wander.

Her stomach grumbled. How long had it been since she'd eaten? She imagined how good a grilled cheese sandwich would taste.

Her nose itched in a most urgent way, as if something had crusted up in her nostrils. She wanted to scratch, but for some reason she couldn't move her arms. There was a moment of frustration, and then her face began to tingle and feel flush. The need to scratch the itch drifted away like a leaf in a stream.

Time passed.

She had no clue how long she had been gone. But now she was back again, surrounded by the vibration and a cloying oily sweetness that reminded her of a quick lube shop. She was lying on her right side, half-folded with her knees near her chest.

Did I fall? Have I had a stroke?

She tried to straighten her legs and roll onto her stomach, but the movement brought a dull ache that hammered through her head. Her arm had fallen asleep and needles of pain now shot from her elbow to her fingers. She tried to cry out, but only a muffled sound came, accompanied by a sticky pain as her mouth twisted and pulled against what felt like tape. She tried again, but the tape held fast.

Her heart began to race. With growing terror she realized she was gagged and her hands and legs were tied. Lying helpless in the dark, with her cheek pressed against a warm concrete floor, a scream curdled up but it had nowhere to go.

Where am I?

Gradually, her heartbeat slowed. The emotional freefall retreated just a bit. And Holly began to piece things together.

Where was I before this place?

She had come home from work. It was hot, and she'd taken a shower and slipped into jeans and a cotton blouse. She began fixing a dinner of macaroni and cheese and turned on the evening news as the water boiled the macaroni elbows.

Someone is knocking at my door.

I answer, and it's a . . . man.

Do I know him?

No.

I ask, "What do you want?"

"I think I know who killed Fiona."

"Who!?"

"May I come in?"

"Of course!"

She let him inside and they talked. He was afraid. Someone was after him. He was scared to go to the police. Everyone knew how the police messed things up. He couldn't trust them to keep his identity a secret. There was a Russian. He thought the Russian had killed Holly. He'd heard that Holly had known Fiona. Was that right?

"Yes. I knew her."

His fear was overwhelming his desire to act. Holly had seen this before. Someone who is ignorant of the criminal justice system and looks upon cops as the enemy. Someone who has been abused. It was important to let him talk and discover what he knew. Besides, he seemed childlike; harmless and confused.

He suggested taking her to a place where she could see the evidence.

"What evidence?"

"Something important. Something linking the killer to the murder."

She agreed, pulling the pot from the stove and turning off the burner, not bothering to eat the meal she had prepared.

That's why I'm hungry.

She pushed herself to remember more.

They got into his car and drove through town. He pulled off the road into an orchard. Something bad had happened. *Pain!* But as hard as she tried, the details wouldn't come.

She tried to concentrate and remember more, but pain lanced through the back of her head. She tried to relax, but the pressure kept building. Nausea. She was falling toward a jagged hole of rainbow light. And then her right arm no longer felt pain. A fresh trickle of blood oozed from her right nostril.

Holly Curtis slipped back into unconsciousness.

Chapter 35

Frank's father had beaten him from the time he was old enough to walk. For dear old dad a stick of kindling from the wood box was every bit as good as removing the belt. A stick was easy. Taking the belt from the loops required a bit of work. Hell, sometimes you just wanted to make sure you pants stayed on while you beat the little shit.

Sometimes.

Fear and shame isolated Frank during his early years. Vietnam provided a chance to vent his anger, both at his father and at the man who gave him a job at the powerhouse and then turned around and fired him so unfairly. In Vietnam you actually got to kill people. Sometimes it was a guy you served with; but you could only frag a bro' if you were very careful how you went about it. Frank got real good at careful.

After he returned stateside, learning that Sidel and the gold were gone nearly caused him to seek a new release—offing orchard workers. Frank managed to suppress the desire, but just barely. Someone would eventually figure out who was strangling transients. It was only the hope that some of the gold might still be concealed somewhere in the powerhouse pipes that kept him from slipping into darkness. The obsession led him down a twisting path toward insanity as the years slipped by and his search proved fruitless.

He managed to keep his blossoming madness a secret. Small towns were good for hiding mental demons. There were plenty of strange souls in rural America. People rarely questioned the quirks in a local boy's behavior, as long as they weren't overtly dangerous. After one of those local boys degenerated into some terrible depravity and was caught, the stories that emerged from people who knew him were remarkably similar. "He was a nice guy, but quiet." "When he was a kid he used to cut my lawn. Always did a good job!" "I never would have guessed he was capable of that. But now that you ask, well, he was kind of a loner." "I saw him all the time, but never really got to know him."

Frank chose not to marry. People irritated him. Being around someone all the time? Not a good idea. He could always find a local barfly when he got horny. But that wasn't often. He came to prefer porn. Over the years Frank amassed a collection of 8mm reels, mostly filmed in third world countries. And more recently, with the Internet . . . *Hoo Boy!*

Still, there were signs that couldn't be ignored. On one occasion Frank stood naked in front of a mirror and painted himself in camouflage colors. Not all of the paint washed off. Frank showed up at work with a bit of color in his hair, on his neck, places where it was hard for him to spot. At the insistence the general manager, he was treated with a visit to a psychiatrist.

Just in case.

It turned out the shrink had also spent time in Vietnam. And he was a bit too sympathetic. Or, maybe he conceded to the possibility that an enraged Frank Brindleman would blame the shrink for getting him fired, and come a calling. So the shrink wrote in the confidential file: *Patient has flashbacks common with PTSD. As long as he takes his medicine he'll be fine.*

Frank kept his prescription filled. And he kept his job. But eventually he began to flush the tablets down the toilet.

He might have gone to his grave after working a lifetime in a place where he was certain there was gold, with no real chance of ever finding another gram of the yellow stuff beyond what he'd seen as a kid back in '69. It was luck, plain and simple, that delivered the answer. Or was it the hand of God? The Devil? Whatever.

Fiona called—out of the blue—to ask what he knew of the powerhouse history. She told him a Russian had contacted her and given what seemed like a contrived story about attempting to track down a distant relative. This led to her discovery of three circular papers in an old briefcase with a swastika stamped into the black leather. As she described the size of the circles and how many holes there were in each, and how far apart they were, Frank nearly exploded on the other end of the line. This was it! The key to the gold! With a huge effort to remain calm, Frank told Fiona he didn't know if the cutouts were meaningful. But he'd be happy to take a look at them if she'd like to bring them by. They arranged a time and Frank practically did hand springs when he hung up the phone.

The disaster began when Fiona arrived without the templates. Right from the start she asked all the wrong questions.

"What are the diameters of pipes in the powerhouse?"

Frank rattled off some dimensions, fighting to remain calm.

I wish I'd taken my medication today.

"And how many bolts hold the eighteen-inch pipes together?"

They were standing near one such pipe, and the abutment where the flanges met was literally before her eyes. He saw her glance at it.

"It depends upon the pipe."

The templates, you worthless bitch! Where are the templates!

She glanced back to the pipe, eyes moving from bolt to bolt, counting. "Some of the holes in the papers are slightly larger. Are some of the bolts that hold these pipes together larger than the others?"

"I don't think so." Frank felt his self control slipping. Finally, he couldn't stand her probing any longer. When the outburst came it was fury beyond reason.

"Why didn't you bring the templates with you?!"

Fiona stumbled backwards. He lunged. Her arms instinctively came up to shield against his attack. He grabbed one wrist, then the other, and they clenched in a brief struggle that ended with Frank in complete control with her arms twisted behind her back and her head pressed against the floor.

"Let go of me!" she cried out. But Frank was now in another dimension.

Force the information out of her, soldier. She's the enemy!

You bet, captain. I've got it handled!

"Where are they?" he yelled, his mouth inches from her ear.

"Let me go!" she protested.

He twisted her onto her back and wrenched her arms wide until they were pinned spread eagle against the concrete. Once he was straddled on top of her she stopped resisting, panting to catch her breath.

The dull realization came to Frank that it had gone too far. For a moment he smelled the sweet gasoline of napalm.

NVA everywhere! They're in the bushes, captain! They're up on that ridge!

Chill man! We've called in an air strike.

After the vision faded, he spoke to the woman he sat atop in a steely flat voice.

"We're going to the tool room. I'm going to let you stand up. But if you resist, you're going straight back down onto the floor. Understand?"

She didn't reply.

"DO YOU UNDERSTAND!"

"Yes," she replied angrily.

The pleasure of being in control took over. In a voice that was almost fatherly and thus all the more frightening, he said, "Good girl. Now get up."

He held both arms from behind as they lurched into the bowels of the powerhouse. He brought her to a chamber where tools lined the walls. There were no windows in the twenty-by-thirty foot room. Frank guided her to a wood spindle upon which was coiled yellow nylon rope. While holding her wrists together with one hand, he pulled off a length of rope, cut it with his pocket knife, and bound her wrists behind her back, then tied her feet with a second length of rope and sat her down against a wall.

"Where are the templates?" he asked, looming over her.

She turned her face away.

Frank knelt down and lashed out with his hand, striking her left cheek, leaving bright red marks. Fiona cried out in pain. She turned back to face him. Her terror now morphed into a rage. With a drilling concentration she said, "Fuck you!"

Frank nearly hit her again, but then reconsidered, a smile creeping softly to his lips.

"Fuck me?" Frank said, amused. "Do you really want to?"

Her eyes grew wide.

"That's what I thought," Frank said, feeling in full control of the situation. "Don't worry, honey," he said in slow drawl, enjoying the panic it brought to her face. "You're not really my type." Frank paused for a moment. "But if you say something stupid like that again, I can certainly make an exception."

She said nothing to further provoke him.

"Okay," Frank continued. "Here's how we're going to do this. I'll ask the questions, you give me answers. Each time you refuse, or if you give an answer I know to be pure crap, you get one point. If you earn three points, you're out. Okay?"

"Out?" She said cautiously. "What does 'out' mean?"

Frank was full of himself by now. "Use your imagination," he said. From the sadness that came to Fiona's face, he knew she understood perfectly.

"Good," he continued. "Now, let's begin."

The questioning went on for nearly an hour. During that time Frank learned everything he wanted to know, and even a thing or two that surprised him. It was only after he sneaked into the museum to retrieve the templates that he discovered she had lied about one crucial fact. They weren't in the filing cabinet where she'd said they'd be. For the first time he felt some regret about having killed her.

It took all of his will power to leave the building without burning it to the ground. That pleasure he would save for later, after the templates safe in his possession and he'd found and removed the gold.

CHAPTER 36

After his hike, Viktor returned to the B&B to shower and change into black jeans and a dark blue denim shirt. He drove his rental car into Langston.

It was too early for what he planned for the rest of the night so he ate dinner at a Mexican restaurant and took in a movie. The quaint little blockhouse cinema, faced in white stucco and turquoise trim, was called the *Ruby Theatre* and it was practically empty on a weeknight. The poster on the marquee was *The Bourne Identity*. Perfect! Lots of action and suspense, even though they got technical stuff wrong. Like when you shot someone with a gun they simply didn't fall down stone cold dead. Sure, maybe a heart shot or direct to the brain and it was over quick. But a bullet to the torso? A tough guy could do plenty of damage with lead in his gut, even if his wound eventually proved mortal. Oh well . . . that was the movies!

By the time he left the theatre, stars filled the night sky. Viktor drove out of town through Turner's Notch and down to the Columbia.

Just a hundred yards up the powerhouse road he turned off onto a short side road that cut down through a thick stand of elms and ended at a small beach near where the water from the race merged into the Columbia. It was a local swimming hole, but what mattered to Viktor was that at night it was secluded and deserted. Someone coming up the road to the powerhouse would never spot his car parked in back of the cement block restrooms. He turned off the ignition, took a flashlight from the glove box, and from beneath the front seat he pulled the revolver he'd bought two days ago.

Viktor found the private gun dealer's ad in a weekly newspaper called the *Pennywise Advertiser.* The *Pennywise* was an angle of American life that amused Viktor. It contained nothing but ads, split up by categories like Vehicles, Building Materials, Household Goods and Services. It was easy to see the sellers were circumventing the taxing authority; not altogether different, in principle, from the Russian black market, except for the absence of drugs; and he suspected that at least a few of the ads which touted herbal cures for everything from warts to sore joints could also be sources for marijuana, if not cocaine and heroin.

The gun ad was listed under Miscellaneous. It read: *Good Used Firearms at Reasonable Prices!!!* There was a phone number but no address.

The man who answered Viktor's call gave him directions to the house. When Viktor drove up he discovered a log cabin with a tin roof and a weedy front yard where a rusting black El Camino with flat tires and a white VW Bug with no tires or fenders or doors were permanently parked. As Viktor stepped out of his rental car, a pit bull, tethered to the front bumper of the El Camino, barked and yanked desperately at its chain.

Viktor passed within a few feet of the dog as he walked to the front door. He was careful not to look at the animal and encourage its efforts to break free.

A man with a face full of suspicion answered his knock. He was fortyish; a slouching couch-potato character who it was easy to imagine was on permanent disability and drawing a monthly check from the state. His greasy black hair was combed to one side, Hitler-style. "Shaddup!" the man yelled at the dog, before turning his attention back to Viktor. "I'm Len," he said warily.

The dog did not pause in its yapping.

"Viktor," he replied, eyeing the dog and its worn chain. The dog's slathering drool now flew in thready gobs as it choked itself trying to get free. Len continued to ignore the pit bull, and Viktor did his best to turn his attention away from the beast.

"You the fella who called?" Len ask suspiciously.

"Yes."

"Where y'all from?"

Viktor expected this question. Len wasn't the first local to react with caution, even fear, when hearing Viktor's thick accent. But Viktor had a creative reply that had worked well so far.

"I'm Ukrainian," Viktor said proudly. He couldn't hide the foreignness of his speech, but he could lie about his nationality. If the man demanded a passport, Viktor was prepared to simply walk away. Americans still distrusted Russians. And probably always would.

"Ukrainian?" Len pondered. "Ain't that one of those parts that broke off from the Rooskies a few years back?"

"Yes." Viktor said with a conspiratorial smile. "We wanted nothing to do with the communists. We are a new country, just like America after it rebelled from the English in the time of your great general, George Washington." He looked Len straight in the eyes to confirm his intentions were above board.

Len burst into a grin as he reached out and pumped Viktor's hand. "About god-damned time you kicked the commies out," he said, nearly crushing Viktor's fingers before letting go. "Always knew the regular folks in them satellite countries was good people. Just like the God-fearin' people livin' here in the good old U S of A. Boy, I'm proud to meet you! Come on in." As Viktor walked past, Len took a final look around to make sure no one else was outside before shoving a deadbolt on the door.

The small living room was lit by a single overhead fixture and dominated by a large oak showcase with a thick glass top. It might have once contained jewelry, but was now filled with handguns laid out on black velvet. Oiled gunmetal glistened softly in the dim light.

Len walked around behind the case and his grin disappeared. "What can I do you for?" he asked with razor calm, suddenly all business.

"I need a handgun for protection," Viktor said.

Len seemed unfazed by what, to Viktor, sounded slightly ridiculous. "You can't be too careful these days," Len confirmed, sweeping his hand across the glass. "Man's gotta pack iron to feel safe anymore. Damned shame." Len seemed pleased by his report on the current condition of life in America. Perhaps he even believed it; Viktor didn't give a damn.

Len selected a key from one of several on a ring at his belt, slipped it into the padlock, lifted up the back panel on the case. His fingers closed lovingly on a short-barrel Colt .38 Special with a walnut handgrip smoothed by age. He handed the weapon across.

Viktor took the gun as if it were a treasure, studied it for a moment, then held the cylinder near his ear, spun the action, listening to the smooth evenness of the clicks. He popped open the cylinder and peered down the barrel. It was a bit worn but in decent shape.

"It's a great little pistol," Len said in a salesman's voice. "A classic American firearm. Had it out on the range last week. Hit the target with every shot. She's a keeper. Now, listen . . . I've had it for about six months and I'm tired of seeing it in the case." He paused, as if running calculations in his head. "I can let her go for . . . eight hundred."

Viktor continued to examine the gun. The price was high even if the gun were in mint condition. The look on Len's face signaled he knew this. The cocky smirk also said Len knew a cooked goose when he saw one.

Viktor was in no position to quibble. What was the American colloquialism? *By the short hairs.*

Just the same, Viktor continued to examine the piece, running a thumbnail where the grip joined metal, quite aware of the value of a tease. People want most what they don't expect to get. Len wanted to sell him the gun, but making him worry a little was a good way to hammer down a deal; and get a little pleasure on the side for making the man suffer.

Len began to fidget. "I'll throw in some ammo," he offered, reaching in back of the case to grab a small box. He thumbed open the cardboard flap to reveal a neat bunch of shiny brass and dull lead.

Viktor glanced at the standard loads. They would be sufficient from close range. He couldn't have expected hollow points or magnums.

Viktor returned to studying the pistol, as if he were not completely decided. Only after an appropriately long delay, and trying not to sound too anxious, he replied slowly, as if it took a great effort to accept the price, "Okay . . . it seems fair, I suppose."

"You bet it is!" Len said eagerly. "How you going to pay?"

Americans! It was amazing how they could overlook the obvious in the name of free enterprise. "Cash," Viktor said. He pulled out his wallet and thumbed up sixteen fifties. Len's eyes widened as he wished he'd asked for more. But a deal was a deal.

As Viktor counted the money a second time, riffling through the crisp bills, he asked, "Is there any tax?"

For Len, this was like sliding a knife in between the second and third ribs. He glanced sideways, as if someone might be hiding in the corner. "It's included in the price," he said, adding defensively, "Government's got its damned fingers in enough pies already. Hell, they're not interested in nothing but putting us little guys out of business!"

Viktor smiled as though he understood. Len couldn't have known that Viktor's smile came because an untaxed transaction also meant an unreported transaction. He handed over the money and took the weapon and the shells.

⅄

Viktor left the road, and under cover of sagebrush and the occasional boulder he crept toward the powerhouse, the revolver securely tucked into his belt. All six chambers were loaded and he had a pocketful of bullets.

The plan was simple. Every German pipe bore a unique identifying number to assist in the installation process. He would break in and record the location of all pipes that might contain gold. Exactly how he would later find and extract the gold was still a mystery. But the first step was to map the pipes.

If only he had the templates! He once again cursed his bad luck.

As he skirted around the side of the building facing the cliff, he saw just one car, an older blue Chevrolet, at the edge of the lot. When Viktor reached the car he placed his hand on the hood. It was cool. It seemed unlikely there was someone working a swing shift in such a small facility. Had the car's owner caught a ride with someone else? Was the car inoperative? After a moment of hesitation, he decided it was late enough at night to be worth the risk.

He crossed to the building, stepped into the band of shadow at the base of the wall, edged along with his back to the brick. When he turned the corner and stepped onto the concrete ramp above the tailrace he breathed a little easier. The gentle rush of water would mask the sound of his footsteps, and the ramp was in almost full darkness.

He walked to the far corner of the building where a chain link fence enclosed a graveled yard filled with huge gray electrical transformers. Transmission cables ran to a metal tower atop the cliff and into the hills beyond. A soft humming filled the air. The hair on Viktor's arms stood up as he came close to the powerful electrical fields in the switchyard.

He found a door, reached out and grasped the knob, turned, pushed, and found it locked. Cupping the flashlight in his hands to narrow the beam, he saw it was a single-key mechanism. Viktor reached into his shirt pocket for the pick set. He took out the L-shaped torsion wrench, selected the medium sized hook pick, inserted the torsion wrench and hook pick, and after a long moment of fiddling the pins moved. Finally there was a satisfactory *click* as the torsion wrench rotated and the bolt slid back. With moist fingers, he turned the knob and felt the door open just a crack. He slipped the tools back into his shirt pocket, turned off the flashlight, pulled the revolver and, with the gun held forward and ready, nudged at the door with his knee. It swung slowly, the latch clicking faintly as it cleared the strike plate, and the hinges began to emit a nasty squeal. Viktor froze.

It took another excruciating minute to quietly inch the door open wide enough so he could enter. He waited to be sure he hadn't been heard. When no one came to investigate, Viktor slipped inside.

CHAPTER 37

The call came shortly after Manny finished a very late dinner. It had been one hell of a long day and he was trying to unwind, sprawled comfortably on the couch, in front of the tube, just a few minutes into a rerun of the Mexican telenovela *Te Sigo Amando*. The ring broke his concentration. He reached to pick up the handset, expecting a pollster or someone offering repair of cracked windshields at a discount price.

"Hello?" he said distractedly, trying to follow the TV dialogue while he listened for the brief pause followed by the fake enthusiasm of a sales pitch.

"Manny?"

It was Alice Jenson. He knew her as one of the few non-Hispanics in the Catholic congregation. In a town not known for its racial and cultural tolerance, many Hispanic children living in and around Langston found toys under their trees at Christmastime because of her generosity. When she learned Manny was a detective she made a point of getting to know him. They became good friends and were on a first name basis. She sounded upset.

"Alice?"

"I'm sorry to call so late. I was afraid to wait any longer. I think there's something wrong across the street at Holly's house."

Manny straightened up on the couch. "Holly Curtis?"

"Yes," she said, the urgency in her voice building. "I thought about calling nine-one-one, but I don't know if it's an emergency. But it might be."

Manny fought the urge to launch a salvo of questions, and instead said in a slow and even voice, "Okay, Alice. Please start from the beginning."

Alice described the man she saw arrive in a blue sedan and told Manny the license number. Next came Jerry Wells and the note he'd left inside Holly's screen door. Finally, the DEA agent, who seemed too abrupt and had purloined the note.

Manny listened with growing concern. From Alice's physical description, and remembering his powerhouse visit and the car parked in the lot, he recognized the first visitor as Frank Brindleman. What possible reason could Frank have for visiting Holly, much less taking her somewhere? The arrival of Wells was equally remarkable. But the last visitor kindled his darkest fears.

A special agent from the DEA?

Special agents didn't casually show up in backwaters like Langston. Was something going down that his department hadn't been informed of?

"Thank you Alice. I'll look into it."

"Tonight?" There was hope.

"Yes, tonight," Manny assured her. He hung up and carefully thought through everything he'd heard, trying to make sense of it.

There was Jerry Wells, camped down on the river. He'd discovered a body and reported it to the police. The DEA agent had asked about him. Would they send a special agent to deal with a retired guy whose main interests were camping and fishing? Hardly.

Manny continued to puzzle it out. If Wells was a wanted man, why hadn't he split when he found the body? The answer came easily. It was the same conclusion Jerry reached earlier. People had seen him camped by the river and would conclude he was the killer if he mysteriously disappeared.

That still didn't explain Wells' presence in the first place. Except . . . one explanation was perfectly logical. A DEA agent showing up tied it nicely together. The conclusion came like electricity. *My fingerprint request turned up something. The FBI just didn't tell me! It has to be narcotics.*

Wells dealt drugs, which meant he had the resources to leave at any time. But it was equally obvious he didn't know the Feds had arrived; otherwise, he would have left, even at the risk of becoming a suspect in Fiona's murder.

Manny remembered the brief encounter between Brindleman and Wells at the edge of the courthouse square. Brindleman served two tours in Vietnam. Brindleman had saluted Wells. That meant Wells was the boss, and the two had likely met through their military service, or at least formed some kind of bond because of it.

Everything now seemed to fall into place. Brindleman used the PUD's resources to store and move the drugs. Who would stop and search a PUD truck? Wells had come to check up on Frank, but he didn't want to draw attention, and what better way to remain discreet than to camp in an out-of-the-way spot down on the river. Only, he got stuck with finding the body.

Or! Maybe Fiona was out jogging and happened upon a drug exchange, or even a meeting with other dealers, near the campsite. They would have had no choice but to execute her. Leaving Wells with a tough choice between fleeing, and making up a story about finding the body.

But how did Holly figure into all of this? And then there was the DEA . . . if it was in fact a DEA agent!

Manny reached for the phone. But he froze as an ugly realization came. Drug dealers were notorious for taking revenge. If they caught wind of police involvement, what were Holly's chances for survival? Someone in the department might be on the take if a cartel was involved. One call from a snitch and Holly would disappear. *Maybe that's why the Feds haven't told us!* It made sense. The Feds knew Manny's department couldn't be trusted.

Manny reached a conclusion. No way could he call in other officers and put Holly at risk. But if he went in solo, and if there were just Wells and Brindleman, he would have a decent chance of taking out both men. He'd have surprise on his side. Even better, if he rescued Holly he'd be her hero.

Manny ran to his bedroom and changed into a uniform and donned his camouflage hunting vest. He unlocked the gun cabinet and selected a Glock 9mm with two thirteen-shot magazines, a pistol grip Mossberg shotgun and a box of twelve-gauge buckshot.

He ran to the garage and laid the weapons and ammo on the passenger seat of the Mustang. They might have taken her anywhere. But Manny figured it was the powerhouse. A chilling thought struck: What if she was already dead?

As he revved the engine and backed out of his garage he resolved that if she was dead he'd make certain there was no need for the courtroom nonsense of a trial.

As he sped toward the East Valley Highway he knew there was one necessary stop before confronting Wells and Brindleman. Manny didn't like Oscar Danner. He was slovenly, and a shitty lawman. But Manny had a hunch the pasty-skinned sergeant knew a lot more than he'd let on.

⅄

A knock on the door came as Jerry slept. Startled awake, his first thought was the sound had come from the dream. But the knocking came again, a soft but insistent rapping.

Who?

Then, as if his thoughts had been read, there came a boy's delicate high tenor.

"Señor Jerry?"

"Pablo?"

"Yes." The boy's quiet voice carried an intense urgency.

"Just a moment." He switched on the bedside lamp and the weak bulb bathed the room in yellow and cast awkward shadows through a cracked shade. Sitting on the edge of the bed he slipped on his jeans. The bedsprings creaked as he stood. He walked into the tiny living room, pulled the deadbolt and opened the door.

Pablo stood in the hallway wearing pants and a T-shirt and no shoes, his dark hair disheveled as though he, too, had recently been asleep. Jerry stepped into the hallway. "Is something wrong?"

Pablo continued apologetically. "I am sorry to wake you, Señor Jerry. But my mother, she said to come up and tell you there is a man on the telephone who needs to speak to you."

Jerry feared the worst. The hospital was calling to inform him Oscar had suffered complications and they needed his permission as power of attorney to operate. Or, maybe Oscar had died. "Did your mother say who it was?"

"He did not give his name." Pablo's face grew more anxious, and Jerry realized how uncomfortable the boy was—a messenger between two adults, late at night, not privy to the nature of the "emergency."

"Just a minute," Jerry said. "I'll be right back."

He went into the bedroom and pulled on a shirt and shoes and rejoined the boy in the hallway.

Rosa was waiting at the office door. "Señor," she said urgently. "Please. The man, he says it is important." She waved him inside the small office and pointed to the phone handset which lay atop the desk, the cord curled like a snake. Jerry put the handset to his ear.

"Hello?"

"Jerry?" It was Oscar, and that was a relief. But his voice was strained and he sounded scared.

"Are you okay, Oscar?"

"Yeah. I'm fine. But I'm not sure you are. Something's happened."

"What."

"We shouldn't talk on the phone. I know it's late, but could you please come over?"

Jerry glanced at the clock radio on the counter. It was five past eleven. "Sure," he replied, relieved that Oscar was all right. But what was putting such concern in his voice? And why did they need to talk in person? "Are you still at the hospital?"

"Yes. How long will it take?"

"Fifteen minutes."

"Good. I'll be waiting. And Jerry. . ."

He waited for Oscar to finish.

Finally, Oscar said, "Nothing. Just hurry."

"Okay. I'm on my way." He hung up and turned to Rosa and Pablo, who stood trying to comprehend what was happening. "Gracias, Rosa," he said.

"Es de nada," she replied. She began to shoo Pablo back into the apartment. He resisted for a moment, looking up at Jerry.

"Is everything okay?"

"Yes," Jerry replied, trying to sound certain. "It's my friend, officer Danner, in the hospital. He got lonely and wants some company."

"Pablo!" Rosa stood with her hands on her hips.

Pablo reluctantly turned away from Jerry. She took his hand and spoke in soft but insistent Spanish. She said it was none of his business what the phone call was about. Pablo didn't protest, but he glanced back, once, with concern in his eyes. Jerry nodded, and winked. It brought a smile to Pablo's face.

In a few seconds Rosa returned, nervous and concerned. "Will you be okay, Señor?"

"Yes, I'll be fine," he assured her.

"Good," she said with finality. "Buenas noches."

Rosa closed and locked the office door.

If Jerry had left just a minute earlier, he would have missed Frank. Or, more precisely, Frank would have missed Jerry. But when he stepped out into the warmth of the evening and stood briefly surveying the street from beneath the arch of the Belvedere's cement portico, the blue Chevy was already parallel parked on the street. Frank Brindleman was about to open the driver's door. Now, he clenched his fist at the good luck of seeing Jerry emerge.

Frank readied himself as Jerry descended the steps. At the moment Jerry turned left onto the sidewalk, in the direction of the hospital, and began to pass the Chevy, Frank pulled the handle and pushed the door open.

Jerry saw the door suddenly blocking his progress. Then he saw Frank Brindleman climb out, holding a revolver.

"Going for a walk?" Frank's words had a nasty bite. He pointed the revolver squarely at Jerry's chest.

Jerry almost laughed, thinking it an awful attempt at humor. But Frank's face confirmed it was no joke.

Frank glanced around and saw they were alone on the street, and returned his full attention to Jerry. "Well!" he demanded, waving the gun anxiously.

Jerry remained calm, completely puzzled by Frank's behavior. "It's a nice night for a walk," he said, eying the revolver. "Why the gun, Frank?"

Frank was at first unnerved by Jerry's reaction. Then anger flushed his face. "Nice try. A really nice try." A maniacal cockiness filled his voice. "We can do this the hard way, or the easy way. It's your choice."

Jerry still had no clue what Frank was up to. "Okay. Let's try the easy way."

Frank's eyes widened with pleasure. "That's good," he said. "A really smart decision."

"So?" Jerry said, still clueless.

"We go up to your apartment and get the templates, of course!"

Things suddenly fell into place. The gold. Fiona's death. The mysterious circles Holly slipped under his doorway sometime that afternoon. Frank had called them "templates." And with that word, Jerry imagined the vast power-house filled with pipes, some of which could easily be identical in diameter to the papers. He realized things were even worse. There was only one way Frank would know he held the templates. *Frank has Holly!*

Frank saw Jerry's face darken.

"You didn't know, did you?" Frank blurted out. "And you didn't believe my story!" The revolver barrel wavered as Frank enjoyed the irony of the moment. Jerry almost lunged, but Frank brought the revolver back straight and steady at his chest.

Jerry glanced down at the revolver, up at Frank's face, and knew this wasn't the best moment.

"So . . . are they upstairs?"

There was no point in lying. Frank was in a manic state and wouldn't believe anything he didn't want to hear; he would insist on checking out the apartment. Jerry had left the door unlocked and the templates were spread out on the kitchen table for anyone to see.

"Yes."

"Let's go." Frank motioned toward the Belvedere with the gun, and Jerry turned and obeyed. As they climbed to the third floor, he found himself torn between hoping someone would blunder into the stairwell, giving him a chance to tackle Frank; and at the same time wanting no one else's life to be in danger. A vision of Pablo coming up the stairs danced in his mind. If Frank began to fire, people would come out, and Frank would have easy targets.

He was relieved when they arrived at his room. Once inside, Jerry pointed to the manila envelope and the templates, hoping this might be the moment Frank let down his guard.

Frank carefully hooked one of the kitchen chairs with his foot and pushed it away from the table. Its metal-capped legs scraped the worn linoleum as it slid several feet before coming to a stop. "Sit," Frank demanded. Jerry sat. Frank moved around to the table's far side. He laid the gun down with the barrel pointed at Jerry. There was no chance to take Frank from this far away, so Jerry settled back, studying Frank's reaction.

Frank gingerly lifted each of the three templates, caressing penciled numbers with the tip of his index finger. Every few seconds he glanced up to make sure Jerry was staying put. Jerry eventually crossed his arms and legs, a clear signal he had no intention of doing anything stupid. This settled Frank and he spent more time studying the templates.

Frank finally folded and slid them into the envelope, apparently satisfied. He looked up. "Great!" He said cheerfully. "And numbered! Just like I knew they'd be!"

Something occurred to Jerry. "I thought you said you checked all of the pipes and that there was no possibility of gold."

Frank laughed. "You really believed that? I'd have had to practically disassemble the powerhouse to make that kind of search. I'd have had to drill hundreds of holes into the pipes. They would have caught me for sure!" He waved the envelope in Jerry's face. "Do you have any idea how long I've been looking for these?" He continued without waiting for an answer. "One hell of a long time, that's how long." His glee was quickly followed by, "I guess by now you've figured all that out, haven't you? After all, I told you the story, didn't I?" The glee intensified. "Yeah, I sure did. Told you the whole ball of wax." Frank's smile faded.

"Okay, get up. We've got business to finish." He picked up the gun from the table.

"Frank—"

"Get the fuck up!" The gun zeroed in on Jerry's chest.

Was now the time? He was still on familiar ground. But Frank was expecting a move. And people in the building would be in danger if Frank went ballistic. Better to wait and hope for a moment when Frank's guard was down. And . . . when people like Pablo were not at risk. And where had Frank taken Holly? Was she even still alive?

"Hard or easy, your choice."

"Easy," Jerry said, and he calmly stood up and walked to his apartment door, then allowed Frank to herd him down the stairs and to the Chevy. When they got to the car Frank directed him to the trunk. After a quick look around to make certain no one was watching, Frank opened the lid. "Climb in," he said. When Jerry hesitated, Frank reminded him, "Hard or easy. I can thump you upside the head if I need to. Or, maybe it would be easier to just put a slug in your spine." It was all the encouragement Jerry needed. He swung one leg over and his foot landed on a loosely folded blue plastic tarp—the kind with nylon webbing for extra strength. He lay down and the trunk lid slammed him into darkness. At that point Jerry knew he'd made a mistake. Better to take a slug or two out here on the street and hope nothing vital was hit. But now, locked in the trunk of a car, there was no option left but to go where Frank might take him.

I never would have let it happen this easy in the old days.

And with that thought Jerry wondered if there was any hope at all.

Maybe this is where it all ends.

Frank took one last look around. The Belvedere's windows were dark. No lights shone in the houses across the street. The sidewalks were empty. Pleased with the way things had gone, he walked around and climbed behind the wheel and brought the engine rumbling to life. He pulled away from the curb, satisfied his work was undetected.

Had he known someone saw his and Jerry's exit, Frank's happiness would have vanished.

CHAPTER 38

Bob Rider had the FBI's computer crunching code all day long. The first break-through came shortly after 11pm.

When the printer finally spit out the photo, Bob studied it, compared it closely to the one of Viktor Anchevsky, and though there were similarities between the two, they were clearly different men. He picked up the phone and dialed, knowing Jim Wheeler would be in the air on a government Citation, headed for Seattle.

"Wheeler," came the voice on the other end of the line.

"Sir, this is Rider."

"And?" There was high expectancy.

"It's not Anchevsky, sir."

"Then who is it?"

Bob looked the photo he held, wishing he knew the answer. "I don't know, sir."

Had Bob been with the FBI for more than a few months, recognizing the man in the photo would have come easy. But during Bob's years at Reed College his time was spent mostly on study. In the few hours not devoted to working on algorithms or writing his thesis, he courted his sweetie. There was no time to read national newspapers or watch the news. The Champoton assassination had never come to his attention.

"Okay. We know it's not the Russian. Run it through the recognition program and let me know if there are any matches."

"Tonight?" Bob was exhausted. He'd called his wife hours ago to tell her the boss wanted him to stay late on an important project. She had not been happy. Having married in December, just a week after he graduated, she now wanted her man home every night. Bob's disappointment over having to work through perhaps till morning flooded his voice. There was a brief pause on the other end of the line.

"I suppose it can wait until morning. Call me when you have the results."

"Thank you, sir."

"Go home to that lovely new wife of yours, Bob. And thanks for staying up so late."

"Yes, sir."

Before he left, Rider started the computer looking for matches. When he arrived back in a few hours' time the results would be waiting. He secured the file with a password and headed home.

$$\lambda$$

As Viktor explored the generator floor, he heard the distant slam of a door. Brisk footfalls approached. He darted behind a cement column and drew his gun. The newcomer clumped down the metal stairs to the generator floor. Viktor fingered the trigger and cleared his mind to concentrate upon shots to the heart or the head.

As he tensed, ready to jump out from behind the column, the walker suddenly veered away. Footfalls receded down the spiral metal staircase of the access shaft and into the bowels of the powerhouse. Viktor lifted his finger from the trigger, took a deep breath and let it out slowly.

As the metallic footfalls faded, Viktor cautiously poked his head out from behind the column. The vast room was again empty. He was ready to head for the back door and a quick exit when he chanced to look up. And there, suspended sixty feet above, on the parking lot end of the powerhouse, near the ceiling, was a perfect place to hide. A massive bridge crane was parked flush against a catwalk that ran along the west wall; its huge I-beam stretched between two tracks that ran the length of the building. The I-beam shielded most of the catwalk from below. From the high vantage Viktor would have a clear view of the floor and the balcony, and views out the south facing windows to the access road and most of the parking lot.

There was a metal access ladder bolted to the wall. Viktor stuffed the gun into his belt and crossed the powerhouse floor. He took off his shoes, knotted the laces together, and draped them around his neck so he could quietly climb.

By the time he reached the top Viktor was giddy. He stepped onto the safety of the catwalk and took several hurried breaths, heart pounding, bright red patches on his palms where he'd tightly gripped the metal rungs. He wasn't afraid of heights. But he wasn't overly fond of them, either.

Three minutes passed before the man came back up the stairwell. He paused for a moment on the main floor, standing beside one of the generators. From the darkness of the catwalk, Viktor peered over the I-beam and saw a middle aged man in coveralls and leather boots. Was this the operator Fiona had described who ran the powerhouse?

The man headed toward a metal staircase fixed to the wall beneath the I-beam and climbed to the second floor. After a few seconds Viktor heard the front door open and then slam shut. He turned and looked out a window and saw the operator emerge into the parking lot and trot across the asphalt and climb into the Chevy. The brake lights flared and the car sped up the access road.

Viktor climbed back down to the powerhouse floor, thinking he was now alone in the building. But as he explored rooms along a lower hallway he discovered a woman, hands and feet bound, with her mouth taped, alive but unconscious. There was a gash and dried blood in her hair. His first impulse was to free her. But there was no compelling reason to make her his problem. He was curious. But he moved on.

Viktor next located over two dozen pipe segments that met the archive specifications for gold bearers. It was too many. He needed the templates.

He was standing near the back of the powerhouse generator floor, considering what else he might accomplish before he left, when he heard the front door open. There was no time to return to the safety of the catwalk, or even exit through the back door. He crouched behind a huge wooden spool wrapped with electrical cable and peered cautiously over the spool's edge up at the balcony.

The operator, together with a second man, appeared from the direction of the entry and walked a short distance along the balcony. The operator held a gun on the new man, but that was lost to Viktor's attention. What the operator pulled from the manila envelope now caught—and kept—Viktor's interest.

Those must be the templates Fiona described in her email!

The operator slid the templates back into the envelope and gave one sharp command to the other, after which the two exited through the side hallway that led to the stairs and the room holding the woman.

Did the woman and newcomer have something to do with the templates? Did the man who worked here know about the gold? Why else would he have kidnapped them both? It occurred to Viktor that the injured woman might be the same Holly Curtis who was named in the flowery love letters he'd found in the roll top.

When Viktor heard a door bang shut he dashed across the generator floor and climbed back up to the bridge crane. At last he had a workable plan. He would let the operator disassemble the pipes and extract the gold. That way there would be no risk of being discovered, and when the operator finished the hard work, Viktor would come down, claim the prize, and tidy up the loose ends.

⋏

As the trunk of the Chevy popped open Jerry saw the brickwork looming beside the parking area and knew where he was.

"Move," Frank said, waving the gun in Jerry's face as he climbed from the trunk. Frank clutched the manila envelope in his left hand.

Jerry stretched out his leg cramps as he obeyed the motion of Frank's gun. They walked together up the steps to the powerhouse door.

"Here," Frank said, tossing Jerry a key. "Open it. And don't try anything tricky. I'll use this gun if I have to."

Jerry slid the key into the lock. It twisted smoothly and he heard the mechanism of the bolt slide back. He pulled out the key and turned the steel knob, pushing the heavy door open.

The arched hallway was lit by bulbs set in wire cages evenly spaced along the walls. For a moment Jerry weighed the possibility of sprinting down the hallway. Frank might miss, or perhaps choose not to shoot at all. Frank seemed to read his thoughts.

"Okay," Frank said. "Let's not do anything dumb."

Jerry again regretted not having made his move outside the Belvedere.

"Hold up for a minute," Frank said once they were inside. "Toss me that key."

Jerry turned and lobbed the key underhand to Frank, who caught it and slipped it into his coveralls pocket. Without ever taking his eyes off Jerry, Frank pushed the door shut and twisted the latch so that it was locked.

"Down the hall," Frank ordered.

They reached a short stretch of balcony above the main floor. A double brass railing ran along the edge. "Hold up a moment," Frank said, holding the gun on Jerry while he fumbled to pull the templates from the envelope.

Is this the time? But where would he run? Back down the hallway to the locked front door? Further down the hallway into the powerhouse? Either way, Frank would find him an easy target. And if Frank emptied the revolver into his body, Jerry would bleed out long before anyone showed up the next day. There was only one hope left. If Frank found the gold, maybe he would settle for leaving Jerry tied up as he made his escape. Someone would come to investigate after Frank disconnected pipes and caused the system to shut down. Whether Jerry was dead or alive, they would know the culprit when Frank was nowhere to be found. Jerry could reason with Frank on this. And even if Frank didn't find gold there was still a chance to talk him out of taking Jerry's life. If he cooperated, it might sway Frank to spare him. So Jerry waited, and hoped.

Frank held the templates and briefly eyed the pipes running along the powerhouse floor, smiled. He refolded and pushed the templates back into the envelope and glanced down the side hallway that led back into the building. "In," Frank commanded. Jerry obeyed.

At the far end they came to a set of stairs. "Down," Frank said. When they got to the bottom Frank directed Jerry through yet another hallway. They passed three doors. At the fourth door Frank said, "Stop. Open it, and hit the light switch just inside to the left." Jerry went in and flicked the switch.

There were racks holding a variety of large wrenches; several pieces of electrical testing equipment lay on a bench. Holly Curtis, bound and gagged, lay in one corner. Her eyes were shut. Dried blood stained her white blouse and crusted in her hair. And now Jerry's hope for reasoning with Frank seemed more of a fantasy than a possibility.

"I'm going to tie you up while I check out these templates," Frank said, the gun pointed at Jerry's chest. "Get down on your stomach. Nice and easy."

Jerry got down as ordered, his left cheek pressed to the concrete. He put his hands behind his back. Frank looped a length of nylon rope around his wrists and pulled it so tight that it began to cut through the skin.

Jerry groaned.

"Sorry about that," Frank said, strangely apologetic. But he didn't loosen the cord. Then he tied Jerry's feet. Finally, he linked the two bonds with a third piece of cord, behind Jerry's back, creating a hobble that kept him from either standing up or working at the knots. Satisfied his captive was going nowhere, Frank stood and walked over to a red metal tool chest, opened the lowest drawer, pulled out a roll of duct tape.

"Got anything to say?" he said with a wicked smile.

Jerry looked over at Holly, bound and gagged, and lost control for a moment.

"For Christ's sake she needs medical attention! She may die if she doesn't get help!"

Frank glared at Jerry. "You pays your money, you takes your chances," he said. It infuriated Jerry.

"And what the hell does that mean?"

Frank seemed amused by the outburst. He began to pull tape from the roll and tore off eight inches. He walked back to Jerry and hunched down in an almost fatherly manner.

"It means," he began slowly, building in intensity and momentum as he spoke, "that she had an opportunity to cooperate, and she blew it. She didn't have your good sense. And if you want to keep all of your teeth, you'll *SHUT THE FUCK UP!*"

Jerry shut up. Frank made sure of his silence by placing the tape across Jerry's mouth practically ear to ear.

Frank stood, stretched, and said, "I've got an inventory of the pipes in the control room. I'm going to compare those with the template numbers. I'll be back." He turned for the door and on his way out flicked off the light switch.

In the dark, Jerry listened to Frank's receding footsteps, and to the soft whistle of Holly breathing through her nose. Beyond those immediate sounds, only the great humming vibration of the massive generators filled the darkness.

人

Denny Nevler stared at the phone on the night stand, regretting that he'd given up smoking. Twice he'd gone into the bathroom, splashed his face with cold water, studied the dark crescents beneath his eyes in the mirror, and returned to his vigil. He now looked away from the phone and began to stare at the wallpaper, losing track of time.

The call finally came. He grabbed the receiver and said, "Denny."

Art Fields' voice whipped back. "I've got Tom here in the office. Hold on while I transfer to the speakerphone."

There was a click, and then he heard Tom's echoing voice.

"Am I coming through okay?"

"Yeah."

"Good," Fields cut in. "Do you have anything new to report?"

"No."

"Okay. Before we get started, there's one additional fact you need to know. We've been waiting for confirmation from Argentina. It finally came four minutes ago."

Denny had no clue what Fields was referring to. Had Dearborn spent time down there? Was that where he was planning to go?

"Tom, would you fill him in?"

"Sure. Denny, you still hearing me okay?"

"Yes. Go ahead."

"Dearborn had money squirreled away in an Argentine bank. We knew of it before Champoton, but no one thought it necessary to deal with. He'd been depositing part of his salary there for years. The account became irrelevant as far as FICO was concerned when he was reported dead. When our staffer was going through his file yesterday, he rediscovered the account's existence. Mr. Fields called an Argentine contact we use for banking matters and learned there was nearly a quarter of a million on deposit."

"Amazing." Denny was impressed by Dearborn's foresight. "What do we do about it?"

"It's already done. We've got a temporary order blocking transfer of the funds. It cost five grand to bribe a judge in Buenos Aires, but now there's no way Dearborn can get his hands on the money."

"Okay."

Fields cut in, impatient.

"Okay, Denny. That brings you up to speed. Tom and I are certain Dearborn will try to make a transfer to some local bank. He might have already set up a wire order. But the money's not going to come in, and when that happens he's going to realize someone knows he's alive."

Tom quickly added, "And when that happens, he'll take off, even without the funds. We've got to keep him from disappearing."

"How?"

Fields answered.

"I'm sending Tom. He'll be in Wenatchee shortly after sunrise. Pick him up at the airport, drive back to Langston, and the two of you will make contact with Dearborn. You're going to convince him to come in, Denny. Tell him there's a jet waiting and that his Argentine account has been blocked."

"What if he doesn't want to come?" Denny imagined the confrontation. Fields' response held not the slightest hint of remorse.

"Tom will be armed."

Denny felt like screaming out how wrong this was. They didn't really expect Dearborn to cooperate, did they? What they really expected was for Tom

Delacorte to impose the ultimate sanction. To remove a potential embarrassment for FICO.

Fields said in a calm and controlling voice, "You with us?"

"Yeah." But his gut was churning. The protest came out even though he knew there was a danger in making it. "He's one of ours—"

"Was," Fields cut him off coldly. "In another life. Now he's a liability, Denny. Understood?"

His shallow words echoed back, "A liability."

"And our job is to neutralize that liability. Are you perfectly clear on this?"

"Perfectly," Denny replied, knowing that *he* would become a liability if he gave any other answer.

Tom tried to sound upbeat as he added, "See you at sunrise." The attempt at levity failed.

"I'll be at the airport."

"Keep it together."

"Yeah, no problem."

Denny hung up, the muscles in his neck bunched and knotted. He tried to work out the kinks, rolling his head to pop the vertebrae. On this particular night he would not sleep. He would not even try.

CHAPTER 39

Pablo stood in the dark behind an evergreen shrub, working up his courage, eyeing the bright red neon: *EMERGENCY ENTRANCE*. It was a frightening place, with the bite of antiseptic whispering through the crack between the automatic doors; a place of polished tile and light blue pastel walls, where he'd once had a cut on his forehead stitched up by a white-jacketed doctor who cast suspicious glances at his mother as she sat patiently in the corner of the small surgery. Shortly, a CPS worker arrived. She was fluent in Spanish and spoke at length with Rosa. Next, it was Pablo's turn to be grilled. And despite Pablo's account of falling off his bike, the social worker remained unconvinced there wasn't some darker reason for his injury. Only after coming to the Belvedere the next day and speaking to one of the other boys who'd witnessed his tumble did she end her inquiry.

Recalling that scary episode, Pablo almost didn't enter. But he knew he had to do something, and going to the police station, especially at night, seemed the worse alternative. With his stomach caught up in his throat, he timidly approached the sliding doors. They swished open. He crossed the rubber mat and walked silently up to the young woman in nurse's whites who sat behind a low counter studying a patient's chart.

"Señora?" he asked in barely a whisper. The woman's head came up. Her light blue eyes softened when she saw the child.

"Well, what have we here?" Her voice was kind but puzzled. She laid down the chart and stood to get a better look. The boy appeared uninjured, and her curiosity grew. Pablo nervously twisted his fingers and struggled for the right words.

"Is there a problem, young man?"

"I need to see someone in the hospital, señora."

"Who?"

"Señor Oscar."

"Do you mean Oscar Danner, the police officer?"

"Yes, señora."

She glanced at her watch. "It's past visiting hours. I'm afraid you'll have to come back in the morning. Mr. Danner is probably asleep by now."

Pablo's words became urgent.

"Please, señora. We have a friend, Mr. Jerry. He may be in great trouble. I must talk to Señor Oscar."

She studied the boy, saw he was trembling, and decided there was no real harm in bothering the sergeant, even if it meant waking him. He could decide whether it warranted calling his office.

"Are you sure you need to see him tonight?" she asked to make certain.

"Yes."

"Let's go and see if he's awake. I'll get someone to cover the desk for me. Wait a minute."

"Yes, señora."

The nurse went into the back and returned with another woman and then beckoned Pablo to follow her down the hallway. When they reached the elevator she asked, "What is your name?"

"Pablo, señora."

She gave a puzzled smile and punched the elevator call button.

They took the elevator to the third floor and found Oscar's room down a hallway that was silent except for the constant bleep of a distant heart monitor. The door was ajar and a dim light shown from within.

She rapped lightly on the door.

"Yes?" came a sleepy voice.

"You wait here," the nurse told Pablo. She pushed the door and entered, half closing it behind her.

From inside, Pablo heard the two adults speaking softly. In a few seconds, she reappeared.

"You can come in now, Pablo."

Swallowing the lump in his throat, he followed her inside.

Pablo was the second surprise of Oscar's evening. Only minutes before, Manny Cruz burst into his room, demanding to know everything about Jerry Wells that Oscar hadn't already revealed. "Someone's life is at stake," Cruz said, nearly hysterical. "So come clean with me Danner, if you don't want to be charged as an accessory."

"An accessory to what?" Oscar said, not really giving a shit about Cruz's threat.

Cruz pointed an accusatory finger at Oscar. "Do you know if Wells is involved in drugs?"

Oscar shook his head in disbelief. "You're kidding, right?"

"I've never been more serious."

"So far as I know, the man is absolutely clean."

"I mean does he deal drugs."

"Trafficking?"

"Yes. Do you think he's involved in trafficking?"

"You're joking, right?" But Oscar could see he was not. "No," he said firmly. "I don't think he is, Manny. It's the most utterly ridiculous thing I've ever heard."

Cruz considered this for a moment, fidgeting. "Are you certain?"

"As certain as I can be. Hell, I can't read minds. But I'd give you long odds."

Cruz settled a bit. "Right," he said, not sounding anywhere near convinced. "Do you have any idea where he is now?"

"As far as I know, he's at the Belvedere, probably in bed."

"What about Frank Brindleman?"

Oscar was finding it impossible to follow Cruz. *What does Brindleman have to do with anything?* "You mean from the powerhouse?"

"Yes."

"You want to know if I know where he is?"

"No." Cruz fumbled to rephrase his question. "What I mean is, do you know of any connection between Brindleman and Wells?"

"No. Should I?"

"If you had your eyes open, you would."

Oscar skipped past being confused and stepped right into being angry.

"What's this about, Manny? Wells . . . Brindleman . . . Is there some connection between them? And by the way, whose life is in danger?"

Cruz turned defensive. "I think there's a big connection, and I'm trying to track it down. As for who's in danger, well, that's confidential for now."

"Who else is working with you on this?"

"That's confidential too."

Oscar settled his head back onto his pillow, staring straight up at the ceiling. With plain disgust he said, "Well, you let me know when everything is no longer confidential."

"Thanks. You've been a real help," Manny turned to leave.

"Don't mention it," Oscar said, equally sarcastic. Manny swished past the privacy curtain and out the door.

Now Pablo was here with fear in his eyes.

"Please sit," Oscar said, patting the bed. Pablo sat. Oscar looked to the nurse and said, "We'll be okay." She left and Oscar said to Pablo, "Now tell me what has happened."

"After you called I went to my bedroom, and I looked out the window and there was a man in a car and as Jerry walked by the man got out and he had a gun. And then he and Jerry came back inside the apartments. I wanted to go and see what was wrong but I was afraid. So I watched out the window and soon the man and Jerry came back out and he made Jerry get into the trunk of his car and then they drove off." Pablo was near tears. "Something bad has happened to Jerry. Somebody has to help him. Please!"

"What did the car look like?"

"It was an older American car with four doors and it was blue."

"And the man?"

"He was maybe Jerry's age. He had on work clothes like the men at the tire store."

"You didn't recognize him?"

"No."

But Oscar thought he recognized who it was, particularly in light of Manny's visit just a few minutes ago. *Frank Brindleman*. But what possible reason could he have for abducting Jerry? Was Cruz right? Was Jerry involved in a drug running operation? But Oscar couldn't justify that conclusion, it simply didn't square up with the Jerry he knew.

He began to consider what role Brindleman might have in all of this. He barely knew the man, having met him only when the sheriff's staff made their annual walkthroughs of the powerhouse. He remembered the fellow as being withdrawn, a bit downtrodden. He was practically a fixture at the PUD, having worked at the powerhouse for years. And that made him an unlikely candidate for drug dealing. But who knew for certain?

Pablo stood quietly and respectfully beside the bed as Oscar mulled things over. Finally the boy broke the silence.

"Señor?"

"Yes, son?"

"What do we do?"

Yes. What do we do? If what the boy said was true, and he had no reason to doubt it, then Jerry was in trouble. But what brought Brindleman to the desperate act of kidnapping? What possible reason could he have? And what was Manny Cruz up to? Was he now down at the powerhouse trying to find Frank and Jerry? Was there some other location they might all be at that Cruz hadn't shared during his brief and explosive visit?

Oscar considered his own physical condition. The angina was gone, relieved by drugs. He was weak, but capable of leaving the hospital. He could give the excuse that he wanted to make sure the boy got home safely. His pickup was at the house, but he could order a cab. Oscar looked to the boy, his face flush with concern. A seemingly random thought surprised him. *He's the kind of kid I'd have hoped for from the girl in the yellow dress.* It made up his mind.

"Do you want to help me find Jerry?"

"Oh yes!"

"Then let's go see if we can figure out what has happened. And if we do, then we'll call the police station."

Pablo's face shone with gratitude. "Thank you, señor!"

"It's okay, Pablo. Now, would you please look in the closet and see if they've left me my clothes?"

Oscar swung his feet over the edge of the bed. He was dressed only in the hospital robe.

"They are here," Pablo said, returning with pants, socks and shoes, and a puzzled look. "There is no shirt, señor."

Oscar realized they must have torn it off at the lodge to apply the defibrillator paddles. "Oh well," he sighed, slipping into pants and pulling on his socks and shoes. He stuffed the loose robe into his pants. When he finished he looked down at himself with satisfaction and chuckled. "It's not the height of fashion, but it'll have to do for now." He reached out and put a soft hand on the boy's shoulder. "C'mon, son. Let's get a move on and figure out what's happened to our Jerry."

CHAPTER 40

Manny's Glock was holstered on his right hip as he climbed the front steps of the Belvedere. For a second he considered waking the manager, but decided instead to go directly upstairs.

When he reached the third floor, he pressed his ear to the apartment door and heard nothing. He pulled the Glock, slowly turned the knob and found the door unlocked. With an adrenaline rush, Manny drove his shoulder against the faded wood, the door flying open.

"Police! Freeze!" He held the Glock with a finger on the trigger but there was no one to point it at. Manny straightened, alert and with the Glock still held forward as he entered the bedroom, finding it too was vacant.

He holstered his gun as fear faded into embarrassment.

Doors began to open and cautious voices sounded in the hallway. He ignored them for a moment, switching on the lamp in the bedroom. He found nothing of interest and returned to the living area, turned on the ceiling light and made a quick search for weapons or drugs. With no search warrant in hand, anything he found would be excluded as evidence in a trial, but he didn't give a damn about procedural niceties. Holly's welfare was all that mattered.

He found nothing of interest except for camping gear piled up against the wall.

He's getting ready to leave.

The hallway voices grew louder and less nervous, more curious and even put out at the disturbance. Manny switched off the apartment light. Several people stood near their doorways and stared at him as he emerged.

An elderly man with wispy white hair and black-rimmed spectacles asked in a bewildered voice, "What's happening, officer?"

"Have you seen the man who lives in this apartment?" Manny demanded.

Puzzlement was replaced by fear.

"No. Is he in trouble?"

"Maybe." Manny now addressed them all. "He goes by the name of Jerry Wells."

Everyone except a teenager with a punk haircut shook their heads. The kid volunteered, "I saw him downstairs earlier this evening. Is he wanted for something?"

A glimmer of hope. "We just want to question him," Manny said reassuringly. "Do you have any idea where he might be?"

"No."

Manny's frustration surged as he glared at the curious faces. "Doesn't anyone know where Wells might be?"

All heads shook in the negative.

A young man wearing only a crew neck shirt and cutoffs spoke quietly to the girl beside him. She nodded in agreement and they disappeared behind a door that was solidly closed and with the immediate sound of a lock being turned. A middle-aged woman in a floral print robe also disappeared behind her apartment's door. One old man wearing a scarlet smoking jacket and sandals, the punk, and a Hispanic teenager wearing jeans and tennis shoes gawked at Manny. He gave up and addressed the three.

"Okay, go back to bed. I'm sorry I disturbed you."

He took the stairs two steps at a time, sprinted to his Mustang, and sped up the strip, through Turner's Notch, down the twisting road to Highway 97. He only slowed when he reached the powerhouse turnoff.

Halfway up the narrow paved lane he switched off his headlights, concentrating on the thin band of asphalt in the moonlight. As he approached the powerhouse, he saw Frank's blue Chevy in the lot. He pulled over and turned off the engine and grabbed a heavy flashlight and his shotgun.

When he reached the Chevy he laid his palm flat on the hood and found it was warm.

Manny circled around the powerhouse, hoping for the advantage of surprise. When he found the access door, he twisted the knob. It was unlocked. He pushed and the hinges squealed. He froze, expecting someone to come running. After a minute no one appeared, so Manny slowly eased the door wide enough to slip inside, shotgun ready, his back against the wall. He scanned the big hall top to bottom, side to side, saw no movement and felt encouraged. With the shotgun held forward and ready to fire, Manny crept towards the control room.

$$\curlywedge$$

From his perch high above the powerhouse floor Viktor saw the approaching headlights. Halfway up the access road they went dark. In the scant light thrown by the powerhouse parking lot lamps he saw the dark outline of the Mustang as it edged to a stop. A lone figure exited. He watched the man approach the building until he lost sight of him when the wall cut off his angle of view.

The operator now appeared at the top of the metal steps of the access shaft. He was winded and paused to catch his breath. Appearing agitated, he glancing around as if ready to take a swing at anything within reach. There were only metal and concrete nearby, and he seemed even more frustrated at not having a convenient target. The templates were in his left hand.

Viktor saw him stiffen and look across the main floor toward the eastern wall. Following the operator's gaze, Viktor saw the same back door through which he had entered open just a crack. He heard the hinges; it was easy to imagine the operator heard the same nasty squeal.

Shortly, a man wearing a camouflage vest over a police uniform stepped cautiously through the door, moving with his back against the wall. He held a pistol grip shotgun, which he swung in an arc as he scanned the room. On the other side of the generator floor, Viktor saw the operator creeping toward a hallway, shielded from the policeman's view by one of the generators.

Viktor settled back, his plan for taking the gold from the operator in jeopardy. But at least he was safe. There was now really only one option. Viktor settled in for the outcome of what was shaping up to be a death circus below.

⅄

After he'd gotten the templates from Wells, the rest of the night's work should have been simple. But as Frank compared the penciled numbers on the templates to his list of numbers there was only one match. It was for the pipe he damaged all those years ago; the same pipe Sidel had removed the gold from.

I must have made a mistake! I wrote the numbers down wrong!

Frank went back through the main floor and then each tunnel and shaft, comparing his list to the raised numbers on each pipe. But after he checked every pipe he realized that he'd written them down correctly.

Another thought occurred. *Wells changed the numbers. He erased the originals and penciled in new ones. Clever bastard!*

As he climbed back up to the main floor, intent on confronting Wells and—if necessary—beating the truth out of him, he heard the telltale squeal of the back door being pushed open.

⅄

Jerry's left thigh had cramped and he was trying to relax and make the cramp go away when the door to the tool room opened. Jerry hoped it might be a rescuer, but it was Frank Brindleman who stood silhouetted in the doorway. He came in and drew the door softly shut. He flipped the light switch, forcing Jerry's eyes to accommodate to the sudden brightness. By the time he was able to see without squinting, Frank had crouched down beside Holly and pressed his fingers against her neck, checking for a pulse.

"Still alive," he whispered. He put one index finger to his lips to signal silence, walked to where Jerry sat with his back against the wall, knees drawn up by the hobble cord, and reached down and stripped the tape from Jerry's mouth.

"Shit," Jerry said, as tears formed.

"Shush up now," Frank said, as he hunkered down, holding the templates in one hand, revolver in the other. Frank pushed the muzzle to Jerry's temple. Jerry flinched as the steel dimpled his skin.

"Speak very quietly and only when you're spoken to, or I'll redecorate the wall with your brains. Okay?"

"Okay," Jerry muttered back.

"Good." Frank tucked the gun into his belt and sat down. He slid his left hand behind Jerry's neck, resting it lightly on his shoulder, as if they were the best of buddies. He held up the templates with his right hand, just inches from Jerry's face.

"See these?"

Jerry nodded.

"They each have a little number, don't they?"

Again, Jerry nodded.

"Did you change any of them?"

"No. Why would I?"

Frank's response was to say, "Shhhhh" to reinforce the need to be quite, and at the same time grab a handful of Jerry's neck and squeeze harder than Jerry would have thought possible. After a few seconds of enjoying Jerry's silent reaction to the pain, Frank relaxed his grip, his eyes gone wild.

"You wouldn't be lying, would you?"

Jerry took several deep breaths, fighting for calm, feeling the burning ache of bruised flesh. "No," he said. "Why would I?"

"Oh," came Frank's acid reply. "Perhaps you wanted to hide the location of the gold. That would be my guess." He paused, as if reconsidering this conclusion. Then, "Yes indeed. That's what I'm thinking. You wanted to keep the location your own little secret." He leaned over, inches from Jerry's face. "C'mon, ol' buddy. The truth."

Jerry stared back. "I did not change the numbers, Frank. For God's sake, you can see that for yourself. Check them. Erasers leave marks. Those are the same numbers that have always been there. Besides, like you said back at the

Belvedere, I didn't know what the templates were for until you told me. So what reason would I have for changing the numbers?"

Frank took his arm from around Jerry's neck. He carefully held each template, studying them one at a time, looking for smudges or broken fibers. As he finished scrutinizing the first template Frank grew sullen. After he scrutinized the second his face hardened. When he finished looking at the third, he laid it atop the others on the concrete and stared at the far wall, eyes glistening with the pain of a man beaten down by life again and again until he has finally reaching the end of all hope. "It isn't fair," he said. "It's my gold, and it isn't fair."

Is this God's way of punishing me for Champoton? Jerry glanced at Holly and was surprised to see her eyelids had opened just a tiny slit. It was hard to tell whether she was aware of her surroundings, or simply drawn to the sound of Frank's blubbering. As Frank's self pitying lament trailed off, Holly's eyes slowly closed. There had been no acknowledgment she was aware.

Frank gazed across the room, confused, lost. There was maybe one last chance to reason with him.

"Frank," Jerry began cautiously. "Maybe I can do something for you."

Frank looked at him, almost with pity. Not a good sign. "What could you possibly do?"

"You need help, Frank. A good lawyer could give you that help. You're a veteran. A court would have sympathy. My testimony might convince a judge to enter orders to make that happen."

There was a short bark of laughter. "Help?" Frank snorted, and he laughed again, totally amused. "You're the one who needs help, so let me clue you in. When that Mexican cop told me a transient found the museum bitch's body I thought it was terrific luck. I had someone to pin Fiona's murder on. And when I recognized you up at the station, it was like some kind of magical gift! I could volunteer a bit of personal history about the 'cold blooded killer' I knew from Vietnam. So here's how you're going to help me. I'm going to make it look like you kidnapped Holly." Frank swept his hand in a broad arc, as if he were talking to Kiwanis or Rotary as the program speaker. *"I recognized how dangerous the man was when I saw him from behind the glass. I was scared, knowing he was a professional killer, but still determined to find a way to ensure that justice was done. Unfortunately, I came along too late, discovering he had executed Holly to cover up his earlier killing of Fiona. I shot him to save my own skin, and to avenge the death of the two women."* Frank's eyes shone with joy. "Sounds great, doesn't it! And what're the police going to do? Question the story of a decorated veteran? Hell, with any luck I'll get a nice piece in the Herald: *Vietnam Vet Saves Taxpayers the Burden of a Trial!"* Frank's booming laughter filled the room. "So I'd say it's definitely you who needs the help, *good buddy!"* And with that final pronouncement he walked to the door and whispered, "Nighty-night," before flipping off the lights, opening the door, and closing it with a gentle finality.

The third-floor duty nurse protested when Oscar told her he was going out.

"Your doctor hasn't approved this!"

He considered telling her the doctor said it would be okay to take a walk if he felt up to it. But it wouldn't say that in his chart. And she would doubtless make a phone call to confirm her suspicion that Oscar was lying.

"True," he said. "But—"

"No 'buts'," she said sharply, walking out from behind the nursing station counter. "You're fortunate to be alive, sergeant. Let's not press your luck." She gently took him by the arm, but Oscar firmly removed her hand.

"It's like this," he said. "The boy's mother will be upset if I send him home alone, on foot. So I'm going to take him back by cab. After I've gotten him safely home, I promise to return."

The nurse scowled. "We should call your doctor first."

"Even if you do, I'm still going to take Pablo home."

She pointed to his hospital gown, tucked in like a shirt.

"Look at you. You're not even properly dressed."

"I'll be perfectly fine. It's still warm outside. The boy and I are leaving." He looked down at Pablo who stood by his side. "Come on, son. Let's get you home before your mother finds out you're gone."

Together they walked away from the nurse, now flustered beyond words. At the elevator, halfway down the hallway, Oscar looked back and saw her behind the counter, punching numbers on the phone.

When they entered the elevator Oscar turned to Pablo and said, "I lied to the nurse. But my little fib doesn't make lying okay, does it?" He smiled.

"No, Señor Oscar," Pablo said, with a complicit smile.

Oscar used the courtesy phone in the waiting room to call for a cab. Within a few minutes an apple green station wagon with *Lone Pine Cabs* in black lettering on the side eased into the emergency entrance. Oscar grinned at the boy who stood resolutely at his side.

"Let's get out of here."

Pablo grinned back, and Oscar realized what an adventure this must be for him.

The cabbie delivered them to Oscar's house, and it was here that Oscar turned to Pablo and said in a patient voice, "I know you want to help me, Pablo. But this may be dangerous and it's no place for a boy to be involved. So I'm going to drive you home after I've gotten some things from the house."

"But I want to help!"

"I know. But if I put you in danger your mother would never forgive me. And neither would Jerry."

"But what if you need me? You are just out of the hospital."

Pablo was right, but it didn't change Oscar's decision. And his earlier admonition to Pablo about telling the truth didn't keep him from telling another lie.

"Pablo, they gave me some special medicine this afternoon that will keep my heart okay. I promise."

Pablo didn't believe it. Not one bit. But he knew he couldn't change the big cop's mind. Pablo looked down at the ground, dejected. "Okay," he finally conceded. "But you don't have to drive me home. It's only a few blocks. I can walk. That way you'll have more time to go help Jerry."

Oscar held out his hand. Pablo stared at it for a moment not knowing what it meant.

"We'll shake on it," Oscar said. "Like men."

Pablo slowly reached with his hand and took Oscar's huge paw and they shook.

"Now I've got to get a few things from inside my house," Oscar said.

Pablo was too proud to even speak. That a policeman would want to shake hands with him! "Good luck, Señor Oscar." Pablo turned and began to walk up the street.

Oscar would have liked to watch until the boy turned onto the street that led to the Belvedere, but his sense of urgency was growing, so after a few seconds he turned for his front door.

After exchanging the gown for a long-sleeved shirt, Oscar got his service pistol from the gun cabinet. He eyed the pistol grip twelve-gauge, reached up and pulled it from the rack, and from the narrow shelf below grabbed a box of buckshot. Nothing was better in close quarters than a short shotgun. It had instant stopping power; even better than a pistol with magnums. He grabbed the spare ignition key from the nail by the refrigerator and headed for the pickup.

It was just a hunch Frank had taken Jerry to the powerhouse, but as Oscar drove through Langston he felt certain that's where they were.

His confidence continued to build as he made the turn onto the powerhouse road. Then, near the end, he came upon Manny's Mustang in the dark. He pulled alongside the convertible, shut off the pickup's engine and turned off the headlights. He stared at the Mustang

"Something's very wrong here," he muttered, looking at the pistol grip shotgun for reassurance. If he'd been in a patrol car Oscar would have used the radio to request assistance. If he'd been on duty he would have a handheld unit. Oscar now regretted the day he'd convinced himself a cell phone was an unnecessary luxury. Then he remembered the emergency call box, just south of the turnoff, where Jerry called nine-one-one to report finding Fiona's body. It wouldn't take more than a minute to reach it in the pickup.

Oscar reached for the key and then heard the crack of gunshots from inside the powerhouse.

No time for that now!

He reached for the shotgun on the seat and then for the box of shells but in the darkness he fumbled and spilled them across the seat and onto the floor. *I have no time for this!* He grabbed a shell from the seat and pushed it into the chamber. He scooped up four more shells and stuffed them into his breast pocket. The Glock in his holster already held a full clip.

Jogging the hundred yards to the powerhouse got him winded and his heart was pounding, but without sharp pain. *At least not yet.* Approaching the building he heard several more shots from inside.

He climbed the steps, hesitated a moment, tried the handle. The door wouldn't budge. There was still no pain around his heart, but it was pounding hard and running around the building in search of another entrance would only make it worse. Oscar reached into his pocket and withdrew two shells and shoved them into the shotgun, stepped back, aimed at the lock. At point blank range, three loads of buckshot disintegrated the door casement around the lock plate.

He reached for the handle and it turned easily, but the door still resisted. He leaned his right shoulder into the door and it broke free, plunging Oscar into the entry hallway.

CHAPTER 41

Jerry knelt in the darkness, struggling to untie the nylon rope. The slippery cord was knotted tight and the hobble kept the knots behind his back. With his wrists tied in a cross he could only use one hand at a time. After several frustrating minutes of failing to work the knots loose by pulling and tugging and stretching, he paused and searched for another way.

When Frank had been in the room with the lights on, Jerry saw tin snips hung on a wall peg, impossibly out of reach for someone trussed as he was. The red tool box against the far wall held the only promise. About the size of a laundry hamper, it might contain something useful. Each of its four drawers had an inset lock, but he wondered if anyone would bother to keep them secured in what was already a secure place. He rolled onto his side and began to inch across the oily concrete.

When one knee bumped into the chest Jerry rolled onto his rear and backed up to it. Curling his fingers under the lowest drawer handle he gave a tug. His fingers slid off the greasy steel. On the next attempt he managed a good jerk and the drawer flew open with a promising rattle.

He rocked into a folded crouch until he could feel inside the drawer, fumbling through the contents, picturing what he felt. A wire bristle brush, a steel chisel with a dull blade, a whetstone, a roll of lead solder, vice grips, pencil stubs, bolts and nuts. Nothing sharp.

Jerry relaxed onto the concrete for a moment before again backing up against the chest, pushing the first drawer shut, and reaching for the second drawer. Four times he gave it a tug but it refused to budge.

The third drawer was also locked.

The top drawer proved impossible to reach; the hobble cord prevented him from stretching far enough off the ground. He considered trying to tip the chest over. But if the drawers were locked they were unlikely to open in a fall. And even if he succeeded, the racket might draw Frank's attention.

Then he remembered the chisel and whetstone inside the lowest drawer. If he could position the chisel over the hobble cord, then pound it with the whetstone, maybe he could crush and weaken the rope enough to be able to break free.

He reopened the drawer. It took what seemed like forever to fish out the chisel and whetstone and drop them onto the concrete. He grabbed one in each hand and realized how ridiculous the idea was. His bound hands moved together. There was no way to bring the whetstone down on the end of the chisel with any kind of force.

Only one option remained and it was maddeningly slow. He twisted one wrist so that the tether cord lay against the concrete; holding the chisel with his other hand he began to shove the dull blade against the tough nylon fibers. Most of the time it slid harmlessly off. He kept at it, refusing to worry about Frank's reaction if he returned. It was now clear that Frank meant to kill both him and Holly.

With excruciating slowness, the cord finally began to fray.

⅄

Pablo lay hidden inside the canopy of Oscar's pickup, listening to the big cop drop the shells and swear. He wanted to push down the back gate and climb out and run around to help Oscar, but he knew Oscar would be angry, and would insist on taking him away from the danger. This would slow Oscar from going to Jerry's rescue.

Climbing inside the canopy had been reckless. He now saw it for what it was: the unwise choice of an inexperienced boy who wanted to make a difference. If he could take it back he would. But that was impossible. He heard

Oscar's footfalls fading fast as he ran up the road, and a new fear crept in. *What if the bad guy comes to the pickup?*

As Pablo sat in the dark he heard three enormous booms in the distance. *What happened?*

Pablo carefully unlatched the pickup's gate and slowly lowered it. He sat on the gate for a moment before pushing off onto the pavement, looking around to discover that he was just a hundred yards from the powerhouse. He recognized the area from when his mother brought him to the nearby park where he and his friends liked to swim; the small park with its crescent of sand and two barbeque pits was almost like a private beach for Hispanics.

Pablo walked around to the driver's door, opened it and looked inside. In the dim cab light he saw the scatter of shotgun shells on the seat and all over the floor. And he saw something else. Mounted on the rack above the rear window was Oscar's old shotgun.

Pablo stepped onto the pickup running board, climbed into the cab, reached up and lifted the shotgun down. It was heavier than his mom's, and instead of a plastic stock like the one at the apartment, this shotgun had a smooth wood stock.

Pablo looked at the shells lying on the seat. He picked one up, broke open the barrel and inserted the casing in the top chamber. He grabbed another shell, his gut turning a somersault as he slid the second casing home. He closed the barrel and cradled the shotgun across his knees, half-trying to convince himself it was only for protection.

And then a sudden *pop pop pop* followed by *boom boom* came from the powerhouse. He waited for Oscar to run out. Another flurry of shots, and Pablo was certain Oscar was in trouble. The first police officer ever to treat him nice was being ambushed. Pablo thought of the times he had visited the rifle range with his mother, and how proud she had been when he began to hit the target; she was even prouder when he hit nothing but the target.

Pablo stretched his legs to the running board and stepped out onto the narrow band of asphalt, looked around to make certain he was alone, then walked with determination toward the building, holding the shotgun pointed toward the concrete steps that led up to the powerhouse door.

⅄

Manny waited after the door hinges squealed, just to make certain no one came. Now he headed for the metal staircase beneath the I-beam crane. He knew of only two escape routes: the door he'd come in, and the main entry on the opposite end of the building. He paused to visualize a quick exit through either one.

The plan was simple. He would climb to the second floor and go to the control room. If he found no one there, he would search the rest of the building. If he found Frank or Jerry, he'd shoot if necessary. Otherwise, he'd arrest them and learn where Holly was.

By the time Manny reached the staircase, Frank had returned from the tool room by circling through a back hallway and out onto the far end of the lower floor. When Manny reached the top of the steps, Frank crept silently into position behind a cement column.

"VC in the tunnel, Private!"

"Yes, sir! I see them."

Frank took aim and fired three quick shots.

When the bullets zinged off the railing, Manny lunged up the last two steps and flattened himself onto the balcony. The narrow cover wouldn't last for long. As soon as the shooter moved for a better angle the six-foot-wide balcony would become useless.

Manny held up his pistol and fired several times in the direction the shots had come from. Return fire chipped the wall inches above his head.

Manny edged away from the shooter. His plan wasn't going to work. *Stupid of me to do this! Stupid! Get up and run for the front door and hope like hell he misses!*

And then the boom of a shotgun came from the direction of the front door. Thump!

Who?

Slam!

And suddenly there was a distant rectangle of light as the door was flung wide. Manny caught a glimpse of the newcomer tumbling to the floor.

Was this a showdown between rival drug gangs? He would be an easy pick on the balcony, from either direction, totally exposed.

Desperate to find cover, Manny stood and sprinted along the balcony away from the front door. The man from below opened up with a new volley as Manny ran. With bullets flying and chips of cement exploding off the wall to his left, Manny dove for safety of the first side hallway he came to.

⅄

Gunfire erupted as Jerry pressed the chisel against the last few strands of the tether cord. He dropped the chisel and strained with his legs to stretch the rope. As the nylon finally parted, another volley echoed outside, accompanied by the *zing* and *ping* of bullets ricocheting off metal and brick.

He slipped his bound wrists under his feet and with his hands finally in front tore with his teeth at the square knots but they refused to unravel. It was taking too long. He stood in the darkness and with small and careful hops he crossed the room until he bumped into the wall. Once he found the door he groped for the light switch. He flicked it and light flooded the room.

In seconds his eyes adjusted and he saw the pair of shears on the wall. He reached up and grabbed them. They were made for metal and lacked a sharp cutting edge so it took several seconds of scissoring the cord until it parted. His hands flew apart.

Once his feet were free he looked across the room to where Holly was lying in the corner, still breathing, still alive. Jerry went over, checked her pulse and found it strong. He untied her hands and feet; Holly stirred lightly as her bonds were released but her eyes remained shut. It would have to do for now. Jerry would come back later . . . if there *was* a later.

He edged the door open and peered out. The long hallway was empty.

More shots rang out. He stepped out and closed the door softly behind. With cautious steps he reached the end of the hallway and began to climb the staircase Frank had earlier led him down, ready to scramble back down if Frank appeared.

There was a pause in the gunfire when he reached the top of the stairs. He looked down the empty upper hallway, wondering if the shooting was finished, just as new shots came echoing.

Up ahead, just before where the hallway ended at the balcony, the control room door stood open. When he reached the door he peeked around the jamb and saw no one inside so he stepped in and closed the door. There was a floor-to-ceiling deadbolt; he rammed it home.

As he reached for the telephone on the main console, something caught his eye—the templates lay at the far end of the console.

He put the handset to his ear. There was no dial tone.

Damnit! What's it take to get a fair break!

He turned to the windows looking out onto the parking lot and saw someone walking up the access road holding a full sized gun. Jerry realized the small figure was Pablo.

How?

The kid was an easy target under the bright yard lights. Jerry raised a fist to bust out a window so he could shout a warning. But he realized this was likely to alert Frank.

Pablo reached the Chevy and paused, looking around as if uncertain.

There seemed to be nothing he could do to help the boy. Then Jerry remembered where he was. He turned from the windows to the master console. The switches and knobs were labeled with small plaques—black letters on white plastic.

FERRY TERMINAL. DECHUTES MAIN. ALTERNATE CHELAN.

Transmission lines. He abandoned the console and moved across to the breaker boxes on the wall. He pulled open the cover on the first.

Entry Lights. Gantry Lights. Yard Lights!

Yes!

He slapped the switch for *Yard Lights* and the parking lot plunged into darkness.

人

For Frank Brindleman the powerhouse had faded away. He was back in Vietnam *in country.* His unit was ferreting out a tunnel system the Vietcong were using to stage raids. Down his team descended into the labyrinth of dirt tunnels, living quarters and meeting rooms. And finally, Frank pinned his first target.

"I'll get him, Sarge!"

Blam, blam, blam.

"You missed him, Private. Try again."

"Right."

But then a burst of fire came from a new direction.

"Look out, Private! There's a new VC coming after you!"

"Right, Sarge!"

Pretty soon there'd be a whole platoon of North Vietnamese. Time to leave. Frank moved back from the—

> *dirt*

column, toward the wall, where a ladder—

> *bamboo*

led to a—

> *trapdoor*

that opened at the main entrance. He would come out behind the new enemy soldier. And then he could exit straight into the—

> *jungle*

without being seen.

⅄

Holly awoke as she felt the ropes being untied. Her first instinct was to scream. She kept her eyes closed. If it was Frank Brindleman there was no telling what would happen next. Holly prayed it wasn't Frank. If it was Frank, she expected rape or death. More probably death, as Frank had yet to molest her. But whoever was untying her said nothing and did nothing improper. If it was law enforcement Holly would have expected at least, "Hello" or "Miss, are you awake?"

Who?

After she heard the door close, Holly opened her eyes. She was alone. Her head hurt like hell, but at least her thoughts were coming more clearly. Somewhere off in another part of the powerhouse she heard gunfire.

Must get out of here!

Her entire body was bruised and sore, but as Holly sat up nothing felt broken. She now began to slowly peel the tape from her mouth and wanted to yell as it finally came free. With tears in her eyes she balled it up and tossed it aside and slowly, carefully, she stood, leaning against the wall for support. There was more gunfire and the urge to escape was overwhelming.

Holly sway-stepped across the room, still woozy from Frank's head blow in the Chevy. Reaching the door she twisted the knob and pushed the door open, at first a crack. When she saw no one in the hallway she pushed it wide.

More gunfire came from the right, so she turned left and moved towards the back of the building. She turned left down the last hallway and found an access door that opened onto a short run of concrete steps into a narrow alleyway that ran along the back of the powerhouse. She saw only two large dumpsters. Holding the handrail she eased down the short flight and walked to the end of the building where she came upon the edge of a parking lot.

As Holly cleared the end of the building and came into the lot the first thing she saw was a young boy with a shotgun. Then the lights in the parking lot went out and plunged everything into the darkness of a half-moon night.

As Holly approached the boy he raised the shotgun and pointed it at her. Holly held up her hands to show she was unarmed and the boy lowered the barrel. As Holly walked up he seemed uncertain.

"Is it loaded?" Holly asked.

"Yes," the boy answered. "It is Señor Oscar's. He is inside."

Holly held her hands out. "Let me," he said. The boy handed the weapon over.

"Now you go away from here. Run to some place safe."

Pablo wasn't certain what to do, but running away did seem like a good idea. Still . . .

Holly ran her right hand along the length of the weapon. When she was a teenager she had hunted birds with her father. Holly recognized it as an old fashioned over-under Remington.

The boy was still standing beside her in the dark. She was about to tell him again that he should run away to a safe place, when a man charged through the open door of the powerhouse and slid to a stop at the top of the steps. At first Holly was unsure who it was. Then the man raised a pistol and shouted,

"Sir! There's enemy out here—"

Before Frank Brindleman could finish his psychotically crazed report to an imaginary sergeant, Holly raised the shotgun and fired both barrels from twenty feet away directly into Frank's chest.

Frank Brindleman tumbled down the steps, finally at peace.

⅄

Viktor was still crouched behind the I-beam when two shotgun blasts sounded outside. He turned to look out the windows, but the lot was now lit only by weak moonlight and his eyes were adjusted to the interior lights. Had he been able, he would have seen Holly holding the shotgun as she collapsed onto the ground.

Viktor waited for more gunfire, but as time passed it seemed to be over. Finally, someone down on the main floor hollered out, "Manny!" The Hispanic cop he'd seen earlier hollered back, "Oscar?" And then, "It was Brindleman, Manny. I think he's got Jerry and Holly tied up somewhere here in the building." And then a new voice, "Oscar, Manny, this is Jerry! I'm free but Holly's still in the tool room!"

Viktor watched the men emerge from their hiding places and gather together on the balcony. A young boy ran in, shouting, "The lady is hurt!" They all ran towards the main entry.

Viktor was about to head for the access ladder when the man who had earlier been under the operator's gunpoint came running along the balcony and turned down the side hallway. Shortly, the sodium lights in the parking lot began to flicker back on. When he re-emerged he held the manila envelope containing the templates. The man walked back towards the main door as Viktor once more cursed his bad luck.

Viktor climbed down the ladder. Safely on the floor, he dashed for where he'd entered, opened the back door, and stepped out into the night with one overriding thought racing through his head: the Mafioso who lent him money would be waiting. If he returned to Russia he would have to face those men, and they would expect to be paid, one way or another.

Without the gold, I'm as good as dead.

The man named Jerry now had the templates, but did he know about the gold? For that matter, who, if anyone, knew about the gold? Maybe Fiona had known? But she would have gone to the authorities to report the discovery. Americans were stupid like that. Did her girlfriend Holly know? Same conclusion as for Fiona. Probably not. Viktor had seen Holly with a head wound lying unconscious on the tool room floor. She might not live. Was that what the kid meant when he said the lady was hurt?

Viktor knew the operator must be dead. Those final two shotgun blasts spelled his end. Had the kid taken him out? If so, that was one gutsy kid!

A distant chorus of sirens floated upriver.

Where can I go?

Viktor saw the gate in the chain link fence that surrounded the transformer yard. The fence was tall, but not topped with razor or even barbed wire. If he went through the gate he could pass among the transformers, climb over the far side, and reach the rocky bank along the water race that led away from the powerhouse.

The sirens got louder.

Viktor edged along the back of the building, reached the gate and entered the yard, felt the tingle of electrical charge, smelled ozone. He picked his way carefully through the field of massive transformers and climbed the fence, swinging his legs carefully, one at a time, over the ragged points at the top before dropping to the ground on the other side.

Three sheriff's cars sped up the access road.

Viktor slid down the rounded river rocks and began crab-stepping his way beside the rushing water. The cop cars screeched to a halt before Viktor was parallel to the Mustang and the pickup.

An ambulance came barreling up the powerhouse road as Viktor crawled to the top of the bank and peered over, seeing in the distance the men gathered around Holly's inert form on the pavement. How had she gotten there? But it didn't really matter. All that mattered were the templates.

Once the paramedics had Holly on a stretcher and moved her into an ambulance, the man named Jerry, the big guy, and the young boy walked up the road until they were close to where Viktor hid; they climbed into the pickup and drove off.

Viktor retreated from the top of the bank and worked his way downstream towards his car so he could leave in search of the pickup. Once he had the templates he would return in a few days, after things cooled down, to finish the job.

Chapter 42

Denny Nevler pulled into Pangborn Field's parking lot at sunrise. In a few minutes the white speck of a Citation jet slipped over the eastern horizon and grew in size as it made a half-circle around the valley, passing across the face of Mission Ridge and then above the Columbia River in a sweeping turn to set up an approach to the mile long strip.

Denny downed one last swig of lukewarm coffee and tossed the Styrofoam cup into a waste can as he walked from the building out onto the tarmac.

As the Citation's engines spooled down the odor of kerosene flooded the morning air. Tom Delacorte emerged from the hatch wearing jeans and a short sleeve shirt, with a stubble of beard. He carried a hard-shell suitcase with reinforced corners of the kind professional photographers use for cameras. Inside the case would be a pistol with a silencer and a high-powered rifle broken down and neatly packed in high density foam.

Tom met the assassin forty feet from the jet.

"Denny," came the focused voice of a killer shifted into top gear.

"Tom."

The assassin had never been friendly with him. Jerry Dearborn was different. You could at least have a pleasant conversation with the man. The image of Dearborn carrying a soccer ball came to mind. Denny had seen boys playing around the Belvedere and one of them carried what he presumed was that same soccer ball. He now found himself hating his job. He glanced at the case Tom held, fingers wrapped almost lovingly around the handle.

"Is the car close?"

Without a word, Denny led the way. Once at the car, Denny slid into the driver's seat and popped the trunk, listening as Tom set the case inside and slammed the trunk lid shut. He came around to the passenger side and climbed in.

"How long is the drive?"

"A little over an hour."

Tom looked at his watch. "It's just past seven. Let's stop and get breakfast."

"Okay," Denny agreed, but his appetite was nonexistent.

⅄

Bob Rider set the alarm on the bedside stand for 6am, knowing he needed to get back as early as possible to check the computer for results. So when he came groggily awake, wondering why his wife wasn't lying beside him, and saw *7:43* in red numerals on the bedside clock, he kicked off the covers and ran for the shower.

Four minutes later he grabbed a terrycloth towel from the rack. The aroma of eggs and bacon wafted in from the kitchen. Karen had apparently decided to take things into her own hands. She had turned off the alarm, and was now cooking his favorite breakfast.

As he pulled on slacks, buttoned his shirt and hurriedly roped a necktie under his collar, he hoped the Beltway traffic would be light. With any luck, he'd be at the office before nine.

Chapter 43

Oscar was again in his private room at the hospital, resting comfortably. There was talk of releasing him later that day. Jerry sat in the room until Oscar drifted off to sleep and then went downstairs to the first floor waiting room.

The nighttime duty nurse suggested he go home and get some rest, but Holly was undergoing a CAT scan and Jerry wanted to know if she was going to be okay. She had, after all, taken out Frank, and all of them were in her debt. The nurse left and came back with a small tube of antibiotic salve for Jerry's rope-burned wrists. He spread the salve on the chaffed skin and settled into one of the waiting room chairs. Twice he drifted off as the hours passed from the dead of night into the dawn of a new day.

As the morning sun shafted through the waiting room windows Manny Cruz came in carrying two cups of black coffee. His hair had fallen into a tangle no simple combing would cure. He sank into the chair beside Jerry's and handed across a cup.

"Thanks." Jerry took a sip of coffee. "Is there any word yet on Holly?"

"They don't know what kind of hemorrhaging might be going on. A helicopter's coming to fly her to Seattle. How's Oscar?"

"He's asleep. The doc says he's in no danger."

"And the boy?"

"I drove him home in Oscar's pickup. The apartments were dark. I'm pretty sure his mother didn't even know he was gone."

"We'll have to do an interview. It's standard procedure, even if he's just a kid. She'll have to be told—"

"That her son is a hero?"

"Yeah." Manny sighed. "If it weren't for him coming along, Holly would have been toast when Frank bolted." He stood, stretched. "Want to go for a walk? I need a cigarette."

"Okay."

Manny led him through the hospital and out onto a loading dock. The rancid smell of spoiled food floated up from dumpsters lined against a cedar fence.

Manny pointed beyond a high bank covered in spreading juniper. "Up there's a spot where the staff go to smoke." He pulled a pack of Camels from his shirt pocket and brought one up, stuck it between his lips, struck a match. He puffed it to life, inhaling deeply.

They climbed a narrow trail cut into the bank and found a flat patch of dirt with a litter of cigarette butts. With just the sounds of morning songbirds and the distant rush of an occasional car on the highway, Manny opened up.

"I have a confession."

"About what?"

"I had suspicions about you. When I spoke to Alice—"

"Alice?"

"The woman who lives across the street from Holly."

"Oh . . . *Alice*."

Manny chuckled. "She called me last night and said you came by asking about Holly. I thought you and Brindleman were tangled up in some kind of drug ring. Of course, I was wrong. Sometimes a guy just misses the boat entirely."

"I suppose." Jerry knew he was being handed his departure ticket. Despite the fatigue he felt better. He fought to keep a smile from coming, but the corners of his mouth lifted just a little.

Manny returned a broader smile of his own. "I'm sorry."

"Apology accepted."

"Thanks." Manny took a deep drag, exhaled a contemplative cloud of smoke. "But there's still something that puzzles me."

"What?"

"You knew Brindleman from before, didn't you? I saw you and him talking after you left my office that first day."

Manny was looking at him with narrow, appraising eyes. Jerry realized he wasn't quite yet off the hook. Close, but not quite. But with Frank dead, the explanation could be simplified without the risk of being contradicted.

"Frank knew me in Vietnam. We served in the same unit for a brief time. When he spotted me, well, he figured I might be able to help him."

"Help him with what?"

Jerry realized there was nothing to do now but share the story. Still . . . what harm could there be in it?

Jerry sketched out Brindleman's tale of the wrench, the gold, and the mystery stalker. Manny eyebrows raised when Jerry described the swastikas on the pipes.

"You're kidding!"

"No."

"So where is it?"

"The gold?"

"Yeah."

"When Frank came back to where Holly and I were tied up he said he couldn't find the pipe numbers that corresponded to the templates. I'm beginning to wonder if there ever was any gold. I think Frank lost his marbles a long time ago. If it weren't for the templates I'd call it a complete fiction." Jerry shrugged. "Who knows for sure?"

"Speaking of which, where are they?"

"In the glove compartment of Oscar's truck."

"We'll need them for the file."

"No problem. I'll be glad to be rid of them."

This seemed to satisfy Manny. He dropped the smoldering cigarette and carefully crushed the butt with his heel until it was completely buried in the soft dirt. "We'd better get back."

Manny left Jerry in the waiting area and went down the hallway to the surgery desk. The nurse said Holly had just been taken by ambulance to a helicopter for the flight to Seattle's Harborview Hospital.

As Manny walked back towards the waiting area, Holly's condition wasn't the only thing on his mind. Everything Wells told him fit, except for the DEA agent Alice had reported. There was more to this story. Manny had no probable cause for a warrant and didn't want to tip his hand, just in case. He needed time to track down the agent, and he wanted Wells feeling comfortable about sticking around.

Manny's radio squawked and he fingered the mike. "Yes?"

"Manny?" came Beulah's voice. "Radio folks say they want to interview you."

Manny closed his eyes for a moment. It was the last thing he wanted; but he'd made a commitment long ago to do everything he could to advance his career, to create a good public image for himself. The old adage now applied: there was no such thing as "bad" publicity. A good interview would be remembered by a lot of people. "Okay, please tell them I'll meet them up at my office."

"Sure thing. And Manny?"

"Yes."

"Congratulations."

"Thanks, Beulah."

When he reached the waiting area he said to Jerry, "I've got to do a media interview at the office. Want a ride?"

"No thanks."

"There's still a loose end or two to tie up, like those templates. Could you please meet me at my office later this morning?"

"Sure."

Manny left, and Jerry was headed towards the front door when a nurse called after him. "Mr. Wells?"

Jerry turned. "Yes?"

"There was a boy who came in a few minutes ago asking for you."

"Pablo?" He expected the boy to be tucked into bed, safe at home in the Belvedere.

"Yes, that was his name. He looked for you in the waiting room and when he couldn't find you he came back and asked if he could see Sergeant Danner. He was very upset, so I sent him up to the nursing station on three. I think he's in Danner's room now. You might want to go see what's troubling him."

"Thank you." Jerry headed for the elevator.

He found Oscar's door partly closed, heard voices inside, pushed it open and walked in.

Pablo was seated on the bed. Oscar was propped in a sitting position and his face was grim. When he saw Jerry, he looked briefly to Pablo. "You go home now, son. And don't tell anyone what you've told me. Promise?"

"I promise, Oscar."

Pablo slid off the bed and came over to Jerry. Unexpectedly, he wrapped his arms around Jerry's waist in an enormous hug, his cheek pressed into Jerry's chest. Then, without a word, Pablo left the room.

Oscar looked hard at Jerry. "I think you're in a whole heap of trouble, my friend. Pablo says two men just came looking for you at the Belvedere. They showed his mother DEA identification. Do you know why the Feds would want to find you?"

Jerry felt as if a tornado had entered the room. It got worse.

"Do you know someone named Dearborn?"

"Oh, shit."

"I thought so," Oscar said. "We've got to do some serious talking and we need to do it real fast. You need to come clean with me on everything, and I do mean *everything*. That is, if you want my help. Otherwise," Oscar nodded toward the open doorway. "I'd suggest you get a quick head start before they figure out you're here."

CHAPTER 44

Special Agent Jim Wheeler flew through the night, landing at the Wenatchee airport shortly after 2am. At the age of sixty-one he found it difficult to sleep on long flights and he was exhausted. He picked up a rental car and drove in darkness down Grant Road and across the bridge into Wenatchee, finally locating the Holiday Inn. He asked the desk clerk for a 7am wake-up call. Within minutes he was sound asleep. One of the nice things about getting old was it didn't take long to conk off in a comfortable bed.

The next morning he placed a call directly to Bob Rider's desk. It was midmorning in D.C., but the cipher specialist didn't answer. He left a message for Rider to call him back as soon as possible. Then he checked out of the hotel and drove back to the airport in the rental.

By the time the three FBI agents arrived from Spokane in a twin engine Beechcraft, Jim Wheeler was frustrated over not having heard from Rider. He now called the main desk instead of Rider's direct line.

"Special Agent Jim Wheeler here. I called earlier and left a message on Bob Rider's inbox. Has he come in yet?" He was brisk. Young people had to learn the importance of punctuality.

The cipher group receptionist sounded on the verge of tears when she said, "Hasn't someone called and told you?"

"About what?"

"Bob Rider was involved in a car accident on the beltway. He's in surgery at Georgetown."

Jim closed his eyes. He let the handset settle a few inches away from his ear. He took a pained breath, then another, before opening his eyes. The agents were staring at him. He let them stare, remembering that Rider had just gotten married. He heard a distant voice and realized it was the receptionist on the other end of the line.

"Sir?"

Tiredly, he lifted the receiver back to his ear. "Have we sent someone to tell his wife?"

"Yes, sir. The Director sent two agents over immediately."

I need the information he was working on. I need it now. But his tongue seemed caught in the back of his throat and his words came like tar. "Is there someone in his section I can speak to right now?"

"Judy Conway is taking his calls, sir. I'll connect you."

The FBI agents at the table were hunched forward. Placing a palm over the mouthpiece he said, "Bob Rider was in a bad car accident this morning."

One of the men removed his glasses, rubbed his eyes. Another said, "Do you want some time?"

"No, stay." They settled in their seats. Shortly, a new voice, a woman who sounded a bit overwhelmed, came on the line.

"This is Judy. May I help you?"

"Judy, this is special agent Wheeler. I was working with Bob Rider on a project. Can you get over to his computer?"

"Of course. I'll have to put you on hold for a moment."

Had he detected an edge of anger in her voice? Did she know he had ordered Bob to work late? With the click of a new handset being lifted she was back.

"What do you need?"

"He was running a photo recognition protocol for me. Can you please check and see if there were any results?"

There were three bursts of tapping on a keyboard and then a moment of silence before she answered. "It shows the search was completed, but he's put a password on it. I can't access the file."

"Shit."

"Sir?"

"I'm sorry, Judy. I didn't mean to say that."

"Of course not, sir."

He felt like an ass and wished it would all go away. *No such luck this time around.* He ground out the words that needed to be said.

"Judy, I need those results. If you can't figure a way to circumvent the password, please call Assistant Director Cross. Tell him I told you to call. He'll give you the necessary information so you can restart the search. Judy . . . this is important. If it weren't, I wouldn't ask."

"Yes, sir."

"Thank you."

She hung up without returning his thanks. He didn't blame her. Jim looked at the three agents who sat silently at the table, their coffees steaming, partly eaten rolls now abandoned on their plates. "Well, there's a shitty start to a day."

Things would get worse.

CHAPTER 45

Marni's eyes had raccoon crescents. Shortly after sunrise, the words on her computer screen blurred no matter how many eye drops she poured in. But the front page article was finally done!

She walked over to Burt Connolly, the production manager, who stood looking out a large window at his press operators scurrying around on the press room floor. The *Courier* was going to print for an unprecedented morning release. Burt was fighting a combination of caffeine shakes and exhaustion. A glimmer of doubt still persisted. They might be sued for libel. But only if they were wrong. And Burt didn't think that was the case. Not at all. And even if they were wrong, how much damage could you do to the reputation of a drifter? And the upside was so glorious. When the copyrighted article hit the wire the national media would arrive within hours. This would put the *Langston Courier* on the map. Yes, indeed! He was imagining just how good it was going to feel to see himself being interviewed on CNN.

ᛉ

Rosa gave Denny Nevler and Tom Delacorte the room number after they flashed their DEA badges and demanded to know where Jerry Wells lived. A young boy stood behind her, but they ignored him. As soon as they disappeared up the stairs, the kid went back to his room as his mother instructed, but he quietly climbed out his bedroom window as soon as he heard his mother's bedroom door close.

On the third floor, Tom took charge, knocking three times, one hand slipped casually inside his jacket, fingers brushing the butt of the gun in its holster. When no one answered, he pushed open the door. They entered and performed the same cursory search Manny had made several hours before. When they found nothing helpful, they knocked on other doors and quizzed residents. No one knew where he was. No one heard him come in during the night.

They went back down to the car and sat as Tom made quiet calculations about where to go next. Denny reached for the radio and turned the volume low, expecting country music. Instead, he discovered a morning news program.

"—you arrive at the powerhouse, Detective Cruz?"

"Around midnight."

"And did you know Jerry Wells was there?"

Tom increased the volume.

"Well, I thought he might be."

"What about Frank Brindleman?"

"Yes, I thought he might be there, too."

"And when did the shooting start?"

Denny said in a stunned voice, "What the—"

"Shut up and listen," Tom ordered, his eyes riveted on the radio. After a few more questions and answers the reporter summed up.

"Well, there you have it folks. Jerry Wells, the same man who found the body of Fiona Ross just last week, once again in the news. And now a word from Cashmere Valley Bank."

The commercial took over and Tom turned the volume down. "Shit!" He said. Then, "We need to call Fields."

Denny pulled out his cell phone. Tom took it and punched the numbers. It rang just once.

"Fields."

"Sir, there's been an incident of some kind. Jerry Dearborn appears to have been involved in a shootout last night. It's all over the local radio. What do you want us to do?"

"Was he killed?"

"No, sir."

"What was his involvement?"

"Not a clue."

Finally, Fields said, "Nothing has changed. You proceed the same as before. Understand?"

"Yes, sir."

"Good." Fields hung up.

"Well?" Denny asked as Tom handed back his phone.

"We find Dearborn."

Denny had hoped the commotion would derail their mission. He sighed and said, "Where do we start looking?"

"This Cruz fellow seems to have an inside line. We need to pay him a visit."

"The radio station, then?"

"Right."

They asked for directions at the Burger King. When they arrived at the radio station they were told the interview took place at the sheriff's office. The receptionist gave them the address and pointed toward the center of town.

⋏

After Manny finished the radio interview, he washed up and poured a fresh cup of coffee, ready to begin searching for the elusive federal agent, at which point two federal agents arrived at his office door. He was grilled—that was the only word for it. When he tried to ask a question, the agent interrogating him said flatly, "We'll ask the questions, Detective." The dark-haired, angular-faced man actually scared him. Manny complied.

He was quizzed about the night's activities. When he said he'd last seen Jerry at the hospital, they thanked him, asked for directions to the hospital, and left.

As Manny walked out into the sea of desks, the receptionist, Beulah, walked up to him looking like she'd just gotten the shock of her life. In fact, she had. In her hand she held a newspaper. On the cover of the paper Manny saw two photos of Jerry, side by side, both in black and white; an older somewhat grainy photo, another photo taken much more recently. The caption screamed:

ASSASSIN AMONG US! Stunned, he laid the paper on the nearest empty desk and sat down to read.

As he finished, he looked up and was surprised to see Oscar Danner, in civilian dress, entering the far side of the room. Oscar looked around, as if checking to see whether or not he'd been spotted, and when he turned in Manny's direction Manny put his head down. When Manny glanced back up Oscar walked over to where the cruiser keys hung from a pegboard. He slipped off a set and headed for the exit.

Manny sat for a moment, trying to figure out why Oscar would want a patrol car. Looking down again at the stunning headline, Manny realized there was only one likely explanation.

Beulah was still standing beside the desk, waiting for Manny to return her newspaper. "Beulah," he said in a voice that now held an element of panic. "I need to borrow your car."

"What?"

"Beulah, I don't have time to explain. I need to borrow your car!"

Beulah was confused.

"Please Beulah! Just give me the keys!"

Stunned, but seeing the urgency in Cruz's face, Beulah reached into the pocket of her uniform and drew out her car keys and handed them to Manny.

"It's a white Nova, right?"

"Yes."

"Thanks, Beulah. I owe you."

And before Beulah could tell Manny that he certainly did owe her, or ask why he so urgently needed her car, Manny practically sprinted from the room.

λ

Jim Wheeler and his team drove from Wenatchee, arriving at the sheriff's office in Langston just minutes after Manny left to follow Oscar. They hadn't listened to the radio and were unaware of the *Langston Courier* headline. When they entered the office a copy of the newspaper lay on the entry table in plain sight. As soon as Jim Wheeler saw the red banner headline and the photos directly below, he called Pete Cross.

It was not long before the first helicopter filled with FBI agents came beating into the valley.

Chapter 46

Viktor planned on a quick exit once he reached his car, but as he worked his way downstream along the steep and rocky bank several police cars and PUD service vehicles swarmed up the access road. A crime scene exclusion zone was established, including a manned barricade on the access road where it joined Highway 97. By the time Viktor reached his car there was no way to drive out because his car was inside the barrier.

He considered walking up onto Highway 97 and either hitching a ride or walking back to Langston; but it was after midnight and his presence would draw attention from the police. And without his car how could he possibly search for the pickup or the Mustang? Viktor couldn't even safely sit in his car. What if the police decided to search the park? They would find him inside and there would be questions about why a man with a heavy Russian accent was parked here at this late hour.

Viktor hung out down by the river in the darkness, keeping a nervous watch, desperately trying to come up with an alternative plan if the gold search proved futile. Could he possibly develop a wine export business? No. That had been a con from the start. He had no business contacts in Russia for selling wine. And for all the promise it might hold for a person with entrepreneurial skills, Viktor was no businessman; he was former KGB and used to working for a government. He wasn't even sure Muscovites would be keen about Langston wines. Russians went for the hard stuff like Vodka, or status wines like French champagne. Langston wines were a complete unknown.

Even if wine sales were an option, it was unlikely they would generate enough cash to quickly repay the loan. The Mafia would be pounding on his door. Would they be sympathetic? More likely they would cut off a few of his fingers.

Viktor returned to the gold as his only hope. It had to be somewhere. And the templates were the key.

As dawn broke Viktor was forced off the river bank. In the dark it was a good hiding place. In daylight, anyone driving along the main highway could see him down on the rocks. He walked back to his car and climbed in.

Two hours after sunrise Viktor finally got a break. Three cars filled with Hispanics pulled up to the barricade, wanting access to the park. After the policeman manning the barricade spoke with the new arrivals, then radioed for permission, he disassembled the wood barrier and loaded it into the back of his patrol car and moved it further up towards the powerhouse.

The three cars drove into the park and began to unload. They eyed the lone driver in his rental car, but no one approached or reported him to the officer on the barricade.

Viktor drove to the access road, turned away from the powerhouse and then onto the highway. No police car came screaming up behind with its lights flashing. After half a mile he knew he'd left undetected.

By the time he reached Langston, Viktor had a new plan. His first stop was the hospital where some or all of the night's powerhouse shootout participants might have gone for treatment. There was no pickup with a canopy or red Mustang in the parking lot or on the street. Entering the hospital to asking questions might provoke a call to the police, so Viktor turned to his next target: the police station.

Viktor found the red Mustang parked alongside several police cruisers. There was no sign of the pickup. He parked half a block down the street and waited. It didn't take long. What next happened was puzzling but promising.

The big fellow from the powerhouse, still dressed in street clothes, exited the building. He keyed open one of the cruisers and slid into the driver's seat. As he pulled out of the lot, Viktor saw the Hispanic cop come racing from the building. Instead of getting into the Mustang or another cruiser, the cop ran to a white car, jerked open the door, jumped in, and quickly backed out. He screeched off in pursuit of the police cruiser which was already turning out of sight at the end of the block.

Viktor followed at a discrete distance.

CHAPTER 47

It was an old log cabin. From the front porch it was a hundred yards to the ski lodge and the bottom of the first slope.

Jerry parked Oscar's pickup around back under the tin-roofed woodshed. If someone came up the road they wouldn't spot the F-150 without circling the cabin. If they did approach, there would be plenty of warning.

After stashing the pickup and making a brief walkthrough of the house, he went out onto the porch and sat in a cedar deck chair, listening to the wind whisper through the pines. A redwing grasshopper sprang into the air, ratcheting into the safety of nearby brush. The air smelled intensely of pitch and dusty summer heat.

After telling Oscar about Champoton and everything since, Oscar suggested Jerry come here while he checked things out. Jerry wanted to call the Argentine bank to arrange a funds transfer, but Oscar said it was foolish to try. There were already federal law officers in town looking for him.

Jerry needed to leave the continent. A freighter or a private yacht would be best. That meant bribing a captain or buying into a crew position. Either would require more than just a little cash. Without access to the money in Argentina he was screwed.

But his deepest regret was not the money. What was causing a bruised feeling in his chest was missing the chance to say goodbye to Pablo. The danger of being caught was too great, and it would also put the boy at risk, so coming straight here was the right thing to do. But the sadness was huge.

He pushed up out of the chair. It was bad to let restless energy churn. Better to get some exercise and let his gut untie from the knot it was in.

He walked to the old ski lodge, intent upon climbing a trail carved into the face of the ski slope. Like Oscar's cabin, the lodge was constructed of pine logs, weathered to a deep brown. Oscar said the cabin had been in his family almost as long as the hill had been in operation—nearly seventy years. Unlike the cabin, which had a cedar shake roof, the lodge had a peaked aluminum roof. The sun dazzled across the metal.

At the front he peered in through large windows at benches and tables stacked near the kitchen area. The cement floor bore a thick coat of dust. Apparently, no one came here during the summer.

He left the lodge and crossed in front of two rows of ski racks and walked up to the base of the rope tow. The rope was removed for summer storage, leaving only the metal post, with large pulleys at the top and bottom, and a small shed housing the electric motor and reduction gears. Growing up around the post were thick clumps of grass.

Beyond the pole was the return trail for skiers. As Jerry walked toward the trail, intent upon hiking to the top of the ridge, something he had just seen—and now recognized—stopped him in his tracks.

The pole!

He looked back with disbelief at the metal base, where several thick bolts ran through the wide flange; fist-sized nuts were tightened flush against the concrete pad. The pole was painted a dull blue, and the diameter was exactly what he'd seen the night before.

He walked over and stripped handfuls of grass and weeds away from the base, and finally found the three-digit number, thickly crusted with paint but still legible.

261

On the other side, where there might have once been something raised in the steel, a small roughened area appeared to have been ground down until it was flat with the rest of the metal.

Someone didn't like that swastika!

Jerry rocked back on his heels, reaching out to touch the three raised numbers to make sure he wasn't dreaming. As he stood, wondering what to do next, he heard a car engine and then saw a police cruiser in the distance, toiling up the gravel road. He was ready to run when the horn sounded four times—the signal he and Oscar had prearranged.

With one last glance at the pipe, Jerry turned and jogged back to the cabin. By the time he was on the porch the cruiser was around the last of the sharp curves, its wheels slashing dirt as the engine strained to climb the final section of road. Oscar's determined face was behind the wheel. The cruiser slammed to a stop and a cloud of dust momentarily covered everything. Oscar flung the door wide, a waxy sheen on his face. "It's a whole new ballgame!" he shouted. In his hand was a *Langston Courier.* He gave it to Jerry.

Jerry scanned the headline; saw the old photo next to the recent one.

"There's no chance of your going back into town. It's swarming with FBI agents. They've been interrogating everyone. Christ! I was luckier 'n hell to sneak off with the car." A wicked grin came to his face. "See that?" He pointed to the dusty cruiser.

"Yes."

"I stole it," he said proudly.

"Stole it?"

"Well, kinda. I just walked into the station, took a set of keys off the pegboard, walked out to the parking lot, and drove off." Oscar let go with a deep laugh. "It was the best way to slip past the FBI. No one questions where a cop is headed."

"So what now?" Jerry knew it was the end, Oscar's exuberance and determination notwithstanding.

Oscar reached around to his back pocket and pulled out a thick envelope. "Here," he said solemnly, holding it out.

Jerry took the envelope and ran a finger under the sealed flap. Inside was money. He pulled out a stack of bills and riffed the edge, all hundreds. "Where did you get this?"

"My retirement account," Oscar said with glee. "Shit, you should have seen the look I got when I told the clerk I wanted to withdraw everything from my IRA. She called the manager and he tried to talk me out of it. The old boy saw all those bucks flying out the door. He warned me the IRS was going to take a big piece of it. And then he remembered my illness. Hell, by now it's common knowledge. Word gets around fast when someone's got one foot in the grave. Anyway, he got all red faced and told the clerk to fetch the cash from the vault. When she got back with bundles of hundreds, I told her to start counting. When it got to twenty-seven grand, I said 'Stop.' That was all I could stuff into my pocket. I hope it's enough."

Jerry couldn't find the words. He wrapped his arms around Oscar and for a moment the weight of the world was gone. When he finally pulled away, intending to tell Oscar about his discovery of the pipe, the sound of gunfire echoed up the valley.

"Who?" Jerry asked.

"No idea," Oscar replied. He looked at the envelope, then to Jerry. "I better go and see."

"I'm coming."

"Like hell."

"I'm coming."

"Jerry--"

"Look, Oscar. I'm better with a gun than anyone in these parts." Jerry stared hard at Oscar, leaving no doubt about whether there would be a debate.

Oscar looked exasperated. "Okay," he said. "Get in the damned car."

But by the time they arrived, it was too late.

⅄

Oscar's first stop was a bank. Manny parked two blocks away. Viktor pulled up a block behind Manny. When Oscar exited the bank and drove through town and then up the East Lake Road, holding comfortably within the speed limit, Manny was certain he was headed for Jerry. Oscar had once mentioned a ski cabin he owned at Kearney Ridge. It had to be where he would meet the assassin. Manny held back a hundred yards, knowing the road had few turnoffs, trusting Oscar wouldn't be concerned about a white Nova in his rearview mirror. When Oscar turned onto the ski hill road, Manny drove past the turnoff and continued up the road until the turnoff was out of sight.

A white Hyundai Accent with an *Avis* rental car bumper sticker on the fender came to the turnoff and slowed. Viktor had seen the police cruiser turn onto the ski hill road. He'd also witnessed the Hispanic cop's puzzling failure to follow. Viktor waited a full minute, and when the Hispanic cop failed to reappear, Viktor faced a choice. Remembering that the big cop had left the powerhouse in the company of the man who held the templates, he turned onto the ski hill road.

In his rearview mirror Manny had spotted the Hyundai turn three different corners to follow him back in Langston, and decided to test whether it would stay on his tail beyond the ski hill road. When the Hyundai failed to appear, Manny sat parked in the breakdown lane, considering his options. If the second car was FBI they would have already called for backup. Shortly, there would be marked cars racing up the road. He had too much invested to let a federal agent claim the full collar, so he turned around.

Viktor traveled nearly two miles before he pulled over to give himself one last chance to turn back from this desperate mission. And just as he came to the conclusion he had no other option, he looked back down the road and saw dust being raised by a car. It was the cop.

No turning back now.

Viktor climbed out of the Hyundai and popped the trunk and pulled out the spare tire.

When the white Nova came around the bend and slowed, Viktor waived a friendly hand to the Hispanic cop he'd seen at the powerhouse.

Manny pulled to a stop and got out. "Howdy," he said as he approached. "Having car trouble?" As he said this he realized the man was changing a flat tire that wasn't flat at all.

Viktor saw the Glock in the cop's holster. The Colt .38 he'd bought from Len suddenly seemed puny. But he had the advantage of surprise. Without hesitation Viktor reached back under his loose shirt and pulled the .38. The cop grabbed for his gun, but by the time he drew Viktor had emptied all six shots into Manny at near point blank range. No heart shot. No head shot.

Manny fired off three rounds before he went down. One struck Viktor in the chest, traveling through to shatter the spinal column directly behind the sternum.

Chapter 48

A voice blared from the phone speaker in the county's emergency call center. "Officer down! Repeat, Officer down!"

Of all the voices veteran dispatcher Connie Trenton might have expected over the radio, Oscar Danner's was not one of them. To her credit, Connie held her focus and responded in the professional way she had been trained.

"Copy that Sergeant Danner. Please advise your location."

"I'm up at Kearney Ridge, near the lodge. I need an ambulance fast. There's also a fire, so you'd better tell the Forest Service to send a pump rig."

"Copy, Sergeant Danner. Hang on. Help is on the way." And then as an afterthought. "Are you okay, Oscar?"

"I'm fine Connie. But Manny Cruz is in bad shape. Please hurry on the ambulance!"

"Right." She pushed a button on her console to open a line for EMS. Once the ambulance was rolling, she opened the main police frequency.

"All officers able to respond please proceed immediately to Kearney Ridge Ski Lodge. Officer Danner reports that officer Cruz is down. Hurry it up folks!"

The FBI was monitoring the sheriff's main channel. Danner and Cruz were by now synonymous with Dearborn. FBI agents consulted their maps, put flashing lights on their dashboards, and took off for the ski hill. An FBI helicopter on the tarmac of the small local airstrip revved its turbines and lifted off. Everyone joined in the mad dash to the ski hill.

The cars which screamed out of Langston and up the East Lake Road were in far too much of a hurry to notice the white Hyundai Accent rental car with an *Avis* sticker, driven by a man who wore a dark blue cap, sitting straight behind the wheel, moving at a law abiding forty miles an hour in the opposite direction. Nor did anyone in Langston give any thought to the car as it continued straight through town, out through Turner's Notch, and onto Highway 97, where it turned north.

Later that afternoon, the Canadian border guard compared the photo on the passport with the face of the driver, thinking for a moment that the driver looked maybe just a bit older, concluded it was just a poorly taken photo, and entered into his log that a Russian national named Viktor Anchevsky had come through.

ᚠ

The FBI Bell Jet Ranger circled as the pilot gauged the wind by the thick column of smoke barreling from the cabin. He found a safe spot near the lodge and set the craft down. Three agents, all wearing windbreakers stenciled with *FBI*, leapt out and ran to Oscar, who was down on his knees, bent over the body of Manny Cruz, sheltering it as best he could from the heat radiating from the nearby inferno.

"Thank God you're here," Oscar said to the agents, one of whom quickly checked Manny's neck for a pulse. There were multiple entry wounds and everything was soaked in blood. The agent straightened up and looked at Oscar. "I'm afraid he's gone."

Oscar had thought out his reaction very carefully. "I tried . . ." he managed to gulp out. The agents pulled Manny's body clear of the scorching heat. Tears streamed down Oscar's cheeks. But not for Manny. The tears were for Jerry. They had done it!

By the time the fire fighters arrived with a pump rig the cabin had collapsed into a jumble of roaring logs. Oscar reported to the FBI that the only person inside was the man he had known as Jerry Wells.

The FBI watched as the fire team fought to keep the blaze from spreading into the nearby forest.

Jim Wheeler later interviewed the local cop who witnessed the gun battle and saw the flames start when a bullet apparently hit a kerosene lantern inside. It did seem a remarkable coincidence that it was his family cabin and his stolen pickup. But the cop said he remembered mentioning the cabin to Jerry earlier, when they went fishing. The pickup had been the easiest vehicle for Jerry to steal from the hospital lot as he could have easily lifted the keys from Oscar's trousers in the hospital closet. Oscar said he was trying to track it down, with Manny's help, when they came upon Jerry and the gun battle took place. When Wheeler talked to another of the local cops about Oscar's story and learned the man was dying of cancer, he decided not to push Oscar for details. At least not until the FBI's forensic pathologist could perform an autopsy.

That autopsy confirmed the remains were the right size to have been Dearborn's. The intense heat shattered the teeth and burned away flesh and crumbled most of the bones. Even if there were adequate tissue for a DNA test, Jerry had no known relatives from which to obtain a sample for a comparison. They found Dearborn's dog tags among the bone fragments, and that finally settled it. The matter was closed.

A few days later Oscar was sitting at home in his recliner, watching a Sunday morning talk show where the pundits were musing about how Jerry Dearborn had slipped through the net one final time. As Oscar reached for a cold can of beer he felt a great velvet sledgehammer strike his chest. He didn't even bother to try and reach for the phone. His fingers feebly brushed against the can, knocking it to the floor. Beer foamed onto the carpet. Oscar slipped toward his final rest, his last thoughts of Jerry and the boy. His mouth formed into a smile. He'd done the right thing. Oscar died a satisfied man.

He was buried not far from where Fiona's body lay.

λ

The following spring a bouquet of wild yellow iris was laid beside Oscar's gravestone by a stranger who drove into the cemetery in a U-haul truck that rode low and heavy with a full load. He sported a beard and wore a dark blue baseball cap. His coveralls were dusty. He said quiet words as he placed the flowers, bowed his head in a moment of prayer, climbed back into the truck and drove carefully down the steep hill and out of town.

The following week, residents would read in the *Langston Courier* that vandals had stolen both ski hill rope tow support posts. Was scrap metal really so valuable that metal posts were now worth stealing? A fund raising drive ensued. There was a short follow-up article lamenting the loss of the antique posts, which originally came from the powerhouse, although no one knew the exact history. Only that they had been salvaged by the old German engineer and installed to make Kearney Ridge a finer place to ski. With funds from the drive, new support posts were purchased and installed in plenty of time for the ski season.

No great loss . . .

EPILOGUE

The Seattle lawyer had been given careful instructions, so when he arrived in Langston two years after the cabin fire and came to the Belvedere to inquire about Pablo, he was unable to tell Rosa anything more than that Pablo had been selected as the recipient of a full scholarship to whatever college he chose to attend.

She was overwhelmed. Her child? A full scholarship?

"Yes. Wherever he wants to go."

"This is wonderful!"

"Is he here now?"

"No. He is up at school. They are having soccer practice."

"And is he doing well with his soccer?"

"Yes. He is best player on team."

The attorney pulled out a note pad and began to write, asking other questions about her son. What was his grade point average? Was he healthy? What kind of kids did he hang out with? What were his hobbies? He gave her his name, address and phone number, so she could maintain contact.

Before he left town he placed a call to the prosecutor's office. When the woman answered, he asked to speak with Holly Curtis.

"I'm sorry. She moved out of the area nearly two years ago. I think she's working for a big law firm on the east coast. Can someone else help you?"

"No, thank you." He hung up wrote on his note pad. The client would be pleased with the news she was alive.

May – 2012

A man now going by the name of *Jerry Collins* sat alone far up in the bleachers at the University of Washington's Husky Stadium, watching the soccer team practice. It was easy to identify the team's leader on the field; a slim Hispanic playing the position of striker. Jerry watched him weave through defenders as if they were ghosts. He scored two goals during the next hour. At one point, even the coach gave him a round of applause. Many of the players ganged around to talk with him after practice ended.

By then, the man in the stands had disappeared.

When Pablo finally exited the locker room, having showered and dressed, he saw a black Mercedes with tinted windows parked at the curb. The door opened, and out stepped a man who had been waiting for a very long time.